Praise for the Musketeers Mysteries

"Delightful . . . Medieval France comes vividly to life."
—Victoria Thompson, author of the Gaslight Mysteries

"Dumas fans eager for further details of the lives of his swash-buckling musketeer heroes may enjoy this . . . Transforms those men of action and intrigue into the king's detectives."
—*Publishers Weekly*

"This is a fun swashbuckling historical mystery starring the four musketeers of Dumas fame. The story line is filled with action as the heroes investigate the homicide while adhering to their original personalities . . . Musketeers and seventeenth-century who-dunit fans will enjoy this changing of the guard from thriller to mystery while retaining the heroic got-your-back essence of one-for-all-and-all-for-one brotherhood." —*The Best Reviews*

"D'Almeida delivers a nice cozy with enough suspects and motives to satisfy the dedicated mystery fan."
—*Gumshoe Review*

D0202233

"*Death of a Musketeer* is the perfect opener for what promises to be quite possibly the most sought after series of books in a long time. While those who enjoy historic fiction will get their fill, those who always wanted more of the musketeers will be delighted to find that the opener takes place during the famous story of the necklace, so aptly penned by Monsieur Dumas. Yet the direction that Ms. D'Almeida has chosen for her characters is startlingly unique and thus the Dumas narrative provides the springboard from which the reader can jump into the new narrative. Showcasing a true flair not only for the period but also for the different places each musketeer has approached in life, this novel only has one flaw: It is over too soon! This is a must-have for the fiction fan, and the sequels will be eagerly awaited by this reviewer."   —*Roundtable Reviews*

"A cracking good book that succeeds on many levels . . . The author might have chosen to pen a cozy tale using Dumas' characters and gotten away with it pleasingly enough, but fortunately she has done a lot more than that. She has managed to tell the tale in the same style as Dumas . . . The characters are all spot on, and the evocation of early seventeenth-century France is just as Dumas had it. A round of applause too, for writing a book set in a period not already overdone and in packing a teasing plot, well-loved characters that spring to life, and plenty of authentic background into a book of just the right length. Waiting until the next book is going to be hard . . . Highly enjoyable!"   —*MyShelf.com*

Berkley Prime Crime titles by Sarah D'Almeida

DEATH OF A MUSKETEER
THE MUSKETEER'S SEAMSTRESS
THE MUSKETEER'S APPRENTICE
A DEATH IN GASCONY
DYING BY THE SWORD

Dying by the Sword

Sarah D'Almeida

BERKLEY PRIME CRIME, NEW YORK

THE BERKLEY PUBLISHING GROUP
Published by the Penguin Group
Penguin Group (USA) Inc.
375 Hudson Street, New York, New York 10014, USA
Penguin Group (Canada), 90 Eglinton Avenue East, Suite 700, Toronto, Ontario M4P 2Y3, Canada
(a division of Pearson Penguin Canada Inc.)
Penguin Books Ltd., 80 Strand, London WC2R 0RL, England
Penguin Group Ireland, 25 St. Stephen's Green, Dublin 2, Ireland (a division of Penguin Books Ltd.)
Penguin Group (Australia), 250 Camberwell Road, Camberwell, Victoria 3124, Australia
(a division of Pearson Australia Group Pty. Ltd.)
Penguin Books India Pvt. Ltd., 11 Community Centre, Panchsheel Park, New Delhi—110 017, India
Penguin Group (NZ), 67 Apollo Drive, Rosedale, North Shore 0632, New Zealand
(a division of Pearson New Zealand Ltd.)
Penguin Books (South Africa) (Pty.) Ltd., 24 Sturdee Avenue, Rosebank, Johannesburg 2196,
South Africa

Penguin Books Ltd., Registered Offices: 80 Strand, London WC2R 0RL, England

This is a work of fiction. Names, characters, places, and incidents either are the product of the author's imagination or are used fictitiously, and any resemblance to actual persons, living or dead, business establishments, events, or locales is entirely coincidental. The publisher does not have any control over and does not assume any responsibility for author or third-party websites or their content.

DYING BY THE SWORD

A Berkley Prime Crime Book / published by arrangement with the author

PRINTING HISTORY
Berkley Prime Crime mass-market edition / December 2008

Copyright © 2008 by Sarah Hoyt.
Interior text design by Tiffany Estreicher.

ISBN: 978-0-425-22461-8

BERKLEY® PRIME CRIME
Berkley Prime Crime Books are published by The Berkley Publishing Group,
a division of Penguin Group (USA) Inc.,
375 Hudson Street, New York, New York 10014.
BERKLEY PRIME CRIME and the BERKLEY PRIME CRIME design are trademarks of Penguin Group (USA) Inc.

PRINTED IN THE UNITED STATES OF AMERICA

10 9 8 7 6 5 4 3 2 1

Those Who Live by the Sword;
The Honor of a Musketeer's Servant;
All for One

~

ATHOS was not used to being looked at with suspicion and hostility, much less suspicion and hostility from mere commoners—a confused rabble of women and children, servants and passersby, the dregs and crowds of early afternoon in Paris.

In fact, the oldest of the three musketeers and the guard of Monsieur des Essarts, commonly known as *the inseparables*—Athos, Porthos, Aramis and D'Artagnan—wasn't used to being looked at directly at all. Though he had now, for some years, lived under a nom de guerre in the ranks of his Majesty's musketeers, Athos normally got treated as the nobleman he was.

No matter how much blond and elegant Aramis preened, and no matter how many yards of lace and gold brocade the splendid redheaded giant Porthos draped himself in, Athos could make them all fade into the background simply by stepping forward and throwing back his head. In his much-mended musketeer's uniform, his curly black hair tied back with a bit of ribbon, the gaze from his dark blue eyes guarded, he looked like what he was born to be: the scion of one of France's oldest and noblest families.

And he wasn't used to people not listening when he spoke; he wasn't used to being doubted; he certainly wasn't used to having his words shouted down.

Yet the words, "I will stand by—" had barely left his lips when the crowd shouted back at him, in confused tumult, drowning him out.

What the crowd shouted—"murder" and "thief" and "hang him"—was not directed at the musketeer himself, but Athos could not have been more surprised if it had been.

He surveyed the scene before him, his face setting into a hard look composed half of determination and half of disdain.

Porthos's servant, Mousqueton, almost as tall as his master and nearly as powerful, looked bewildered, held by five guards of the Cardinal. And around them the crowd surged. Behind them was the armorer's shop, where Porthos had sent Mousqueton to arrange for Porthos's sword to be mended.

It was a low-slung building, and its wide door normally stood open to the outside street—to allow the inner air, warmed by the forge, to cool. But now the heavy oak doors were shut and there were muscular locals standing in front of them. When the musketeers had come to find the long-delayed Mousqueton, they'd stumbled on this scene of confusion and public disorder and just managed to step in front of the guards dragging Porthos's servant away.

Athos raised his hand towards the crowd, palm out, an imperious gesture. His assumption of authority quieted them for a moment. Into the silence, Athos poured his words, "I will vouch for Mousqueton. He is my friend Porthos's"—he indicated the redheaded giant just behind him with a head tilt—"servant and I've known him long. He is not a murderer."

He abstained from swearing that Mousqueton was not a

thief because, in truth, Porthos had recruited the then famished waif into his service upon Mousqueton's trying to steal from him. And even now, when he had for many years been employed in a steady if not necessarily respectable position as a musketeer's servant, Mousqueton was known to supplement Porthos's irregular pay in various and creative ways. Athos would be loath to say how many times the young man had shown up at one of their assemblies carrying a bottle, which he swore had just fallen from an overloaded cart, or a chicken, which he claimed had been run over by a cart and to which Mousqueton had felt compelled to give mercy.

But Athos was sure, as he was sure of breathing, that Mousqueton would not murder anyone. And yet his words met with the sneer of one of the guards holding Mousqueton's arm. "A fine thing to say, monsieur, when he was found next to the murdered armorer. And the armorer's best sword in this ruffian's hand!"

And on this the crowd shouted again. "Murderer" and "thief" and other things. Things about the musketeers and their servants, duelers and bullies and riffraff all.

Athos felt his hand fall onto the hilt of the sword strapped at his waist. "Do you call me a liar?" he shouted above the abuse of the crowd, "Do you doubt me?"

His voice, or the outrage in it, again brought a few moments of silence. But another of the guards said, "Well, monsieur, it is not as if it is not known that this man"—he shook Mousqueton, whose hands were tied together and who looked too bewildered to resist—"is a thief, all too fond of taking that which doesn't belong to him—eggs and bread and wine."

"But . . ." Porthos said, stepping forward. He was twice again as large as most other men, redheaded and dressed—as he normally was—in a splendid suit of golden brocade in the latest court fashion. But he looked as bewildered as his captive servant. "But, surely . . . taking a loaf of bread or an egg is not the same thing as killing someone, or even stealing a sword."

"Doubtless he killed in the heat of the moment," another guard said. "When discovered in theft."

"We've told you he wouldn't kill," Porthos said.

"Yes, yes," Athos said, impatiently. His hand held so tight onto the hilt that he felt as though the metal itself might snap under the force of his fury. "And they do not believe us, Porthos. They doubt the word of the King's Musketeers."

"With all respect," one of the guards said, in a voice that denoted he had none, "it is not your word we doubt, so much as your knowing anything about this. We found this man unconscious and holding a sword next to an armorer that had been killed with that sword. No one else was in the shop. No one else was seen to come in. He is the murderer."

And on this the crowd started shouting again, demanding Mousqueton's death. And Athos—furious at being ignored, feeling his face cool as blood drained from it—pulled at his sword, removing about a quarter of it from its sheath. He would have got it out altogether, and challenged all five of the guards of the Cardinal to defend themselves against his fury, had not a hand held onto his arm, forcing the sword back down.

Athos turned to look into the cool gaze, the intent green eyes of his friend Aramis. Tall, slim and blond, Aramis was admired by half the women and not a few men at court. He claimed a wish to become a priest. He claimed that his passage through the musketeers was just that—a temporary exile on his way to taking orders. But there were very few duelists in Paris who would dare cross swords with him. And the grip of his white, elongated fingers felt like bands of iron on Athos's arm.

"Will you stop me?" Athos hissed back at him. "I can

fight all five of them. Not bad odds, one of the King's Musketeers against five guards of Richelieu. And the rabble will melt. You know they will."

"No, Athos," Aramis said. "You forget the edict."

"The . . ." Athos said, and realized, as if on a wave of blind fury that seemed to obscure his gaze, that indeed, he had. Oh, not the edict against dueling. That had been in effect for many years. Aramis's own downfall, as a young divinity student, had come about because he had killed someone in a duel. But the edicts just drafted had a new force.

Dueling might have been illegal before, and brought the King's displeasure down on your head. It did not, however, bring down your head, itself. The new edict called for any nobleman caught in duel to be beheaded in the public square. And while it was said his Majesty hadn't signed it yet, the Cardinal was bringing it before the King every day. Who knew if he'd not signed it, just moments ago?

Athos took a deep breath, trying to control his anger. Many years ago, in the grip of a lesser fury, he'd killed the woman he loved, the woman he'd believed had lied to him and betrayed him in a grotesque way—a way likely to destroy his and his family's reputation forever. Then, on a wave of doubt and remorse, he'd entered the profession of musketeer to punish himself for that crime—as other men might enter a monastery to expiate sin. And yet his anger remained within him, in a confused coil with his overwhelming guilt.

That the rabble dared yell at a musketeer—That they thought they were safe—That his eminence's minions, themselves, would dare lay hands on a musketeer's servant—

"That's well," he said, forcing his fingers to let go of the sword. "That is all very well. But you have an innocent man, and the guilty one is still at large."

The guard who'd first spoken—a mean man, with a

ferret-like face and sparse moustaches—looked as though he was thinking of another insult to heap on the musketeers. But his imagination or his courage failed and, instead of speaking, he gave Athos a stiff little bow. "Very well, monsieur. If that is so, you may be able to prove it to his eminence before the man is hanged. For now, we are taking him to the Bastille, to wait his eminence's pleasure."

Mousqueton seemed to wake at those words. His eyes wild, he stared at them. "The Bastille!" he said, with the terror that the name of that infamous prison never failed to evoke. It was said that men disappeared into it never to be heard from again.

"Certainly the Bastille," the guard said, almost primly. "For where else could we trust you to stay that your master might not break you out?"

This time it was Athos who put his arm out, to restrain Porthos's hand as it fell on his sword. The larger musketeer did not protest it, just stared at Athos, as the guards dragged Mousqueton away and the greater part of the crowd followed.

"Come," the fourth member of their group—an eighteen-year-old Gascon, named D'Artagnan—said. "Come." Though he was the smallest—and youngest—of them all, the dark eyes in his olive-skinned face were full of cunning and Athos knew for a fact that his head was always full of thoughts. People like D'Artagnan looked at life as a game to be well played, a game in which it was important to be always two or three moves ahead of the adversary.

"Come," D'Artagnan said, again. And, turning, led them into a nearby alley.

"They're escaping," one of the mob called behind them, clearly having forgotten that they weren't accused of anything.

"Well, if they escape, we still have their servant," one of the guards said, chortling.

It took all of Athos's willpower, while grinding his teeth so it hurt, to keep from going back and punishing the insolence.

But D'Artagnan reached back and grasped the threadbare sleeve of Athos's second-best doublet, looked up urgently at his friend and said, "No Athos. No. It is no part of honor to fall into a trap."

He led them right, then left again, seemingly at random, until they came to an area where there was no one else around. There D'Artagnan stopped, and turning his back to the blind wall of a garden, he looked at his friends.

"By the Mass," Porthos said. "You should have let me fight them. They took my poor Mousqueton!"

"Your poor Mousqueton will be well, Porthos," Aramis said.

"Well? In the Bastille?"

"Surely well, in the Bastille," Aramis said, throwing back his head and with it the blond, shining curtain of his hair. "Surely you don't think that they would mistreat him, much less kill him? Not when they know we will be going to Monsieur de Treville with our grievance as soon as we can get to his office. And that Monsieur de Treville will want to ensure Porthos's servant is treated fairly. The Cardinal is not so foolish that he'll overplay his hand this soon. He would only risk the King's ire."

"But . . ." Porthos said. And opened his hands as though his words had quite failed him. "The Bastille!"

Most musketeers, most guards of Richelieu, probably most of the people who knew the giant musketeer would think he was stupid. Athos, who had been one of Porthos's closest friends for many years, knew better. Porthos was an observant man, an intelligent one, and quite capable of sudden, blinding insight into the souls of men. However words themselves were Porthos's foe, one that refused to be drawn out into the light of day. And in moments of emotion, like this, Porthos's lack of facility with words managed to make him seem young and almost small.

"He'll be safe, even in the Bastille for a while," D'Artagnan said, taking the lead. "We will, of course, as Aramis says, go to your captain, Monsieur de Treville, and ask him, at once, to make sure that Mousqueton is well and that we have the time needed to prove his innocence."

"But," Porthos said, and clutched at his red locks in despair. "How could it come to this? I only asked him to go and get my sword repaired!"

"I was listening in the crowd," D'Artagnan said, gravely. "While you were . . . disputing with the mob, I was talking to some of them, and they say that the armorer was found killed—run through with his best sword. And Mousqueton was found unconscious next to him. And you must know that Mousqueton's reputation . . ." He floundered, doubtless catching some hint of annoyance in his friend Porthos's look. "Well, everyone knows how fast Mousqueton's fingers can be, Porthos."

"But he wouldn't steal a sword," Porthos said. "To what purpose? And if he ran the armorer through, why would he be unconscious? I mean Mousqueton. Surely he wouldn't faint at the sight of blood! He is my servant. You did tell them that, D'Artagnan, did you not?"

D'Artagnan shrugged. He looked up and his gaze met Athos's. D'Artagnan looked more troubled and worried than his calm words would lead anyone to suppose. "Porthos, they say that a hammer fell from its peg nearby—probably in the fight—and chanced to hit Mousqueton on the head, just as he killed the armorer."

"God's Teeth!" Porthos said. "Are you telling me you believe Mousqueton killed him?"

"Mousqueton is your servant, Porthos, as you said, he cannot be a stranger to blood and killing."

"Yes, but . . . it is one thing to kill someone in a duel," Porthos said. "And another and quite different to murder someone by stealth."

"But we don't know if it wasn't a duel, Porthos," D'Artagnan said. "Or a fight."

Porthos shook his head. "What would he have to fight with the armorer about? Good man, he was, let me have repairs on my sword on credit. He knew Mousqueton . . ." Words failing him, Porthos simply opened his hands.

Athos could have said many things, among them being, that the way life was, it was quite possible that a sudden altercation had arisen, or sudden anger. Or he could have said that Mousqueton was, after all, a little inclined to ignore the eighth commandment. But the whole situation—Mousqueton being unconscious when found, and clearly unable to give a coherent account of himself, even by the time his master had arrived on the scene—seemed skewed. Surely, it couldn't be. The circumstances were just too strange. And the guards had been all too quick to seize upon Mousqueton as a culprit.

Perhaps they had accused Mousqueton out of pique against the musketeers. Or perhaps, just perhaps, because they were hoping to hide the true culprit, if they moved fast enough.

Athos took his hand to his forehead. "I do think, D'Artagnan, that this is all a little too convenient. And, though Mousqueton is doubtless human, and could doubtless have lost his temper, I must say that his being found unconscious does not seem natural."

"No," D'Artagnan said. "Fear not. I agree with you. The whole thing is too convenient by far, for Mousqueton to be found unconscious with a bloodied sword in his hand. I don't for a moment believe it all happened like that, with no one else being involved."

"But what can we do to prove it?" Aramis asked.

D'Artagnan shrugged. "What we always do. We'll find out what happened. We ask people who might know something. We examine the armorer's shop."

"And we prove Mousqueton innocent!" Porthos said.

"And we prove him innocent," D'Artagnan said. "Others among us have been accused of murder before," he looked at Aramis. "Surely the fact that Mousqueton is a servant doesn't make him any less our responsibility."

"No," Aramis said, doubtless remembering the circumstances under which he'd been suspected of murder, circumstances far more incriminating than even Mousqueton's.[1] "No. Perhaps more our responsibility, since he's more defenseless than we are."

"Yes," Porthos said. "We are his only family, you know? He was an orphan when I took him into my service."

"Well, then," Athos said, and though he heard the amusement in his own voice, he knew he was in dead earnest. "Let it be for our servants as it is for us. We'll prove him innocent or die trying. One for all—"

"And all for one," his friends answered in a single voice.

---

[1] *The Musketeer's Seamstress.*

The Antechamber of Monsieur de Treville;
The Inadvisability of Tempting
a Musketeer; The Limits of the Possible

✎

PORTHOS didn't doubt that Monsieur de Treville would be able to do something about Mousqueton. After all, Monsieur de Treville, captain of the musketeers, often stood somewhere between a father and a confessor to his musketeers. He was the one who got them pardons from the King when they were arrested mid duel. He was the one who protected them from trouble when their amorous adventures landed them in hot water.

And he had been the one who, those many years ago when Aramis killed a man in a duel with Porthos as his second, had looked after them and given them a place to hide and identities to hide under. He had also, through the various travails in which the four friends found themselves involved, stood by their side and protected them. Porthos was sure that Monsieur de Treville could do something.

But when they arrived, the antechamber was crowded. Oh, it was normally crowded, serving the musketeers as gathering place, sports chamber and training room. The entire room—a huge, well-proportioned room of Italianate influence, furnished with fine mosaic floors and columned expanse—was the setting for impromptu mock duels—battles for position and place—in which the musketeers tested their mettle and fought with such abandon that a stranger might imagine they wished to kill each other. On the stairs, the more adventurous ones fought, gaining and losing a step or two, at the risk of eye or ear or limb.

Normally when in the antechamber, Porthos, Athos, Aramis and D'Artagnan whiled away their time fighting on the stairs—either against each other, or the four of them shoulder to shoulder against any challengers. But this time they were in a hurry and, as they came into the room, Aramis searched among the throng of musketeers for a harassed looking young man in the livery of Monsieur de Treville—one of his attendants or clerks, who made it his business to announce when someone might have an urgent need. He cut through the crowd to approach the small darkhaired gentleman and whisper in his ear.

As the gentleman turned to go through the dueling crowd on the stairs and Aramis turned back to his friends, Porthos heard behind him, "I'd say they're worried. I hear Porthos's servant was arrested for murder."

"He let his own servant be taken?" another voice said.

"Worse. He let his servant be taken by Richelieu's guards," another said.

And yet another quipped in, in the tone of someone who would ape Aramis's style of dressing and manner, without the slightest hint of the blond musketeer's suave personality, "Well, murder surprises me, but we all know he's a cursed little thief, don't we."

As Porthos felt his hand drop to the hilt of his sword, another voice said, "Oh, no. I wouldn't say that." Porthos halted his movement, but when the voice finished, "I'd never call Mousqueton little," Porthos's hand pulled up and his sword with it, glinting by the light coming in through the lead-paned windows of the antechamber.

"You dare," he heard himself bellow, before he was

even sure what he was about. "You insult me and my servant? In my hearing?"

Turning, he faced a group of five musketeers—it was plain they'd been the ones speaking. For one, even though the antechamber was so crowded that it would have been difficult for any individual person to move, everyone around them had managed to move back. They, themselves, looked as though they'd been stopped in the middle of taking a step back—but had done it too slowly to quite manage to meld with the crowd behind them, which managed to look as though they had always been back there, looking with interested eyes at the five and the irate giant redhead with his sword in hand.

Porthos's eye alighted on each of the suddenly pale faces. Yes. As he expected. Three of them he didn't know by name, though they'd probably been on the same side in a hundred street battles, when the cry of "to me, Musketeers" went up and any musketeer in range came to support his comrades.

The other two he knew all too well. One of them, Roux, who shared with Athos the superficial resemblance of being tall and dark haired—though his eyes were not dark blue and he did not have the same air of nobility—had for some time now taken to wearing the same old-fashioned, Spanish style tight doublets and flaring breeches that Athos favored. The other, Bernard D'Augine, was his best friend. Blond and slim like Aramis, he aped the blond musketeer in everything, from his fashionable clothes, to his habits of speech, and that annoying habit that Aramis had of turning his hand to contemplate his fingernails when he was about to say something particularly cutting.

In his defense—at least that Porthos knew—D'Augine had not taken to claiming that his passage through the musketeer corps was just a temporary detour on his way to becoming a priest. This, and this alone saved Porthos from wanting to cut his heart out right there. But he was not feeling particularly charitable for all that. "Draw," he said, through clenched teeth. "All five of you draw. Let's see if you're match for my steel. Let's see if, in my place, you would have been able to keep your servant from being arrested."

He was dimly aware—as one atop a runaway horse is aware of the screams of those surrounding him—of Aramis's voice saying "Porthos!" And of D'Artagnan's putting in, "The edicts."

He answered D'Artagnan. "Don't worry. This is not dueling. It's slaughter. I am going to—"

Before he had a chance to say what he was about to do, the voice that everyone in that antechamber obeyed rang from the top of the stairs. "Porthos! Athos! Aramis!" And, after the slightest hesitation, since Monsieur de Treville was not, after all, his captain, "D'Artagnan."

The mass of men in the antechamber shifted again, parting like the sea before divine will. A clear path up the stairs was suddenly evident and through this loped Aramis, followed by Athos, who managed to rush while looking as if he weren't doing so at all, and finally D'Artagnan, who tugged at Porthos's sleeve on the way and whispered, "Sheathe."

Porthos turned and sheathed, as he started up the stairs after his friends. Even at that moment, if one of the five had dared speak again, he feared he must turn back and massacre them, simply for the principle of it.

But there was no sound behind him, as he made it all the way up the stairs and got into the office in last place, just as Monsieur de Treville—taking his place behind a massive and cluttered desk—waved at the rest of them to take chairs.

Being invited to sit, in Monsieur de Treville's office, was a rare occurrence and usually reserved for the delivery of bad news. Normally a conference in the captain's office was restricted to one of two functions—informing the musketeers how far they'd trespassed on their captain's goodwill and how they'd need to present really good reasons for their conduct or be dismissed; or listening to their problems and offering solutions.

Either type of conference usually took no more than a few minutes, though the musketeers could often swear that the first type took whole days or perhaps weeks. But now, something was very different. Worrisomely different, Porthos noticed, as he settled himself on a small chair with a cushioned seat, whose dainty proportions hadn't been designed even for the normal musketeer much less someone of Porthos's overlarge and over-muscular frame.

He held his breath and tried to keep his weight at least partly on his feet, afraid that if he shifted it to his behind the chair would splinter and crash to the ground in pieces beneath him. But even this concern wasn't enough to keep him from noticing that Monsieur de Treville looked ashen pale, and his brow was knit in a frown of worry.

"The devil," Porthos's mouth blurted out. "Don't tell me Mousqueton's case is that difficult, Captain."

The captain's dark eyes turned to Porthos, in something like wonder. Many people who met Porthos looked at him in wonder when he spoke at all. It seemed to be against the laws of nature that someone that tall and that bulky, let alone possessed of the type of features that made people think of Viking longships, should be endowed with the French tongue and speak it without the least hint of an accent. Other people were surprised when Porthos perceived their intentions or saw through their motives. Because Porthos was not facile of language, and sometimes in fact said quite the wrong word at the most inappropriate time, people tended to assume he was stupid.

But Monsieur de Treville had known Porthos for years,

and knew, furthermore, that none of his friends would associate with a dumb person because, all of them being quick of mind, the intercourse with a mental inferior would grate. Porthos knew he knew this, yet he looked upon Porthos with an astonished, wandering look for a long while.

At last he sighed. "It's not Mousqueton, Porthos." He frowned slightly and leaned forward on his desk, interlacing his hands atop of it. "I'm afraid it is far more complex than that, and perhaps . . ." He shrugged. "You could not have chosen a worse time, nor could have poor Mousqueton, to put himself in the hands of Richelieu."

Porthos felt bewildered "But we didn't choose—"

"No, of course not," Monsieur de Treville said, and looked up, his dark eyes, despite their worry, managing to look somewhat amused at the idea of Mousqueton voluntarily getting arrested by Richelieu. Monsieur de Treville was from Gascony, D'Artagnan's compatriot. And, like D'Artagnan, he had the olive skin of the region, the quick eyes, the piercing gaze, and the sense of humor that surfaced even at the moment of greatest tension. "No." He looked around the room, fixing each of them with his gaze in turn and arresting, at last, on Aramis. "I would guess you know what this is about?"

Porthos now turned to Aramis, arguably his best friend among the inseparables, in utter bewilderment. "Let me tell you what this is about," he said, before Aramis—who was studying his nails—could speak. "Captain, I don't know what you've been told, but here is what happened. I broke my sword, and I sent Mousqueton to the armorer to mend it—you know, the one on Rue des Echarps. I didn't have money for it, but Mousqueton and the armorer knew each other, and I thought they could . . . well, Mousqueton often arranged to trade one of my old cloaks or something, you see . . . So, anyway, I sent him. And next thing we know, he'd been arrested for murder and attempted theft. And you know he never stole anything." And then, with sudden recollection of his servant's habits, and seeing the quickening of humor in Monsieur de Treville's eyes. "Well, not as such. Getting the occasional loaf of bread or bottle of wine isn't stealing. It's . . . it's keeping from starving." He said, opening his hands in a show of helplessness.

And Monsieur de Treville, who knew just how often Louis XIII's encumbered finances meant that he must delay paying his musketeers, and to what straits his musketeers could be driven, nodded and opened his hands a little in sympathy. "Yes, I know the facts of the case, Porthos. The musketeers all bring me news sometimes before the principals of the event, themselves, know. In fact, just before you arrived, I was going to have you called, in case you'd chanced to come in, because . . ." He paused, and looked, this time to the chair by Porthos's side, where D'Artagnan, the youngest and smallest of them all, sat, prim and proper like a schoolchild. "D'Artagnan," he said. "Did nothing about what happened strike you as odd?"

"Only one thing," D'Artagnan said. "Why five guards of the Cardinal were right there, on hand, to arrest Mousqueton. It might mean nothing. They might have simply been getting their swords mended, as Mousqueton was, but . . ." D'Artagnan took a deep breath. "All the same they seemed a little too quick, almost gleeful to arrest him. Of course with the edict hanging over our heads, they knew we wouldn't dare fight them, and yet it seems a little . . ." He seemed to hesitate. "Intemperate to arrest the servant of someone like Porthos, on no more than the cry of the mob."

"And to take him to the Bastille!" Porthos said, in a tone of outrage.

Monsieur de Treville nodded at D'Artagnan and turned

to Aramis. "And you, Chevalier, I believe know why they were so quick to arrest him, even if none of us can be sure what brought them there?"

"Yes," Aramis said. "Or rather . . ." He hesitated. "I believe I do, though since I intend on taking orders as soon as it is possible, I'm not very interested in these worldly affairs." This was roughly, Porthos thought, the equivalent of an ant not liking to be immersed in sugar. Aramis was always alive to every rumor and knew the heart of every conspiracy. He watched as his friend, apparently unaware of the irony of his words, looked at his nails again and scratched, absorbedly at one with the index nail of the other hand. "But I have heard that a certain duchess who is close friends with the Queen . . . That is, I heard that who some of their correspondence has been intercepted, and that the Queen fears the duchess will be taken from her as . . . as so many of her friends have."

"I see," Monsieur de Treville said. "And you lack all knowledge of the contents of this correspondence."

"I've been given to understand," Aramis said. "That someone of a suspicious turn of mind might think that it fomented conspiracy against him or even . . ." He shrugged slightly. "A plot to assassinate him."

"You speak in riddles," Porthos burst forth. "Who is this duchess? And what can she mean with the Queen? And what does all of it have to do with my poor Mousqueton? And when you say duchess, is she yet another of your seamstresses?"

The shocked look from Aramis might mean anything—including that the duchess was indeed one of his seamstresses, the name Aramis had used for many years to signify whichever noble lady he was, at the time, having a carnal liaison with. But before Aramis could answer, Monsieur de Treville cleared his throat calling their attention.

"I'm not going to credit Aramis's rumor," he said. "But

I have heard rumors myself and, what's more . . ." He shrugged. "As you know, I have friends among the guards of his eminence as, doubtless, he has friends among my musketeers."

"If I find the dogs," Porthos said, understanding that by friends Monsieur de Treville meant spies, "I will cut out their tongues."

"You'll do nothing of the kind," Aramis interposed. "Do you not think that Monsieur de Treville knows who they are? A known spy is almost an ally. You can make sure he knows only what you want him to know and furthermore that he knows a lot of things that aren't true."

Porthos, who was quite bright enough but disdained this type of underhanded intrigue, turned to the captain, only to be met with a nod of acquiescence. "Indeed, my dear Porthos," he said. "I beg you you will leave his eminence's pet musketeers alone," he said with the hint of amusement. "However, this is how it stands—rightly or wrongly, his eminence has interpreted some correspondence which he intercepted between the Duchess de . . . well, I need not name her, only to give her her nom de guerre, Marie Michon, and the Queen. And he has taken it into his head that the purpose of the two ladies' conspiracy is to kill him and install another one in his place, in the King's favor." He shrugged. "I'm sure it's all overblown suspicion, however . . ." He shrugged again. "You can see how this would make him wish to have one of your servants in his power."

"I see nothing of the kind," Porthos said. "What has poor Mousqueton to do with duchesses and queens?"

"Well," Monsieur de Treville fixed the four with a slightly considering gaze. "It is an open secret, though certainly not openly discussed, that the Queen owes the four inseparables a favor. This being so, she might be convinced to abandon her interest in this conspiracy and, in fact, to denounce her friend wholly to the Cardinal, in order to avoid the inseparables' servant being condemned on a murder charge."

"*Dents Dieu*," Porthos said. "You'd think that if she's indebted to us, they'd try to arrest one of us, not our servant."

The look the captain gave him was grave enough it would not have been out of place at a funeral. "Undoubtedly they did and they will, Porthos. Mousqueton was probably simply the easiest prey at the time. They know how loyal the Queen is, and that she might commit whatever folly for her friend. She has near disgraced herself for other friends in the past."

"But . . ." Porthos said. "But . . . I would not want the Queen to compromise herself for my sake." And after a hesitation, "Or even Mousqueton's."

But at the same time that he spoke, Athos said, "Do you mean to tell us, sir, that Cardinal Richelieu ordered the armorer murdered solely in order to entrap Porthos's servant?"

"If he thought that would result in saving his life?" Monsieur de Treville said. "Yes, I do believe he would do so, do you not?"

Porthos could easily believe that Athos did not. Athos was a noble person—not just born a nobleman—and often had trouble believing the intrigues and dishonorable maneuvers that seemed to be part of living at court. And as much as all of them hated Richelieu, Athos's noble spirit sometimes shrunk from what that gentleman would not stoop to do.

"But . . ." Porthos protested. "What are we to do? How can we save Mousqueton without compromising her Majesty?"

"There is only one way," Monsieur de Treville said.

"We must find the true murderer and expose him," Aramis said. "If the true murderer is exposed, then they will, perforce, have to let Mousqueton go."

Porthos thought through this. Yes, that was undeniably true. Even if it had been one of the guards of the cardinal, it should be possible to expose his guilt. "But we will need time," he said.

Monsieur de Treville shrugged again. "I'll talk to the King, my dear Porthos. I understand you practically raised the young man, and that he's almost like a son to you. And you have this comfort, Porthos, that the Cardinal will not easily dispose of so valuable a hostage. There will be no rush to execute Mousqueton. Not when he has hopes of bending the Queen to his will by virtue of her indebtedness to you."

Porthos felt somewhat reassured but not as much as he'd wish to be. He couldn't avoid the thought that at this very moment, his poor Mousqueton was in a place reckoned as one of the antechambers of Hell.

Their being dismissed, he stopped at the door, and turned inside for a final question, "Captain . . . would it be possible for me to see him?"

Doubts and Fears;
The Ever Vanishing Musketeers;
Only One Thing To Do

∽

THEY walked out of the captain's office and out through
the antechamber, while the crowds of rowdy musketeers
parted for them as though they were infected with a dread
disease. Athos noticed it only with part of his mind, while
the rest of it worked at what the captain had said.

Although no one in Paris would have classed a single of
the inseparables as naive—D'Artagnan being the only exception and him people would only call naive until they got
to know him better—from Athos's perspective all of them
were naive, or at least more trusting than himself. He cast a
look sideways at each of them in turn.

Porthos seemed confident that the captain could at least
keep Mousqueton from being executed for a good while.
This might or might not be true, of course. It all depended
on how fast Mousqueton lost his value as a hostage and on
whether the person who had committed the crime was
someone Richelieu valued. Athos could hardly imagine
Rochefort being handed in for the sake of sparing Porthos's
servant. No, for his right-hand man, the Cardinal would
fight as for his own life.

And the whole idea that the trap had been set for Mousqueton just because he happened to be alone and away from them—and if this were engineered by Richelieu, it would need believing just that—was disturbing. Did this mean each and every one of them was in similar danger? Each and every one of their servants? "Aramis," he said, speaking as though out of his dreams, without looking at his friend. "And D'Artagnan." He took a deep breath, bracing for what he was about to say, and any questions that might follow. "We must send messages to our servants now, if you know where yours are. Grimaud should be at home. Ask your servants to meet Grimaud at my home and stay there. And for neither of them to go out without at least one of us."

There was a silence, and for a moment, Athos believed his friends would argue, but instead, what he heard was a deep sigh from Aramis, followed by, "Oh, Bazin will not like that."

"I understand," Athos said. "But I believe his safety must trump his preference in this matter."

"Yes, I believe so too," Aramis said. D'Artagnan didn't say anything. They walked back, and into the captain's compound, where they found three servants to take hastily scrawled notes to their servants. Porthos waited by, silently, as if deep in thought. Athos would like to believe that Porthos's being deep in thought meant he was thinking of something sensible.

The problem with the redheaded giant—beyond his open warfare with language—was that Porthos's brain seemed to work in a very original manner. Perhaps this came from his having been raised, wild and almost illiterate, cut off from civilized interaction, in a distant domain. Or perhaps it was just the way Porthos's genius—and it was genius—worked.

But while he might be the only one of them to think of examining the pattern of blood drops at the scene of a crime[2], and while this might be the key to the entire murder they were trying to solve, the truth was that Porthos's ideas were often impractical, or disregarded such minor things as what other people might think or the possibility of being arrested for something.

Athos badly wanted to get Porthos to tell them what he was thinking about, but chances were the answer would muddle more than enlighten, so he kept quiet, as they walked back out of Monsieur de Treville's residence, and onto the street once more. They walked, four abreast, down the street, forcing everyone else to take long detours around them, and to cast them almost fearful looks. Athos realized their steps were perfectly in rhythm, which, given their varying heights and walks, was somewhat of a miracle, and smiled despite himself.

In his life, he'd lost title and honor, wife and domain. But his friends made it possible for him to wake every day and do what must be done, no matter how many ghosts had haunted his remorse-plagued sleep.

At the next crossing, Aramis paused, and the rest of them stopped, one step forward, and turned to look at the blond musketeer.

Aramis tilted his head back to look at them, a frown of deep thought on his regular features. "I wonder . . ." he said.

"Yes?" Athos said.

Aramis nodded, but his mind seemed to be very far away. "That is," he said, "I think I should go to the royal palace. After all, Mousqueton's . . . friend . . . Hermengarde, lives there. Surely, if he did do this or if . . . if the problem is with the armorer, Hermengarde will know?"

"Mousqueton did not do this!" Porthos said, harshly.

---

[2]*A Death in Gascony.*

"No. I don't believe he did, Porthos, except maybe if it was in self-defense. Imagine that the armorer has some reason to hate Mousqueton. Imagine that . . . shall we say . . . the armorer thought he wanted to kill Mousqueton and advanced on him. Can you doubt that Mousqueton has seen enough swordplay to instinctively pick up a sword and . . ."

Porthos snorted. "Mousqueton might have seen swordplay, but that doesn't make him an expert. Surely you'd seen swordplay before you came to me because you wished to fight your first duel. If I hadn't taught you to wield a sword, how would that duel have gone with you?"

Aramis shook his head. "But he would be fighting against someone who is not a dueler."

"Granted," Porthos said. "But all good armorers are *trained* in the weapons they make. They study them and work at them and wield them in practice, so that they can tell how the balance should be and whether the weapon they just created is any good. And this one, Langelier père, was the best armorer in Paris. Not the most expensive but the best. I went to him because though his swords and knives were not ornate, they were the best balanced and the sturdiest. I know. I used to teach fencing." He shook his head gravely. "My poor Mousqueton would not have a chance."

Aramis sighed. "You don't know. People do strange things in the grip of fear."

Porthos shrugged. "By all means," he said. "Go and ask Hermengarde, but I don't think you'll find anything. If Mousqueton had felt any animosity towards this armorer, count on it, I would have heard."

Athos knew the interminable discussions Porthos and Aramis could get into. They resembled the bickering between brothers and often gave the impression they had been going on since the beginning of the world and would go on until the final trumpet. In this one, Aramis, contrary to form, was not using the longest words he could find in his vocabulary, or the convoluted argumentation methods taught to him by his Jesuit masters, but doubtless, that too would come, if Athos allowed the discussion to continue. Which Athos had no intention of doing. Instead he cut in. "Aramis, you cannot go alone."

Aramis graced him with a sudden smile. "I cannot? And why not?"

"But you just saw . . . you just wrote a letter to Bazin, telling him to go and stay with Grimaud. Surely, you don't think that you'll be safe, if our servants aren't?"

Aramis shrugged. "Bazin is notoriously bad with a sword," he said. "If someone attacked him, he'd probably either bless them, or—if we're lucky—hit them over the head with a crucifix. And since he doesn't normally carry a crucifix about on his person, I'd have to guess the blessing part. I"—he smiled again—"am not Bazin."

"I cannot approve of your risking yourself this way, Aramis," Athos said. "After all, with the edict hanging over our heads, any duel could be a death sentence."

"Not if you kill your enemy and his seconds, and there are no witnesses," Aramis said. "That will keep you from being arrested."

"Aramis!" Athos said. He could well understand his friend's frustration at the idea that they were, yet again, in a situation where it was not safe to conduct business alone and without chaperonage. But then again, he must see the situation as it was. "Why do you believe you will be attacked, and not merely entrapped?"

Aramis shrugged. "If I'm entrapped, I'll attack."

"I could go with you," D'Artagnan offered.

"I would prefer you don't," Aramis said. "If, as you believe, the Cardinal is seeking to entrap the Queen by taking Mousqueton—if, as the captain believes and as it is rumored, the Cardinal imagines conspiracies against his life . . . Then if I go alone to the palace, and they see me talking to Hermengarde, they will think that I am just talking to yet another woman." He gave a little smile, quite different from his previous ones—half filled with rueful self-mockery. "You must know it is believed I'll sleep with any woman at all. However, if I am with D'Artagnan, the Cardinal will wonder if we're trying to circumvent his plan to entrap Mousqueton. Or if we're part of some plot to kill him." He looked at his fingernails. "You must see it can't be done."

"Must I?"

Aramis smiled, and this time it was yet another smile—his suave, practiced courtier's smile that gave the impression he could glide over trouble and not feel it. "Indeed you must. Fear not. Nothing will happen to me."

And with that, he walked away. Athos, staring after him, crossed his arms on his chest. What could he do? He might feel as responsible for his younger friends as if they were his children or his vassals, but he couldn't tell them that. It would only enrage them. The second possibly more than the first.

He looked back at his other friends, to realize there was only one remaining. D'Artagnan, looking back at Athos with an expression between amusement and worry. "Porthos must have walked away while we were arguing with Aramis," D'Artagnan said.

Athos nodded and repressed a wish to sigh. "Indeed. Which would not worry me as much, if I didn't know how Porthos's mind works. Or doesn't."

"Yes," D'Artagnan said. "Me too. I wonder what he got it in his head to do."

"If we are lucky," Athos said, "he's gone to Athenais to ask her opinion of all this. Athenais will keep him from doing something foolish." Athenais was Porthos's longtime lover, the younger wife of an aged notary. She had met all of them under trying circumstances and had earned the respect of them all and, possibly, a little of Aramis's fear.

"If he's gone to Athenais," D'Artagnan began, doubtfully, "you know, what I should do . . ." he said, and hesitated. Then, as though acquiring renewed courage, continued, "You know, it is possible this is not the Cardinal's trap. Or at least that it wasn't set by him. It is not unusual to see five guards of the Cardinal walking around town in a group."

"Though it's more likely to see them sober than it is to find five sober musketeers," Athos said, only half joking.

"Yes, very paltry fellows, the Cardinal's men. Comes from serving a churchman," D'Artagnan said, and a humorous light danced in his dark eyes. "But all the same, they walk all around town in groups, as much as we do, which is what results in so many duels between the musketeers and the guards.

"So, they might have been passing by, and might have seen an opportunity. Perhaps they are of the trusted few who know that the Cardinal needed a hostage. Or perhaps they just recognized Mousqueton and decided to avenge themselves on Porthos through him."

Athos shrugged. "Well, that does not matter. It would still be the same, once the Cardinal had hold of him. A mind such as Richelieu's cannot have failed to see Mousqueton as a pawn in a game where he can entrap the Queen. Or lead her to entrap herself."

"Indeed," D'Artagnan said. "But it makes a very great difference towards two purposes, you see?" He lifted his hand and counted on his fingers. "One, if the trap was not set on purpose, it is not likely the Cardinal will try to entrap the rest of us, or our servants." And as Athos opened his mouth to reply, D'Artagnan said, "Not that I suggest we risk ourselves unnecessarily. But the qualifying term there is unnecessarily. I realize the Cardinal might think circumstances offered him a really good opportunity to entrap us, and might seek to replicate them from now on. But even so, he's unlikely to get anything set up in time."

"In time?"

"Right now. Today. These things take time."

"I suppose," Athos said, frowning. He could see that D'Artagnan had some maggot in his brain and some plan that would, more than likely, be foolhardy. If not as foolhardy as Porthos—or at least not as unheeding of consequences—not very far off. He narrowed his eyes at his friend. "Why today? What do you intend to do?"

"Well, I thought," D'Artagnan said. "You know the place I come from. Not very . . . well . . . being the son of the lord didn't mean I was that far above the peasants. And in my youth," he said, quite unheeding of the irony of saying these words when the beard growth was still uncertain upon his chin, "I used to associate with farmers and crafters, and all manner of people."

"Yes?" Athos asked, trying to get the boy to tell him the nonsense he intended, so that Athos, who was old enough to be D'Artagnan's father, could stop him before he got hurt.

"Well, I thought I could borrow one of Planchet's suits of clothes—"

"And look like a scarecrow," Athos said, because Planchet, D'Artagnan's servant, was taller than Athos himself and thinner than anyone Athos had ever seen—as opposed to the young Gascon's broad-shouldered figure, which came no higher than Athos's shoulder.

"Well, probably," D'Artagnan shrugged. "But that is all to the good and only adds to the image I'm trying to create."

"Which is?"

"That of a young man, from a farmer's household, just come from Gascony to earn his living in Paris. You see," he rushed ahead as though he feared that Athos would contradict him, "Gascony is so poor, what with all the wars and invasions and all, that it is not just noblemen who can't provide for their sons there. Even well-to-do farmers, if they have more than two sons, often send one to seek his fortune in Paris."

"I fail to understand why you would want to pretend to be a peasant seeking employment," Athos said, half-guessing where this was going and dreading it. D'Artagnan would walk in where angels feared to tread. No, he would dance in.

"Because then I can go to the neighborhood of the armorer," D'Artagnan said. "And ask the people in the neighborhood if someone might have wanted him dead. If this is not a trap of the Cardinal's, there's a good chance that the person who murdered the armorer was someone in the family or one of his acquaintances. Only someone in the neighborhood will know who's likely to have done it."

"And so," Athos asked, folding his arms. "You intend to leave your post as guard and go work as a chamber pot emptier at some inn?"

D'Artagnan laughed, the easy laughter of youth. "I was hoping," he said, "for some more distinguished position. Perhaps swine feeder." He shook his head. "But no, I did not intend to take a post. Tell them I have another thing waiting, you know, but I'm just . . . looking around for another, in case the first one doesn't come through. That way, I have an excuse for not staying there too long. And if I meet a likely lass around my age, I may return, and claim it is for her sake . . . and ask a few more questions."

Athos thought a moment. The boy was right. If this was not a plot of Richelieu's—and no matter how much power Richelieu had, he couldn't be held accountable for every crime in France—then it must be something that had happened in the man's family and neighborhood. He looked down at D'Artagnan, who was looking up at him, his eyes shining with mischief and that repressed excitement the youth always seemed to feel when they were in the middle of an adventure.

The boy might be right. But he could not go alone and unprotected. "I'll come with you," Athos said.

D'Artagnan's eyes widened. "No. Everyone would know you for what you are."

"But I'll borrow a suit of Grimaud's!"

D'Artagnan's lips stretched in a convulsive smile, which he seemed to control only by a great effort of will. "Athos, my friend, no." And to what Athos was sure was his own bewildered countenance, he added, "My friend, you could dress in rags and soot, and you'd still look like one of the noblest men in the land." He bowed a little. "Which you are."

"But—" Athos said. Oh, he was proud of his ancestry and his family name. For their sake, he had renounced his domain rather than drag that noble name through the mud by associating it with his marriage to a branded criminal. But he didn't think, if he should dress as a commoner, anyone would guess his true origins.

"Trust me," D'Artagnan said, with a slight smile. "Everyone who meets you knows you come from a noble background. I don't think there's anything you can do to make yourself look as a commoner. Cloaked and hidden, your posture must yet announce your quality to the world."

Athos sighed. He didn't want to believe it, but the truth was, there were many people who'd told him the same in the past. That there was something about him that stood out. And hadn't he seen it, in his duels with strangers, that they always demanded to know his true name—that they always knew his name was one of the noblest in France. And yet. "But D'Artagnan, I don't want any harm to come to you. You are the youngest of us."

"And you are the oldest. Do not let it disturb you. No

harm shall come to me. I can't take my sword, but I shall take a dagger, and you know, if I've survived the snares we've escaped so far, I won't be that easy to kill."

He bowed slightly, almost formally, to Athos.

And Athos, standing alone on the street corner, watched him walk until he turned right and disappeared from sight, headed for the Rue des Fossoyers, where he would be getting an outfit for the expedition.

So, Aramis has gone to the palace. To see Hermengarde, he says. And D'Artagnan has gone to look about the neighborhood where the armorer lived. And I? What can I do? He stood on the street corner, and his mind went back to the interview with the captain. Monsieur de Treville had looked more worried than he should. As though he were not absolutely sure he could keep Mousqueton from harm in Richelieu's prison.

If that was true, what could Athos do? Only one thing came to mind. *I must,* he thought, *go see if this is Richelieu's plan, myself.*

Night was falling, the streets of Paris filled with the curious red of a wintry sunset. Athos squinted at the sunset, then at the crowds of commoners, noblemen, whores and musketeers pouring out for an hour or two of amusement.

And he turned and headed towards the compound that housed the Cardinal Richelieu and those he commanded.

Grief and Comfort;
Where Mousqueton's Reputation
is Tarnished; The Merest Acquaintances

⚜

TURNING towards the royal palace—the so called hôtel de ville—brought an already familiar bittersweet ache to Aramis's heart. Last winter, when he turned this way, he'd been on his way to see his *seamstress*, Violette, Duchess de Dreux, one of the noblest women in the land and, in Aramis's eyes, the most beautiful woman in the world.

She'd been a friend of Anne of Austria's, come with her at the time of the Queen's marriage and forcibly married to a French nobleman who spurned his new wife's charms, charms that Aramis had been more than happy to enjoy. It seemed to him, these many months after she'd been cruelly murdered, that he'd only realized how much he loved her and how much he'd miss her after she was lost to him forever.

Her face haunted his dreams. He'd wake in the middle of the night and swear he'd just heard the tinkle of her musical laughter. His hand would stretch to find only cold bed, and no Violette, and he'd come awake in stark loss, as though it had just happened, as if she'd just been taken from him.

And he'd find himself, at a duel, or a game, a night of

drinking or in the middle of a conversation with his friends, thinking "I must tell Violette of this," only to realize he'd never tell Violette anything at all, because she was gone forever. And it was all he could do, at such moments, to turn his face and hide the tears that prickled at his eyes.

He couldn't have brought D'Artagnan with him now. Because while he was alone and walking towards the palace, he could pretend that he was going to see Violette, and that she would be there, in her startlingly pink room, waiting for him with a smile. And walking through the streets, he walked as if in a revery, dreaming of her soft hair beneath his face, of those lips that, on kissing, felt like animated velvet.

Only at the entrance to the royal palace did he wake. He had to, because he was not going to the entrance nearest Violette's room, nor would instructions have been left with the musketeers on guard duty to let him pass. Instead, he approached an entrance a friend of his was guarding, and bowed slightly. "D'Armaud," he said. "I have some business within."

D'Armaud, a young musketeer who aped Aramis, but with the greatest of admirations, looked at him doubtfully. "I don't think it will do you any good, my friend, to try to plead the case of Porthos's servant with the King yourself. Or even with the Queen. You know they don't receive—"

Aramis laughed, and shook his head. "No, that is not it. I must go tell Mousqueton's girl what happened to him. She is a maid within. I wouldn't bother with it, but, you know, Porthos likes the boy, and he thinks, you know . . . the girl should know."

"Oh," D'Armaud said, looking doubtful. But he stepped aside and let Aramis through.

Aramis knew the palace as well as he knew his own quarters. For years now, he'd stood guard at the palace door and, long before he'd become Violette's lover, he'd taken his pleasure with many of the ladies in the palace. And given, he hoped, pleasure in return.

He crossed a courtyard, ran up a staircase, wound around a hallway, until he came to a place where a door stood ajar. At this door he knocked, ever so lightly.

A formidable white-haired matron emerged, and looked surprised at seeing Aramis. "You're on guard tonight, monsieur? I'm sure her grace—"

"No, no. None of that," Aramis said, smiling through what felt like frozen lips. Had he been so obvious? Did everyone know of his latest flirtation? He could have sworn he'd played it dark and deep. He could have sworn it was all hidden. By the Mass, he was a fool. "I'm here to speak to Hermengarde. I believe she is a maid here?"

The matron raised her eyebrow at him, as she would at any gentleman, he supposed, who asked to speak to one of her maids. Her hard, dark eyes implied that she knew how these affairs ended.

Aramis shook his head. "She's friends with the servant of my friend Porthos and he—"

"Oh, the poor boy who was taken for murder," the matron said, taking her hands to her chest. "Do you know when he'll be hanged? Have they announced it, yet?"

"We're hoping never, madam," Aramis said, stiffly. "We're sure Mousqueton didn't do it."

The matron patted him on the arm. "And much credit it does you too. But there, you wait here, I'll have Hermengarde fetched to you."

She walked down the hallway and he heard her talking to someone, then she came back, nodding to him as she passed him and returned to her lair, leaving him to wait in the hallway, outside her door, like a petitioner before royalty.

After a while, he heard light, fast steps, and, in moments, Hermengarde appeared. She was a little, blondish slip of a thing, and always managed to look to him more like a waif than a full-grown woman. She stopped awkwardly in front of him, and made him a very tottering curtsey, before looking up to show a face ravaged by tears.

"Monsieur," she said, and her lips trembled. "Monsieur. I'm sure you have bad news of Mousqueton and, oh, monsieur, I wish this hadn't happened."

"But no, my little one. Not bad news," Aramis said, finding himself speaking in the tone he would use for a little kitten or a frightened horse. "I'm sure you know he was arrested, but we've been told that nothing bad will happen to him and—"

"Nothing bad!" Hermengarde said. "But . . . he's in the Bastille! They torture people in the Bastille."

To this Aramis could counter with nothing but a bow. Searching frantically in his sleeves, he found a lace-edged handkerchief, and handed it to her, and looked away as she wiped her cheeks. "I'd like to talk to you, Hermengarde," he said while she did so. "Perhaps you can tell me something that will help us free Mousqueton?"

"Oh no," she said. "At least I don't know of anything . . ." She shook her head.

"Well," Aramis said. "You've helped us with these things before, and surely you know many times people don't even realize what they know, and are all innocently keeping the secret, which if known would set their loved one free."

"I . . . I don't think I know any secrets," Hermengarde said, looking up, and her lip started trembling again, doubtless heralding another flood of tears.

"No. But the point of those secrets is that one never knows," Aramis said, and offered his arm to her. "I know you to be a brave girl, and surely you will help us to free Mousqueton."

She took his arm and he led her, almost by instinct, to a small garden, in what used to be the part of the palace where Violette lived. If anyone of the many people who crossed paths with them thought it odd for a musketeer to walk arm in arm with a crying maid, no one said so. Not even the occasional musketeer who saluted Aramis as an equal.

It wasn't till they exited through an arched gateway into the tiny walled garden where in summer the fragrance of roses was almost overpowering and where now, in late February, only the skeletal twigs of the bushes stood, their arms raised to a lowering sky from which all light had fled, did Aramis realize where his feet had brought him. He sighed, remembering the many times he'd sat with Violette upon the marble bench under the tree. And how many times he'd kissed her, in the rose-scented nights that were now irretrievably gone.

Startled at his sigh, Hermengarde looked up. She looked surprised and blushed as if she'd caught something indecent in his gaze. "Oh. You miss her," she said. "The Duchess."

Aramis nodded, gravely. What he couldn't tell his friends, what he couldn't tell the many women who courted his favors and with whom he could not become involved because none of them could ever hold the place in his heart that Violette had held, he could tell this little waif of a maid. The words tripped from his tongue. "I'll miss her the rest of my life," he said, factually. "We used to come here, on summer nights. It is a little-used garden. And we used to sit on that bench there, under the tree, and face the entrance of the garden. Because if we saw no one else come in, we knew that no one was close enough to hear our conversation."

"And so no one will hear our conversation tonight?" Hermengarde asked, sagely.

"Exactly, my dear," he said. "No one."

He led her to the bench and they sat, the marble's ice-cold

temperature seeping through his venetians and his underwear and settling like a chill upon his whole body. "Now," he said, softly, in the tone he'd been told he should use for confessions, and which he'd used, to much good effect, to talk to women in all walks of life. "Tell me what you know of Mousqueton and the armorer. You said you didn't want for this to happen. As I don't doubt you didn't. But what do you think happened, and why?"

"Oh," she said. And then, quickly. "They said that Mousqueton killed Monsieur Langelier père."

"They said . . . and do you believe it?"

"Oh, no," Hermengarde said, hastily. "At least, if he killed someone, it would have been Pierre Langelier."

"Pierre Langelier?" Aramis asked.

"The son," Hermengarde said, and blushed.

"You know Monsieur Langelier's son?"

"Yes, of course," she said, as if it were a strange thing for him to ask her. "I was born in that street, you see. My parents live a few doors down from Monsieur Langelier. My father is a smith. It was only because my godmother, Madame du Pontus, is the palace's fifth housekeeper, that I had the good fortune to be appointed to this post."

Aramis, who had more than once seen her duck food, or worse, flung by the noble guests of the sovereign wondered how she could call it her good fortune without irony. But then he didn't know how much worse her life would have been without such preferment, so he said nothing about it. Instead, he asked, "And Monsieur Pierre Langelier fils?"

"Oh, he wanted to marry me. And my parents approved of it, because they know his parents and . . . and he stands to inherit the armory . . . or I guess has inherited it now. And . . . you see . . . Mousqueton doesn't even know who his parents are. His first memories are of running wild on the street, purse cutting and . . ." She blushed. "Oh, I know he is fortunate and that his position with your friend cannot lead to anything less than great recognition and fortune, but . . . But . . ." Her lips trembled. "My parents didn't view it that way."

"I see. So, they wanted you to accept Monsieur Pierre Langelier's suit."

"Oh yes. Oh, very much so. And the last time I talked to Mousqueton, you see . . . I told him I didn't think we should see each other again, and he left in a fury. I told him I could not help but do what my parents wanted, and that my parents wanted me to marry Pierre. He . . . he accused me of wanting to marry Pierre. He said Pierre and I . . ." She blushed. "He accused me of things I'm sure I've never done. Not with anyone but Mousqueton."

"I see," Aramis said, though he did not in fact see much of anything, except that this made things worse for Mousqueton.

Hermengarde looked up and seemed to read his expression. "But no, monsieur, you can't think that. You can't believe it. Because you see, Monsieur Langelier père had snow white hair, and Pierre has blond hair. Golden, like yours, monsieur. And he's almost as elegant as you are, monsieur. He was a late-born son. Even in the darkness of the room with only the forge for light, it would be obvious they were not the same person."

Aramis inclined his head, not to let her see his expression darken still further. That was true, as far as it went, and he was sure she thought she was telling him the truth and that it was impossible for Mousqueton to be guilty. But what if he had come to demand that the father refuse his son consent to marry Hermengarde? And what if the father had refused? He'd seen the way Mousqueton spoke of Hermengarde and if they had been intimate, as her words seemed to imply . . .

Men did all sorts of stupid and criminal things for women they loved. He'd all but cut himself from the living for the sake of his lost Violette. And look at Athos. If Aramis read his hints right, Athos's entire life had been blighted by his love for a woman who had duped him into marrying her. And at young D'Artagnan, involved in a complex affair with his landlord's wife. Or sober, honest Porthos, who went to Mass even more often than Aramis, but who committed regular adultery with his Athenais, the notary's wife. There was no explanation for it, and no inequity to which a man in love would not stoop and consider himself justified.

"And the other thing," Hermengarde said, her voice rising defiantly. "Is that he had no reason at all to kill Monsieur Langelier, because I'd sent him a note just this morning." She sniffed, and wiped her nose with the handkerchief he'd given her, which looked like a repulsive mess now. "You know . . . I've . . . that is, I found that my monthly course was missed, and it could only be Mousqueton's. So I told him I would marry him as soon as he cared to make me an offer." She sniffed again. "So it makes no sense at all he should do this."

To Aramis too, this made no sense at all. Oh, he supposed Mousqueton's enemies could say that he had lost his mind and sought to steal the sword to use the money from its sale to finance his marriage to Hermengarde. In fact, he could not imagine how she thought they would live on Mousqueton's very irregular salary.

But then he thought if she married before the pregnancy became obvious, there was no reason at all that she couldn't continue working after the brat's birth. She'd just give it to nurse to her relatives, or to a hired maid. There were those who took them in by the dozen, and while one heard horror stories, most of the children survived with little outward injury.

And Mousqueton would have continued to live with Porthos. And more likely than not, Porthos would become a fond almost-grandfather to the child. Aramis could see it all in his mind's eye. He could see Porthos, fond of the little one, and sacrificing a bit of his self-indulgence to keep the young couple happy.

They would be no worse off than Madame Bonacieux, D'Artagnan's lover, who was a personal maid to Queen Anne of Austria and could leave the palace no more than a few nights a week. Though truth be told far more often than she told her husband that her mistress could spare her, because most of the time, she took a detour up D'Artagnan's stairs, and into the young man's bed.

Aramis sighed heavily, thinking of D'Artagnan's love. Athos was known to say the youth lived in a fool's paradise, but Aramis wished he had his paradise back, fool's or not. "I see," he said. "And this note you sent to him?"

"Yes," Hermengarde said. "And I had his answer by present." She smiled. "Monsieur Porthos taught him to write, but I must say his handwriting is abominable. And his spelling." She smiled more broadly. "You see, I learned to write, myself. Some ladies opened a school and taught the children. But I can say Mousqueton . . ."

"Spells and traces his letters like Porthos," Aramis said, amused.

"No, really? But it is often that way, when you have these big men, with their way . . . I bet Monsieur Porthos was too restless to sit and learn his letters when he was little."

Aramis didn't think there was any need to tell her that the truth was that monsieur's old and crusty father found it unnecessary for his son to learn to write and, in fact, believed that such gifts could emasculate his tall, redheaded son. "And what did the note say?"

"He said he would request my hand of me tonight and of my father tomorrow. You see?" She looked up at Aramis, tears trembling in her eyes. "There was no reason at all for

him to kill poor Monsieur Langelier père. I can't think why
he should do such a thing."

"Well," Aramis said, but without much force. "We . . .
we don't think he did it. Monsieur Porthos is sure he's innocent."

"Like he was sure of your innocence," Hermengarde
said. "When everyone said that you'd done murder. I'm
sure with such friends on his side, Mousqueton will be
fine."

Aramis nodded and took his leave of her, and managed
to get himself lost in a maze of hallways before he saw his
own tear-streaked face in a mirror he was passing. For a moment he was disoriented, as though this were a stranger,
whom he had to find a way to console. And then he realized
that the woebegone face looking blankly at him was his
own, and in his own eyes he read what he was thinking of.

Hermengarde was with child—or probably was—and
Mousqueton might very well be lost to her. And Aramis's
own Violette had been carrying his child when she'd died.
He tried to think whether his son or daughter would now
have been born, but he kept getting muddled in the months,
his mind confused.

What he wanted, what he craved was to wind back time,
to make Violette's death not have happened, and to return
her warm and living to his arms, with the baby that was
theirs, and whom he would have contrived to raise to carry
on his name. The tears in the reflected eyes multiplied, and
he groaned, under his breath.

Pulling another handkerchief from his sleeve, he looked
at it blankly, surprised, because he didn't normally carry
more than one handkerchief. The initials were RH—Rene
D'Herblay, the name he'd given up when he'd taken up the
uniform, but which still survived in the embroidered handkerchiefs his mother sent him—and so this was his handkerchief. That meant, he must have given another

handkerchief to Hermengarde, and that could only mean that he'd give the little maid the handkerchief of the Duchess de Chevreuse.

He smiled at his own reflection in the mirror, as he erased all traces of his tears. Walking to a window, he unlatched and threw it open, to allow the cold night air to efface the last vestiges of his grief from his pale, easily marked skin.

Then he closed the window and walked down the hallway to a door, where he stopped and scratched at the wood.

"Open," a sultry voice called from within. He opened.

The Duchess de Chevreuse stood at a writing desk, dusting with sand a sheet of paper that she had, presumably just written. She looked at him with a smile. "Chevalier," she said, "but how enchanting of you to come. I was just about to send you a note."

He went in and closed the door.

Hammers and Swords; The Tendency of Objects Not To Fall; Where Porthos Decides It Would be a Bad Idea To Drop Objects on His Own Head

❧

PORTHOS didn't know when his mind had become attached to the high unlikelihood of Mousqueton's having dropped a hammer on his own head. He just knew that it had. Of course, it would have been far easier to ask the question of Mousqueton, but he judged from Monsieur de Treville's expression that such an interview would be a hard thing to arrange.

And so, Porthos was left with the explanation that the guards of the Cardinal had given for having found Mousqueton unconscious next to the murdered armorer. And all he could do was to interest himself in the matter personally, as it were.

At any rate, Porthos had found, through the many crimes he and his friends had got involved in—and truly, what was it that had brought so many sudden deaths into their path all of a sudden?—that more than people's conversations, more than confessions or lack thereof, more than the deceptions and counter deceptions of humans, what made sense to him were concrete facts: where blood had fallen when it erupted frm the body of the murdered person. And how far the man had to walk after being hurt, or else, whether there was another way into a room.

Words were all very well, Porthos thought. Certainly, Aramis seemed to derive an immense amount of pleasure from fiddling around with them, arranging them pleasantly and, sometimes, twisting them around to give them meanings that nature never intended. Words were to Aramis as wigs were to certain men, who liked to sport a different head of curly hair for every day of the week—utterly unnecessary but a source of great pride and joy.

Porthos didn't begrudge Aramis this joy. At least he didn't begrudge it when Aramis was using the words for purposes other than bludgeoning Porthos with them. When he was using them for that purpose, Porthos tended to become rather ill-tempered, because most of those words made no more sense to him than if Aramis were to speak a foreign language. Which, in fact, he found, Aramis often did, speaking Latin or Greek, or who knew what else, and making the chore of understanding him yet more difficult.

And Athos . . . Athos hoarded words like a miser hoards gold. And when he spoke at all, it was as likely to be in his own words as in the words of some great writer dead a thousand years or more.

The one whose words made the most sense to Porthos was D'Artagnan. Not that the young man was always straightforward. But he tended to use his words to serve a purpose, and not just to make himself feel this way or that. And words, as far as Porthos was concerned, were just— tools—tools with which he was, he confessed, devilishly clumsy.

So he would leave words behind. He was sure, just like Aramis intended to question Hermengarde, that Athos would go and question someone or other at the palace. And D'Artagnan would, doubtlessly, find some Gascon to give him information about something. As many Gascons as there were in the capital, and as clannish as they tended to be, the surprising thing would be if he didn't find someone to give him information.

But all of this involved words and understanding the words of others, and Porthos simply did not have the patience to deal with that. So, instead, he would deal with hammers and swords—things that could not lie and that very rarely spoke in words. Well, at least not unless one was dead drunk. And even then, Porthos was fairly sure that the swords and the hammers didn't talk so much as the wine roared in his head.

He walked away from Athos and D'Artagnan as they were trying to convince Aramis not to leave. Why they were trying to do that was quite beyond Porthos's ken, since, after all, Aramis had always done exactly what he wanted to do and would doubtless continue to do so. He walked along gradually narrowing streets, till he found himself on the street where the armory stood. It was still closed. Or perhaps, he thought, it was closed again.

After all, he thought, the armory wouldn't be open now, because—and he cast a surprised look up at the sky—night had fallen. A look around sufficed to tell him the streets were quite deserted. Unlike parts of town where there were taverns, or hostelries, there was nothing here to call the custom passersby. Only homes, and closed stores.

From the homes, usually right next to the stores, came voices and the occasional cry of infants. None of the homes were very large or very sturdy—just barely more than hovels, made of stone. The house next to the armorer's was a little larger, and perhaps in this area it passed as a wealthy residence. Porthos supposed so, after looking at it appraisingly. He also judged, from the light of fire and probably candles emanating through the cracks in the wooden shutters of the room most distant from the armorer's, that everyone would be gathered there, probably having dinner.

This meant, if he was going to break into the armory, now would be the best time to do it.

He walked towards the door, as though he had every right to be there. Although he doubted that very many people would be looking out of doors at this time, he had long ago learned that when doing something reprehensible or—in this case—highly illegal, it was best to proceed as though one were doing something official and perfectly legitimate.

The door was heavy and, to Porthos's eyes, looked like oak. In the almost complete dark, he found the lock on it, part by touch and part by sight. It was a sturdy lock. But then Porthos was an unusually sturdy man. In fact, he had often been compared to the giants in the Bible—and he was never sure the comparison was meant as flattery. He had often thought when he retired from the musketeers he would devote his life to replicating the feats of Hercules, at least those that didn't involve dressing up as a girl, which he had the vaguest of ideas Aramis had once told him Hercules had done. Of course, Aramis might have been lying. The fact that Athenais once, for the purpose of hiding him, had dressed Aramis in a fashionable green dress[3] still seemed to rankle Porthos's friend.

So he set his hands to the wood, one massive hand pushing against a panel of wood, while the other seized hold of as much of a lip as there was on the other side of the door and pulled. His first attempt at applying force caused the lip of the wood to crack and splinter. However, it also pulled the door slightly out of true, giving Porthos a firmer grasp on that side of the door. With that firmer grasp, well past the lip that covered the joining of the two halves, Porthos pushed and pulled again.

Meeting with resistance, he thought that the lock might

---

[3] *The Musketeer's Seamstress.*

have been forged by the late armorer who, as Porthos had told his comrades, was known for metals of exceptional resistence and strength.

But just as he thought it was a lost cause, he heard wood splinter, as the lock, under pressure and not breaking, parted company with the more fragile oak. The side of the door that had been under the lip of the other side let loose and swung inward into the shadows of the armory.

Porthos paused, long enough to recover his breath, and then entered the armory in turn.

It was warm. Even during a winter night, the armory retained some of the heat of the forges, a heat augmented by the banked fires—the embers of the last fires, now covered in ashes, to keep them smoldering but not burning—glowing in the massive hearths.

The armory looked like a very large smithy, with two large forges and a succession of smaller ones. Porthos did not doubt that if Monsieur Langelier had been born and lived in a village that was exactly what he would have been, his talent for weapons notwithstanding. He'd have run a smithy and shod horses and mended plows and shovels as often as he would get to mend the occasional sword or create the occasional knife. Or rather, far more often, for those were the services that people in villages needed more often.

Even if there were a seigneur, in a village, it was not to be thought he would engage in dueling all that often. Not even with the lords of neighboring villages. Well, at least not, he corrected himself, scrupulously, unless he chanced to be of the same disposition as D'Artagnan's late father, who seemed to duel with even his best friends, just to keep in practice.

But, generally, in such small, confined societies, even the most bellicose of lords had to keep on good terms with his neighbors, and certainly couldn't afford to duel any of them to the death.

In Paris, however, people of Monsieur Langelier's abilities could obtain ample reward for them, and do nothing but work upon swords all day long. The evidences of this work, in the shape of swords in various stage of finishing piled in corners and hung upon walls and depended from racks on the ceiling. Even in the dark, Porthos could catch glimmers of their shapes and his practiced eye could have told which ones were finished—by and large the ones on ceiling racks and walls—and which ones were not—mostly the ones in piles, in various places throughout the workshop.

Without light, he could tell nothing else, but fortunately Porthos, in what Athos doubtlessly would call one of his strangely provident turns of mind, had thought to stop on the way here and provide himself with two candles from his lodging. Not that stopping had interrupted his thoughts or given him much pause. Or that he had even thought of what he might use the candles for. If he were forced to explain his decision to bring candles in so many words, he would say that he realized he would need light to see by, and that an armorer's, after nightfall and closing, was unlikely to provide that.

Now he made sure that the door was closed again and met as nearly as it could, so no light escaped from within. Then, in darkness even deeper than before, he went to the big hearth. Using one of the pokers nearby, he moved aside some of the ash from atop the embers, and touched the wick of one of the candles to it, then smiled and sighed as the light came up, pure and white.

The candle was made of the best wax, the sort of wax often burned at cathedrals during Mass. Heaven only knew where Mousqueton had got it, though of course Porthos hoped he hadn't stolen it from the cathedral.

He didn't think so. Mousqueton was of a larcenous frame of mind, but not an impious one. Now, stealing it from one of the merchants who sold to the cathedral before they could make delivery, that was something else, and he wouldn't answer for it that Mousqueton hadn't done so.

At any rate, the light was much better than anything that anyone had any right to expect from a single candle, and Porthos dripped some wax onto one of the large anvils, and stuck the candle to it as it hardened. Then he looked around.

Given the benefit of the light, and his reasonably sharp eyesight, he could see this was where the murder had happened—right there, next to the anvil, where a dark stain marred the dirt floor.

Porthos looked up, almost instinctively, at the weapons hanging over the forge. Swords. Just swords. But . . . Porthos was sure that they'd said that Mousqueton had been felled by a hammer falling from the rack over the anvil.

Well, let's imagine then, he thought, *that there truly was a hammer hanging up there amid the swords.*

He frowned. It seemed a very unlikely thing to imagine. The racks were affixed to the ceiling of the workshop, more than ten feet up. At least Porthos presumed so because he was a very tall man, and yet with his arm extended he could not reach the tip of those swords. He could tell that these were the armorer's best swords—shining examples of the sword-maker's art. Which explained, of course, why they were hung so far up and out of reach of anyone who might come into the workshop and perhaps momentarily manage to distract the armorer with talk.

The inferior swords were hung from the wall, where the enterprising might reach them, but not these. So why would anyone hang a hammer—a tool of the trade—that far out of reach?

It made no sense at all. First, all the hammers Porthos could see were either dropped here and there, haphazardly, or stacked neatly near one of the anvils. In either case, he thought, they were where they could be quickly reached.

And besides—he frowned up into the dark recesses of the ceiling from which the racks hung—*wouldn't a hammer falling from that distance onto someone's head kill them? Instead of just stunning them? Well . . . perhaps not. Perhaps if it only hit a glancing blow. And it would depend on the size of the hammer. I guess I'll have to try it to see.*

Porthos was, in fact, very much a man who could not believe without seeing. Aramis, once, mid-argument, had flung at him that he was a doubting Thomas. Porthos could perceive from the tone of voice and the expression on Aramis's face that the blond musketeer meant this as a terrible insult. It had missed its mark. As far as Porthos was concerned, Saint Thomas was the only man who had handled Christ's resurrection the way it should have been handled.

After all, if your teacher and master, who claims to be the son of God himself, has just returned from the dead, wouldn't you want to make sure it was him and not some fakery, by putting your fingers or hand into his wounds? Else, how would you know it wasn't just something painted on, and the look on the man's face a mere casual resemblance? And if you were going to go out preaching this as truth to the whole world, how could you *not* need to know for sure?

He shook his head in dismissal of Aramis's odd notions, notwithstanding that Aramis was a good man and a better friend. Porthos must remember this, and perhaps he should try to argue with him less. Aramis could not avoid the blindness his excellent education had created in him.

Meanwhile Porthos, who was far from blind, discerned in the corner an instrument somewhat like a shepherd's crook, which was used to bring swords down and put them up onto the ceiling racks. He loped over to get it, and returned to select a hammer to hang up.

Here he was faced with an immediate problem because while swords had means of hanging from the hooks on the suspended racks, hammers did not. There was no handle, no loop of leather, no way he could hook that hammer on the shepherd's crook, and get it hanging from the rack. Which left . . . balancing the hammer on the shepherd's crook and hanging it up there.

Porthos looked at the hammer, the handle of which was big enough to fit his own hand, but for which most men would need two hands, and the head of the hammer, which was almost as big as Porthos's own head. "Right," he said, and wandered off in search of some sort of material to make a loop. He found it in the form of a pile of leather strips in the corner, that, by the look of them, were used as some sort of polishing implement.

He tied a couple of the longer strips to the hammer handle, then using the crook, gently inserted the loop into one of the hooks on the rack, then looked up at the hammer hanging amid the swords. So far so good. If there had been a hammer hanging on the rack, that would be what it had looked like. Now, if that hammer fell, and hit someone on the head . . .

Porthos frowned upwards. The hammer was too high for the result of such a blow to be unconsciousness. Even a casual blow, glancingly struck, would kill a man when coming from that height and endowed with the speed and force of its fall. He could not try it on himself. Of course, he could not try it on anyone else either. Not that he expected to have any volunteers.

So, what was the good of putting a hammer up there, except to prove to whomever came in after him that hammers could indeed be hung up there? None that he could think of.

He frowned at the swords up there. But then, how could Mousqueton have got those swords, again, without getting hold of the shepherd's crook? Oh, Mousqueton was ingenuous and able, both as a servant and a thief. Porthos had seen him steal bottles from locked cellars and meat from the spit without the owners being any the wiser. But . . . a sword? Wouldn't the armorer think it odd, if Mousqueton went to get the crook, to pull out the sword?

Besides, this was an armorer to which Porthos sent Mousqueton often enough. There was no possible way the man did not know of Mousqueton's sad failings when it came to the eighth commandment. Just like anyone who had a passing acquaintance with Aramis knew of his almost inimical relationship with the seventh. No one in his right mind would allow Mousqueton near his property or Aramis near his wife.

But Porthos knew all this was no good. His friends might believe him. His friends might understand that Mousqueton could not possibly have stolen the sword. But his friends either already understood, or were willing to pretend they believed that Mousqueton was innocent. To strangers, he couldn't possibly explain how stupid the whole story was.

Well, first because Porthos couldn't hope to explain much of anything else. His words would get tangled, even if he tried to explain things people already knew or with which they were in utter agreement. But, beyond that, in this case, people would simply tell him that Mousqueton would have asked for the sword, as if to evaluate it, and then killed the armorer with it.

Which was utter nonsense, of course. If Mousqueton asked the armorer for the sword, the armorer was likely to laugh in his face. If it was Langelier's masterpiece, neither Mousqueton, nor Porthos, nor indeed Monsieur de Treville could have afforded it.

So it left Porthos to figure out—and prove—whether the hammer could be brought down from the rack or not.

He wondered what could make the hammer fall? Shaking the rack, definitely. Taking a deep breath, he took the flat end of the shepherd's crook, and set about shaking the rack back and forth.

The swords swayed and trembled, and hit each other with an infernal racket, sounding much like a madman loose in a bell tower and having hold of the ropes to the bells. And yet, neither sword nor hammers fell. Porthos hit the side of the rack with the hook, with enough force to set the rack swaying on the chains that suspended it from a ceiling beam.

Through the deafening racket, he barely heard the voice from outside, "Holla! What goes on in there? Who is there?"

Monsieur D'Artagnan Searches for a Position;
Bread, Soup, and the
Friendship of a Gascon;
A Clatter in the Night

❧

D'ARTAGNAN felt oddly excited about going in search of a position as an apprentice or as a day laborer of some sort. Perhaps, he thought, it was that he had never done that. He had come to Paris to look for employment in the musketeers, but he'd come with a letter from his father.

And the letter being stolen, he had yet to obtain that position he had once dreamed of. So, now he would like to try his luck and see if he could obtain another position, without such help or such problems.

Wearing Planchet's suit, which had, in truth, been made out of the suit that D'Artagnan himself had worn to town and which had been altered to fit Planchet. Of course, now that it had been altered—by Planchet's able needle—wearing it was akin to wearing a much too long tourniquet. But D'Artagnan could endure it for a few hours. Much harder was the lack of a sword by his side. He kept reaching to the side and finding it bare, and feeling lost, as if he'd left some essential part of himself behind.

It was true, since for almost a year now, he had lived by

the sword. The sword earned him the respect of his fellows as well as his income as a guard of Monsieur des Essarts. Now, going into the working class neighborhood, where the houses were either much smaller—and only one story—than even the ones in the area where he lived, or tall, flimsy looking towers where each floor seemed to be inhabited by an impossible number of screaming babies, he realized that people walked much closer to him, and occasionally jolted him.

It was sunset, and women rushed home to prepare the main meal of the day, while their husbands rushed home to eat it, and sons, whether apprentices in nearby workshops or merely street-playing urchins, were called home by the tolling of their empty stomachs. None of these people saw any reason to steer clear of this short young man, with the dark hair and the curiously ill-fitting suit.

As for D'Artagnan he found himself quite at a loss for what to do next. He was not normally of a retiring disposition and since coming to Paris had struck many more friendships than with just his closest friends. And he'd found himself in situations he'd never before faced and made himself known.

But he'd never been in a situation he didn't quite understand as something other than himself. He'd never had to present both a humble and yet unremarkable appearance. He'd never had to be . . . common. He understood, as people walked past him without a glance, that even in his childhood days, when he had mingled freely with farmers and merchants and behaved like one of them, they had not behaved to him as to one of their children. He'd always been Monsieur D'Artagnan's son, and, as that, accorded more respect than he would have otherwise had.

He felt a smile play on his lips, as he thought to himself that he was a fool, lecturing Athos about fitting in, when he, himself, seemed to fit in all too well, and to—thereby—be able to achieve nothing.

And just as he thought this, he passed a small house with a shop. Like most houses in this area, the shop was part of the house, the door open to allow people in and out, even as the business of living went on on the other side of it. Judging by the smell of freshly baked bread, and by the people coming out carrying various forms of bread, the place was a bakery. But what attracted D'Artagnan, more than the aroma, which caused his still-adolescent appetite to wake up and his stomach to growl, was the voice emerging from it—clearly the voice of a father giving orders to a daughter and a son. "Now, Belle, what are you doing? And, Xavier, did I tell you to put that tray there?"

The words were innocuous, save that they were said in the curious mix of French and the Gascon tongue that only transplanted Gascons used. D'Artagnan took a step in the door, almost unable to help himself. The family looked like his people too—or at least like most of the people around his province, even if his father hadn't been one of them—small and dark, with straight, black hair. It was, for a moment, like looking back at a bakery in Gascony, as he watched the father take a tray out of the oven and swiftly hand the loaves of bread to his daughter who handed them out.

A quick look up discovered D'Artagnan lurking in the doorway, as customers streamed in and out and jostled him as they went. The father of the family looked intently at D'Artagnan, then away as though he'd forgotten him, to shout an instruction to his son to go tell his mother to have dinner done "momentarily," since they were running out of both baked loaves and customers, as those rushed home with their prizes.

The boy, probably only a couple of years younger than

D'Artagnan, vanished through a door at the back, and the father and sister continued dispensing loaves, till eventually all the loaves were sold and the late-arriving customers went away empty-handed. Then the father strode towards the door, clearly to close it.

D'Artagnan, waking from his revery—in which mingled memories of his mother, his father and the servants who had helped raise him, all scented with his longing for home, and the melodic syllables of that *Langue Gascona*, which had been his first speech—nodded to the man, politely, and took a step back.

But the baker, his hand on the door as if to close it, darted the other hand out, and grasped D'Artagnan's arm. "Hold, lad," he said. "Hold."

D'Artagnan looked back, and realized only as the man patted his shoulder and said, "Don't be afraid," that his look of shock at being thus unceremoniously held, had been mistaken for fear.

"Don't be afraid," the man repeated, and shook his head. Then, looking one way and the other down the street, said in a low tone of voice, "Are you hungry?"

D'Artagnan was hungry. Famished, in fact. Strangely, Monsieur des Essarts paid his guards far more regularly than King Louis XIII, with his permanently entangled finances, did. But that meant nothing, when it all came down to it. The pay of a guard was never enough, not once his servant's upkeep and his own, and the inevitable drinking bouts with his friends, were taken into account.

The last time D'Artagnan had eaten fresh bread had been when Mousqueton had brought a couple of loaves and sworn they'd been lost by someone on the street and he'd simply picked them up. And he could smell, now that most of the loaves were gone, the meal being prepared for the family—hints of garlic olive oil, and the unmistakable odor of meat.

But he knew he was not hungry the way the baker meant, and the part of D'Artagnan who was the son of a seigneur, an armed man, entrusted with both protecting and looking after peasants, bridled at the thought that he had been confused with one of the urban poor, one of those unfortunates who needed food, or would perish of hunger.

Caught in this stream of conflicting emotions, he found himself as unwilling to speak as Athos, as clumsy with words as Porthos, and could only shake his head.

The baker frowned. "Proud, aren't you?" he asked. "Proud like the devil, and never had to ask anyone for anything back home, did you? No doubt your father does well enough as a farmer or a tinker, or whatever, and you never knew one day of stomach-churning hunger. Aye. I remember my days, when I first came to the capital. My father . . ." He shrugged. "Too many of us at home, and I'd guess you know that too, no, boy?"

D'Artagnan, an only son, nodded mendaciously, and the man continued volubly, in a low, paternal tone. "Look, there is no shame in it. I was never hungry, not once, not for a moment, when I was in my father's house. He was a baker, see, and the bread we ate might be stale, if times weren't so good. But there were always vegetables from the back garden, and a chicken now and then. And then I came to Paris. The things you hear of Paris! Everyone is wealthy and eats beef every day. I thought, of course, I would live like a nobleman."

The man shook his head as though at youthful folly. "Ah, idiot child that I was. But you see, in Paris, I didn't know anyone, and before I got myself an apprenticeship at a bakery and saved enough to open my own . . ." He shrugged. "I was hungry many times. Lodgings had to be paid, as had food. An no vegetable patch in the back." He patted D'Artagnan's shoulder with a hand that left white streaks of flour. "But there, there were other Gascons. Like you, I would be called by the language and stand there and listen to it, because it reminded me of home. And Gascons look after each other. Have to, since our cursed land has always produced more boys than food, and more rocks than both."

D'Artagnan, pummeled by the flow of the man's generous talk, could only swallow, and smile, and manage to speak in a small voice. "I'm not hungry," he said. "I mean, not that hungry, though your bread smells very good." And though he was aware that he should, truly, exploit this opening and find out what he could about the death of the armorer, he could not bring himself to do it. He'd feel as if he were taking advantage of a kind, generous family. "And I was . . . thinking of buying some, only I was listening to you speak, you know . . . our tongue, and I forgot . . ."

The baker smiled. "Buy it, were you? With what coin? No, please, don't tell me more lies, lad, there is no need."

The huge hand grabbed D'Artagnan by the shoulder. "You're hardly older than my own son, and even if you're more sturdily built, I know what you eat like at your age. I tell you what, if you'd do us the honor." As he spoke he pulled D'Artagnan into the shop and closed the door behind him. "If you're not that hungry, just come and give us the pleasure of your company, Gascon to Gascon, and eat at our table tonight."

To that, there was nothing D'Artagnan could oppose and he let himself be led, by the shoulder, through the dark doorway at the back into a small, crowded kitchen where there stood what seemed to be an overflow of flour barrels, other barrels and bundles of miscellaneous supplies, a small, dark wooden table, and a huge hearth, at which a dark, plump woman worked.

She turned at their entrance and seemed to take it as normal that her husband should come in with some waif off the street. The two children, boy and girl, were already seated side by side at the table, with a bowl of soup and a piece of bread in hand, and squirmed aside to make space for D'Artagnan as a matter of course.

D'Artagnan wondered whether the baker did this every day and how many waifs he fed. As he took his place beside them, he found a piece of bread and a bowl, overflowing with vegetable soup with some small pieces of what appeared to be pork dropped in, were set in front of him.

He watched as the baker sat and talked to his wife of how much they'd sold and of what type of bread, while she served him and then herself, from a large pot of soup she'd set in the middle of the table.

D'Artagnan had resolved, before he ever sat down, that he would eat little, and show no unusual enthusiasm for the food. Part of this was his pride, revolting at his pretending to be a mere homeless, rootless Gascon waif in Paris. The other part of it was his absolute certainty that these people—no matter the actual facts of the matter—should need the food more than he did. He had his commission as a guard, after all, as well as his career, which he was sure would be long and illustrious. He aimed for nothing else than the post Monsieur de Treville held.

And while he had absolutely no idea what ambitions lay in the future of a baker in Paris, he was sure they would be more limited than his. So, with absolute certainty that he would not let himself eat too much of these poor people's food, he took a mouthful from his spoon.

The flavor exploded in his mouth, like a surprise, bringing with it the tastes of his childhood but much improved, unexpectedly sweeter, one playing off the other. He saw the baker looking at him, and he swallowed hastily, before taking another spoonful, feeling suddenly more ravenous than ever.

The baker laughed. "Cooks well, doesn't she, my Adele?" He half embraced his wife, who made a playful motion to swat him away. "Eat what you will, lad," he said. "There is plenty, and it is a compliment to the house."

And D'Artagnan, not able to protest against the commands of his body, ate a full two bowls and a full half-loaf of the crusty, dark bread, before he could slow down. And wished he could, on some excuse, take this food back to his comrades. Though he could well imagine the reaction of aristocratic Athos faced with dark peasant bread and vegetable-heavy soup.

He was so amused by this image that it shocked him as the baker said, "Have you a job? Or do you want me to look about for one for you? We don't need help at the shop right now, as it happens, but I'm sure—"

"Oh, no," D'Artagnan said, quickly, fearful that he would find himself helped to a job as he'd found himself helped to food, and thereby forced to live a double life for the rest of his time in Paris, standing guard at night and working during the day in a bakery, and possibly, eventually, keeping a wife and children in each place. "Oh, no," he said. "It is not like that. My father . . . you see . . ." and deciding, quickly, to go on a variance of his real story. "My father used to be in service with Monsieur de Treville, you know, as his valet, and he sent me with a letter to Monsieur de Treville's valet, as used to be his apprentice. Only though they want me to work for them, they don't have need of me right now, so they said as I could start tomorrow. It's just the last week has been rough."

The baker nodded. "Monsieur de Treville will look after you, right enough," he said. "And most of his staff are from our land." He smiled slightly at D'Artagnan, "So you were lost, were you? Or exploring Paris?"

D'Artagnan decided this was the time, if ever, to bring the subject around to what he needed to know. "Well, the thing is," he said. And managed to look embarrassed, which in fact he was, though not over what he appeared to be. "I heard that there had been a murder this way. Some musketeer's servant was caught at it, I heard at Monsieur de Treville's. And of course, well . . ." He shrugged. "I've never been anywhere anyone was murdered. My village was not that big."

The baker smiled, but something like a shadow passed his eyes. "You are lucky," he said. "Being of a generation from Gascony which didn't see enough death." Then shrugged. "Not that I'm sure that the musketeer's servant did it, mind."

"But, dear," his wife put in. "Everyone says as he was caught, with the sword in his hand, and his arm all over blood."

"Adele," her husband said, looking at her seriously, but with the twinkle of humor in his eyes. "I saw the boy taken, as did you, with all those guards around him. There was no blood on him, not even a few drops as someone will have if they stab any person or animal nearby. And the other thing is, they said he was unconscious, and what musketeer's servant would fall unconscious after stabbing someone. For you're not going to tell me he collapsed at the sight of blood, because that I won't believe. Always pulling their swords in and out of their sheaths, are those musketeers, and I wouldn't trust them for a moment, be it with my food or with my daughter, but murderers . . . that they're not." He smiled at D'Artagnan, suddenly and startlingly. "Overgrown boys, all of them. Much mischief, and all that, but also high ideals, and wanting to rescue others. Not the stuff of which murderers are made."

D'Artagnan, stunned by the idea that anyone could call Athos—Athos!—an overgrown boy, and imagining the response of Alexandre, Count de la Fere, no matter how submerged under his nom de guerre, to such an assessment of his character, could not find words to speak, and before he could, the boy, Xavier, said, "Only they say he'd lost consciousness at a hammer that fell from the overhead rack and hit him on the head."

The baker snorted. "Yes, and that's likely enough, isn't it? Xavier, you've been in the shop, as have I. There are no hammers on the racks, overhead. Only swords and such. Besides, as high as those racks are, if a hammer had hit the boy on the head, he'd not be unconscious, he'd be dead, and his brain, likely as not, splattered all over the floor."

"Yes, but . . ." Xavier said. "Something must have happened."

"Ah, you see," the baker said, and then suddenly, "What is your name, son?" to D'Artagnan.

"Henri," D'Artagnan said and then, acutely aware that to pronounce his father's family name would give away his true origin, "Henri Bayard."

"Well, Henri, what I say is that we don't know the half of the story, and that it will all become clear in time, and it is none of our business. You and Xavier might find all this very exciting, and stuff to dream on. But the thing is . . ." He shrugged. "Murderers are not usually grabbed at the scene of the crime like that. It's not usually that simple, is it?"

"I . . . I don't know," D'Artagnan said, startled at his own capacity for lying. "I've never been close enough to a murder to . . . to observe it."

"And lucky you should count yourself."

"But then . . ." D'Artagnan said, contriving to seem disappointed—which he was. Or at least frustrated at his inability to question the man. "But then you don't believe this was done by the musketeer's servant?"

The baker shrugged. "No. Or at least, I don't believe it was, though sometimes people do things you don't expect and would never have thought of them. But why Boniface, such a nice young man, with a sunny disposition—oh, light with his fingers, but everyone must have a failing—should feel the need to murder the armorer is quite beyond my reckoning. You see . . ." He shrugged. "He came around to the armorer's a lot. Monsieur Langelier, in fact, had plans for him."

"Plans?" D'Artagnan asked, shocked. Almost as shocked as to find that here Mousqueton went by Boniface, his name before he had become Porthos's servant.

"Well . . ." The baker smiled. "Ah well. That is probably all ruined now, because her brother would never allow it, not and have to pay out money from what—I hear—is already a much eaten inheritance for her dowry. But you see, besides his son and heir, the armorer has a daughter."

"Faustine," Belle said, and giggled, as if the name itself were very funny.

"Aye, Faustine, twenty-five if she's a day, and no one has ever looked at her twice."

"She has cross-eyes," Belle said, and made a face.

"Now, child," her mother said, mildly. "That is not charitable."

"Neither is she. Temper like a viper and a tongue like the devil," Belle said.

"Well, and all that might be true," the baker said. "But Langelier always said she would have a good enough dowry, something, you know, to start a shop, or to buy a house, or to do with what she wanted. She and her husband. And a boy like Boniface, well set up and kind, even if he was a musketeer's servant . . . well . . . And eventually the musketeer might make something of himself too— not to mention that half of them are grand seigneurs, noblemen in disguise, here to escape some debt or work out some crime . . . well, Boniface would be all right, might still be, I daresay. And Langelier thought, what with all that, he couldn't do better than marry him to his Faustine. So he'd been talking to him, slow like, leading him gently by the reins, as it were." He broke another piece of bread and bit into it. "You see, the young man never had money for the sword repairs his master asked for, and so he was in obligation to Langelier . . ."

D'Artagnan saw it, perhaps too well. He'd seen Mousqueton with Hermengarde, the little palace maid, and he knew how attached they were. Would Mousqueton's temper flare if he felt he was being blackmailed into marrying the cross-eyed viper? "But at Monsieur de Treville's," he said, hesitantly, "they say that he is . . . that is, that he is friends with a maid at the palace."

"That would be Hermengarde," the baker's wife said and shook her head.

"Ah, yes, Hermengarde," her husband said. "Cute little thing, Hermengarde, but . . . well . . . you know, like us. Starting out on her own with nothing to call her own besides whatever education she brought from her father's house, which will not be much, and her palace connections, but that just makes her a devilishly uncomfortable wife, because she'll never be home.

"No, they couldn't tie the knot, Hermengarde and Boniface. Not that they needed to, because Langelier wanted Boniface for his daughter and his son, Pierre, wanted Hermengarde for his own."

"Seems odd," D'Artagnan said, and though the innocence of the words might be a put-on, the frown that accompanied them was quite genuine. "That they are . . . friends and being courted by siblings."

The baker laughed. "Odder things have happened, my boy. It has long been my experience that with whomever you might be friends as a youth, in the end you marry the woman who will be best for you as a wife. And though that was not needed for me, not with my Adele, and my baking skills and the little bit I had set aside, sometimes the better woman for someone is the one who brings money with her. Because money can buy freedom and security."

"But . . ." D'Artagnan said, and the protest was genuine,

wrung from his still-romantic heart, a protest against life in general, as well as against forced marriages. His lovely Constance, the woman he was sure he loved like no other, was married to a man she didn't love and whom, as far as D'Artagnan could discover, she had never loved. "But . . ." He shook his head. "What about love?"

The baker shrugged. "Well, if you are lucky you will love the woman who is best for you."

"But not always," his wife said, frowning slightly. "And a bad woman will ruin you faster than anything else."

D'Artagnan looked at her, startled. "So you agree with Monsieur—with your husband, that . . . that they would in the end have married the children of the armorer?"

"Monsieur Ferrant," the plump Adele put in. "And yes, of a certainty they would. For what else is there, when you need to eat? And what woman wants to bring children into the world without a certainty for their future? They would have married the Langelier children, and been . . . if not happy, resigned to their life as siblings-in-law. Others have in the—"

An unholy clatter interrupted her words. It sounded, D'Artagnan thought, like a horse running through a field of metal; like a bell tower collapsing to the ground; like the end of the world.

"What," he said, and, standing, found his hand going to the place where his sword normally hung. Not finding it, he cast a look around, to see if anyone had noticed his gesture. But the entire family, standing, seemed as much shocked as he.

The clatter ceased, and D'Artagnan repeated, "What—"

The baker's wife crossed herself and spoke through almost bloodless lips. "It's coming from the direction of the armorer's. Mind you, it's the ghost that's walking." She crossed herself again. "It's what happens when someone dies by the sword, like that."

Her husband opened his lips, but D'Artagnan never found out what he would have said. Because before he could, the clatter started up again, and D'Artagnan was out the door, running, finding that Xavier was running by his side.

Towards the armorer's shop.

The Palais Cardinal; The Shadow of a Shadow; The Devil by the Tail

∽

"**I**F you'd wait here, monsieur," the Cardinal's servant said, bowing deeply, as he led the musketeer away from the antechamber, the counterpart of Monsieur de Treville's musketeer-packed waiting room.

The Cardinal's antechamber was, perhaps of a less bellicose nature. His men were less noisy, less provoking, less enthusiastic. Not that the guards tended to be less fanatic in their devotion to their master than the musketeers in their loyalty to Monsieur de Treville, and not that many of them didn't serve out of conviction. In fact, when occasion had come to engage them in words, Athos had often found that they served the Cardinal out of absolute belief that he was the best thing for France and that under his capable hands the kingdom would become the first power of the world, the envy of all of Christendom.

And it might well be so. Athos was intelligent enough and learned enough to concede that Richelieu had done much to restore a treasury and a prestige squandered in the wars of religion and destroyed in a thousand internal and petty disputes. None better than him to agree that Richelieu could be said to be better for France.

At any rate, it would be very hard to be more damaging than the previous two monarchs, who had sowed dissension like a bountiful crop and well-nigh brought the kingdom to the verge of tearing itself in two. Richelieu—for though it made Athos gnash his teeth, it could hardly be imagined to be Louis XIII—led a prosperous and stable France, where people could at last imagine they had a future.

But the future they had was not the future Athos wanted. Oh, he was neither as remote nor as deaf to what passed about him as he pretended to be. He knew what the people said on the street—that Richelieu had curbed the power of the great noblemen. That he'd given the sons of merchants and accountants a place in leading France. That he made it impossible for the princes to squander what the artificers made.

What Athos saw was different. Surely, some noblemen had grown too great and, used to a weak royal authority, had become little princes in their own right. And clearly, though he would never say it aloud, Athos was impartial enough—in his own mind—to admit that simply to be born to a great house, or a great position, didn't necessarily qualify one to carry that position. Look at Louis XIII who let his minister reorganize the kingdom and his life, while he played at cards, or complained of being bored.

But he also couldn't help thinking that this new class coming through—these functionaries, these smart accountants, the sons of men who didn't know their grandfathers' names, would be no better. They might be cleverer, but nobility had always been able to hire the clever to do their bidding. But at least nobility—when things worked the way they were supposed to—was raised, if not conceived, in the expectation of being of service to those under their power. That meant even the ones who did not behave responsibly felt they should.

But only let these newly educated functionaries out into the multitudes. They would feel no obligation to be of service and, like Richelieu, everything they did would be for their own aggrandizement.

Athos felt his lip curl in disdain as the servant who appeared to be Richelieu's secretary led him from the crowded antechamber into a private chamber, surrounded by tall bookcases, with a writing desk pushed against a wall, in front of the sole window. There were upholstered chairs. Just two.

"If you'll take a seat, Monsieur le Comte," the Cardinal's secretary said. "His eminence will be in instantly."

Athos opened his mouth, closed it. He didn't want to know how the Cardinal's secretary knew a secret he would have killed to preserve, but he wasn't about to show his discomfiture, either. Instead, he sat down, and looked incuriously towards the nearest bookcase, which showed many of the titles his own bookcase had sported, back in his domains.

It seemed to him it took an unduly long time for the Cardinal to join him, but he hadn't expected anything else. After all, he'd come, by himself, to the enemy's lair. He knew the enemy would try to enforce his superiority, or at least the superiority of his hand. Athos, who played card games—even when he always lost—knew he'd have done the same himself.

But at length the gentleman appeared. "Monsieur le Comte," he said, and smiled slightly as he crossed in front of Athos and towards the desk by the window. A candelabra rested on the desk, casting the light of six candles upon various sheaves of paper and all that was needed for writing, including quills and ink bottles. Selecting a piece of paper and an ink bottle, the Cardinal spoke, offhandedly, over his shoulder. "To what do I owe the honor?"

Athos, who had once been a voluble and near garrulous child, had learned in his later life to be quiet, almost taciturn, as sparing with his words as though they were debts he must pay back, once spent. "I believe you know, your eminence," he said.

Cardinal Richelieu wrote broadly, with an expansive gesture of the hand, then folded the sheet and sealed it. "What am I supposed to know? How may I help you, milord?" Leaving the sealed sheet upon the desk, he turned around, his fingers interlaced at his midriff, his bright dark eyes filled with curiosity.

Not, Athos thought, curiosity to know what brought Athos here. No. That he knew, and Athos would swear to it. He was, however, interested in seeing how Athos would react to his slighting manner—how Athos would respond.

And though Richelieu was a very different type of person from Athos's late father—in fact, the late Count de la Fere would have hated Richelieu as well as everything he stood for: his camaraderie with the lower classes and the casual way in which he pushed aside the older families of France—in that moment he reminded Athos of his father.

Athos's father had been one of those people never very at ease near children. An only child, who in turn had sired Athos late in life, Monsieur Gaetan Count de la Fere had treated Athos as an object of intense scrutiny—at a distance—until Athos had been breeched. And then, suddenly, Athos's father had decided that Athos was a man, or at least a youth. It was as though nothing existed, in the late Count's mind, between the mewling infant and the striding man. And so, he'd expected Athos to be proficient at horseback riding, competent enough with a sword for the honor challenges that might befall any noble, and cultured too, so that his speech wouldn't lead his inferiors to sneer at him.

Athos, a dutiful son, had learned the riding and the sword fighting from the masters provided and, though struggling, always managed to exceed the prowess of those far senior to him. Even the Latin and the Greek pressed upon him by yet another set of masters, the poetry, the diction—even that he learned, and effortlessly.

Of the rituals and demands his father enforced on him far too young, there was only one that Athos had resented, but that one he had resented absolutely and with a raging hatred. Because every night, from the age of seven or so, he'd been brought into his father's study and sat, across from his father, at a table that had been designed as a chessboard, and upon which elaborate, expensive china pieces were set.

Athos didn't resent that his father expected him to play chess. He didn't even resent that the late Count gloried in winning games over his small son. What he resented—the memory that still made the bile rise at the back of his throat—was that the rules of the game had never been explained to him. Night after night, he'd sat there, and learned all the moves by trying them the wrong way first. Night after night, day after day, he'd brooded on the losses. And every night his father smiled at him, with the exact same smile that the Cardinal was now giving him.

Something to the movement of the Cardinal's eyes made Athos realize he'd been inching his hand towards his sword, and he pulled it back by an effort of will. The day after his father had died, in a ritual composed part of grief and part of relief, he had taken the beautiful intaglio chess table, and all the chess pieces. He'd smashed the chess pieces in the depths of the garden, before setting fire to the table.

Now his fingers itched for the fire to set beneath the Cardinal's feet, but he bit the tip of his tongue between his teeth, instead, holding it till he tasted blood. But he pushed a smile onto his lips, and what he hoped was a pleasant expression into his eyes, and looked up at the Cardinal. "Do you truly mean, your eminence," he said, filling his voice with wonder, "that I know more than you do?"

There was a dark shadow beneath the Cardinal's gaze, just like the first time that Athos had managed to take Father's queen. For a moment, Richelieu was discomfited enough to show frustration. And then the urbane mask descended again. "I suppose," he said, with the ill-grace of someone who has been bested, "you come about the servant?"

"The—Oh, yes," Athos said, as though the recollection cost him effort. "At least, the servant is part of it."

The Cardinal's eyebrows shot up and Athos had to avoid grinning. He thought the Cardinal's expressions could be much like Aramis's, remembered that Aramis's mother had once loved the Cardinal, and thought all in all he would not make the comparison near his friend.

"Well, I say part of it," he said, "since Monsieur de Treville seems to believe there is much more involved. Something about a conspiracy or correspondence." He made a dismissive gesture with his hand. "You know I don't listen to court gossip, so your eminence cannot possibly hope for me to remember all the details, beyond the fact that somehow poor, light-fingered Mousqueton has delivered himself into the midst of a plot." He opened his hands. "Truly, not difficult. It seems one cannot cross the street these days without falling into a plot against your eminence. I would wonder—do you not?—what one could be doing to bring about such hatred."

The Cardinal smiled, a pale lips-only smile. "Keeping back the deadwood of the old noble houses," he said, his eyes full of insult.

"Oh, then," Athos said, feeling quite proud of himself and, in fact, quite Aramis-like. "It is a good thing that all the branches of one's own tree are in good working order."

For a moment, for just a moment, he thought the Cardinal was going to choke, but he didn't. Instead he narrowed his eyes at Athos. "Monsieur le Comte, let us make an end to the fencing. When it comes to fencing you are better with steel than with words, and you see, I have long ago given up the sword, in trade for the cross and the rosary."

"I see," Athos said. "And I see you expect everyone else to do it as well, through your edicts."

"My edicts . . ." He opened his hands, in a show of helplessness. "I do what I can, Monsieur le Comte, for France. I would keep her young men alive. I would keep them from dying in senseless duels."

"You would keep the young noblemen incapable of defending their own honor," Athos countered, parrying expertly. "Till all they can do is put an end to their own lives."

"On the contrary. Their lives will be better than ever. They are encouraged to come to court. The king's palace shall be the most glittering gathering in the house."

"To the court where they can be kept dangling, hoping for royal largesse. In other days they would have been supported by their own domains, and remained there, making sure their domains were taken care of as they should be."

"Ah, you can't blame me if not everyone's mind is of a provincial turn."

"I can blame you when everyone's mind takes a mercantile tone."

"Objections to wealth, Monsieur le Comte? Is it because you have none? Perhaps the cousin who has charge of your estates needs to be replaced by yourself? Perhaps it is time, enfin, to return home."

"I will let you know when I feel such a desire," Athos said. And managed a smile through his tight lips. "And until then, perhaps we can discuss Boniface?"

"Boniface?" Richelieu asked. And he'd got Athos angry enough that Athos enjoyed the shock and surprise behind the word.

"Certainly," Athos said. "Porthos's servant. Boniface is his given name, only changed to Mousqueton by Porthos, who thought Boniface didn't quite fit such a belligerent master."

"Indeed. Monsieur du Vallon and his reasoning are ever such a delight."

"Indeed they are. He often sees through things other men take for granted. I would not disdain him."

"Disdain him? Monsieur le Comte, you injure me. I'd never underestimate any of you." He narrowed his eyes. "You are all such different temperaments and have such complementary abilities. And yet, you're also versatile and so often exchange roles. Take you . . . I'd have said if you needed guile and planning, you'd have provided yourself with an escort more capable at such. Your friend Chevalier D'Herblay. Or perhaps that young cunning Gascon. So why alone?"

"Because, your eminence," Athos said, inclining his head in a perfunctory bow and, tired of sitting while his foe stood, standing in turn, "I have not come with guile. Or with any complicated plan. I have, in fact, come to offer your eminence my services."

"Your services?" Richelieu said, and now sounded completely shocked. He couldn't have looked any more surprised had Athos grown a second head right there, in front of him. "Do you mean to tell me . . ." His hand reached for the chair opposite the one that Athos had just vacated, and held onto it, as if for support. "That you are ready to abandon Monsieur de Treville's service, and you chose mine instead?" He looked up at Athos's face with a speculative, evaluating look. "I'm honored beyond my deserts, but won't your friends resent it? Won't they think some pressure must have been brought on you to change allegiance so dramatically? Are you doing it for the freedom of this . . . what is his baptismal name? Ah, yes, Boniface? Because if you are, noble though it is, I must tell you, the exchange is a bit high, a count for a servant."

Athos should have been offended. Athos was offended. That he would consider trading the allegiance to Monsieur de Treville, who guarded the King himself; that he would ever think of letting the Cardinal put his stamp on him. Richelieu must be mad. Only of course he wasn't. What he was doing was trying to anger Athos, to see what lay behind the hand Athos clutched to his chest. And Athos, unlucky at cards though he might be, was not such a bad strategist. "No, your eminence. Considering all the good people in your service, Monsieur de Rochefort and all those fine sword fighters—what is the name of the one that D'Artagnan wounded two days ago? I can't quite remember, but I hope he's doing well. Has he recovered from his wound?"

The Cardinal's face betrayed only the slightest hint of annoyance before closing into a placid look. "No. If you mean Herve, poor fellow, his Maker has called him home."

"Oh. You have my sympathy. The poor man. And twice D'Artagnan's age too. But at least he'll be joining his comrade who helped him fight D'Artagnan and who died of his wounds at the scene of the duel."

The Cardinal made a gesture of impatience, hastily suppressed. "But if you haven't come to offer me your services, may I ask . . ."

"But I have come to offer you my services," Athos said. "I said so." He lifted a hand, as he saw Richelieu open his mouth. "No, pray, allow me to explain. I came to offer my services, but without leaving Monsieur de Treville's service. No, before you seek to insult me by insinuating I am willing to spy for you, let me stop you. There are insults, your eminence, that will make me forget that you've given up your sword."

"I trust your honor better than that, Monsieur le Comte. You would not kill an unarmed man."

"I wouldn't trust my honor, Monsieur le Cardinal. I am,

in fact, human, and flesh and blood can only stand so much."

The Cardinal inclined his head. "I won't accuse you of wishing to play a double role, then," he said. "At any rate, it is more likely that your friend Aramis or your friend D'Artagnan would succeed at such a game. But if you want to take up my service without giving up Monsieur de Treville's, what else am I to understand? I have enough people to guard entrances and doors, and if you mean that you'll stand such a sort of double shift, again, much as I regret to tell you, it is not the thing that is worth the life of a servant who murdered someone."

Athos wasn't about to argue that Mousqueton hadn't murdered anyone. At any rate, he would bet that Richelieu knew that already. Instead, he inclined his head, and looked at the pattern of the carpet upon the floor for a while before speaking. "No, no. While I am a good guard, I claim no particular acuity. After all, it was past my guard that the Duchess de Dreux was murdered. Forbid the thought that your eminence should likewise succumb to murder while I guarded the entrance."

Richelieu shuddered, the shudder unmistakable, then focused his gaze on Athos, with renewed sharpness. "So you know of the conspiracy to kill me. I assume Treville told you so. And Treville being Treville, and no more likely to understand conspiracy or plotting than you are, I presume he foolishly told you that I am holding Mous—ah, Boniface, to get the Queen to confess to her part in the conspiracy." He raised eyebrows at Athos. "Do you play chess, Monsieur le Comte?"

"No, your eminence. My father did. You remind me a great deal of him."

This got him a quizzical look. Then the Cardinal shrugged, minimally. "Ah? Very well. However, I am sure you know that a Queen is worth more than a pawn. The trade won't be made."

"I quite understand," Athos said. He allowed his more typical smile, tinged with a good deal of bitterness to elongate his lips into a smile. "I am not one of those who reposes a great deal of belief in the natural benevolence of women."

A long enquiring look back, and Richelieu opened his hands wide, not quite in a show of helplessness, but more as though he were laying out a hand of imaginary cards. "What, then, do you propose to do?" he asked. "I have something you want—that is your servant back. And you have, presumably, something to offer me in return, else your coming in like this and wishing to deal would seem even more foolish than it is."

Athos allowed a dry chuckle to escape him, without betraying the slightest expression of amusement. "A good description of the situation, your eminence. And the only answer I can make is that I've come to strike a bargain with the devil."

The eyebrows went up. "Truly? How strange of you to seek him in the home of a churchman."

"Not so strange, when you think about it, your eminence," Athos said. "I do not listen to gossip, but one cannot help but hear some portion of it, as one goes about one's business."

The Cardinal said nothing. This meant, Athos supposed, the time for talk was over. He nodded, as though acknowledging the end of a part of the game and the beginning of the other. As much fun as it might be to needle the Cardinal, Athos had come here for a purpose.

He opened his hands in turn, displaying his palms. "I want Mousqueton's freedom. Mousqueton's freedom and his exoneration from these ridiculous charges."

"And I want a strong France where noblemen can't challenge the power of their sovereign," Richelieu said. "We all want things. The question is, what do you propose to do about it? And what can you do about it?"

"In return for the freedom and life of Porthos's servant, I offer my services in unraveling the conspiracy against your eminence."

A surprised look. "Oh? I thought you meant to offer me something of value?"

Perhaps Athos deserved that, for the unprovoked insults against the Cardinal, or perhaps this was just the way of the Cardinal's enjoying himself in turn. Athos bowed his head slightly, in acknowledgment of a hit, and answered back, "I'm sure it has value enough. You are aware that in the last year we have unraveled murders that baffled everyone else."

"And bested me not a few times? Yes. But for that, you had the help of your friends. Am I correct in saying that this time you are on your own, and that none of your friends knows of your effort, much less is prepared to help?"

Athos opened his hands, displaying his symbolic cards. "Alas, I can only offer myself," he said, while in his mind he calculated things quickly. There was D'Artagnan, on whose loyalty and cooperation he was fairly sure he could count. And there was Porthos, who would protest at the idea of doing anything for the Cardinal, much less anything to defend the Cardinal. But he would do it, nonetheless, for the sake of Mousqueton. And Aramis . . . ah, Aramis. There was no telling what Aramis might do. Even when he told you what he was going to do.

Not that Athos didn't value Aramis as a friend—he did. And not that he believed that Aramis would knowingly betray him, or any of them. Their friendship had been tried in too demanding a course for him to have any doubt that they did indeed stand one for all and all for one.

It was more the way that Aramis's mind ran, deep and convoluted and often hiding from himself what he himself thought. Aramis knew of the conspiracy and, in fact, Aramis might be part of it. Athos didn't think so, at least not knowingly, because much as Aramis despised Richelieu, he did not condone of murder. A man he wanted out of the way would be challenged to a duel or manipulated into exile. And if neither of those applied, then neither would murder.

And yet, he might very well refuse to help save the Cardinal's neck, or work only halfheartedly to save it. "I can't promise my friends, or not yet," Athos said.

The Cardinal watched him. Finally, he nodded. "I cannot give you the servant's liberty without some surety you can do what you promise," Richelieu said. "So this is the deal I offer you, Monsieur le Comte. I shall promise you nothing will happen to the boy for the next week. No torture, no condemnation. But you must deliver me the conspirators meanwhile or . . ." He clasped his own neck, with one hand, as if to indicate hanging.

Athos nodded, staring. It wasn't till he was outside the Palais Cardinal—having crossed the great antechamber where all conversations stopped at his approach and didn't resume again till he was too far to hear their words—that Athos thought there was another outcome the Cardinal hadn't considered, and one for which he was sure of his friends' approval.

He could discover who had, in fact, killed the armorer. And then Richelieu would have to free Mousqueton.

Meanwhile, he had a week. A week, and Mousqueton would be safe meanwhile. And he could work to find the real murderer. If he needed to pry into the conspiracies of the court to find something to keep Richelieu quiet meanwhile, it wouldn't hurt. The court was so rife with conspiracies, he was unlikely to find anything concrete.

He was putting on his gloves, preparing to go back to his lodgings, when he heard a soft cough behind him. "Monsieur Athos?" a well-known voice said.

Athos pivoted on his heel, to see Rochefort, the shadow of the Cardinal and, many said, the Cardinal's evil genius. He was looking at Athos with an expression of interested amusement in his single eye. His other eye socket was covered with a patch. The last time they'd seen each other alone, Athos had held the upper hand. He rather suspected that Rochefort imagined he had it now.

"Yes?" he said.

"His eminence asked me to have a talk with you. If you would follow me."

The Bravery of Youth; Porthos's Defense;
Ghost Tale

❧

OUTSIDE the door to the armorer's, Xavier hesitated, and D'Artagnan took advantage of the moment, to run ahead. There was a crowd outside the door, and a large man had just knocked on it and was calling out.

No one answered him. As D'Artagnan approached— since everyone was keeping a safe distance and looking rather like they were ready to take to their heels—the big man turned around and said, "No one is answering. Perhaps it's just a cat locked in there? A cat would make a lot of noise. There was once a cat locked over in the potters and he—"

"Don't be daft, Francois," a voice shouted from behind him. "How would a cat reach the swords?"

D'Artagnan didn't know why, but he did not want anyone to come in with him, and he found himself saying, "Perhaps. Or perhaps it is a ghost."

At his conspiratorial accents, even the big man stepped back a little. Which allowed D'Artagnan a chance to slip past him, open the door, and slip into the dark armorer's.

Of course, it only occurred to him afterwards, as the dark, clammy air of the workshop closed around him, that he was alone. In the armorer's. Where a recent murder had happened.

Monsieur D'Artagnan père, a man of certain convictions and wise maxims, had once told his son, when D'Artagnan was just a small boy, that the probability was that there was no such thing as ghosts, and that it was very important for D'Artagnan to know that. On the other hand, it was important to keep in mind that the ghosts themselves might not know it.

It seemed to D'Artagnan, now, in the dark workshop, his nose filled with the smell of coals and metal polish as well as that curious metallic tang of smithies and an underlying smell of sudden death, that he heard his father's voice again. He swallowed loudly, and hoped these ghosts—if there were any here—knew that they didn't exist.

In the dark he took a step, two. And he found a huge hand clamping tight over his mouth. He put his hand to his sword belt, but he was wearing neither sword belt nor sword, and squirmed in the grip of another huge hand that had clasped his shoulder, in an attempt to turn around and kick his captor—who he was quite sure was corporeal—where it would hurt, when a well-known voice stopped him.

"D'Artagnan," Porthos whispered in his ear, in his whisper which had an odd habit of booming at unexpected times. Not loud enough, D'Artagnan hoped, to be heard outside the doors to the smithy, but one could never be sure. "D'Artagnan? What are you doing here? And dressed that way."

D'Artagnan did his best to answer, which was easier thought than done, due to the huge hand still clamped tightly across his mouth. He let out a hiss of exasperation, lifted his own hand and, delicately, prized one of Porthos's fingers away, enough to say something that sounded like "pfffff" but was in fact, "Let me speak."

Porthos jumped a little. "Oh, sorry," he boom-whispered, while pulling his hand away from D'Artagnan's face.

D'Artagnan, in turn, took his finger to his lips, in the

universal gesture of recommending silence and said, in quite a low whisper. "There's a crowd outside. Don't speak. You boom when you speak."

Porthos nodded and looked an enquiry at D'Artagnan.

D'Artagnan sighed. He said, thinking as he said it. "Well . . . You can't get out. Not through there. There is a crowd out there too. So . . ." He chewed on his lip, thinking, as he looked around the darkened smithy. There was a candle burning on one of the forges, its light too little to make it beyond a circle perhaps as tall and wide as D'Artagnan himself. Well, and a little more of it making it, attenuated some distance. He could see the swords overhead and, near the embers on the hearth, a pile of something that might be coal or metal. But that was about it, except for the light of the embers. There was a crowd outside the door. Porthos couldn't leave without being stopped by the crowd. And since he was Mousqueton's master, things could get ugly rather quickly. He would not put it past the crowd to try to arrest Porthos. And one of the ever-obliging guards of his eminence might be nearby. The last thing they needed was to be arrested or worse, to fight a duel in full view of a lot of people, a duel that could—at a stroke of the King's pen— become their last.

No. Something more cunning must offer. And, as D'Artagnan thought it, the plan presented itself, emerging from his head like a rather shifty Athena from Zeus's head. He grabbed at Porthos's gold-lace edged sleeve. "Listen," he said, standing on tiptoes to whisper as close as he could to his giant friend's ear. "Hide behind that pile of . . . whatever it is, there. And I will . . . do something that will bring the crowd in here. They don't have torches. At least not yet. The moment they enter here, you mingle with them. Remember, I'm your servant—" and at Porthos's look of rebellion— "your other servant. And as such, you were looking for me, and I'm a bad, bad boy, and in a lot of trouble."

Porthos looked doubtful. "But—" he said.

"Not a word. My name is Henri Bayard."

A look of relief in Porthos's eyes battled with a stubborn expression of confusion, but D'Artagnan, no matter how much he knew his stubborn friend's need for concrete explanations was not so foolish as to spend his time—now—explaining to Porthos why he must be Henri Bayard.

At any minute, someone—perhaps the big, brave guy—would open that door. Worse, they might think to get torches, and then they would see Porthos and D'Artagnan and . . . all there was to see before it could be hidden.

"Go," D'Artagnan told Porthos, in the tone that brooked no dissent. "Go. Now. Do not wait. Run."

Porthos hesitated a moment, then ran to hide behind the pile of material, whatever it might be. D'Artagnan hoped it was not coal, as it would seem rather odd when Porthos reemerged—for him to be covered in soot. But then again, D'Artagnan was entrusting the success of his plan to a man whose mind worked in such an odd way that people not familiar with the inner architecture of his thoughts often thought him dumb, or at least simple.

But Monsieur D'Artagnan père, other than wise advice on ghosts, had also told his son that when going into a duel, one must always fight with the sword he had. There was no use, and it would only lead to no good, to keep wishing after the sword he couldn't get. Porthos was the accomplice he had, and it was up to D'Artagnan to make the most of it.

Taking a deep breath, he blew out the candle on the forge, then let out a long, haunted scream, and after it, "Help me."

At the scream, he fancied he heard feet scurrying away, but at the "Help," the door was pushed open. In the doorway stood the big man and behind him ranged his friends and neighbors.

D'Artagnan, hoping it looked natural, threw himself down as though he'd lost consciousness. The steps approached. The big man knelt down. "What's wrong boy? What happened?" He put his hand, roughly, on D'Artagnan's neck, and announced, in tones of relief, "He lives."

Xavier was there too, on the other side, and D'Artagnan had a brief moment of panic, as he realized the story he'd told the Ferrant family in no way accorded to what he'd given Porthos. But there was nothing for it, now, and he blinked, and pretended to come to, and said, in a trembling voice, "There was a creature . . . very tall and dressed all in white, and a red light enveloping him, as he stood at that forge there." He pointed. "And he was . . . beating something. Looked like a sword made of men's bones." He shuddered at his own imagination and was quite glad to see not a few people in the crowd hastily crossing themselves.

"It's the devil," one of the men in the crowd said. "Come to collect the soul of whoever murdered Langelier."

"A likely story," Porthos's voice boomed, from the back of the crowd. Arms crossed, Porthos forced his way amid the locals, using his shoulder as a battering ram, as he was known to do in any crowd, Monsieur de Treville's antechamber included. "More likely you were in here to take a look at the scene of the crime, Bayard. And you left me without a servant to get me my dinner."

"You're his servant?" Xavier asked, his voice trembling. "But I thought you said you were going to be Monsieur de Treville's servant."

"Oh, he is that," Porthos said, and at that moment, on a wave of relief, D'Artagnan could have clasped him in his arms. "But the captain is letting me borrow him until Mousqueton is freed." Even in the dark, it was possible to see the glare he gave the gathered crowd, as though daring them to say that there was another outcome possible than Mousqueton's freedom. "But Bayard thought he was too good to be the servant of a mere musketeer, didn't you, rogue?"

He reached down, and with a realism that D'Artagnan couldn't have anticipated, got a firm hold on D'Artagnan's ear. "Up you come. I need someone to take a letter from me to the Princess de—" He stopped, as though he'd just avoided committing an indiscretion. "You know well who. And then we must pick my outfit for the encounter."

The crowd—possibly daunted by the idea that Porthos, whose suit managed to shine even in the scant light of the embers and the little coming in through the open door, might have a better, more impressive suit that he kept for encounters with princesses. And Porthos, holding fast to D'Artagnan's ear, and pulling it just a little too high, and a little too fast—just enough, D'Artagnan judged, to look as if he were dragging him—led him to the door of the armory and down the street.

No one followed them, though D'Artagnan could hear them arguing, still within the shop, the words "ghosts" and "murder" emerging now and then.

"Porthos," D'Artagnan said, after a while. "It might interest you to know that this is not one of my favorite modes of walking with a friend." And to his friend's blank look, D'Artagnan sighed. "You are holding my ear, Porthos."

"Oh," Porthos said, letting go of D'Artagnan's ear. He looked over his shoulder, then back at D'Artagnan. "What are you doing here, D'Artagnan?" he asked. "And why are you calling yourself Bayard?"

D'Artagnan calculated in his head the chances of Porthos understanding what he meant in the time available and without too much argument, and sighed when he could not raise the number above less than a chance in a million. Not that Porthos was stupid. Porthos was in no way stupid. But his mind worked on concrete details and on small points, and he would want D'Artagnan to explain why exactly he'd chosen the name Bayard, or else why he'd picked that exact color of russet suit from Planchet's wardrobe.

Instead, D'Artagnan shook his head. "I'll explain later," he said. "For now, tell me what you have been doing? How came you to raise that racket in the armorer's?"

Porthos gave him a sheepish look and shook his head in turn. "You see," he said, and opened his big hands, as though to illustrate his helplessness, "I found that I couldn't drop hammers on my head."

D'Artagnan raised his eyebrows and gave his friend a level, attentive look. "You had for a moment considered that this might be a good plan?"

Porthos sighed. "Not a plan," he said. "Not a plan as such. It's more . . ." He bit his lower lip as though in deep consideration. "You see, I thought it was odd that if a hammer had fallen on Mousqueton's head it should not have dashed his brains out altogether."

"If it were a glancing blow . . ." D'Artagnan said.

Porthos looked at him, with that air of mute misery he displayed when he was trying to think of words. Porthos could think of everything at all, but words caught on his tongue and refused to flow out as did the words of normal men. He hissed in frustration, and D'Artagnan waited for the words, looking at Porthos, betraying no impatience.

"You see . . ." Porthos said, and again he opened his hands, to show his lack of weapons, or perhaps his utter helplessness before the alien foe that was language. "I have been at Langelier's before, and I had an idea, though I confess I'd never looked very closely, that the ceiling beams were too high. They could not be reached with a hand."

D'Artagnan frowned. "You mean, you could not extend your hand and reach the beam? But surely, Porthos, one cannot reach most ceiling beams with one's hand."

"Of course," Porthos agreed, amiably, but his tongue

came out to touch his lips, and he made a grimace like a man in pain. "But I mean that you can't touch whatever you hang on the rack that you hang from the beams."

"Thereby making it impossible for anyone to retrieve a hammer easily," D'Artagnan said. "And making it so that no artificer in his right mind would hang a hammer from such a rack."

"Yes," Porthos said with audible relief. "You understand."

"Yes, I believe I do. And so you slipped away to go to the armorer's and verify the height of the ceiling beams without telling us what your intentions were."

"Did I not?" Porthos said, looking guilty. "I thought I had. Only I was thinking very hard on it, and it didn't seem to bear the trouble of explaining." He looked down at his feet. "I hope I value Aramis as I must, his being one of my best friends, and the noblest man in the whole world, excepting only Athos and . . . and perhaps yourself, D'Artagnan."

"No, don't strain your courtesy," D'Artagnan said, fighting hard not to laugh. "It is not fair to include me in the same class as Athos or even Aramis. Let's establish our two friends are the noblest men who ever drew breath and go from there."

"Well, yes. And I know Aramis is my friend, and a kind friend too. But he asks questions, and he would want to know what I was going to do, and why, and he would . . . push me half to death, before I could explain what I was about to do. And by that time I might very well be confused on the why and the when."

D'Artagnan nodded. He'd seen the process many times. "And Athos would try to convince you it was too dangerous."

"You understand," Porthos said.

"Oh yes, I understand, for you see, he tried to convince me it was too dangerous for us to go out at all, by ourselves, for however long it took to solve this murder. And then he tried to convince me that he could come with me and pass as a plebeian in this neighborhood."

Porthos looked at him in shocked horror. "Good men," he said. "They are. And noble, and Athos is so learned. But sometimes I wonder . . ."

"Where he gets his ideas," D'Artagnan said. "Yes, so do I." He spoke entirely without irony. Oh, D'Artagnan was cunning enough, and he understood the complex words that frustrated Porthos's tongue and ear. But he also understood how Porthos's mind worked better than he understood Athos's or Aramis's minds. Perhaps because he and Porthos, though noble born enough, had not after all, been raised as high nobility. It was a different country, almost, the level of pride and honor at which Athos had been brought up.

Porthos gave D'Artagnan the smallest of smiles, as though gratified to be making common cause with the Gascon, then shrugged. "At any rate, when I got there, I lit my candle, and I realized that there were indeed no hammers hanging from the upper racks. Nor should there be, since they could not be easily reached. You needed this hook thing I called the shepherds crook, just to remove the swords from their hooks."

"So it was unlikely that Mousqueton could grab a sword quickly without anyone stopping him, and, therefore, it is unlikely he was stealing it."

Porthos looked pained. "I have learned," he said, primly, "that it is never a good idea to say it is unlikely for Mousqueton to steal anything at all, D'Artagnan. When I first met him, he managed to steal my monogrammed handkerchief from my sleeve, without my ever feeling him touch me. And I know at least one case where he stole two pigeons in a cage from a shop where they were the only livestock." He shook his head. "Not that I intend to speak of these cases to anyone."

"Please, do not," D'Artagnan said. "No one needs to know who doesn't already."

Porthos touched the side of his nose in a conspiratorial way. "This I know," he said. "But you see, I thought it was still possible that someone who didn't know Mousqueton—particularly someone who didn't know Mousqueton or myself—would say that he had asked Monsieur Langelier for the sword, and then run him through suddenly when he least expected it."

"They wouldn't say that if they knew Mousqueton or yourself?"

"No, because anyone who knew Mousqueton would know that he would never run a man through like that, in cold blood. And anyone who knew me . . ." He shrugged. "Anyone who knew me would know that I have no money for an expensive sword. And, what's more, would know Monsieur Langelier knew it also."

D'Artagnan nodded. Having walked all the while they spoke, they were now well away from the neighborhood of the armorer's and at the point where they must choose whether to turn in the direction of Porthos's lodgings or D'Artagnan's. D'Artagnan motioned towards the alley which would lead them to the Rue des Fossoyers, where he lived. "Come with me," he said. "I must change out of this suit."

"Of course," Porthos said, good-naturedly, and followed him. "So I thought perhaps they had hammers up there. Not . . . Not that I could see them there, and I don't think anyone would have their work hammers so far up they would need a tool to retrieve them, but then . . . perhaps they'd made a hammer or two, to see how they would sell, you know . . . and hung them up there."

"Unlikely," D'Artagnan said.

"Very, but I was thinking, you see, of what people would say."

"Of course," D'Artagnan said. "And so . . ."

"I put a hammer up there, hung it with a bit of leather. And then I swung the rack, to see if it would fall."

"And did it?" D'Artagnan asked.

Porthos shook his head. "Never did. And, you know, I could not allow it to fall on my head, but I'm sure we can get some large melons or something of that nature. I would wager you, if I can make it fall, coming from as far up as it would be coming, even a glancing blow would be enough to crush a melon. Or a human head."

Frowning, D'Artagnan nodded. "You may be right," he said.

"I know I am," Porthos said, with that complete absence of arrogance and absolute certainty in his own experience that was his hallmark. "So it is quite impossible for Mousqueton to have done it. Of course, I already knew Mousqueton couldn't do it, but . . . I didn't have proof."

"Yes, yes, and proof is very important." They had reached D'Artagnan's door, and D'Artagnan opened it and started up the stairs, to his lodging. Porthos followed.

"Planchet," D'Artagnan said, "will be with Grimaud, so it would be perhaps a good idea for us to go there, after I have changed."

"Certainly," Porthos said. "Perhaps we may speak to Athos about the hammers and . . . and the impossibility of the whole thing, and perhaps he can lay that impossibility before Monsieur de Treville."

Thinking that while Athos would be more than happy to lay the impossibility before Monsieur de Treville, it was highly unlikely that the captain could do anything more about it, D'Artagnan started to cross his vast front room, empty except for a table at which the four of them often held their war councils. And stopped. On the mantelpiece was a letter in a hand he knew much too well.

He stopped and broke the seal and was momentarily

overwhelmed by the familiar perfume of Constance, Madame Bonacieux, the wife of his landlord, D'Artagnan's lover and, incidentally, the first true love of his young life.

All of which made him frown at the shakiness of the hand in which she had written: "Please meet me at the palace as soon as you can. Monsieur de la Porte will make sure you can enter. Tell him I am expecting you. Yours, anxiously, C.B."

He turned to Porthos, letter in hand.

"Bad news?" Porthos asked.

"Not . . . I hope not, but Constance wants to see me," he said. "As soon as may be. I will change and go to her."

"You know," Porthos said, slowly, "Athos will never forgive me if I let you go alone. Perhaps I should accompany you now?" And then, in a rush, "Oh, I don't mean I will go with you to see Constance. I don't . . . have the need to see her. But I will accompany you to her door and wait for you. You know how Athos worries."

And D'Artagnan, looking up at his friend's eyes, knew how Porthos worried, also, and wasn't cruel enough to refuse his offer. "I would be very grateful to you," he said. And added with a hint of mischief, "But only if you promise not to drop hammers on my head."

Porthos looked shocked. "Melons," he said, drily. "Not Gascons." And before D'Artagnan could decide whether his friend was joking or not, he added with a smile, "Everyone knows your average Gascon head is hard enough to break any hammers dropped on it, no matter from what height."

Instead of Love;
The Many Forms of Forgetting;
Where Athos Sometimes Was Correct

✑

ARAMIS entered the room, as the Duchess de Chevreuse sealed her letter, dropped it on her desk as something of little importance, and turned towards him with a smile. "My friend," she said, and extended both hands.

The Duchess de Chevreuse had to be close to Athos's age. Aramis wasn't sure exactly how old she might be, but he knew she was on her second marriage and that her son, Louis Charles D'Albert, a godson of the King's, was now six and that she'd given birth to a daughter just the year before. But no one would have believed it, looking at her.

Blond, with soft, well-shaped features, Marie Aimee de Rohan, Duchess de Chevreuse—or Marie Michon[4], as she called herself in the midst of her impetuous adventures and intrigues, which had made her the scandal of France and the amusement of the rest of the world—looked no more than seventeen.

---

[4] We now come across M. Aramis's seamstress, as depicted in Dumas. We don't know if M. Dumas lacked knowledge of Aramis's earlier affair with Violette, Duchess de Dreux, or if, for the sake of a more popular narrative, he chose to focus on the Duchess de Chevreuse, whom historians have called Richelieu's most voluptuous adversary.

Her hair retained the intense gold shading which was usually the mark of the very first youth, and her intent blue eyes projected an expression of complete innocence.

Yet she stepped into Aramis's arms with the ease that betrayed a woman who had had more than one husband and who, at this time in her life, entertained several lovers from various orders of nobility.

Aramis received her body in his arms, with a sigh—half of relief and half of desire. He was no fool. He knew that she was no Violette. Oh, he might have thought when he'd first started seeing Violette that he was only one of the musketeers and servants that she took to her lonely bed that her husband had spurned.

He might have continued to think so with his brain, but in his heart he knew that Violette was his and his only. As he was hers. He would have been offended—and fought a duel—had anyone told him that his Violette was seeing anyone else.

It wasn't like that with Marie. In fact, he had no illusions at all. He thought of Marie as he supposed Athos thought of the bottle. Something in which to lose himself when the pain grew too intense to bear and the futile longing for what could never again return so strong that he could hardly think against the force of it.

For the last several months, when that longing got too strong, its buffets impossible to resist, he'd come here and satiated them on the warm lips, the pliant flesh of the Duchess.

Now he kissed her, ardently, his tongue invading her mouth, his hands roaming the heated expanse of her velvet-dressed body. She responded in kind, her hands bold and searching, loosening his doublet and slipping beneath it and his linen shirt to raise a hundred points of desire from his flesh.

"Ah, D'Herblay," she said, as he pulled away to draw

breath, and she looked up at him smiling, her eyes dazed with desire. "Nothing like the sword to make the muscles of a man stand out." Her hands went lower and struggled for a very brief time with the fastenings of his breeches, then found their mark. Clutching it, she looked up and favored him with a dazzling smile. "I do so love a man with a good sword."

Aramis groaned, and picked the lady up by her waist, surprising a delighted squeal from her. "Ah, Marie Michon," he said, because he knew it pleased her to be addressed that way. "I've heard you're quite good with the sword yourself, now and then."

She giggled. "Only when some gentleman lets me borrow it."

"Well, my friend Porthos was the one who gave fencing lessons, but I learned from him, and well enough to win duels, so let me see if I can teach your grace something useful." Joining word to action, he dropped her on the bed, and pulled up the mass of her skirts and petticoats, beneath which she was, of course, bare. He ran his hands up her stockinged legs and caressed her, until her eyes looked wholly unfocused, the eyelids half-closed over them, "D'Herblay!" she said.

He grinned at her. "Are you begging me to unsheathe, milady? Is this where you wish to test my steel?"

"Yes, yes, a thousand times yes," she said, impatiently. And then, as though remembering herself and her sense of humor, "What good is a duel if all you do is brag to the other man about how fierce you are, but you will not show your mettle?"

Aramis unfastened what remained fastened of his clothes and plunged into the safe haven of her body, so suddenly and so completely he raised a small shriek from her, though not one that could in any way be considered a protest. He took a deep breath. "Have I wounded you?"

For her only response, she raised her body and pressed against him, and he lowered himself upon her, kissing her beautiful face, her soft neck, burying his own face into the soft, scented mound of her breasts.

Anything, anything at all, to avoid thinking of another body, another pair of breasts, now taken from him by the only rival he could not hope to best.

Violette's breasts had been smaller, but firmer, her neck longer and her features, though not as universally celebrated as those of this Duchess, had a sort of arch sweetness that made him fall at her feet at the sight of them. And while he had not been her first lover, nor the second, nor, indeed, he very much doubted, in the first dozen, she was somewhat less bold than De Chevreuse. Or at least she liked letting him set the rhythm and rarely pushed against him in that impatient manner, telling him to stab forcefully or not at all.

And yet, this woman too was sweet, and her scent of spice and some indefinable exotic mixture tantalized his senses. And his body responded with deep-seated pleasure to her advances and, in the way of things, he pursued release eagerly, till his body gave it to him, blotting out thought and—for a moment—breath and awareness of self with it.

He came to while being rather rudely shoved aside, and because the lady was inconstant, but never rude, he opened his eyes in shock, to find her glaring at him. "D'Herblay," she said, crossing her arms on her not inconsequential chest, from which he seemed, somehow, to have torn enough lace and ruffles that her left nipple stood up among such a nest, looking like a slatternly version of its more demure right-side sister, still sheltered by fabric.

"Yes?" he asked, dazed, as he pulled away and fastened his own disarranged clothes.

To his surprise, she answered him with a bubbling laugh and, looking up, he found her sitting up and smiling at him. "It won't do, my friend. It won't do. This is much like sending a challenge to duel to the wrong man." She shook her head. "At the very least, you'll offend the offended yet more, and you'll offend a whole other group of people." Looking up at what must be his very bewildered expression indeed, she laughed again. "How abominable you are, D'Herblay. You have no idea at all what you have done, do you?"

He shook his head, checking that he was indeed now decent, and adjusting his doublet.

"Who is Violette?" she asked.

The name, pronounced in the light of day, made him tremble all over and look up. "Vio—" he said, but could not pronounce the rest of it. Not here. Not in front of this woman.

"You don't even know, do you? I'm sure," she said, drawing herself up in turn and rearranging her clothing. "She would be heartbroken if she knew you forgot her name as soon as she left your bed. And yet"—she gave him a calculating look—"you remember her in the throes of pleasure, which seems to indicate that she has bitten deeper than I would have expected. Who is she, D'Herblay? Are we going to hear the announcement that you have decided to forsake your vocation and to marry, after all?"

"No," he said, horrified, wishing she would drop the subject. Sometimes he found himself quite willing to agree with Athos that women were the devil.

"Oh, good. You're not so lost. Because, of course, it would not do. I suspect you could no more be faithful to a wife than I could be faithful to a husband. So I'm very glad you're not willing—quite yet—to marry your Violette," she said, and, on the instinctive, immediate reaction to the name, she looked surprised.

"I'd marry her in a second, madam," Aramis said, primly, hoping this would stop the flow of words. And hoping above all it would stop De Chevreuse pronouncing a name he tried to avoid even thinking too loudly, in the privacy of his own mind. "Were it possible."

The Duchess was sitting in the midst of her disarrayed clothes that rose like a frothy foam of fabric at her waist. She looked like a picture some Italian painter might do, slightly altered. Venus rising from the sea, perhaps, though the sea probably shouldn't be on a bed. At his response, she widened her eyes. "Oh, married is she? My condolences, D'Herblay, but I must own that leaves the field open to the rest of us who are perhaps not quite so skilled as to imprint ourselves upon your mind and heart so indelibly."

The idea that his love for Violette was based on skill—that type of skill yet—made Aramis start. "She's not married," he snapped. "She is dead."

"Oh," De Chevreuse said, and, as her face fell, "Oh, but her name was not Viol—"

"Please don't pronounce it," Aramis said. "Please don't. She was that to me. It was the name she first gave me, and to that name we clung." He shook his head. "Have mercy on a bereaved man and don't drag your fingernails upon a still raw wound."

She tilted her head sideways and regarded him curiously. It was very much the expression of a cat studying a small animal squeaking past. "How odd," she said. "I believed you quite recovered from that incident, if indeed you had ever felt it."

"What you believed matters not," he said, and turned his back on her, walking to the wall and pretending to be all-encompassingly absorbed in the portrait of a small child on that wall. Probably one of Marie's daughters, he thought, as there was some resemblance to the mouth and the eyes.

He heard her get up and come towards him from behind. He felt her hand resting so half her fingers touched his neck and half his shoulder. "I could give you a child, you know?"

His head turned around so fast that it felt as if he'd dislocated something, and his normal suave manner deserted him. "What?"

She smiled at him, a contented smile. "To be sure I can. I can conceive very easily and I've had . . . bearing is easy. I've had more children than the obvious, you know? It's not so bad—a trip to the country, and later, you send the baby to the father who can then do with him or her as he pleases." She gave him an understanding look. "Someone bound to be a cleric could always claim it was a nephew of his and have him—"

"I am an only child."

"Oh, that hardly matters. It's only a polite fiction. The popes themselves have done. Everyone knew the nephews and nieces were truly—"

"No."

"But yes, I tell you it would be the easiest thing. All society really would care for, of course, was knowing the child was of the first blood. And my children are always lovely." She looked at him speculatively. "And if I have one with you, then he can't help but be lovely. I feel sure the Lady your Mother would approve. Just because she means you for the church, it doesn't mean—"

"Maman!" Aramis said, his mouth gone dry with feelings he couldn't even describe. "Oh, yes, everything I do in life must be with the object of pleasing *Maman.*"

This got him an odd look and then a small nod as though De Chevreuse had decided he could not possibly but be telling the truth. "I thought," she said smugly, "that was the origin of your great grief, for everyone knows the Duchess de Dreux was carrying her lover's child. I never thought that lover would be you, though I knew you were one of her—" She stopped, abruptly, and Aramis was shocked to realize the reason she had stopped was probably because he'd strode towards her, and was now holding her small face in the vise grip of his large hands.

He didn't know what his eyes showed, but he was sure they were intent. And, since he'd not meant to come here and hold her face; since, in fact, he had never thought of doing it; indeed since he couldn't make himself let go of her, he must assume there was something very scary about his expression.

The impression was confirmed by a little squeal escaping De Chevreuse and then her hand coming up to cover her mouth. He looked intently at her a while longer, before his mouth found its own way to the words he must pronounce. "Do not ever pronounce the name of Violette again," he said. "Not in my presence. Not if you live a thousand years and see me every day. I am a sinful man, despite my best intentions. I've had many lovers and will probably have many more, whether I take orders or not." He paused. There was something in her eyes that told him only the fact that his gaze was still intent, his hands still immobilizing her face, kept her from giggling. "Violette was not one of those lovers, taken to satisfy a human lust. Something happened between us. Though we were never married, it was the first time I understood the biblical order to leave your mother and father and cleave to your wife.

"Violette and I were like that, one body, one blood, one flesh. As long as I live, though what you might call grief might die down—will die down, I daresay, since human memory does—I will be half a creature, a half of me having been ripped away and sent to an early grave. I will never know wholeness again till, God granting it, I meet her again in the ever after and we can be one once more. A child . . ." His mouth went dry again, and he had to stop, while his eyes filled with unaccountable moisture. "Should there have been a child from her, I would have moved heaven and Earth to have him by my side and to make him my heir. Other than that, a child is of no consequence to me. I've lived since I can remember in the expectation of being a priest one day, and of leaving no descendants. My lands and title will devolve on a distant cousin with a numerous family, and I wish him joy of them."

Now his body allowed him to pry his fingers away from De Chevreuse's face—as though he were prying them away against their will. She looked at him, her mouth half-open, like a startled child. And Aramis thought that he'd ruined it, now. He would be leaving here never to return, the one palliative he'd found for his pain over Violette's death gone forever.

He stepped away and bowed correctly. "My apologies, your grace. I regret having upset you or scared you. It was scarcely my wish to do so. I beg you will forgive me and that when we meet again, you will show no signs of your anger at me."

"Oh, but I'm not angry at you," she said, suddenly. "And you'll come see me the day after tomorrow, of course."

He raised his eyebrows. "After my . . . insufferable behavior?"

She grinned at him, raising an ingratiating dimple on her cheek. "Your behavior," she said, "insufferable though it might be, shows you to be a man of deep passions and sudden anger." She shrugged. "It is in my nature, you know, to embrace danger. Much of my life has been lived in seeking it out and following it wherever it may lead."

"Oh," Aramis said, and stopped, remembering the rumor, more or less confirmed by Monsieur de Treville. "Your grace wouldn't be happening, right now, to be involved in a conspiracy?"

She flicked her fingers, casually. "I am always involved in a conspiracy," she said.

"To murder the Cardinal?" he said.

She looked surprised, her eyes wide. "Oh, I'd devoutly love a conspiracy that does that, or even attempts it," she said, eagerly. "Is there one? And can I join it?"

"Unlike you," Aramis said. "I don't court danger for the

love of it." And then, with punctilious exactitude, "Unless it's in duel where I must, of course, defend my honor."

"We women do not have that choice," she said. "All the swords we have must be borrowed."

"Those," he said, thinking of his fingers grasping her face while fury ran like a grief-dark river through his mind, "must be danger enough."

She shrugged. "But I do not know of this conspiracy you speak. If someone wants to murder the monster, I must, of course, support them. I've found no one brave enough to try it yet, though." As she spoke, she darted the smallest of looks at the folded missive on her writing table, and then quickly away.

Aramis was almost absolutely sure that she was lying about knowing nothing of a conspiracy. And yet, he was also almost sure he had seen something like surprise quickly followed by relief in her eyes when he'd mentioned the conspiracy. Surprise because he knew it? Relief because he didn't know her part in it?

"I'd take care, milady," he said. "Your correspondence with the Queen has been intercepted, and the Cardinal is sure it betrays a conspiracy against him."

"His eminence thinks that the fact I still breathe, never mind my being in the same city as her Majesty, is a conspiracy against himself. It is all very silly."

"Perhaps so, but remember he has the power to separate your head from your neck, and that's a danger too large to court. Take care, my lady."

"I always take care. I will see you the day after tomorrow, D'Herblay, since you anticipated our meeting today."

It was so clearly a dismissal, he could not help but take it. On his way out, passing the table, he managed to cast a glance on the name on that missive, and was startled to find the name and styling of her Majesty's illegitimate half-brother, Cesar.

The Spider's Web;
Where Old Enemies Are
Much Like Old Friends;
The Loyalty of a Worthy Man

⌘

"SIT down, Monsieur le Comte," Rochefort said. He had led him into an office that was the exact, if poorer, replica, of his master's. Where Richelieu's study was surrounded by a profusion of bookcases, each filled with leather bound volumes with gilded edges and covers, this one had only two bookcases. And where Richelieu's chairs were majestically carved and ornamented, Rochefort's— while looking quite comfortable—were undeniably utilitarian affairs. His office also lacked a writing desk. What it had in its place was a sword, mounted on the wall, a sword that looked much like Athos's ancestral sword, mounted on his own wall.

"I wish you wouldn't call me that," Athos said. "You might know it, and the Cardinal might know it, but other than courting my vengeance if you reveal it, there is nothing you can earn by letting me know you have my secret. I don't use the name. What I have done has darkened it forever. Perhaps some yet unborn La Fere can resume it with pride, but I can never. So long as I live, that name must remain unknown."

"Or at least until the crown has forgotten the small matter of your wife," Rochefort said, casually, shrugging. "That's normally why people take the uniform, isn't it? To serve a while until one's crimes are forgotten and the King owes one enough he'd never dream of punishing them. And then one can return to one's former life, untouched."

Athos felt a muscle work on the side of his jaw. "Do not mention . . . the lady. I committed no crime," he said. "But as for returning . . ." He shrugged. "There are events and . . . and decisions that alter one forever. I don't think I would be the best custodian for my lands or my people."

Rochefort said nothing to this, simply sat down and joined his hands on his lap. "You're not going to require," he said, "that I call you Athos, are you? It is a demmed silly name. A demon, wasn't he?"

"A mountain," Athos said. "A mountain in Armenia on which a famous monastery is set."

"A monastery!" Rochefort said, with every sign of alarm. "Are you then, like your friend who calls himself Aramis, merely wearing the uniform of the King's musketeers until you can exchange it for the habit of a priest or a monk?"

"I?" Athos said, almost in shock. "Heaven forbid. I hope I have as much faith as the next man, but if I find myself inadequate to care for my lands or my people, how much more inadequate am I to look after God's affairs? No. I'll remain myself. The name is just . . . what it is."

Rochefort shrugged. "Those of us who serve the Cardinal," he said, "are not ashamed to do it under our own names."

"Perhaps," Athos said, "because you had nothing left to lose." And let the idea sink in, seeing the sting of it at the back of Rochefort's eye, even as the man looked away. Rochefort was, as Athos knew, as noble as himself—a man from an ancient family.

They'd been on the opposite sides of the secret war

between King and Cardinal for so many years that the two of them knew each other as well as old friends might. Two things divided them beyond their opposing loyalties— which either considered inexplicable—that Rochefort was willing to stoop to the most dishonorable actions in pursuit of his master's aim; and that Athos had no expectations, ever, of regaining the honors he had lost, while Rochefort was hoping to rebuild his domain and the fortune his ancestors had squandered.

"His eminence says you have agreed to work for him on this matter of the . . . conspiracy," Rochefort said, politely.

"On this matter only and only because he's holding Mousqueton, Monsieur Porthos's servant, as a hostage to this."

"I understood you offered," Rochefort said, drily.

"One offers, when one is compelled," Athos answered with equal dryness. "I do not want the boy harmed. You know Porthos. He took to the boy as though he were his own son." He held back from saying that Porthos had already lost one son. Not that he wasn't sure Richelieu knew this. There were very few things in France that escaped the attention of the éminence grise. But either Rochefort knew it and it didn't bear mentioning—or he didn't know it, and Athos would spare Porthos's pride. "It would be devastating to lose him."

Rochefort raised an eyebrow, "Is he perhaps, in fact—?"

"Not that I know, or Porthos knows," Athos said.

"Or find it necessary to tell me?"

Athos shrugged. No use making Rochefort and Richelieu think that their hostage was, in fact, more important than he was. "That I know," he said, "Porthos met him when he came to Paris. I understand Mousqueton tried to relieve Porthos of some of his possessions and . . . Well, you know Porthos."

"Mostly I know his prowess in duel, but yes. I have heard rumors about Monsieur Porthos's soft heart."

Athos inclined his head. He supposed that there were rumors about all of them and that somewhere, if not actually written down, in the Cardinal's hand, there was a list of their weaknesses—Porthos's soft heart and his vanity; Aramis's faith and his inability to stay away from the fair sex; D'Artagnan's tendency to leap before he looked and his romanticism and Athos's—he paused. He knew himself well enough to realize he had faults aplenty. But he was at a loss to choose which of them would be the fatal one. His drinking? His reluctance to deal with any women at all? Or his shattered and embittered heart, forever burdened with the sense of guilt for having killed his wife. She might have been a criminal and her death an execution, but in the dark of night, Athos stared dry-eyed into the darkness and suspected very much that he'd made a mistake and slain the only woman he'd ever love, the woman whose memory still haunted his every moment.

"So you offered to help us with this conspiracy to murder the Cardinal," Rochefort said, suddenly businesslike, as though something in Athos's expression had scared him. "And I think perhaps you should know what we know for a fact and . . . and what his eminence fears."

Athos did not say that his eminence's fears might have very little to do with reality. He knew that this was probably a slander. The Cardinal was many things, but none of them was either coward or insane. In fact, he was—always, in Athos's experience—realistic and exact and fully aware of the truth of a situation, no matter how much he chose to distort it in his favor. Instead, he settled himself, with his hands folded on his lap, and waited.

Rochefort seemed surprised he had passed up a chance to engage in a battle of wits. "His eminence," he said with something like a twang of disappointment in his voice, "has intercepted some correspondence between the Queen and some of her friends."

Athos inclined his head. "Not the first time," he said. "Nor the last."

Rochefort shrugged, as though to signify this did not matter. "The Queen is very loyal to her brother the Emperor," he said. "Sometimes it seems inexplicably so. She has also conceived the most vehement dislike of his eminence, for no reason anyone can understand, since you must know his eminence has always had her best interest—" He stopped, and shrugged and Athos was very much afraid he'd allowed a chuckle to escape him. "At any rate, you see, the Queen's loyalties are divided, and having the King's best interests—and, aye, those of the kingdom—at heart, the Cardinal can't help but monitor her conversations. We are not going to beg pardon for doing what must be done."

"I assure you, Rochefort, we never expected you to beg pardon."

He got a look of dubious enquiry for that, followed by an exasperated exhalation. "The thing, my dear Count, is that . . ." He hesitated. "This correspondence hinted that there would be a great change in France soon, and it was clear they meant that the Cardinal would be dead and . . ." He paused. "And the throne might be better managed. We believed the implication was that they meant to murder the King."

He paused. Athos caught himself halfway out of the chair, rising by the force of his arms upon the armrests, and he forced himself to sit down again. He noted Rochefort's gratified expression at what Athos was sure was his alarmed face, and Athos forced his face to relax; forced himself to discipline his emotions. This was Rochefort and Rochefort was an echo of the Cardinal. They—both of them—told the truth only when they couldn't tell lies, or when the truth served their purpose better than a lie. The chances of this being truthful were less than none.

Yet, Athos's voice still sounded altered and distorted by emotion, as he said, "You cannot know what you're saying. You cannot mean it."

Rochefort was looking neutral, his pleased expression gone. "I wish I didn't," he said. "Though in the beginning it was just . . . a suspicion, or less than that. A thought that the matter should be followed up. A vague idea that things were not all they seemed to be. So I . . . followed up on it. The Queen's correspondent, the Duchess De Chevreuse, who you know, is like the worst half of her majesty, and has already been responsible for one miscarriage of her majesty's, for encouraging her to behave in a very irresponsible manner in the halls of the palace . . ."

"Or at least that was the reason given," Athos said.

Rochefort shrugged minimally. "We intercepted correspondence of the Duchess's, next. The names this brought to us were a little . . . odd. It appears Madame la Duchess has for some time entertained correspondence with Captain Ornano, the governor of the house of Monsieur, the brother of the King."

Athos, completely confused by the introduction of the governor of Monsieur, the heir apparent, Gaston d'Orléans, could only raise his eyebrows and try to appear more knowledgeable than he was and yet less enlightened on the matter than he felt he should be.

Rochefort smiled and shook his head. "Perhaps I should explain," he said. "I understand your friend Aramis is quite au courant of every possible affair in the court. I judge it will not be a surprise to you if I say that we've had some strange reactions to the announced marriage of Monsieur to Mademoiselle de Montpensier?"

"Is he to marry her?" Athos asked.

"But . . . It has been announced by his majesty himself," Rochefort said, as though shocked that anyone at all could have missed this all-important news. "Surely—"

Athos shook his head. "My only interest in the royalty is to serve them," he said. "Not necessarily in the person of the present occupant of the throne." And, added, hastily as Rochefort raised his eyebrow in turn, "No, I don't mean anything disloyal by that. I am a musketeer of the King's and I will serve him to the utmost of my understanding and my ability. That is not what I meant. I meant . . ." He steepled his hands, then shook his head. "When I was . . . fifteen, I ascended to the dignity of Viscount de Bragelone, the junior title in my family. As such, my father judged that I should be knighted according to the true and ancient rites. What occasioned the knighting—the performing of an act of valor—all that matters not. It was an organized tourney, in which I could display my prowess." He was aware of a rueful smile distending his lips. "Such as it was, at the time. Good enough for my father's blessing, at any rate. And he took me to the Abbey of St. Derris where the crypts hold the bones of the kings of France. There he made me aware that the occupant of the throne such as he is, remains, for all he is our sovereign and King, a passing being—a mortal like all other men. What I must serve, he then told me, and made me understand, is the monarchy of France. The present occupant is merely the . . . vessel of that sacred line, that power which represents and rules all of the kingdom."

In Rochefort's eyes, for just a moment, there was something of a fellow-feeling and a look of understanding. "As I assume the Cardinal would say, we must worship the presence of Christ in the sacrarium and not the vessel itself."

Athos shrugged. "I would say something akin to that. But while one might, on occasion, destroy the sacrarium, one should never destroy the King. Which doesn't mean one should take a great interest in his life or that of his relatives, either. I have gathered, from gossip, that the King's marriage is an unhappy one, and the only reason that matters to me is that it reduces the chances of France's having an heir and, therefore, lays the kingdom open to the depredations of foreigners intent on seizing the throne. My only interest in Monsieur, therefore, is that he is the heir to the throne and stands between us and a disputed throne. Whom he marries signifies little, next to the imperative that he marry and sire children for the crown."

"It is the Queen Mother's only interest, also, I believe. That and that Mademoiselle de Montpensier carries with her a large dowry as well as all the ancient dignities and powers of that branch of the Bourbons. Her mother was a Joyeuse and the Queen made much of her and . . . indeed, of the daughter. In fact, you could say the Queen Mother has been planning this match since before Monsieur was breeched. The sum of this all is that, Monsieur being seventeen, the King has granted permission for the marriage to take place." He looked at Athos, half in wonder, as though meeting a strange creature, and half in amusement. "If you do not listen to gossip, it is possible you don't realize this would throw into disarray several people who have an interest, direct or indirect upon the throne and the fate of Monsieur and any heirs he might sire, in particular."

Athos frowned. He did not, in fact, take any interest in gossip. However, he had been born and raised as a nobleman, sitting night after night at his father's table, in their domains de la Fere, and listening to the discussions that washed up in their rural province, like echoes of a far-off sea. And then, after all his ambitions and hopes and desires had come to an end in the person of a beautiful blond woman marked with the fleur-de-lis of infamy upon her peerless shoulder, he'd come to court. There, he could no more hope to avoid being immersed in gossip than a fish could hope to avoid being immersed in water.

And the gossip ran rife, of course, as it would, since the twenty-five-year-old King had no heir and his fraught relations with his wife made it very unlikely indeed that he would have any. For a time—and perhaps still, though Athos refused to enquire—there had been a running pool among the more daring of the musketeers about who might sire the heir of France.

Oh, not themselves. The duchesses, princesses and minor noblewomen at court might disport themselves with the dashing young men, though even they—themselves—were not so zany as to allow their heir to be conceived by one such. Stories might abound—they always did—about how this or that heir to this or that domain favored this or that nobleman. But it was all nonsense, and of this Athos was fairly sure.

The Queen, like Caesar's wife, must be above reproach and as such, she could not have it rumored about her that she slept with this or that musketeer—and in as crowded an environment as the palace, the gossip would fly far and wide, if she so much as favored one of them with a look or permission to kiss her hand.

No—the names on whom the hope of an heir for France rested, at least to believe some irreverent musketeers, were higher and more carefully guarded: Buckingham had for a time been a favorite, lending an air of intrigue to every one of his visits to France; then came Richelieu himself, though it was rumored by many that he had indeed made the attempt and been spurned; after that were many would-be contestants—almost every nobleman in France, truth be told.

But to Athos it had always seemed that—though the gossip didn't scandalize him as it scandalized Porthos who had more than often threatened to duel someone for it—as much as they ran pools and gossiped and amused themselves with such, the musketeers didn't believe the Queen would stray. Nor indeed did anyone else.

In fact, considering the position of queens as almost

strangers and often suspected of insufficient loyalty to their adopted land, it seemed strange to Athos that any of them ever strayed. It was a brief pleasure, surely, and not worth the beheading that would follow.

Therefore, everyone expected the throne to, eventually, devolve on Monsieur, Gaston d'Orléans, the King's younger brother. And after that, he knew that some families were waiting, in the full expectation that neither of the royal brothers would produce heirs, and the throne would thereby devolve to them. "I have," he admitted, "heard the princes of Conde and Soissons speak as though they quite counted on the throne being theirs one day. In fact . . ."

"In fact?"

"In fact, to the extent that I've paid attention to such gossip, which, if you permit me, seems exaggerated considering his majesty is still young and, though not in the best of health, might yet live for decades—it was to worry that if ever it came to such a pass, those two houses between them might tear the kingdom apart." And, afraid that Rochefort would think this fear hyperbolic, "They have pride and greed enough for that."

"I agree, they do," Rochefort said, his voice expressing his surprise that Athos and he might agree on anything. "And I confess they were two of the people on whom the news of Monsieur's intended marriage fell heavily. They cannot, after all, count on the throne, if Monsieur sires a child at eighteen. So, you see . . . they were unhappy. All the more so since Monsieur de Soissons has for some time been trying to make his own arrangements with Mademoiselle de Montpensier."

"You think the Duchess de Chevreuse is acting for them?" Athos asked. It didn't seem an impossible idea. After all, De Chevreuse had a reputation for intriguing for the sake of the intrigue itself.

"It is possible," Rochefort said. "All the more so since

there are intimations that the fair lady has had some veiled correspondence with the two of them. And we've heard their names fall in conversation with the Queen."

"But then her interest in this Captain Ornano must be . . ." Athos said. "That he might yet convince the Prince to refuse to marry Montpensier."

Rochefort smiled. "You are wasted in the musketeers, Monsieur le Comte," he said, and bowed. "If you worked for the Cardinal, your genius for intrigue would be rewarded as it deserves."

"If I worked for the Cardinal," Athos countered, "my good manners forbid my explaining what I would deserve, since you, yourself"—he gave a small bow—"have that honor. Reward would not be exactly the word for it though. Remember my father made me a speech on serving the monarchy."

"We each serve it as we see best," Rochefort said.

"And if De Chevreuse is doing this," Athos said, changing subject, "what proof have you it is not at the behest of Soissons, who perhaps still wishes to marry Mademoiselle de Montpensier?"

"Or her dowry," Rochefort said.

Athos bowed. He knew why most men married. He had not done so, but that was perhaps to his detriment. Certainly, considering whom he had, indeed, married, to the discredit of his good sense and judgement.

"It might be at the behest of Soissons," Rochefort said. "But the truth is, she has talked to the Queen about replacing the Cardinal with someone more amenable."

"Which you must know is the dream of most of the nobility in France, and not exactly treason in itself."

"Perhaps not, but we know how attached our King is to Richelieu."

"Or how attached he pretends to be," Athos said, remembering more than a few times when Louis XIII had shown himself overjoyed at his musketeers thwarting some plot of the Cardinal's.

Rochefort bowed. "But you must see," he said, "that it would be the worst for the Queen if the King's brother were to have children before . . . the royal marriage is fruitful. It would be a reproach to her, and, doubtless, lead to her loss of importance. So you must see . . ."

"That she would lose by it, yes. That she would conspire against her husband and her kingdom thereby, no, I do not need to see that."

"Perhaps not," Rochefort said. "But the Cardinal and I would very much like it if you should investigate in that direction, shall we say."

Athos all but paled. Through one of their previous adventures, they had managed to keep the crown on the head of Anne of Austria, despite the Cardinal's best efforts to unseat it. Was he truly fated to remove it this time? The Cardinal, with his fine lessons on the theory of chess, should understand that the knight was more often used to protect the queen than the pawn. If it came to that, Athos would have to resign himself to the loss of Mousqueton.

Or perhaps, he thought, ensure his freedom by other means.

But what could he do if the Queen, herself, was part of a play for the King? The horrible prospect put a shiver up his spine.

A Fortuitous Meeting;
Where Three Friends Are Better Than One;
The Impossibility of Two Musketeers
Dueling One Guard

$\mathcal{S}$

D'ARTAGNAN hurried to the palace with a confused and worried mind. Oh, he did not doubt Constance, whose nature was as her name, nor did he fear that she might entangle him in some plot. But he did fear that a plot was already in place and might entangle himself and Constance without mercy.

On the way to the palace, he responded to Porthos's questions as to what D'Artagnan had been doing near the armorer's, with half syllables, which not only led Porthos to believe that D'Artagnan had been seeking additional work, but to heartily approve of it, because, as he put it, the pay in the guards seemed to be as bad as in the musketeers, and that was as irregular as the very irregular finances of their sovereign.

D'Artagnan didn't bother arguing how unfit it would be for him to take a position as an assistant baker, or even an armorer. Porthos was, after all, the only one of them who had ever done work for pay. He'd been employed as a dance and fencing master upon first coming to Paris. And he was a proud man—or at least, he liked to wear clothes

resplendent enough to put the royalty to shame, and he told
a great many innocent falsehoods about his familiarity
with princesses and duchesses. Yet, he could consider with
equanimity a course of action—becoming employed as a
servant, under an assumed name—which would have made
Aramis speechless, caused Athos to challenge someone to
a duel for accusing him of it and which, had D'Artagnan
given the idea his full attention, would have made
D'Artagnan blush.

There was absolutely no reason to argue with Porthos,
and D'Artagnan was concerned with far weightier worries.
The note from Constance worried him, after what might
have been the deliberate entrapment of Mousqueton. If
they were right and if the Cardinal were so desperate to get
leverage against Anne of Austria and to make Anne of Austria confess to some plot that he would stoop to entrapping
Mousqueton, would he not prefer to entrap one of them?

He'd looked at her letter, and it did look like her handwriting, but would not the Cardinal, in all but name and
honor the King of France, be able to command someone to
imitate the hand of a woman who lived at court and who
had, doubtless, written notes to various people living there?

He felt a shiver down his spine, even as he gave his
password to Monsieur de la Porte and got admitted into the
palace—or at least into the dark gardens adjoining the
palace. Because his eyes were sharpened by his awareness
of danger, his mind prying the edges of every dark corner,
every lengthening shadow, he was alert and ready, and
dropped his hand to his hip at the sight of a man walking
towards them.

The words, "Who goes—" were on his lips—the training of years as a guard in the long watches of the night. But
he got no further than that because his eyes had recognized
the tall, slim figure, the glimmering blond hair, the fashionable attire of his friend Aramis.

"Aramis," he said, at the same time that Aramis's voice echoed back, "D'Artagnan."

The two stood in the winter garden, surrounded by bare trees, looking at each other. D'Artagnan was surprised to see something very much like hostility in his friend's eyes.

It was only when Aramis said, "He made you come after me, did he not?" that he understood the mute resentment in the green eyes.

"Athos?" he said, and, to Aramis's nodding, "No. I convinced Athos that you—and I too—must be allowed to investigate this by . . . having freedom of movement. I am here because I got a letter." He felt himself blush. "From Madame Bonacieux," he added, with reluctance that came not only from laying open his affairs to his friend, but also from his consciousness that Aramis's lovers were of a much higher level in society.

But Aramis didn't seem to catch the implication, nor to be inclined to deride D'Artagnan's choice of society. Instead he leaned in close to his friend and said, worriedly, "Madame Bonacieux? She has sent you a note? What did she say?"

"Nothing, except for asking me to meet her."

Aramis gave him a curious look. "Is this normal, then?" he asked. "For her to send you a note ordering you to come to her at the royal palace?"

D'Artagnan shook his head. "No," he said, and blushed a little. "Normally she comes to see me. She has the keys to my lodging, and she will come in any time of day or night that she can get away. I assumed . . ." He cleared his throat. "I assumed she did so today, coming into my lodging and leaving me her note, since I was not there and neither was Planchet. Unless, of course, she sent the note earlier, while Planchet was still there. Why are you looking at me with such an expression of reproach, Aramis?"

Aramis's expression of reproach did not abate, but he

frowned harder at D'Artagnan. "My friend, sometimes I am reminded of how young you are and that you are, in fact, far younger than I, myself, am or remember being. How can you, at such a time as this, come to a summons written on a note, without any warranty that it is from someone who means you well? Did you at least take the precaution of not coming in the way she told you to? Or the way she expected you to come?"

D'Artagnan frowned. "I came the way she asked me to, and gave word to Monsieur de la Porte."

Porthos said, "Surely you can't think that Monsieur de la Porte is betraying us? He has always been on the side of the Queen. His—"

"Porthos," Aramis said. "We are now in such territory that I'm not absolutely sure the Queen means us well. And I know the Cardinal means us ill."

"What do you mean you don't think the Queen means us well? We have always been her devoted servants, and in fact, we have allowed her to remain on the throne and we—"

Aramis's finger darted out, and stopped D'Artagnan's lips. "Shh," he said. "Shhh. Do not be foolish. Doesn't even the Bible exhort you not to put your faith in princes?"

"But—"

"No," Aramis said. "The devil. I'm starting to suspect, with Athos, that this whole thing is deeper than we thought. Where is Athos, speaking of him? What is he doing?"

D'Artagnan shook his head. "I presume he is back at his lodgings, with the servants. He did not tell me he intended to do anything else. At least . . ."

"At least?"

"At least since I disabused him of the notion that he could pass for a peasant looking for work," D'Artagnan said.

Aramis's chuckle echoed like a clap of thunder, all the more surprising because until it sounded, his features had been so grave and tense and full of foreboding. Now he grinned at D'Artagnan. "Surely even our friend could not—"

And at that same moment, Porthos lunged past D'Artagnan's shoulder, sword out, so quickly that D'Artagnan was forced to dart out of the way or be trampled. And in darting out of the way, he noticed a motion. Something dark moving past his line of sight towards Aramis. At the same time, Aramis had his sword out, and his cloak wrapped around his arm, and was defending himself from two adversaries at once.

D'Artagnan in turn found himself fighting two men, attired all in black and wearing what looked uncommonly like monkish cowls. They had sword and dagger out, each of them, and there were at least six. They fought fiercely, with quiet intensity, their only noise being grunts of surprise when their attacks were parried, or sudden exclamations of pain, when first Porthos and then Aramis put his sword through one of the adversaries.

Faced with two of them, D'Artagnan, for the first time in his life, found himself sweating to hold his own in a duel. He'd fought two guards of the Cardinal before, and wounded them both. He'd fought more than two of them, sometimes, truth be told. But this—this was something quite different. These men fought with unerring ability, as though each of them had been as well trained as D'Artagnan himself had been by his battle-veteran father. It was all he could do to meet each of their thrusts and push them away.

In his mind, his late father's voice echoed, in quiet reproach, *never be happy that you are parrying each of an enemy's thrusts, my son. The truth is that if you're only parrying you have already lost, for you're never attacking. You have to be lucky every time they attack, and they only have to be lucky enough to let the sword go through once.*

But though his father had trained him on how to respond

to sudden attack, and given him intensive practice on dueling two experienced swordsmen—often recruiting his friend, Monsieur de Bhil for the occasion—he had never trained him in fighting two people who were intent only on murdering him.

"Holla there, what goes here?" a voice called, out of the shadows.

On that sound, one of the adversaries lunged, and his sword blade thrust towards D'Artagnan. D'Artagnan had only the time to interpose his arm to push the blade away from his chest. And then his opponent was gone; vanished, as though he'd come out of the night, and left via the night itself.

And D'Artagnan realized, only then, that he'd been wounded and his arm was bleeding profusely. He watched the blood drip from the cut which had pierced both the velvet of his doublet and his flesh and, from the pain of it, had grazed the bone of his forearm.

"I see, musketeers with their swords out," the voice that had spoken out of the shadows said again. "Dueling, were you?"

Into the relative light of their position—in the middle of the garden where neither shadow of tree nor of wall fell on them—strode Jussac, one of the Cardinal's favorite guards. "Porthos, Aramis, D'Artagnan. Tell me, who was dueling whom? Not that it matters, as you have undoubtedly been dueling, and therefore you are all arrested and you'd best hope that the new edicts weren't signed tonight, else you shall all be beheaded by first dawn."

Porthos answered only with a long stream of swearing—inventive swearing, D'Artagnan noted, even in his shocked state, his hand holding his wounded arm up and staring in disbelief at the stream of blood pouring forth. He was fairly sure whatever the Cardinal might or might not have done to or for his niece Madame de Combalet, it could not be what Porthos had just said he did. Mostly because it was anatomically impossible and probably fatal.

He felt light-headed and as though he would presently lose consciousness; only Aramis touched him on the arm and said, "D'Artagnan." And D'Artagnan, looking up from his arm, realized that Aramis had put away his sword, and was holding up one of his immaculate, embroidered, silk-edged handkerchiefs, and trying to remove D'Artagnan's doublet.

"Can you remove your arm from the sleeve without my cutting it away?" Aramis said. "Your doublet might be salvageable with the insertion of some panels. I'm sure Mousqu—Well, one of our servants should be able to help with that. Only I must tourniquet your arm as soon as it may be, else you will bleed out very quickly."

As though in a dream, D'Artagnan opened his doublet and removed his arm from its sleeve and watched Aramis tie the handkerchief around his arm. A gulp escaped him when Aramis tightened the handkerchief, and then Aramis made D'Artagnan lift his arm. "It will help stop the flood," he said.

Meanwhile, the guards of the Cardinal had come into the light, and it was de Brisarac and Jussac and about six underlings. Jussac, apparently under the control of an idea that dominated all others, said, "Which of you wounded the boy? What were you dueling over? I thought you were inseparables."

"I knew you had deformed moral structures, to serve the Cardinal so willingly," Aramis said drily. "I did not know that you also had subnormal wits. Why would we be dueling each other, Jussac? We are friends. We are, indeed, inseparables."

"The first time I met the boy, you were all dueling him," Jussac said.

"Oh, that was because I had only come to town, and made their acquaintance," D'Artagnan said. "Now I know them better than that, and I would never duel with all of them at once."

"So you would duel them one at a time," Jussac said.

Aramis gave D'Artagnan a warning look and said, "I wish you wouldn't speak, my friend, not while your head is clouded by blood loss. You see that Monsieur Jussac is determined to judge us before he has any facts." Then turning to Jussac, he said, "We were crossing the garden, together, as you see. We were looking for our friend Athos, who said he might come and help supplement the guard today. And out of nowhere, we were ambushed by men in black wearing monkish hoods. What you saw was our effort at defending ourselves, nothing more. It was no duel, with appointed time and seconds, but surely, even under the Cardinal's rule, a man is still allowed to defend himself when in fear for his life?"

"I didn't see any men," Jussac said, mulishly, jutting out his chin. "What I saw was the three of you, with your swords out. And since I know you've fought each other before . . ."

A stream of invective escaped Porthos, prompting Aramis to say, "Porthos, I don't think the Cardinal can have done that."

"And why not?" Porthos asked, in a challenging tone.

"Because I think you'll find," Aramis said, "that only women have that organ."

"Oh," Porthos said, and frowned. "But I meant it in the sense where things aren't really true, but the spirit of them is, anyway."

"The metaphorical sense? Even in that sense, that is not something I'd ascribe to the Cardinal," Aramis said, absentmindedly and then, examining D'Artagnan's arm. "I think the bleeding is slowing."

"Well," Jussac said. "Porthos can have the pleasure of explaining to his eminence his views on anatomy and metaphor, both, since I know his eminence will be overjoyed to see you. As will, might I add, most of our comrades. If the edicts have been signed tonight, which will cause you to die in the morning, we might even throw a party."

"Ah, yes," Aramis said. "I've long known that you were afraid of us."

"Afraid? Us?" de Brisarac asked.

"Indeed. Else, why would you hope the law would rid you of us? Why else, but that you, yourselves, could not defeat us?"

De Brisarac reached for his sword, but Jussac held his arm. "No," he said. "You do not want to answer to his eminence for that. We'll simply arrest these miscreants, and they can tell his eminence their pretty tale."

"It is not a pretty tale, you fool," Porthos said. "Here. Come here." Without ceremony, the giant musketeer grabbed Jussac by the arm and dragged him over to where he'd been fighting his enemies. "Do you see that? The ground is fairly hard, but even so you can see my footsteps and, see, two others."

"So, you were fighting these other two and they—"

"Don't be more foolish than you can help being," Porthos said, and D'Artagnan had to suppress a wish to giggle, since that was a comment more often heard from Aramis to Porthos. "Look there. I wounded this man. See the blood? And before you tell me it's D'Artagnan's, note how the drops vanish into the shadows there. And here." He forcibly led the guard another way. "Here, see, was where Aramis wounded his adversary. Look how he ran into the night, pouring blood out of him. Why, if the boy had bled that much, instead of simply looking white as a ghost, he would be a ghost."

The guard made a noncommittal sound in his throat.

And Porthos said, in a tone of utter, sneering disdain, "Your Cardinal is in many ways a man without honor. But he is not stupid. If you should go to him with that story, and I told him mine and showed him the evidence, I would not be the one arrested. Nor you, I dare say, since it is not a crime to be a fool. But if I know the tender mercies of the gentleman you serve, he would be furious you ignored attackers, loose in the grounds of the royal palace. And even more furious that you showed yourself for a fool. Now, I don't know how true this may be, but I've heard stories of what happens to those who displease the Cardinal."

Jussac was quiet a long time.

"Come, Jussac, you know he is right," de Brisarac said, in a resigned tone.

"Very well," Jussac said, in a tone that sounded more like challenge than like surrender. "We will follow your so-called attackers, but heaven help you if we find they were your accomplices."

"How could they be our—" Porthos started.

But Aramis made a gesture to silence him. And as the guards vanished into the night, in the direction the figures had disappeared, he turned to D'Artagnan. "There, you have stopped bleeding. Now, if you can walk, we will go to Athos's lodgings and see if we can unravel this very confusing hour."

A Ghost Walking; A Musketeer's Conscience; Where Athos Understands Porthos's Difficulties

❧

ATHOS left Rochefort's office by way of a side door to the Palais Cardinal. He stumbled blindly past the guard there. And stopped.

Walking past him, down the darkened alley into which the door opened, was a ghost. It was a ghost he'd often seen in the dark, but never while wide awake. The ghost of the woman he'd once killed.

Tall, slim, though her heavy breasts and slim waist were disguised in a heavy cloak, Athos could tell she was indeed his late wife. Her carriage, the way she held her head, the pale blond hair that swept down to her waist—all of them belonged to Charlotte, Countess de la Fere.

Her name was on his lips. He wanted to pronounce it, to beg her pardon, to besiege her to look at him, to forgive him for having killed her. But she was so clearly there—solid, as solid as he was.

He thought, for a moment, madly, that perhaps Charlotte had had a sister—someone who looked exactly like her. But as she approached the door, without noticing him—not unbelievable, since he was wearing a musketeer's attire and had his hat low over his eyes—she raised her hand to show the guard something. And on her hand, Athos saw a very small silver ring, with the glimmer of a pinkish stone. The ring that had once been his mother's, the ring he had given his wife.

And the guard spoke to her, the guard answered her. He called her "milady" in English, as though she bore an English title, and she inclined her head to him as she went past.

Athos, pierced by regret, shock and confusion, remained standing where he was, long enough that the guard—a young man and, as such, brash and full of his own prerogatives and, after all, in his own territory—asked him if he needed anything more and suggested that perhaps he needed to move along.

Moving along was easy—at least physically. Athos allowed his feet to be set one in front of the other, insensibly carrying him away from the Palais Cardinal and towards his own lodgings, his mind benumbed. He'd hanged his wife. Of this he was as sure as he was sure he was alive, breathing, male, and Alexandre, Count de la Fere, now living under the penitent name of Athos. He had married the sister of his curate. She was well beneath his dignity, but so beautiful and seemingly so pure and pious that he couldn't but fall in love with her.

A week after her elevation to the dignity, they'd been out hunting together. The countess, more eager in the chase, had spurred her horse ahead with such vigor, and charged with such intent blindness that she hit her head, hard, against the low branch of an overhanging tree, falling from her horse in the process.

Coming across his wife, to all appearances dead, the young count had panicked. With trembling hands, he'd cut her dress, to allow her to breathe more freely and perhaps recover consciousness.

They'd been married for a week. He'd enjoyed to the full the pleasures of his conjugal bed. He had not, however, seen his wife naked in the full light of day. Now, on a clearing on his lands, he saw her shoulder—and upon it, though small and very faded with cosmetics—was the brand of a criminal, the fleur-de-lis.

The shock and horror of that moment still made him reel, more than twenty years later. Branded criminals were adulterers, thieves, even murderers who had been branded between condemnation and execution, so that should they escape they would never be safe. It was the brand of infamy.[5]

Athos didn't think—though it was hard to tell, looking back and trying to judge the feelings of that much younger man—he'd ever experienced anger. He didn't think he'd ever moved beyond shock and throat-tightening horror. The wife whose position in life, by itself, would have caused Athos's father to tell him he had besmirched the dignities of his life, had turned out to be yet far more unworthy and in a way that Athos couldn't explain away by invoking her sweetness or her purity or even her beauty.

The sheer enormity of having picked, as the mother of his future children, a woman depraved enough to deserve

---

[5]Though it is clear from Dumas that a fleur-de-lis meant the criminal was intended for the gallows, though the manuscript explicitly says it, the compiler of this account has not been able to find confirmation on this point. As far as Ms. D'Almeida can determine, the only criminals to be branded were those whose crime fell very short of death. While one can understand Athos's rage at being duped, his killing of his wife upon finding the brand on her shoulder would be seen as overreaction, when merely divorcing her and having her immured in a convent would serve the purpose. And though Athos is remorseful, it is because he thinks the brand might not have been legitimate and never because he doubts the brand is worthy of death. It is one of those instances in which one must bow to the material of the time, and even M. Dumas's—flawed though we've seen it to be—interpretation of events, and assume there was more to this than was recorded or at least than was recorded and survived to the twenty-first century.

that brand upon her shoulder had crashed about his head like a thunderstorm. He could only think of what people would say, should they ever find out. How, for the rest of his life, he would be pointed at and laughed at. How, should he ever marry again, his children too would be tainted with his dishonor, his mind-crushing miscalculation.

Unable to be angry, unable to think, he'd gotten a roll of rope that he kept in his saddle. He'd hanged his wife from a low hanging branch. He'd disposed of his affairs as though he had died. By the time evening fell, he was on his way to Paris with only Grimaud, who had once been his father's valet and who had watched over Athos from earliest childhood.

Now, in the twilight of late winter, in Paris, twenty years after, he felt a headache forming. *How can Charlotte be alive?*

He'd hanged her. He remembered that. Though truth be told, he didn't remember staying around and waiting to make sure she had indeed died. Such was his mental state at the time, that he thought he'd hanged her, then ridden away, disturbed by the last feel of her body in his arms.

Was it possible that as soon as he'd galloped away—if not before—the branch from which he'd hanged her had snapped? She'd been unconscious when he strung her up, so it was quite possible, though perhaps not probable, that she had survived a few minutes. Athos knew that what caused first damage when being hanged—at least when there was no substantial drop to ensure the executed broke his neck in the fall—was the frantic struggle against the rope. Being unconscious might have preserved her life longer, and if either branch or rope had broken shortly after . . .

He walked through the darkening streets. So suppose Charlotte had survived. Why had she not sought him out? If she were innocent—a possibility he had tormented himself with for so long—would she not have written to him, explained her case, made it known why she'd been branded and which enemy had managed it? If she truly loved him . . . Wounded though she might be by his having believed the worst about her, would she not have tried to reconcile with him?

Even now, even though he had reason to believe she was truly a criminal, wouldn't he take her back in a second, if it could be proven to him that she hadn't been guilty? Wouldn't he?

He knew from the straining of his heart, from the sting of tears behind his eyes, that he would. But his wife was in town, and she'd not contacted him—she'd not, to Athos's knowledge, made any effort to see him. In fact, though Athos had recognized her from the turn of the head, the way she stood, from the elegant slimness of her body and that moonlight-blond hair, she hadn't seemed to notice him at all. She hadn't seemed to recognize him.

Had he not haunted her mind as she haunted his? Not even in rage or wish for vengeance?

And she had been going into the Palais Cardinal, with every appearance of being well-known there. Surely, if that was true, the Cardinal would have told her about Athos, about who Athos was and what he was doing. She would know exactly how he lived, and anyone who knew him would have good reason to believe how remorse blighted his life.

So he would have to believe that she had not contacted him because in fact she did not love him and never had. He had been a rung on her climb, and his reaction to her perfidy had only meant that she would avoid him in the future.

It was the logical conclusion, and it should have made him feel better. He had, for so long, carried remorse over what he'd done, and doubt over whether it had been needed. Now his question had been answered and he was, in fact, fully justified. So why didn't he rejoice? Why did he feel as though a band of iron had tightened about his heart?

Looking around, he realized his feet had brought him to his lodgings. He unlocked the door and climbed up to his room, having decided to find some of those bottles that he had hidden from Grimaud's sometimes astringent searches of his belongings. That Grimaud thought his master drank too much, Athos understood. That the man—who had in large measure helped to raise Athos—thought himself entitled to make it harder for Athos to find liquor when his mind was taken with this fog of grief and hopeless mourning for what hadn't been nor could ever be, Athos accepted. But he could not—he simply could not—allow Grimaud to keep him from drinking entirely.

Grimaud thought that if Athos didn't drink, he would be awake and more aware of his surroundings. Athos would agree that was true. But he also knew, with absolutely unflinching certainty, that there was a great anger that lived just beneath the surface of his mind. That anger could be dulled and covered up by drinking. Without it, Athos wasn't sure what he would do—what he would have done by now.

His lodgings were a tall, narrow slice of a bigger building. There were three floors and a basement, but each barely large enough to contain more than a room. It had a little landing at the bottom of the stairs. The upstairs floor was entirely Athos's—consisting mostly of his bedroom, but also of a room decorated with an ancestral portrait and sword, and furnished with a number of comfortable chairs. Here he kept a few of the books he had packaged and brought with him, and a few other books he had acquired over the years. Books, like wine, could dull the pain and make him forget the anger, at least for a while. And here he and his friends often met, to discuss what they should do when faced with a dilemma.

On the bottom floor, there was a dining room, and the

kitchen at which Grimaud's labors often managed to produce meals that could have graced the kitchen back at La Fere—meals that were, more often than not, wasted on the master who would have preferred to drink his dinner.

As Athos was about to set his feet on the steps, he heard a voice say, "Monsieur, monsieur. I have bound wounds before. Please do not tell me how to do it."

The voice was undeniably Grimaud's, and undeniably it spoke the truth. Athos's first thought was that one of the servants had got wounded and that Grimaud was binding his wound, while discussing it with the other servant. Perhaps, in fact, Mousqueton had escaped the Bastille, through either cunning or luck, and was wounded, and this wound Grimaud was attempting to bind. But there was no possible way their servants—by now as much comrades at arms as they, themselves were—would call each other monsieur.

They perhaps liked Bazin a little less than the other three, but even he would never be addressed as monsieur. They called him Bazin, and might roll their eyes at his pious pronouncements, and yet they did what they could to keep him safe and they remained his friends.

"Grimaud," Planchet's voice said. "He faints. My master faints."

This was a completely different matter. What D'Artagnan would be doing in Athos's kitchen, and why he should be fainting, was totally beyond Athos's comprehension. But Athos was almost old enough to be D'Artagnan's father, and the young Gascon, with his quickness of mind, his cunning, his brilliance with a sword and his unswerving loyalty to his friends, was exactly the son that Athos would have liked to claim. There was between them a bond that was only half friendship. The other half was Athos's almost desperate wish to protect the young man from the strokes he himself had suffered at the hands of fate.

The idea that D'Artagnan was wounded or ill carried him all the way into the kitchen and onto a scene of the purest mayhem. There was blood all over, on every possible surface. The kitchen table, at which Grimaud normally prepared food, and at which Grimaud ate—no matter how often Athos told him he could serve him there, also, if they were alone. Grimaud insisted on serving the man who would always be Monsieur le Comte to him either in the dining room or in Athos's own room—had bloodstains, and a basin filled with blood-colored water. Bloodied rags littered the floor. There was blood on the servants, blood on Aramis's incredibly elaborate doublet, cut according to the latest and most daring fashion, in blue velvet and flame-colored satin, and on Porthos's cheek and the ends of his red hair.

In the midst of all this, D'Artagnan sat, stripped to the waist. There was blood all over him too, blood on the various ligatures wound around his arm. And, as Athos watched, the rest of them, not seeing him, had rallied around D'Artagnan with the obvious idea of preventing an imminent collapse. Aramis was supporting the young man, and Porthos was helping—one hampering the other, in the way the two of them were likely to, when they both acted out of the best intentions and without coordinating intents. And, standing by D'Artagnan, Grimaud—Grimaud, who sometimes could behave as though alcohol were the enemy of man, as the puritans in England believed—was pouring something amber colored into D'Artagnan's half-open mouth.

"D'Artagnan," Athos said, shocked. "What is here?"

The boy sat up straight at Athos's voice, as he hadn't at the swallow of what Athos guessed was brandy. He pushed the glass away, as though embarrassed by it or by his weakness, and he looked up at Athos, trying to force a smile onto a much-too-pale face. "It is nothing. A scratch. A wound hardly worth mentioning."

"Wounded," Athos said, and because this was something he understood, he turned without one more word, and took his stairs, two steps at a time, to his bedroom where, from the bottom of his clothes press, he extracted a jar that the Gascon himself had given to him months ago. Back to the kitchen, jar in hand, he stretched it to Grimaud. "The ointment that Monsieur D'Artagnan was so good as to give me when I was wounded, Grimaud. You remember its effect on me, and I'm sure it will have a like effect on him."

Grimaud, used to his master's ways, took the jar and uncorked it, while he directed Planchet, "You will have to undo that ligature, Planchet," and, to D'Artagnan's quickly suppressed moan, "There's nothing for it, Monsieur D'Artagnan, and it was your fault as well as mine, for Monsieur le Comte is exactly right. If you'd reminded me you'd given us a pot of the ointment, we would have used it to start with."

Athos, who had enough experience with wounds, not only from attempting to bind his own, but from binding Aramis's and Porthos's too, after duels when servants weren't available, moved to help Planchet and soon had managed to remove the bandage without causing D'Artagnan to do more than bite his lower lip and grow twice as pale.

He examined the long, deep gash beneath. He would not put his finger in it to test the hypothesis, but he was almost absolutely sure that the sword had cut to the bone. "How did this happen?" he asked. "How did you get cut like this, D'Artagnan? Was it while you were pretending to be a servant? Did anyone take a sword to you while you were unarmed?"

Perhaps something of his anger at the idea showed in his eyes, because D'Artagnan looked alarmed. "No, Athos. No. It happened after that, at the royal palace."

Athos raised his eyebrows as he slathered the wound with the ointment from Gascony, whose miraculous, but proven, claim it was that had any wound not reached a vital organ, the ointment would cure it in no time. In their trip to Gascony, Athos had found this ointment was universal, and perhaps explained the madcap character of the Gascons, who would rather fight than speak. Or for that matter, would rather talk than eat or make love. Knowing they could impunely escape wounds had made them willing to receive the worst wounds without dying, and they had lost all reason to restrain themselves.

"I went to the royal palace at . . . That is . . . There was a note . . ." He blushed. "From Constance."

Athos felt his expression harden. Right then, all he could think about was that Constance Bonacieux, D'Artagnan's lover, had somehow betrayed him. But he just stopped himself saying so, when Aramis looked up at him, and said, in a slow, sullen voice, as though he resented having to reveal even a little of his private life. "It was my fault," he said. "I'm sure it was me they were trying to kill, or kidnap, or do who knows what to."

Porthos grunted at this. "It could have been me," he said. "I had, you know, just called a lot of attention to myself by setting the hammer swinging into the swords, and it is not unlikely someone realized what the truth was, despite D'Artagnan's clever story about the ghost. And you know, if they knew, there were reasons they might have been angry at me."

"Plebeians, you mean," Aramis said, his words tolling with absolute disdain. "If you're about to convince me that the six men in cloaks who attacked us were in fact from that neighborhood, I am not likely to believe it, my friend. No man who hasn't had extreme learning in swordplay could possibly have fought like that. Nor was their attack, coordinated and seemingly planned, a mere revenge for what they would doubtless think of as a mere prank in the workshop."

Athos, listening to all these disconnected words, found it hard to formulate a question of his own. From what he could gather, while he was at the Palais Cardinal, his friends had been running around town, each in his several ways, doing his best to call attention to himself and—incidentally—to cause as much trouble as humanly possible.

He started and discarded several lines of enquiry. He knew that asking Porthos about taking a hammer to swords would only cause a flow of words more likely to leave him bewildered than not. And he rather suspected that asking Aramis about why he believed this was his fault would only cause him to say some nonsense about some woman or other—or possibly worse—about some point of theology and divine retribution. And D'Artagnan, whose lips Grimaud was, again, solicitously wetting with brandy, did not seem able to assemble more than two words without succumbing to blood loss.

Athos, normally so fluent with words and so ready with classical quotations, suddenly felt a great empathy with his friend Porthos, to whose lips words would never come when called.

Having fastened D'Artagnan's bind, he crossed his arms upon his chest. "What have you been doing? All three of you? For you must give me leave to tell you that it seems like you've all gone around like madmen, attempting to get killed."

Where the Importance of Melons Must Outweigh that of Hammers; Brandy and Blood; A Musketeer's Trust

✑

OF all of his friends, D'Artagnan retained his greatest admiration, not to say hero worship, for Athos. Oh, it could be said in many ways that the young Gascon revered all his friends. How could it be otherwise? His father had raised him in awe of those servants of the King. He had trained him to use his sword as one of them could be expected to use his. For the longest time—in fact, since he'd first been breeched—D'Artagnan's entire ambition had been to wear a musketeer's uniform. In that uniform, he hoped to follow the footsteps of those other sons of Gascony who had made themselves famous, if not rich, in the capital.

Indeed, he viewed Porthos as a new Ajax, and lived in silent admiration of Aramis's worldly ways, his understanding of court gossip and his easy grasp of the more obscure points of theology—save for the patent meaning of the seventh commandment. Aramis's influence had greatly improved D'Artagnan's mode of dress and of wearing his hair, and Porthos's not-quite-voiced exasperation had taught him to use his sword better and to move his feet with the grace of a dancer, as his giant comrade did.

Still, when all was said and done, Athos was the one of

the musketeers who commanded D'Artagnan's near vener-
ation. If D'Artagnan could have chosen to be any man at
all, he would have been Athos. It wasn't that he was blind
to Athos's defects of character—in their time as friends, he
had come to know Athos's deep grief and the things he used
to hide it, from wine to his sudden, blind rages. But he also
knew that Athos held himself with an iron-strong will and
to principles so high that he would never stoop to doing
anything dishonorable. In fact, the more he knew Athos, the
more he'd come to admire him, for the faults he did not allow to affect others, as much as for his obvious nobility of
character. Still young enough to need guidance, D'Artagnan had chosen Athos as his mentor and the tutor of his
mind.

To see Athos this angry at them cut him to the quick.
The emotion was increased by his patently weakened state,
his having lost enough blood to feel dizzy and vaguely nau-
seous. To Athos's words, he could only say, "Oh, pray,
don't be so furious. We didn't do it to vex you."

This brought him an intent look from the blue eyes so
dark that they might as well be black, and a slight frown
that was, strangely, apologetic. "I didn't suppose you did,"
Athos said. "I am fairly sure the three of you were just proceeding in the way you normally do." He pressed his lips
together, as if this were a great crime, then looked up at
Aramis. "I told you not to go to the palace."

"I had to," Aramis said. "I had to speak to Hermengarde."

"Alone? Are you perhaps courting Mousqueton's girl-
friend?"

"No," D'Artagnan said, jumping into the conversation,
because he had seen Athos and Aramis fight before, and it
was not something he wished to see again. Porthos and
Aramis fought all the time, the sort of amiable squabbling
that caused one to think of a litter of newborn puppies in a

basket, stepping all over each other and nipping at each other's ears with no malice and no rancor—or memory of injury—held.

But perhaps because they were so highborn and trained to it, as great noblemen were, when Athos and Aramis argued it was all pale, drawn faces, and the sort of look that true enemies gave each other, not friends who merely disagreed on some point. Besides, this one fact was the sort of thing that would make Athos very irate, and an irate Athos could be an unbearable Athos. As the oldest and noblest of all of them, the erstwhile count held himself responsible not just for D'Artagnan, but for all of them. But his wish to protect them often demanded that they obey him, something that Aramis more than the others rebelled against. So he intervened hastily, trying to deviate the conversation. "No, but the armorer's son wished to."

"The armorer's son?" The question came from both Porthos and Athos, at once.

D'Artagnan shrugged. "At least that is what the neighbors thought. That the armorer's son, the young Langelier, wished to make Hermengarde his wife, while the armorer wished for Mousqueton to marry his daughter."

"The armorer's daughter?" Porthos asked, bewildered. "Is that what they told you? I cannot credit it. Mousqueton never told me."

D'Artagnan was much too kind to explain that, given Porthos's sometimes ambiguous relationship with the French language, it was quite possible that Mousqueton had indeed told him, but that the whole thing had got twisted in Porthos's own mind into a conversation about some different subject—as perhaps the price of swords, or maybe even of fish. Instead he said, "I don't know how seriously Mousqueton would have considered it, but the neighbors—at least the Gascon baker I spoke to—and his family, seemed to take it quite as a given."

Athos was frowning at D'Artagnan. "I wish you wouldn't speak," he said. "You have bled a great deal."

D'Artagnan, despite dizziness induced by blood loss and not improved by brandy, shook his head. "Oh, it is nothing," he said. "Planchet, could you give me my shirt?" And then to his friend, "I just got slightly cut. Most of what appears to you to be blood comes from washing the wound and getting the water mixed with blood, so that there seems to be a great deal more of it than there ever was."

Athos looked at Aramis over D'Artagnan's head, and because there didn't seem to be hostility in that look, D'Artagnan didn't feel obliged to speak up. He had the impression that Aramis had shrugged. "It is bad enough," he said, in a low voice. "As you saw, the cut is very deep and, in fact, he bled a great deal, in the palace gardens, before we could stop it. You must not be so alarmed though. I stopped most of the bleeding there. The very little he bled here can't have made his case much worse."

And Athos, who appeared thunderstruck and at a loss for words, shook his head. He looked at D'Artagnan allowing, for just a moment, a glimmer of humor into his severe countenance. "All of you, my friends, tempt me to say, with Monsieur de Treville, that such noble men shouldn't risk themselves in such foolish ways."

Aramis gave a soft chuckle, echoed by D'Artagnan himself, and Porthos snorted in amusement. "He only says that when he is pleased with us, usually because we have risked ourselves in foolish ways. Only let us be taken by the guards of the Cardinal without a fight, or let us do the prudent thing and abandon a scene of trouble, and he will proclaim us the most scurvy and worthless men who ever lived. And he will give us no quarter."

Athos inclined his head, but the tension in his bearing seemed to have broken. D'Artagnan, who was starting to read his friends very well indeed, suspected that Athos had come in furious at something and that this anger had colored the scene that had greeted him. Ire mingled with worry had made him, for a moment, wish to pick a quarrel with any of them, so that he could either justify his annoyance or stop worrying. And Aramis would have risen to the bait.

But perhaps his own confusion had helped or perhaps Athos's sense of humor had reasserted itself. He sighed, in exasperation. "Let's suppose we take this from the beginning and one at a time, then. D'Artagnan, am I to understand that you gathered information from a Gascon family?"

D'Artagnan nodded. "I was starting to think I couldn't do it at all," he said. "You know . . . lie to someone. But this bakery was very busy and it smelled and sounded like home." He shrugged. He had wanted to come to Paris and seek his fortune. He had been blessed indeed to make friends with the best of the musketeers within days of his arrival. He would be the worst of wretches if he let his friends know how often or how much he missed the province of his birth. "So I went in and the baker invited me to dinner, and . . . well . . . I heard the neighborhood's gossip. I would doubtless have heard more, but there was this big eruption of noise from the armory, and I . . . well . . . I went in and found Porthos."

Athos's observant eyes looked towards his larger friend. "And you, Porthos?"

"Well . . ." Porthos took a deep breath. "I remembered to take a candle, but I totally forgot to procure some melons."

Aramis snorted. "Porthos! Melons are not in season, and what can your lack of melons have to do with your making a racket in the armorer's? What were you even doing in the armorer's?"

"Well . . . I'd heard that Mousqueton had lost consciousness after being hit a glancing blow by a hammer that fell from the high rack over the forge."

"And you realized, as I did," Athos said, "that you had been in that shop a lot of times, that you knew the ceiling was very high, and that you didn't remember seeing any hammers hanging from the rack." He looked at Porthos with something approaching benevolence. "But with your turn of mind, you needed, of course, to go and test the idea."

"Well . . . I didn't drop hammers on my own head."

Aramis, to D'Artagnan's side, rolled his eyes. "Something for which we should be very grateful indeed. But why did you need to make noise?"

Porthos shrugged and Athos shook his head, and asked him, "Did any of the swords fall? Or the hammer if you managed to hang it there?"

Porthos looked relieved and shook his head, and Athos nodded. "And that brings us to you, Aramis. You went to the palace and you spoke to Hermengarde, which brings us to . . ."

"She said she . . . she had decided to marry Mousqueton," he said, lamely, not wishing to discuss Hermengarde's possible impending motherhood with the servants present.

"Hermengarde is with child, sir," Grimaud said, and gave Athos a sideways glance. "Or at least Mousqueton believed so and believed the child was his."

D'Artagnan, by the corner of his eye, saw Porthos pale and sit down. "With child?" he said. "This too, Mousqueton did not tell me."

"He would not," Grimaud said, and shook his head. "Not until he had made up his mind what to do and worked the plan over with Hermengarde, which he had just done when . . ." He shrugged. "You see, they've all of them"— he looked at Planchet and Bazin in a corner of the kitchen— "gotten used to coming to me for advice. Because . . . because I am older, and I have raised children."

Athos nodded at this. "So he came to you for advice?"

"Certainly, when he had his letter. And he wanted to know what I thought and how Monsieur Porthos would accept it if Mousqueton were to get married."

"What did you tell him?"

"That Monsieur Porthos was the kindest of all masters, and that he was not likely to take it amiss if Mousqueton married, provided between the two of them they found some way to support themselves and their child. And Mousqueton, you know, sir, the last thing he wanted was for his lover to be forced to give up their child or to leave him at the door of some church, to be raised out of charity."

"No," Porthos said. "That's how Mousqueton himself was raised, and I would have guessed that he would endure any number of trials to assure that his child didn't suffer a similar childhood. But . . . How is Hermengarde taking all this?"

"I told her," Aramis said, his shoulders squared, his face resolute, "that we would do all we could to ensure Mousqueton's freedom."

D'Artagnan noted a look from Athos. "And what in this made you believe you were the target of this attack? What could possibly have crossed your mind to lead you to think—"

Aramis shook his head. "You know I have a new . . . friend."

"If by that you mean a new seamstress, or a new niece of your theology professor, or whatever you're calling it these days, yes, I am well aware of that," Athos said, drily. "Else how to explain the disturbing profusion of perfumed note paper arriving at all hours."

By the corner of his eye, D'Artagnan watched Bazin cross himself. Since he knew what Aramis's servant, whose greatest ambition in life was to become a lay brother in whatever order his master chose to serve, thought of his master's carnality, it was a confirmation of Athos's guess.

Aramis only nodded. "Well . . . I have . . . something of that nature." He stopped, suddenly, and looked around, with a worried eye. "Can we speak of this in private?"

"In the kitchen?" Athos said. "Not likely. And surely you're not suggesting you don't trust our servants. We are, after all, fighting for the life of their friend."

"Yes, that is all very well," Aramis said. "And I am sure each and every one of them is more than willing to do what must be done for our brave Mousqueton. However . . ." He paused, and hesitated. "There are dangers attendant to this situation, dangers, shall we say, that do not proceed from the murder and do not devolve upon Mousqueton alone."

Perhaps it was, D'Artagnan thought, the return of Aramis's habitual roundabout manner of speech that made Athos's lips go taut once more. But D'Artagnan knew this could not be allowed. "I believe," he said, in a tired tone, "what Aramis means is that there is some danger attaching to his seamstress. I'm not going to speculate, but it could be anything, from an irate husband to . . . something more serious. We know how high Aramis—who is, after all, so punctilious about his clothes—looks for a seamstress who can sew a straight seam, do we not? Is it so strange that he would not wish to speak of it in front of our servants, not because he doesn't trust them, but because he believes the knowledge could bring danger to them?"

Exhausted by his long speech, he leaned back against the edge of the table, in time to see a grateful smile from Aramis. "Thank you, D'Artagnan," Aramis said, in a voice that revealed D'Artagnan was not by any means the only one to notice that Athos was more tightly wound than normal. "You have, as usual, made light in the dark."

D'Artagnan bowed slightly, but Athos was frowning.

"Well, then let us adjourn upstairs, to my sitting room, to discuss the matter. I . . ." He frowned more intensely, as though the admission were being torn from him reluctantly. "I too have something that I should discuss and which is perhaps too serious to allow innocents to be involved in."

"Planchet, my shirt," D'Artagnan said again, imperiously. The boy had been holding his shirt the whole while, looking at it with an expression of utter dismay on his freckled face.

"It's all over blood, sir," Planchet said, lifting the offending garment. "As is your doublet."

"Grimaud," Athos said, "if you would be so kind as to help Monsieur D'Artagnan to my chamber, and offer him any of my shirts or doublets he would care to take."

D'Artagnan felt a sudden relief, for he had been afraid they'd need to send Planchet home for replacement clothes and he, himself, was starting to think that there was some danger involved in their going out of doors alone. As far as he could determine, each of the three of them had assumed he was the culprit in the fracas in the palace gardens. And Athos, himself, seemed to have some secret.

He allowed Grimaud to lead him out of the kitchen and help him up the stairs. Grimaud assisted him with small movements, a touch on the elbow, a support of the arm— all without seeming to, D'Artagnan noted and wondered how many times Grimaud had escorted his drunken and querulous master this way. And how many times he must have lead Athos up these stairs when Athos was far more wounded than D'Artagnan was now.

All of them, D'Artagnan knew, worried about Athos. Aramis might be the only one who worried for his soul, but Porthos and D'Artagnan spent plenty of time musing on the state of his body. As, doubtless, did the devoted and absolutely loyal Grimaud, who now led D'Artagnan to a room far better appointed than should have been expected of any musketeer living in Paris. Most of the furnishings there declared as loudly as words that they'd been brought back from Athos's ancestral domains.

Grimaud extracted a linen shirt—much finer than anything D'Artagnan had ever worn—and an old-fashioned and worn doublet from one of the clothing presses, and clucked at something within the press. D'Artagnan, who had heard the sound of glass or ceramic just before that, looked at Grimaud, and their gazes met in perfect understanding.

As Grimaud helped D'Artagnan into the shirt—a little long, but not much larger than D'Artagnan's own, or at least not large enough to look ridiculous, since D'Artagnan was much more sturdily built than the muscular but spare to thinness Athos—D'Artagnan said, "Has . . . has your master been suffering a great deal from his old trouble?"

Grimaud sighed. "Not so much, sir. Now and again though the . . . since you joined their group, the troubles of a different sort have kept him from brooding on his own quite so much as he used to. And with Monsieur le Comte, you know, it is memories and . . . and the thought of what might have been that brings his trouble about."

"You mean that having found himself faced with murders has been good for my friend?"

Grimaud inclined his head. "I've thought so. There is nothing, you know, like a little intrigue and a lot of danger in the present to keep the past at bay. Only today, when he came in, Monsieur D'Artagnan, I will confess that I looked into his eyes and I thought . . ."

"You thought?"

"I thought he looked as though he'd seen a ghost."

Where Aramis Talks of Conspiracy and
Athos Talks of Ghosts;
The Honor of a Nobleman

∽

"**D**ID you see a ghost?" D'Artagnan asked, as he came into the salon where his friends had been speaking desultorily, while waiting for him.

Athos looked at him, surprised. The boy was wearing clean clothes—Athos's, but they looked, Athos thought, better on the Gascon. And he looked as if he was just slightly weakened. Perhaps a little dizzy from the medicinal application of brandy, but he wasn't stumbling near enough to allow him to speak foolishness.

And yet, when Athos looked up at him, he wondered if it was foolishness. Instead of ridiculing D'Artagnan, he shrugged and said, "Where did you come by that notion?"

"Grimaud," D'Artagnan said, simply, as he settled himself into a chair, "said that you looked as though you'd seen a ghost."

Athos tilted his head to the side, examining the Gascon. It had been sometime in the last few minutes, while Aramis had been coy about his seamstress and Porthos had made the usual mess out of his attempts at explaining his actions, that Athos had realized he would have to tell them what he had seen, as well as what he had done.

He wasn't sure which of his pieces of news would cause the most uproar amid his friends—the sudden resurrection of a long-dead countess, or the clear-eyed way in which Athos had walked into the Cardinal's trap, rather than allow it to close on his neck when he least expected it.

He sighed deeply. "I have, in a way," he said. "Save that I believe a ghost would have disconcerted me less. But first, I'd like to know what Aramis has to say about . . ."

"The attack?" Aramis said. He had sat himself down on one of the more elaborate armchairs, immediately beside Athos, probably, Athos thought, because he didn't want Athos looking directly at him as he questioned him. "As I said, all of you know about my . . . friend."

"Seamstress," Athos said, both amused and confused that Aramis was not using the term he usually used.

Aramis shrugged. He'd pulled a handkerchief from within his sleeve, and was examining its lace edging with utter care. "She . . . is a lady of the highest nobility and she resides in the palace."

"I would expect nothing less," Athos said.

Again Aramis shrugged, when in the past he would have looked either very gratified or somewhat upset when they penetrated the meaning of his words. He looked up at Athos, sidewise, and his green eyes seemed full of worry. "Well, after I spoke to Hermengarde, I went to my friend's lodgings. I . . . well . . . for various reasons I was in need of a friend and she was the nearest."

Athos nodded and forebore to say anything. He was fairly sure the reason was that Aramis had had to walk along certain hallways which awakened memories of his dead lover, Violette. He'd noticed that when the four of them had to go to the royal palace for any reason, Aramis avoided that area of the palace like the plague. And, in fact, since the most common reason they had to go to the palace was to stand guard there, he did his best not to go inside at all, but to take a post outside, near the entrance, and stay there.

"Well, while I was in her room we . . . argued. It is possible . . . That is . . . I angered her, and she is a woman of strong passions. I would not swear that she did not send assassins after me. Though I wouldn't believe it likely. But I . . ." He half rose and sat himself again, and gave Athos a look so full of piteous protest that it was plain he very much wished himself elsewhere, and he very much wished not to have to go on with his revelations.

Athos said nothing, just continued looking his enquiry at his blond friend. If Aramis thought he could escape telling what worried him, he did not know what Athos, himself, would have to reveal.

Aramis sighed, heavily, as though realizing no one would facilitate his escape. "As I was leaving her room," he said, "I saw on a table, a letter, written and sealed to someone . . ." He took a deep breath. "Enfin, to Caesar, the duke of Vendôme, the half-brother of the King." As though he'd spent all his speech braving himself for this, he said, "I was going to simply show you her handkerchief, but I gave it to Hermengarde to dry her tears, and then I ruined one I thought was mine on D'Artagnan's arm, in the palace. Now I find I still have mine, and am at a loss to find which handkerchief I did ruin." He shrugged.

"Well, where did it come from?" Porthos asked.

Aramis shrugged again. "I found it on the ground at my feet, in such a position that I thought it could only have dropped out of my sleeve, and since it was clean, I used it to tourniquet D'Artagnan's arm."

"It's in the kitchen," D'Artagnan said, starting to rise. "Perhaps we should get it, before it is fed into the fire?"

Porthos, seated beside the youth, put a massive hand on his shoulder. "I'll go, my friend. It is not likely I'll understand this intrigue of court ladies and handkerchiefs."

Though Athos thought this was the absolute truth, he said nothing else, nor did any of them, until Porthos galloped back up the stairs, a square of blood-soaked linen and lace in his hand. He handed it to Aramis. "It is most certainly not yours, though it might very well be the handkerchief of your seamstress. In which case, I'd very much like to know why you were carrying three handkerchiefs along on your sleeve."

"He uses them as safe conducts," D'Artagnan said, sounding somewhere between tired and amused.

"Safe conducts to three ladies?" Porthos said. And added fervently, "Sometimes, Aramis, I get the sense that you wish to sleep with every woman in France."

And Aramis, looking down at the handkerchief with an expression of the greatest horror, said, absently, "I do. Twice." And as he said it, he passed the handkerchief to Athos, allowing him to see the embroidered initials in the corner, MAR.

"Marie Michon?" Athos asked, at the same time that Porthos, having reached some sort of conclusion from what Aramis had said, exclaimed in a sullen tone, "If you so much as look at Athenais . . ."

Athos's look at Aramis was quick enough to capture the expression of horror on his face. Madame Athenais Coquenard was Porthos's lover of some years now. She was also—though born to minor nobility—the wife of an aged accountant, and well past thirty. On all these counts, she was disqualified from the pool of women that interested Aramis. On the other hand, it was hard to deny that she was indeed one of the women of France and that Aramis had, therefore, just declared his intention of sleeping with her. Twice. Athos would have laughed, were it not for the fact that he had a strong feeling if the girl wanted Aramis—or in fact, himself—he would find himself in her bed before he could think twice.

Aramis, realizing where his words had led him, turned to Porthos. "Oh, be still, Porthos. I was only . . . That is . . . You know that Athenais is not a woman." And, as Porthos bristled at this, rapidly he added. "She is something far beyond woman, something that, to own the truth, terrifies me a little. I'm afraid should I pursue any intimacy with her, she would suggest I wear a green dress."[6]

Porthos didn't smile. He nodded, thoughtfully. "Well," he said. "She scares me a little too, but the thing is that . . ." He shrugged. "Some of us like to know we are courting a woman who could, if needed, take us in combat. Though perhaps not in fair combat," he added, even more thoughtfully. "I'm sure Athenais is not an amazon."

Aramis nodded, but turned towards Athos. "Yes, Marie Michon. We've been . . . I think . . . using each other for some months now. But you know she is . . . that is, there is no intrigue, in the palace, in which she does not have her dainty hands. Which leads me to thinking of what Monsieur de Treville said." He shrugged, again. "It is entirely possible I am wrong," he said. "It is entirely possible that the letter concerned private matters. The lady is, as we all know, as much involved in affairs as she is in intrigues."

"Yes, this is quite possible," Athos said. "And yet . . ." He got up. He would have to tell them his story, and he hesitated. He would have to tell them everything, including the detailed story of why he'd left his domains to become a musketeer. He'd more or less told it to them before, in bits and pieces and, sometimes, he was sure they knew much more than they showed. But he had never explained to them, exactly, what he'd felt . . . What he still felt for Charlotte.

"Is Marie Michon the nom de guerre of the Duchess de Chevreuse?" Porthos asked.

---

[6] *The Musketeer's Seamstress.*

"What?" Aramis said. "Yes, but you are being insufferably blunt. You must know I was avoiding pronouncing her name."

"Why? Is it like a magical invocation? Of the sort we're not supposed to do? You said she was as fond of affairs as of intrigues, and you must know this means you might as well have pronounced her name, because we are not so stupid as not to know that all of the court speaks of both of these characteristics of the lady."

"Yes, but one should hardly be so blunt as to admit like that, to one's friends, that one is enjoying a highborn lady's favors."

Porthos shrugged, looking bored, then lifted his huge hands, and counted off arguments on his fingers. "First," he said, "from what I hear, the strangeness of this would be if, given the slightest interest in bedding her, you hadn't managed to do so. From what I understand there is a line down the halls from her room, and there have been musketeers called in simply to make sure turns are taken in an orderly manner."

"Porthos!" Aramis said.

Porthos ignored him, and touched the second of his fingers. "Second, we are alone and without our servants, so I fail to see what good secrecy would do us. And third . . ." He touched a third finger. "And third, did you truly propose to discuss how you suspect her of involvement in a conspiracy without ever once mentioning her name?"

"The lady," Aramis said, "is not as you paint her." He spoke through his teeth and had his hand on his sword hilt, but Athos noticed he seemed curiously detached. It was as though he felt he should defend the lady's honor, and as such was going through it as though it were a play that he must perform, but without any of the feelings of outrage that would normally have colored his actions or motions. What was Aramis, arguably the most romantic of them all, since he was in love with the idea of woman, even when he was merely whiling his time away with the current specimen between his arms, playing at, to be sleeping with a woman he cared for so little?

"Well, I'm merely saying what everyone repeats," Porthos said, not seeming the least bit embarrassed. "They all say that she will take as a lover anyone who is comely enough, so I have long expected that . . . well . . . you are comely enough."

Athos looked towards Aramis to see how he took this announcement and found his friend making what he thought was a heroic effort not to laugh. "I think I should thank you, Porthos," he said slowly, "for the compliment, but indeed . . ." He shrugged. "Well, I've been seeing the lady. And while her favors are not as widely given as gossip would have you believe, the truth is that part of the reason I settled upon her is that she will not expect from me that which I cannot give."

Porthos, who had looked disposed for battle, darted a quick, sympathetic look at his friend and said nothing.

And Athos nodded. "You are probably right, Aramis about . . . er . . . Marie Michon being involved in something she should not be. But why do you think she would try to kill you because of it?"

"I don't know," Aramis said. "It's just . . . I might have said something that irritated her also."

"I've heard many things of the lady," Athos said, "but none of them that she was in the habit of murdering her lovers over trifles."

"Oh, not that, it's just . . . I had the feeling I left her on less than good terms."

"And she had cloaked assassins ready to follow you and attack us?" D'Artagnan said. "And she would send six men to attack you? You must pardon me, Aramis, but though the lady has graced you with her favors, do you mean to tell me she has such a high opinion of your sword arm?"

Aramis shook his head. "I don't know. All of us are taken as gods with the swords, you know, to hear court gossip."

"Demons, more like," Athos said. And gave a look at D'Artagnan. "At least the Gascon there. He's often been compared to a demon with a sword."

He hesitated, and flung out of his chair, with an impatient movement. Walking to the door to the stairs, he called, "Holla, Grimaud. Bring us cups and half a dozen bottles of the burgundy."

He couldn't really hear Grimaud's answer, an indistinct blur of syllables, such as they got at a distance, but he answered back, "Now, Grimaud. Your service and not your opinions are needed."

Despite the distance, Athos could swear he heard Grimaud's sigh with full clarity. After a while there were steps up the stairs, accompanied with a tinkle of crockery. He and Planchet emerged, Planchet carrying four white ceramic cups on a tray and Grimaud bearing bottles.

Though Athos had brought with him or, over time, sent for glasses and porcelain from his domains, normally he and the others drank out of serviceable ceramic mugs, which bore the distinct advantage of being sturdy and of large capacity. Even so, he didn't know what to make of the fact that Grimaud had opened all the bottles. He set them on the table, side by side, his lips pressed into a tight line of disapproval, and Athos thought the fact that all the bottles were uncorked was meant as a reproach to him. As if to point out he couldn't control himself.

Grimaud poured wine in each cup and handed one to each of them. D'Artagnan looked at his own dubiously. "I'm not sure if it's such a good idea after all the brandy."

But Aramis spoke up. "Drink it, D'Artagnan, for I'm

sure that Athos will let you have accommodation for the
night, and truth be told, I don't think you should go back to
your lodgings. Not in your state."

Athos waved the servants away, tossed back a cup of
the full-bodied wine, then poured yet another and drank
it. And found Aramis watching him with a cool look.
"When you drink so much, Athos, it can only be because
you wish to make yourself drunk. And if you wish to
make yourself drunk, it can only be because—as you accused us earlier—you have been running all about, trying
to get yourself killed."

Athos frowned at him. "Wide off the mark, my friend,"
he said, quietly. "Wide off the mark. When I wish to get
myself drunk, it is that I am very much afraid I might kill
someone. And not in duel."

Aramis's eyebrows went up. He took a sip of his wine,
and said, almost fearfully, "Athos, you must tell us—what
have you done?"

"Well," Athos said. He walked towards the window, and
looked out through the small panes of glass towards the
street immersed in darkness. "I know you will, all of you,
consider me disloyal, but I could not consider that Monsieur de Treville would have any hold over the Cardinal.
Not if the Cardinal felt that his own life or interests were
threatened."

"No, I don't consider you disloyal," Aramis said.

"Nor I, either," D'Artagnan said, his words slightly
slurred by the drink. "The thing is, I thought that Monsieur
Treville might very well be able to delay the execution of
Mousqueton, but only that. There would be little else he
could do."

"It has occurred to me," Porthos said, "that there
wouldn't be much the captain could do. I mean, they . . .
they torture people in the Bastille, and if he couldn't keep
Mousqueton from being tortured, then he couldn't keep

him from being executed. People will confess to anything under torture."

"So you all agree with me," Athos said, as he drank yet another cup of the wine. It would take a while to take effect. All the more so, because he had long since grown used to the wine as a palliative for his distress. But even so, the more he drank, the more he would look to his friends as though he had justification for any wild words, or wild thoughts. He was glad too that there were only three candles lit in the room, so that perforce the details of his expression would be obscured to their eyes. He walked from the chairs to the window, then back again.

"You are behaving like a caged lion, Athos," Aramis said. "And this, again, is never good."

Athos shrugged. "I think there's very little good in recent events. Let me explain first, my reasoning, when the three of you left me standing alone on a street corner while you went to investigate multiple and disparate things." He walked towards the window again. "I thought that since the captain could do next to nothing against the Cardinal, it would come down to the Cardinal in the end, and we would have to deal with him directly.

"Now I couldn't imagine living like this, waiting for the Cardinal's trap to spring, so I . . ."

"So you did what you always do, and ran headlong into the trap?" Porthos asked.

Athos gave his large friend a surprised glance. Sometimes one forgot that Porthos, for all his difficulties with language, had a mind sharp enough to see through people's motives. He shrugged and felt his cheeks heat. "You could say that," he admitted, at length. "You could say I did, for you see, I reasoned that if it finally came to the Cardinal wanting someone to . . . to defray the conspiracy, I would . . ."

"No." Aramis had half risen from his seat, his features

contorted by something like anger. "You cannot have meant to deliver the Queen to the Cardinal, for that must be your whole plan."

Athos frowned at his friend, and finished drinking the cup of wine he held. "It might be," he said, and dipped his head a bit. "But I will admit, my dear Aramis, that the situation seems to me somewhat more complex than that."

He had the gratification of seeing Aramis raise eyebrows at him.

"I mean," Athos said, "that there might indeed be some sort of conspiracy at work, though most of the part where the Cardinal thinks it applies to him . . . well, it seems to have originated whole cloth out of his mind." He poured himself more wine, then said, "As far as my conversations, first with his eminence," he said.

"Athos," Porthos said, in shock, his hand going to his sword hilt, then forcibly away, as though he had but remembered that Athos was his blood brother, and one of those who had so often and unstintingly risked his life for Porthos. As though only awareness of that kept him from drawing, even right here, in Athos's own lodging.

Athos looked back at him, pleased to note that his eyes were becoming unfocused through the action of the alcohol. "Well, Porthos . . . I needed to do something. And no, Aramis, I was in no hurry to implicate our Queen in anything. In fact, as the Cardinal so kindly reminded me, a Queen's value by far trumps a pawn's, so that I would not even consider such an exchange." He shook his head. "But I . . ." He drew a long breath. "I have told his eminence that I will try to unravel this conspiracy against him, if conspiracy it is." He frowned, as he dredged from the depths a memory fast becoming clouded by the wine, the exact words and implications of what the Cardinal had told him. "Aramis, you who are up on all court rumors—have you

heard of the Queen and . . . Marie Michon courting Ornano, the governor of the Prince's house?"

"Oh, that," Aramis said. "I heard some rumor that they
were opposed to the marriage of Monsieur, his being the
heir apparent and all. But I'm not sure . . ."

"I'm not sure either, except that the Cardinal seems to
think that this means they are in a conspiracy to kill him,
which he seems to have got from some correspondence
between the Queen and Marie Michon. He also hinted—
though I cannot credit it—that they intended to kill the
King. Or rather, Rochefort hinted that. It is, I'm sure,
something destined to spur me on into investigating this
conspiracy the Cardinal pretends to see."

"And will you investigate it?" Aramis asked. "How?"

Athos shrugged. "That, my friend, I do not have the
slightest notion about. The Cardinal himself hinted that I
do not . . . That I lack the cunning, and the contacts to penetrate this sort of court intrigue. I confess . . ." His gaze
was now fairly unfocused, which promised that by the time
he got to talking about what he feared, his brain would be
fogged enough that perhaps he could avoid making a complete fool of himself. "I confess my intention was simply to
buy time—to have Mousqueton unharmed, until we could
find who killed the armorer."

"Right," Porthos said. "And that's the sort of thing we
know how to do."

Athos looked at him, and lifted his cup of wine a little,
in a silent toast. "That is indeed, Porthos, but perhaps this
case is a little more complex?"

"How more complex?" D'Artagnan asked, and, from
the way his voice sounded, he was quite a good bit ahead
of Athos in pursuit of a good drunk. "So far . . . well . . . if
it was not Mousqueton—and don't glare daggers at me,
Porthos. I don't believe it was Mousqueton—then it seems
likely it was something happening in the man's life.

Something, perhaps, having to do with his wish to marry his daughter to Mousqueton. Perhaps the daughter decided to kill the father and implicate Mousqueton."

"Right now," Athos said, "I am quite willing to believe anything of any woman. But it seems a little odd to be judging a creature we don't even know, save for a report that she is cross-eyed." For some reason, this struck him as funny, and he added softly, "I will remind you, D'Artagnan, that being cross-eyed is not a proof of being a murderer. In point of fact, it has been recorded, throughout history, that various people have been cross-eyed without being murderers."

D'Artagnan looked up at him, his expression vacant, which probably meant that, being further on the road to drunkenness than Athos, he would not retain any of this. Athos must remember to ask Aramis to relay to the boy what he heard. Because Athos didn't think he could repeat it. Right now, Athos shook his head, and poured himself another cup of wine.

Porthos frowned at the cup as Athos took it to his lips. "Athos . . . I don't mean to count, but I think that is your fifth."

"Sixth. I figured I needed at least that, to . . ." He shook his head again. "Look, I don't know what we can do to investigate the conspiracy, but . . . Aramis, on the off chance the conspiracy exists . . . And frankly, I don't like the idea that Marie Michon is writing to Monsieur de Vendôme. We all know he's hated the King ever since they were very young, and the hatred has only grown with time."

Aramis sighed. "You can't deny it's a sad thing for a sovereign to have been married ten years, and still lack an heir to the throne."

"I can't deny it," Athos said. "But I do find that perhaps Richelieu's iron grip on France is causing more conspiracies than it should. If every lord were still independent in his own domain, it would be far more difficult to consider Paris, and what happens in Paris, all-important."

The others didn't say anything, though Aramis nodded.

And after a while in silence, Porthos said, "But that is not why you are looking like you died on your feet and are looking for a good place to fall over." And then in a rush, "Or, forgive me, perhaps it is, but I've never known you to look like this . . . well . . . not since . . ."

Athos could well imagine what the *since* was that took up his friend's mind. He felt his jaw set, and a muscle work on the side of it, like a metronome to his anger and sorrow. Another woman, another . . . He shook his head, again. "No," he said. "No, though for all I know that might be tied in. I can't imagine the lady in question thinks well of me, or has any kindness towards me," he said. "She has to have heard of me from . . ." He shook his head again. "She would . . . You know . . ." And suddenly, one question rising foremost in his mind, he asked. "Why didn't she come to me? If it was all a misunderstanding . . . why didn't she explain? Surely she knew I loved her still?"

He looked out at his friends, who, at that moment, through the foggy veil of his emotions, looked like so many figures, sculpted in stone, their features blurry. He saw one of them thrust his head forward. It was the blond figure, and it was Aramis's voice which spoke out. "What do you mean? Who is this 'she' you speak of?"

"My wife."

"Your . . ." Porthos said.

Athos felt suddenly very exasperated with his friends. He was not sure what he had told them before, but he was sure it had been enough for them to piece together something of his past. "I . . ." He normally told this story in the third person. He didn't know how to tell it any other way. And yet, this time he must. "When I was very young, shortly after I inherited the domain from my father . . . well . . . I needed a wife and I knew that. My father had neglected to arrange a marriage for me, and I was in no hurry to find one through the usual channels. The daughters of my neighbors bored me; the prospect of marrying a stranger through some arranged exchange filled me with dread.

"I am . . . in the normal way of life, rather reserved and would prefer to keep private, or only in the company of my close friends. And the idea of coming to Paris, of leaving my domains, made me feel as though my heart was breaking. You see . . . I was very fond of my domains. I had great plans for orchards and vineyards, and I'd grown up there, amid the rolling ground, and I knew all of my peasants from infancy. I looked forward to living the rest of my life there." He shrugged, dismissing this as one would dismiss an impossible childhood dream. "And then, suddenly, one of the parishes on my land came vacant and the new incumbent was a young man, almost my age. Very pious. Fervent, in fact. His beautiful sister lived with him. I was aware that in the eyes of the world, she was as far below me as one of my own peasants. But she was so beautiful, so chaste, so religious. I fell in love with her and spent many a pleasant evening talking to her brother in their little cottage. In the way of things, I, who had never fallen in love before, fell in love with this beautiful blond woman and I married her. One week after she'd been elevated to countess, we were out, hunting. She hunted like Diana, a swift rider and an exacting markswoman. She was riding ahead of me, and turned back to say something. As she turned, she went under a low branch. It caught her and pulled her off her horse." He stopped, because he could hear his voice tremble, on the edge of tears. Fortunately not being able to see his friends' faces made it easier, but he heard Porthos draw breath as though to say something and, right now, pity was more than he could endure. "I dismounted and ran to her, naturally. She had lost consciousness. I panicked, also naturally, and took my hunting knife and cut her dress away, to give her the room to breathe. Which is when I found that she was marked with a fleur-de-lis.”

This time he couldn't avoid hearing someone—he thought Porthos—say “*Sangre Dieu*” under his breath.

“I, after all my careful picking, and my refusal to be drawn in to a contracted, loveless marriage, had given my hand, my lands, my honor, to a marked criminal. You must understand . . . I was as in love as anyone can be, and I was a callow youth. It would have been better, perhaps, if my father hadn't raised me away from the world and its fashions, if he hadn't kept me from society. If I'd been sent to Paris, years before, for a while, and spent some time with young men my age, I might not have fallen for Charlotte. Or, if I had, since she was so very beautiful and so very accomplished, I would have had more resources of mind and heart to turn my crushing pain into something more manageable. I had none of those. Thoroughly provincial, I could think only that my honor was crushed forever. I could divorce her. I could judge her publically, for having imposed upon me. In . . . in my domains, the feudal law still held. As such, I thought that I could . . . justly condemn her. Only . . . it wasn't like that. If I tried her publically, all my tenants and all my serfs would know of it. It would be spoken about till the end of my life. I could not do that. It wasn't in my mind-set.

“So, still shocked and grieved, you realize, my mind roiling, my heart in turmoil, I took her, and I lifted her and put around her neck a noose from my saddlebag. And I hanged her from a low branch. Only afterwards, when I was riding away, did I think that because I had not exerted my authority through the normal channels and in an open way, this would be believed to be a murder—that whoever found her would think someone had murdered, and doubtless would think of me.

"Well, I was sure I could defend my actions, but I had started all of this because I wished to keep my family and myself from notoriety. So I did what I could to keep the talk down. I arranged things so that a distant cousin of mine would come and administer my domains in my absence. And I took some possessions from my house, but not too much. I let it be known that I would be going on a long voyage and didn't know when I could return. I didn't explicitly say my wife would be with me, but I let it be understood that she would be. That she had, in fact, gone ahead of me. I thought that way, if no one found her, it would be believed that we had left on some voyage together and, if I chose to come back in many years, I could do so and mention she had died, without exciting comment. And if she were found, I would be far, far away, and even though they might suspect me, no one would search for me.

"By nighttime I was on my way to Paris, with Grimaud. By the end of the week I was installed, as you see me, and I'd spoken to Monsieur de Treville, an old family friend, and obtained a post in the musketeers. Since then, every year, I've considered returning. But I've found I have very little interest in revisiting the site of my misguided idylls. And even if I did, I'd prefer it if the present generation has passed away, and no one there remembers how much in love I used to be."

He was pacing again, between chair and window, his steps rubbery, the room seeming to tilt under his feet. Through his window he saw lights come and go, like torches in the night. Carriages, he supposed, or perhaps parties of people walking and carrying a torch or a lantern. Though this was not a place known for revelers, there was some foot traffic, at night. "I thought it a little odd that I never heard of her being found, or even of her missing. We were somewhat lost in my hunting preserve, but after all, other people hunted there, if no one else, my cousin when he came into residence. And if someone had found her, they could not at all be at a loss about who she was. She was wearing her clothes. But no one found her, and I simply waited and was happy of a momentary respite."

He stopped, his mind in confusion, thinking he hadn't been glad of a respite at all. All this time, all the years he'd been away from La Fere, he'd been waiting for doom to come upon his head again. The one time he'd been happy in his life had ended in the greatest dishonor and pain. The one time. And now, he wasn't even happy, but he had his position and his friends. He had been waiting for something horrible to happen. And it might well have had.

"And what happened?" a voice asked. He thought it was Porthos. "Did they find her?"

Athos heard a very odd sound, half cackle, half sob escape his lips. "No. No, my friend. I found her. Today. Outside the Palais Cardinal."

"What?" another voice asked, almost certainly D'Artagnan's. "But how can her body . . ."

"It wasn't her body. Or rather, yes, it was, but she had moved it herself, she still being very much alive."

"You never verified that you had killed her?" Porthos asked.

Athos shook his head. "I couldn't. Even such as I did . . . it has tormented my mind and heart . . . all these years."

"And are you sure it was her?" Aramis asked. "You know women can look devilishly alike, and after all this time . . ."

Athos nodded. "Aramis, I've dreamed about her every night since it happened. In my heart, I've never really stopped thinking about her. Her image is etched in my heart and seared in my soul. I could never not recognize her. It was her, but she went by me as if she didn't recognize me . . . which . . . perhaps she didn't, but . . . Why the Palais Cardinal?"

There was another soft bout of swearing. From its definite near-pious characteristics, and the soft voice in which it was pronounced, Athos was sure it was Aramis. He tried to protest that he truly wanted to know, but his tongue had, unaccountably gone thick and unyielding. So had his legs, which presently stopped obeying him and lost all force under him.

"Porthos," Aramis's voice said, as though from a long way off. "You help me carry him to the bed. And you'd best stay here. I think both he and D'Artagnan are quite out of human reach, just now. I . . . I have some things to do, and I will return in the morning."

"Things to do?"

"I know a man," Aramis said, "who might tell me who this blond servant of the Cardinal is. I'm hoping, I'm almost praying, that she is not . . . whom Athos thought she was."

And Athos, lost between consciousness and a deep, black abyss of nothing, wanted to explain he wouldn't prefer that. Then he would still be waiting for them to find her body.

But his mouth could form no more than a long, low moan, and, as he felt Porthos lift him, he plunged fully into the black nothingness.

The Garden after the Fall;
Where Aramis Knows Several Men;
The Cardinal's New Right Hand

⌘

ARAMIS stepped out into the cool night, to find himself as if in a prefiguration of the Garden of Eden. Granted, at best Paris was a built-over garden of Eden, but now at the end of winter, when the night wasn't quite as icy as it had been, it was possible to imagine the night perfumed with newly grown flowers, with soft, ripe grass, with the promise of the coming spring.

He looked at the stars above, and thought of his friends, up in Athos's lodging. Porthos, perhaps because he had heard Athos's story, had felt unusually fearful of attack. He'd told Aramis, in a perfectly serious tone, that since they still didn't know why they'd been attacked in the gardens of the royal palace, it was not unheard of for them to be attacked in their own lodgings. And he did not feel confident with the three of them being in separate rooms.

Aramis had thought of explaining that people who broke into musketeer lodgings were, by definition, desperate enough to face practically anyone or anything. Or of pointing out that he doubted anyone at all, who knew Athos well enough to know where he lived, would find it a good idea to break into his house.

He did neither. Both of those might be true and sensible, but, in point of fact, neither mattered. Porthos felt threatened, and therefore they'd managed to lay Athos and D'Artagnan, side by side, on Athos's bed, which had, fortunately, been brought from his domain and was therefore large and sturdy enough to fit another two musketeers, if needed, without their needing to touch.

Porthos had brought a chair from the sitting room, and half lain upon it, wrapped in his cloak. For good measure, Grimaud, who clearly felt as threatened as Porthos did, even without hearing Athos's story—which he possibly already knew—had set a rotation of servants on guard outside the door.

So, Aramis thought, this was a paradise where the fall had occurred. And a serpent lurked somewhere out of sight. This thought sharpened his eyes, as he looked around. And he saw enough shadows lurking that he tightened his pace. And when the shadows detached from doorways and the darkened mouths of alleys, he started running, to avoid them.

It rankled to run, as he'd never before turned from offered combat. But he remembered the fight all too vividly, and he was not about to allow himself to be caught. There were far more of them than of him, and under those circumstances, it would not be a fight, but a slaughter.

He took various turns, blindly, with only one thought in mind—to get to the portions of the town where taverns were still busy and the streets thronged with strangers. There, even should his pursuers set on him, he would be more than able to call to his aid those musketeers nearby—and in the area where taverns clustered, there would be a lot of musketeers.

By the time he reached the nearest of these streets—Saint Antoine—he was running full force, and careened into the crowd of prostitutes and late-night drinkers like a man diving into a tawdry sea. Like water, they closed about him, carrying him along, in their revels.

He took several turns at random, and whenever he could, he turned to look back. Soon he was glad to note not a single man cloaked in black in sight. Not that there might not be black-cloaked people who were in no way related to those pursuing him, but on these streets you were more likely to find peacock colors and a blazing display of jewels that would shame Porthos himself.

He turned and turned again, surrounded by the smell of wine, of perfume, of sweaty bodies, taking care always to be in the thick of the crowd. A woman's hand—at least he hoped it was a woman's—took rather disconcerting liberties with his breeches, and a wishful sigh echoed from the direction the hand emerged.

Aramis resisted curiosity, which told him to turn and look, and walked on. At one of the edges of the drinking district, the one closest to the Palais Cardinal, he found himself quite free of pursuers.

He headed at a fast clip for the Palais Cardinal, or rather for a small tavern near it, where some of the Cardinal's more . . . assiduous servants ate their evening meals, and often stayed by to drink their evening drinks. It wasn't frequented by guards, as such. Or even by the Cardinal's secretaries. No. Here came the keepers of the Cardinal's clothes, the people who cleaned the Palais Cardinal and those who cooked for him.

While Aramis stuck out in there, like a lion at a congregation of ants, he'd been coming to the place for so many years that his entrance, in his well-cut suit, his plume-trimmed hat, occasioned not even a stare. The men ignored him. They usually did. The truth was that, for all that Aramis claimed to know a man, mostly—as Porthos was always quick to point out—he knew women. And women who made their living from scrubbing and cleaning were still, and ultimately, women. Women who had trouble resisting Aramis's pale blond hair, his sparkling green eyes, his well-molded lips and his soft, whispering voice.

Aramis had first come in here out of a fascinated interest, like a man who sets out to explore an unknown jungle. He wasn't of Porthos's cut. He didn't view these places, attended by laborers and humble artificers, as the true source of humanity's best. Aramis thought that, all other things being equal, the best of humanity should come better washed, and, if at all possible, more fashionably attired.

But he knew that servants found out as much or more about their masters, as did their best-trusted secretaries and their guards. Sometimes more. It was, after all, highly unlikely that even the Cardinal had a personal secretary wash his underwear. So he'd started coming here, night after night, when he could spare the time from more urgent pursuits. And now, after all this time, he could come into the darkness, illuminated by sputtering candles made of bacon grease, with hardly a flinch and without actually attempting to avoid the touch of his fellow customers.

He made his way between tables packed with drinkers, to the one table at the back where he usually sat and listened to the conversations, while doing his best to dispense spiritual advice.

He'd no more sat down, and asked his server—the burly son of the tavern keeper—for a pint of their best wine, when a woman emerged from the shadows and sat across from him, giving him a brilliant smile.

She was very young—maybe no more than sixteen or so—which in this environment was the only explanation for her still possessing all her teeth. She was also somewhat pretty, or would be, with her little round face washed, her blondish hair properly combed, and wearing something other than a formless grey sack. Her name was Huguette, or at least that's what they called her, when they weren't calling her "pretty" and "sweet" and other such names.

Aramis had heard that she worked in the Cardinal's kitchens, and he suspected that she engaged in a bit of prostitution on the side, just for the fun of it. Whether this was true or not, she was clearly unchaperoned, unguarded, and quite, quite determined to make the conquest of the fine-looking gentleman who consented to sit among them.

Today was no different, as she sat on the bench across from him, and pulled up her legs, so that the sack fell, and her legs were displayed from the thigh down. She wasn't to know that those thighs, with their bony knees and the almost too thin legs, excited nothing in Aramis but a profound sense of pity. In fact, long as it had been since he'd seen D'Artagnan's bare legs, and unexciting as he'd found the occasion, he would probably say that D'Artagnan's legs—hair and all—were far more luscious. All Huguette made him wish to do was buy her a loaf of bread and a slice of meat. But he'd tried that at first and found that she considered it payment in advance and became, therefore, even harder to evade.

So he'd taken a sip of his wine—more to prove friendly than because he had any wish to drink it, since the vintage here was vinegary and quite a few steps below Athos's excellent burgundy, of which Aramis had not drunk more than a few sips. In fact, faced with how incapable of self-defense the wine had made his comrades back at Athos's house, Aramis felt not at all like drinking. He said to Huguette in his softest, most clerical voice, "Good evening my daughter."

She gave him a look full of mischievous fun. "Your daughter, am I? Coo. I knew you gentlemen were strange, but not that strange. Even Rochefort is not that odd."

Aramis refused to rise to the bait, either of pretending to

believe her misunderstanding, or wishing to explore Rochefort's strangeness. The idea of what Rochefort might or might not want to do in the privacy of his chamber left Aramis completely uninterested. It was what Rochefort did to France, in full light of day, and with the Cardinal's orders to back it up, that made Aramis's heart beat faster. Usually with fear. He took another sip of his wine, to disguise his confusion, and Huguette laughed softly.

None of the other women were coming near today, which, probably, meant none of the other women were in the tavern. Aramis would have preferred to get his gossip from a more informed source or, at least, since he didn't think that Huguette was ill-informed, from a more stable source. But if Huguette was all there was, he would have to cater to her topics, and he would have to approach the subject, he judged, via Rochefort. Though he refused to ask about Rochefort's habits, in general.

"So," he said. "Is the blond lady one of Rochefort's friends?"

"What blond lady?" she asked. "There are so many."

"The one who came in earlier," Aramis said, and relayed what he remembered of Athos's description without the superlatives, which he was sure were only how Athos saw her, and in no way connected to reality—or only very little.

Huguette raised her knees a little, bringing her grimy bare feet closer to her body, on the bench. "Are you in love with her too?" she asked.

"Too? And of course I'm not in love with her. I've never seen her."

Huguette looked wishful. She had eyes somewhere between green and brown, and large, all out of proportion to her face. She stared at him a long time, then sighed. "You'll be in love with her," she said. "As soon as you see her."

"Doubtful," Aramis said, thinking of the only woman

who had ever commanded his love, though he'd had a continuous stream of beauties grace his bed. Violette had not been branded with a fleur-de-lis. "And who has fallen in love with her, that you should say I'll fall in love with her too?"

"Oh, everyone," she said and sighed. "Everyone who sees her. But you shouldn't fall in love with her, you know? Because she's not very nice. I've heard her talk to the Cardinal, and she says that she has . . . killed people." The huge eyes stared out at him, with what seemed to be very sincere shock.

"Lots of the Cardinal's people kill other people," Aramis said, and shrugged.

The girl sighed. "Yes, I guess they do. But not, normally, with poison. Or not while they're in bed with them."

Aramis raised his eyebrows. He was so completely taken aback, he was surprised into blurting, "I'll take care never to be in bed with her."

"See that you do," Huguette said, very seriously. "I've heard that she has killed three husbands and a lover."

"And does she have a name," Aramis asked. "This sinner?"

"Why do you want to know? Do you want to meet her?"

Aramis shook his head. "No. But I think it will be easier to stay away from her if I know her name, and where she's likely to be."

"Most people just call her milady," the girl said. "You know, in English. The last husband she killed with slow poison is said to have been an English earl. So she gets the title, you know. But his family was very suspicious and as soon as he died, they set about investigating his death, and she found things too hot for her in England, and so she came here."

She hugged her bony knees, in a curiously unselfconscious and childish gesture. "I bet you no one else could tell you her name, but I can, because I heard her talking to Rochefort, and Rochefort was calling her Charlotte."

Aramis felt as though an icy finger had run down his spine beneath his clothes. Whatever else was said, he was sure that Athos had referred to his wife as Charlotte. "Was she . . . was one of her husbands a count? A French count?"

The tavern waif shook her head, then shrugged. "I don't know," she said. "He might have been. But . . . You know they're all dead, so what does it matter. There is a guard, in the palace, who calls her the black spider. He's sensible at least, but most of the others aren't. They say she's so pretty that she must most certainly be as good as an angel." She sighed. "I find that men can be very stupid."

Agreeing with her, and counting out his money to pay the server, Aramis was about to say his farewells when he heard the next words tumbling out of the young woman's mouth. "It is all very well, you know, but I heard her price for working for the Cardinal. I know that you're a musketeer, which is why I feel a little naughty talking to you, and I know that you and your friends are forever fighting the guards of the Cardinal. But I also know that you look so kind, and I know you speak so sweetly, that it can't probably be provoked by you." She shrugged, completely unconscious of the irony of her words. "But I also know that when you do fight the guards, it is in duels, and it is all fair and correct. But milady is not like that. And I heard her tell the Cardinal that there was a musketeer she wanted dead. It appears he has done something to her, some time ago. Only I guess he wasn't a musketeer then."

She looked at Aramis, eyes wide, lips trembling a little. "She has found out he has become a musketeer, and her price for whatever she's doing for the Cardinal is a safe conduct to be allowed to do what she wishes to this musketeer and his friends."

"Do you remember the musketeer's name?" Aramis asked, cold sweat now trickling down his body, and his mind clenching in panic. "Anything that might tell me who he is?"

"His name is Athos," Huguette said. And, quite unaware that Aramis felt as though he'd just turned to stone, "I remember because it's an odd name. Like yours."

Where Monsieur Aramis
Attempts to Investigate;
Creditors with No Sense of Humor;
It Is Better to Bless Than to Fight

✺

Aramis, having left the tavern in good time, and finding himself, as of yet, devoid of followers, stood in a narrow alley, removing his gloves and slipping them back on, a trick he had when he was in something of a puzzle.

He could return to Athos's house, but he could not imagine why he would be needed there. After all, the two most affected by alcohol were sleeping and, if he knew Porthos, the one least affected by alcohol would be snoring—and loudly too. This meant that Athos's chamber was the last place to seek repose. As for the sitting room, he supposed he could sleep on a chair, or rolled upon his cloak on the floor. In fact, he'd slept in far worse conditions, when the King's honor demanded that they march to battle. He remembered nights in arms, spent sleeping standing up, against a wall, under the pouring rain.

He had no wish to repeat that experience, though he was fairly sure he would, when next the kingdom embroiled itself in war with its neighbors over someone's religion or someone else's vacant throne. Until then, he had absolutely no interest in recollecting the hardships of battle by putting himself in discomfort.

Thoughts of his bed, its soft mattress and immaculate linen sheets, came to mind. Only he remembered the tone of voice in which Huguette had told about the woman, Charlotte. If she was one of the Cardinal's minions; if she was even half so dangerous as Huguette believed . . . Well, it would be all up. Perhaps Aramis was becoming as afraid of shadows as his friends had been under the influence of alcohol, but he still couldn't dispose of the conviction that the last place he should go was his lodgings. If she had asked for Athos's life—and by extension their lives—as recompense, then heaven only knew what information the Cardinal might have given her, and what it might mean as far as their being safe in their own homes and in their own beds. And if he went home now, he wouldn't even have the relatively ineffective Bazin as a guard.

And yet, he couldn't imagine going to Athos's house and crowding upon the already crowded floor or the even more crowded bed. He could, he thought, ask Grimaud for his bed, and he was fairly sure Grimaud would give it to him too. But Grimaud was old enough to be Athos's father, which meant, in the end, that he was almost old enough to be Aramis's grandfather. No good could come of this. Aramis could obtain his bed, but he would find himself unable to sleep for the remorse.

The other part of it was that he did not, very much, feel like sleeping. His body was charged with a sort of electrical energy, and he could not help but want to do something. Part of it was, he very much feared, that he wasn't sure he could go home and sleep. Not with the idea that Athos's wife was far worse than anything that Athos could represent with his story and that she wanted all their lives. If Huguette had not exaggerated—and though the girl could be fairly zany, in the past he had found her rather purple information, if anything, on the side of understated—then this woman was of the type that could not possibly have tolerated the injury that Athos had done her. He and everyone associated with him would be slated for death and this would most certainly include the friends that everyone knew spent most of every day with him.

Aramis was very much afraid even his well-appointed bed would not soothe him into sleep. And he certainly didn't want to go back to Athos's lodgings, wake his friend and tell him that the wife he'd thought dead was not only alive, but she was no common grade of criminal or fugitive. No, she was the sort of criminal or fugitive who could climb to the top rungs of society and destroy all those who stood in her way.

Aramis became aware that he was holding the tip of his tongue between his teeth, as though he were forcibly attempting to keep himself from telling the absent Athos the bad news. Which meant he definitely wasn't ready to face his—who would be extremely hungover—friend. And he wasn't ready to seek comfort in his bed, supposing there were no sharpened stakes waiting at his own doorstep, which at the moment was a somewhat unwarranted supposition.

So . . . So he would go to the armory, he thought. He had heard Porthos's description, and D'Artagnan's account of local gossip, but he was quite willing to bet that there was a nightlife in the area also, and that those abroad at that time would be more willing to talk to him than to Porthos or D'Artagnan. After all, people were more respectful of someone who was obviously a nobleman and wasn't afraid to command their respect.

Of course, Athos could probably do the nobleman act better than Aramis, but Athos was more likely to scare them into silence than to get them to speak. Aramis they tended to think of as a fool and a dandy, and as such they viewed him as quite inoffensive.

With this happy thought, he set off at a fast clip towards the neighborhood of small close houses where the armory was. It had the advantage of being—he supposed—the very last place where anyone would look for him, just now. And it should keep Aramis happily occupied till dawn when perhaps he would be ready to brave his friends.

What he did not exactly count on was on finding the streets around the armory as empty as those of a ghost town, where everyone had suddenly died in the privacy of their houses, leaving the outside areas haunted only by shadows. Aramis took a moment to reason that, after all, he was used to musketeers and to taverns, to wenches who prowled the night and to courtiers. He was not used to people who actually woke up in the morning and worked. He supposed those would need to sleep at night.

Yet, unwilling to turn and go back to his friends, he, instead, walked around the armory. He tested the front door which, doubtless as a follow-up to Porthos's interesting adventure, had been chained. Then he walked around, noticing how close the armory was to the house. Leaning one on the other, in fact. He wondered if there was an internal connecting passage and went along to poke his head in the narrow space between the two—so narrow, in fact, that it was hard to get his hand in between the two walls. Which he was in the process of doing when he heard a crunch of feet on gravel behind him. He started to turn around, but before he could someone or something swept his hat from his head. And something heavy hit him hard on the back of the head and the world went black.

He woke up in complete darkness and being jolted about. His first thought was that he was in a carriage, but judging from the jolts, he was being carried around in something that shook all over the place—which meant a

not very good carriage, he supposed. He reached up, only
to find out that if it was a carriage, it was a very small one,
since he was confined, in a sitting position, with his back
bent over forward, in a space barely large enough to contain him. A frantic feeling of the space around him dis-
closed that they had taken his sword and—apparently—his
hat as well.

His first, terrifying thought was that he was in a coffin.
But if he were in a coffin, the coffin was still being carried
around and not confined in the ground. And besides,
Aramis had never seen a coffin the shape his enclosure appeared to be—fairly high and rectangular at the base, and
covered over by a domed space.

Because his head hurt like blazes, it took him a moment
for the shape to connect in his head to the only thing it
could be—a storage trunk, of the sort used to deposit tools
and clothes, or anything else. It smelled faintly of sap, so it
must be fairly new and made of wood. And, now that his
eyes were accustomed to the darkness, Aramis could tell
that there was a small crack all around, through which light
and air came. There was also a hole which was clearly a
keyhole.

Aramis peeked through this keyhole and to his shock
saw light of morning and also what appeared to be a swath
of countryside. And someone's back, dressed in rough
homespun. He was being taken somewhere in an open cart,
by men dressed in homespun. Probably men who did not
know him and whom he did not know, though it was always
possible, of course, that they were wearing disguises.

In Aramis's mind, he had a view of the trunk, with him
inside it, being dropped into a hole in the ground and covered over. That, doubtless, would be a solution to his having penetrated some portion of De Chevreuse's conspiracy.
Perhaps to other things too. Perhaps the whole thing with
the armorer was that it was part of the same conspiracy. It

would explain the guards' presence on the scene so soon
after the murder and their eagerness to take Mousqueton
in. In fact, as far as that went, it explained a lot. Including
why Aramis was now inside a trunk.

Well, he might in the end finish his life in a hole in the
ground while still alive, but he would be damned if he allowed them to do it while he was still and well behaved.

Raising his fist, he pounded hard on the lid of the trunk.
"Hey," he called. "Hey, you above, let me out."

"Ah, woke up, have you, sleeping beauty?" A rough
voice, with a plebeian accent, answered him. "Well and
good, now be quiet and no harm will come to you."

"Why should I be quiet?" Aramis said, pounding on the
lid again. "What are you doing to me?"

"You'll see," the man said. "And soon enough. Let's just
say you'll be put in a safe place, from which you'll never
get out, not in a thousand years."

The image of the hole in the ground, and dirt being
shoveled in on top of him made Aramis shiver. "There are
no places safe enough," he said. "My friends will come for
you, you'll see."

"Oh, don't be going on about your friends. Rest assured
they will be taken care of, and they won't be coming for
nobody when we're done with them."

Aramis, despite himself, heard a moan escape between
his lips. "You'll find them harder to deal with than you
think," he said, in a low voice, from which he could barely
keep the sting of fear. Oh, sure, Athos, Porthos, D'Artagnan were all able men and capable of turning the world up-
side down at sword point. They were, however, as
vulnerable as all other men to being taken in, fooled, cajoled and/or destroyed by a woman's wiles.

Unless he much mistook his understanding of the man,
and Aramis was not in the habit of misunderstanding anyone, Athos was still in love with the frightening creature.

And as for D'Artagnan and Porthos, he would not give them a chance in a hundred of withstanding the charms of any female who approached them the right way and played the victim. They were even quite likely to overlook the fact that she looked uncommonly like Athos's lost and found wife.

The response to his threat was a chuckle. "Oh, good with a sword, your friends are," the man said. "But they are not very good with their minds. Trying to find you would require that they think and that, I fear, between drinking and wenching, they won't find much time to do."

Aramis considered shouting back that they didn't drink that much, but then again, he'd left two of them behind in a profound drunken stupor, so that would not work. And as for wenching . . . well . . .

He thought of the wench most likely responsible for this—for it wasn't to be supposed that Athos's wife by herself would come up with the brilliant idea of capturing and boxing up Aramis. Not for a moment. It was more likely that she would think of boxing up Athos. And probably setting fire to the box afterwards. He rolled his eyes. So the person responsible for this would more than likely be De Chevreuse, who wanted Aramis out of her affairs. Did she truly intend to have her henchmen drive him to the countryside and bury him alive?

Shallow and frantic though their connection was, Aramis could not help but think that he could not possibly mean so little to her that she would want him to die such a horrible death. Perhaps she didn't know. He knocked on the top of the box, this time more politely. "Pardon me, but does Marie know what you mean to do to me? Did she give you orders?"

"What?" the man said, and banged what seemed like a gigantic fist atop the box. "You dare use her name? All while you're intending to marry your highfalutin hussy, you dare use my sister's name? Let me tell you, my boy, that though she gave us no orders, as you presume, she will be more than happy to know you will not return to the world and the society of men until you do right by her. And pay back what you owe."

"Beg your pardon?" Aramis said, hearing his voice squeak with alarm. "Your . . . sister?" He wasn't aware of Marie Michon, aka De Chevreuse, having brothers who concerned themselves in her affairs. Truth be told, if they did, they would be the busiest swords in France, just keeping her name from being stained by rumors.

"Beg my pardon all you want. It is Marie's pardon you'll be begging in the end, and on your knees too. And don't think you'll convince us to let you out by using that well-bred voice, Pierre. We know where you come from. We know how you grew up. You're not going to impress us by dressing all in fashionable velvets and by speaking as though you were born to rule a kingdom."

Pierre! Aramis might be many things, but Pierre certainly he was not. Porthos's given name was Pierre, but Aramis would need to be insane to think anyone had mistaken him for Porthos, even on a dark night and while his face was obscured.

No. He'd been between the armory and the house, as he would have been if he'd been coming out of the inside, and about to go into the armory. As if he were the new owner of the armory, the son of the murdered armorer. A vague memory of D'Artagnan's account of the gentleman emerged. Something to do with his being in love with Hermengarde, doubtless the highfalutin hussy.

This being that way, and these men obviously intent on making Pierre marry someone by the name of Marie, this meant . . . That they weren't going to bury Aramis. In fact, they were hardly likely to hurt him. And when they opened the box and saw his face in the full light of day, they would have to let him go.

But when would they open the box? He put his eye to the keyhole again, in time to see a swath of trees go by, at creeping speed, on the other side of what appeared to be a country road. From the daylight it would be nearly noon. If they'd come away this slowly, it was possible he wasn't that far away from Paris. But how far away did he need to be to make it devilishly difficult for him to get back?

And he must get back. He absolutely must. His friends must be warned that the Cardinal had a new minion, and one who would be looking for their blood.

Where D'Artagnan Wakes Up
in a Strange Bed;
The Doubts of a Loving Heart;
A Woman of Dazzling Beauty

∽

D'ARTAGNAN woke up with his hand on a mound of silken-soft hair. He tugged at it, experimentally, and was answered with a low grunt that brought his eyes fully open and showed him someone who was most definitely not his Constance. For one, the person in his bed had dark hair. For another, from the width of the shoulders and the doublet stretched across them, he was male. He was also, as D'Artagnan realized, once he'd blinked the sleep from his eyes, Athos.

A glance above showed him he was in Athos's bed, in Athos's lodgings. And that Athos was asleep, curled entirely away from him, save for his loosened curls. Athos was still wearing his full day attire, including his sword, in its sheath strapped at his waist, which bespoke his either having collapsed on the bed, dead tired, or his having been carried to the bed by Porthos and Aramis, who probably had carried D'Artagnan to bed also.

D'Artagnan sat up, experimentally, to a chorus of what sounded like bells, and a pull of nausea from his stomach.

His eyes hurt with the light. His arm hurt too, but he wasn't so confused he did not remember he'd got wounded the day before in a duel. He'd been about to go see Constance. He remembered that. And then there had been men in black cloaks who fought as if possessed by the devil. And he had got wounded. After that, Porthos and Aramis had brought him to Athos's place, and they'd proceeded to make him drink more alcohol than he'd ever drunk before. And since he'd met the three musketeers, he'd drank quite a bit of liquor in almost painfully strange combinations.

He glared at Athos. Athos had given him brandy and wine, he remembered. What he couldn't remember was why. He was sure Athos had been angry, or at least at that edge of anger to which he allowed himself to go without ever tipping over. And he was sure, angry as he'd been, Athos had felt a need to get drunk. It had been a deliberate effort. One doesn't order up six bottles of burgundy all at once unless one means to get most seriously and intently drunk.

"Athos?" he said, slurring the word. But his comrade only grunted again, and curled yet tighter upon himself. "I see," D'Artagnan said.

What D'Artagnan needed was a good pail of cold water over the head, and then to find breakfast in the nearest tavern. He'd lost blood, and he'd never taken more than wine. That was a recipe for disaster.

He swung his feet off the bed, picked up his sword which—at least in this case—his friends had been kind enough to remove and prop against the wall, and sheathed it. Then, he stood up. They'd never removed his boots, which was fortuitous, as he did not wish to struggle with them.

Porthos was asleep on the floor, next to a chair, all rolled up in his cloak. D'Artagnan wondered if Porthos too had gotten drunk, and decided it truly wasn't worth his while to look for Aramis. For all he knew, he was perhaps on the other side of the bed, between bed and window, or maybe under the bed.

Instead, D'Artagnan opened the door, tiptoed out of the bedroom, and stepped over Planchet who was asleep in the hallway. He stared at his servant for just a moment. Planchet could not have been drunk, could he? There was no saying. Perhaps they'd finished up whatever wine their masters had left. Should D'Artagnan wake Planchet up? That was very doubtful. After all the young Picard had a worse head for wine than anyone that D'Artagnan knew, Bazin—who could get drunk off communion wine—included. If he had been drinking, he would be irascible and also sullen. And D'Artagnan was in no mood to drag a sullen, dismal servant behind himself.

So, he would go without Planchet. And joining action to word, D'Artagnan tiptoed down the stairs—avoiding waking anyone else who might be suffering from hangover in some other place in the house—and into the front hall, then opened the front door and slipped out into the bright morning.

He hadn't lived in Paris so long that he had learned to be indifferent to the city in the early morning hours. Perhaps because he rarely woke up this early—though sometimes he went to bed this early—he loved the look of the buildings under the early dawn light, enjoyed the pealing of morning bells that called various monastic orders and convents to matins, and enjoyed seeing people with their morning faces, still fresh and surprised by the daylight.

He enjoyed it so much, in fact, that before he had gone more than one block his sour mood and his frown had vanished, and he was thinking clearly, as he breathed in the cool, clear air.

Constance had sent him a note to meet her at the palace. Of this he was sure. She had sent him the note in some distress, and this was not normal, because when Constance was in distress, she came to see him—she did not send him notes. That meant the situation must have been unusual, and, as such, she must have needed him more than ever. And he had failed her.

So, he was willing to concede that he'd been attacked and wounded and finally made very thoroughly drunk by his very misguided friends. But did this excuse him? Would Constance forgive him?

And suddenly he was not hungry at all. He just wished to go and see Constance as soon as possible. He took the shortest route possible for that purpose, and got to the royal palace before the sun was fully up in the sky. The man on guard, he noticed, was De Jacinthe, one of his friends from the musketeers. He was a little confused when D'Artagnan told him he needed to speak to someone—a lady—within. It wasn't until he was on the point of giving his Constance's name, that his mind caught up with his racing mouth.

Yes, yes, Aramis had his affairs with married women. Countesses and duchesses and the occasional foreign princess, at least to believe gossip. But the thing was, gossip there was, and aplenty, and only the fact that most of the husbands of these illustrious beauties had their own amusements and could not care less what their wives did in their spare time, kept it from being a problem, leading possibly to a duel or worse, to the setting aside of the lady.

Porthos, whose lover, Athenais Coquenard, was married to a mere accountant, had to be far more circumspect with his behavior, because Athenais could and would suffer, should it be discovered that she had a gallant. How much more so would Constance suffer, whose husband was twenty years older than her and besotted and far more alert and capable of obtaining revenge than Monsieur Coquenard. Let alone that he could turn D'Artagnan out, or demand that D'Artagnan pay him back the several months his rent was in arrears, there was the very real possibility he would divorce Constance. And much as D'Artagnan longed to marry his ladylove, he much doubted that anyone who had a say in it, including her godfather who was steward to the Queen's household, would allow her to marry a penniless eighteen-year-old guard with not a pistol to his credit.

He sighed. No. He must be discreet. And being discreet, he cast about for the name of a lady whom he could claim to be courting without in any way being compromising. The only name that came to mind was that of Mousqueton's inamorata, Hermengarde, and her name D'Artagnan gave with no remorse.

De Jacinthe sent word for her to come receive him, and when Hermengarde appeared at the door, her blushes and confusion on seeing D'Artagnan lent a credence to his story that the musketeer could not possibly have anticipated. She led him into the palace, and it was only once inside that she turned to him and smiled. "You've come to see your lady, have you not, Monsieur?"

It occurred to him, belatedly, that she might take it amiss that he'd given her name when it was another he wanted to see. He looked at her, somewhat fearful of incurring her wrath, but found her smiling at him and shaking her head, indulgently. "She was very worried about you, yesterday, and she confided in me and asked me if there was any chance perhaps that you were out and working on behalf of my Mousqueton."

D'Artagnan shook his head. "I was . . . I think I was." He told her, rapidly, everything that the baker's family had said.

Hermengarde smiled. "Oh, that is so much nonsense. His daughter, Faustine, is a true fright, and Mousqueton would never marry her, if she were the only woman in the world. Though you know, it is his fault that the Langeliers entertained such thoughts, because he was so jealous of young Langelier that he used to go to the armorer's simply to be around and make sure he wasn't saying anything about me or that I . . . that I wasn't visiting. So he had to justify it and he pretended he was courting Faustine. But for all the money Monsieur Langelier would have given her, Mousqueton has too much sense to want to be married to a cross-eyed shrew. And as for me . . ." She shrugged. "It is said that Pierre Langelier spends as much money as he makes—and he makes a lot, for he was his father's best apprentice—upon the gambling tables. I don't think being married to me would have made him any better and, anyway, you see, I am probably carrying Mousqueton's child, so it is all to naught." She smiled hopefully at D'Artagnan. "Have you heard anything of Mousqueton? How does he fare? Is he in health? He has not . . ." She crossed both her hands at her chest. ". . . been tortured? Has he?"

"No, no. That of a certainty he has not," D'Artagnan said, and was rewarded for his lie—or at least his affirming of something he could not at all know—with a bright smile. Encouraged, he continued. "And I shall do my best to find the true culprit soon and to ensure that he shall not be detained much longer."

"Oh, good," Hermengarde said. "And then we may speak to Monsieur Porthos and get married."

D'Artagnan was sure of it, though he did not inform her, because if Mousqueton hadn't already, it would be useless to attempt it, that making Porthos understand what the situation was and what they meant to do might prove considerably harder than it would at first seem.

Instead, he sent Hermengarde to Constance to inform her that he was waiting. As Hermengarde was about to turn away, she turned to D'Artagnan. "Oh, your friend Aramis lent me such a pretty embroidered handkerchief yesterday, to dry my tears. I'm sure I was very silly to be crying at all. It must be a side effect of my condition, for never have my tears been more abundant." She smiled shyly. "At any rate, I have washed the handkerchief, and here it is back again."

She handed D'Artagnan a square of lace and D'Artagnan, who was quite sure that in the confused babble of last night, between brandy and wine there had been a talk of monogrammed handkerchiefs, looked uneasily down at the monogram, which was MAR. Since he knew for a fact that Aramis was in another life Rene Chevalier d'Herblay, he could but marvel at those initials. And then he remembered the Duchess de Chevreuse who apparently—and for reasons known only to her, or to those more adept at court intrigue than D'Artagnan—called herself Marie Michon. He put the square of lace into his sleeve, and thanked Hermengarde, determined to ask Aramis what all this could mean at the first opportunity.

Not many minutes went by, before Constance came out of the little door through which Hermengarde had disappeared. D'Artagnan started to her, with both hands extended, but the lady made no effort at all to meet his hands. Her own were kept where they were, at the end of her crossed arms.

Instead of the affectionate greeting which the twenty-something blond was likely to give him, frosty accents echoed from her soft and luscious mouth. "So I see," she said, "that my summons are for nothing. I call you to me with the utmost urgency, and you decide to ignore me and instead"—she gave a pointed look to his arm, where the bandages were perfectly obvious by the lump beneath the borrowed shirt and doublet—"you choose to go to the duel you'd set before."

"A duel?" D'Artagnan said. He stared at her aghast. "Who told you there was a duel set?"

"Someone," she said, primly, "has said it. It is common

knowledge at court. I heard someone say you and your friends had a duel set for yesterday. And you must know that his eminence is daily in expectation of getting the King to sign that edict which would make it fatal for you to fight. And yet, the marchioness tells me that you would have fought anyway, for you care nothing for your life, nor for how much you'd leave me desolate, should you die. No, you'd rather be killed and leave me quite alone."

The words came out in such a torrent that D'Artagnan's mouth dropped open in surprise. "Constance," he said. "You cannot meant it."

"What, that you should not fight so many duels? Of course I mean it. How many times have I imagined—"

"No, that you believe all this nonsense about my meaning to fight a duel. I never did."

"You weren't home when I delivered the note on my way to visit Monsieur Bonacieux."

"Yes, that is true, I wasn't. I spent most of my afternoon trying to find out something about who might have killed the armorer that Mousqueton is accused of killing. You must know, my dear, that we cannot let the poor boy rot in the Bastille. Not when . . . well." He couldn't bring himself to give away other people's secrets, so he finished in a halting tone. "Well, Hermengarde loves him, you know."

Constance, who had been examining D'Artagnan's features, as though desperately trying to fix in her mind any reason to believe him or disbelieve him, now sighed. "I cannot believe you. I'm sorry. I left the note, and you never came."

"I came," D'Artagnan said. "I came and Porthos with me. Ask whoever was at guard last night, to whom I gave Monsieur de la Porte's password. I came, and in that courtyard over there, before I could get to you, we were attacked by six men in dark cloaks. They . . . They wounded me," he lifted his arm slightly, in vain hope for sympathy. "And then some guards of the Cardinal appeared, and they accused my friends and I of dueling. 'Dueling' he said. Among us. And when Porthos proved to them that it wasn't so, they let us go, but by then I had lost so much blood, that the only thing to be done was to take me to Athos's place. And then I don't remember much of anything, save that, for some reason, I was given more brandy than I've ever drunk, and some excellent red wine."

At this point, he realized Constance was crying softly. He said, "No, no. What's this?" as he fished madly in his sleeve for a handkerchief. He found a square of lace and gave it to her. "Don't you believe me?"

"I know I believe the drinking," she said. "But I don't know how much more. You don't understand my fears," she said, and touched her eyes with the handkerchief. "I know you're out there, free, and so much younger than I, and I know how all the ladies of nobility make it a point of picking out the most handsome of the musketeers. And I am not noble-born, not even of very good family. All I have is my gentle upbringing, my familiarity with the Queen and my beauty, such as it is, and sure to fade fast, as much as you worry me."

D'Artagnan said, "To me you are more beautiful than any princess."

It is almost sure his honeyed words and that charm of manner for which his countrymen were known would have carried the day. It would, that is, had not the fair lamenter's eyes fallen upon the square of lace in her hand. And then she stared at it, in something like horror, dropped it on the ground, and stomped on it with the tip of her dainty, slippered foot. "As beautiful as any princess, am I? Am I as beautiful as any duchess, also?"

Bewildered, D'Artagnan said, and meant it, "To me you are the most beautiful woman in the entire world."

She sneered at him. She actually curled her lip in disdain and said, "Oh, I am done with you. I know you Gascons and your love of words, often empty of all meaning. How long have you been sleeping with the ladies of the court? Oh, answer me not. Probably before you met me, and probably it will go on long after you've ceased to care for me. I will not speak to you anymore. I will not . . ." She shook her head. "I married Monsieur Bonacieux at the behest of my family. Until I met you, Monsieur D'Artagnan, my heart was as innocent and untouched as that of a young girl in a convent. I could have lived my whole life long without knowing love. But you woke me to that emotion, and now it turns out it was all a lie." She stomped again on the square of lace on the ground, then reached into her own sleeve and threw a key at his feet. "I shall not be needing the access to your lodgings that you so kindly bestowed on me. It was only a matter of time before I detected you in some other woman's arms."

And D'Artagnan, who in his whole life had only one lover, and that lover Constance Bonacieux, stared at her in horror, quite convinced his beloved had taken leave of her senses. Such words as came to his mind—mostly her name and protests of his innocence, he knew too well than to say. Indeed, he didn't recover his voice till she had left and until, reaching down, he retrieved the maltreated handkerchief and saw that it was the one he'd meant to return to Aramis.

"The devil," he said to himself. He had suspected it all along, but the thing was that Constance had never given him a chance to defend himself. And that she could believe in his perfidy like that, without need of proof, without a single doubt. That cut into the center of his young heart. "Perhaps Athos is right," he told himself. "Perhaps all women are the devil."

In this sullen mood, he left the courtyard, and went through the door barely saying a word of thanks to De Jacinthe. In fact, his rejection of all of the fair sex lasted exactly until he walked less than twenty steps from the palace entrance, towards his lodging, and saw a beautiful woman cowering against the wall, while two rough-looking men, with knives, tried to convince her to come with them.

"You'll come with us," one of the men said. "And there will be no debate. You are too tasty a morsel to escape us."

The woman was indeed a tasty morsel, D'Artagnan thought, as he rushed to her rescue. She had hair so blond and so shiny that it might as well be pure moonlight. It was braided simply down her back, over a pale grey cloak edged with some sort of fur. Her features were as beautiful as her hair or her attire, something that didn't seem quite real. Oval, perfect face, huge grey eyes, that matched her cloak, a straight nose, and lips so full and promising that they quite cast Constance's into shade. In fact, while Constance was beautiful, this woman was stunning.

His sword out of its sheath, D'Artagnan rushed in, and—in a mood of reckless chivalry—charged the two ruffians. "Leave the lady be," he said. "Or face me."

Clearly his demeanor was more fearful than he'd thought, for they didn't even wait for him to come near, but instead took to their heels. D'Artagnan, somewhat bewildered by so easy a rescue, reasoned that perhaps they were, out of reason, afraid of guards. Or perhaps they'd mistaken his uniform for that of a musketeer.

He now found his hands taken in both of the cool, soft hands of the woman, who was as beautiful as an angel. "Oh, my hero," she said. "You've saved a foreigner from a fate worse than death."

Her accent, though present, didn't so much sound foreign as like the accent of someone who'd spent a long time abroad. But then, D'Artagnan was quite willing to understand he knew nothing of accents.

He did however know of beauty, and this beautiful woman was curtseying to him. He bowed in return, removing his hat.

"Henri D'Artagnan, madam," he said. "At your service."

She smiled. "I am Lady de Winter," she said. "And quite a stranger and friendless in Paris. I wonder," she said, "if you'd do me the honor of dining with me tonight?"

Before D'Artagnan had fully recovered, he found himself in possession of the beautiful woman's address and the time to present himself at her door. And standing there, in the full sun of morning, he thought that if Constance was going to accuse him of dallying with well-born ladies, by the Mass, he was about to give substance to her accusations.

The Importance of Private Correspondence;
No Gainsaying the Count

⟨∼⟩

PORTHOS woke up with repeated knocking outside the door. Opening his eyes, he saw that he was in Athos's room, though he had slipped to the floor. Athos was still asleep on the bed, though D'Artagnan was nowhere to be seen. And there was a repeated, insistent knocking outside the door.

His first attempt at a reply having come out as a grunt, Porthos cleared his throat and said, "Yes?"

The door opened and Grimaud's worried face peeked into the room. "Monsieur Porthos," he said, with a worried look at his master on the bed. "There is a letter come for Monsieur D'Artagnan."

"Well, then give it to him," Porthos said, speaking gruffly. On the bed, Athos stirred. Grimaud looked worried. Porthos, following his glance, saw Athos sit up suddenly and pull out his sword in the same moment.

Grimaud said, "You did not remove his sword," and then dove for cover behind the chair. Whether the sound of his movement or his words called Athos, Athos rose from the bed and jumped down from it and, silent as the grave, charged towards the chair.

"Stop!" Porthos yelled, not at all sure the sword would not pierce through the chairback and hit the cowering

Grimaud. "Athos, are you mad?" he asked at the same time he got his own sword, which he had leaned against the wall, and managed to deflect Athos's charge just in time.

The sound of metal on metal caused Athos to open one of his eyes, but all the same, he still made a half-hearted lunge towards Porthos, which Porthos averted easily. And then Athos's eyes were both open, his forehead wrinkled, and his mouth set in a grimace of pain. "What are you doing dueling me, Porthos?" he asked, in a tone of great outrage.

"I would ask rather," Porthos said, baffled, "what you are doing dueling me." And joining action to words, he lowered his sword and sheathed it.

For a moment it hung in the balance, but then Athos lowered his sword as well, and glowered at Porthos from beneath lowered eyebrows. "I couldn't have," he said. "You must realize I was asleep."

Porthos sighed and refused to say that yes, he was perfectly aware of this and vaguely shocked that Athos could duel in his sleep. Instead, he just said, "Grimaud came in. With a letter."

Grimaud emerged from behind his chair, at first cautiously, until he ascertained that his master's eyes were both open—or a given value of open—and looking vaguely in his direction and focused enough that he might actually know who Grimaud was.

"Ah, Grimaud," he said, in the tone of one considering a problem, as he stretched out his hand. "The letter."

"The letter," Grimaud said, "is for Monsieur D'Artagnan."

"Oh," Athos said, putting his hand down and frowning. "Then perhaps you should give it to him?"

Grimaud sighed, as though he were faced with madmen everywhere he turned. "Yes, I would, sir, if I had the slightest notion where he might be."

"Well, I would assume at his house," Athos said, though there was a touch of insecurity beneath this declaration, and he was frowning ever slightly more. "Or did he sleep here? I have some fantastical memory of waking up with his hand on my hair, but I went back to sleep immediately after." He turned his frown on Porthos.

"We put you both on the bed," Porthos said. "You and D'Artagnan, when you could not walk."

"We?"

"Aramis and I."

"And where is Aramis, then?"

Porthos looked around, as if he expected Aramis to materialize next to him out of clear air. Which, in fact, he did expect. After all, you never knew where Aramis might be, but he might be anywhere.

Grimaud cleared his throat. "Monsieur Aramis," he said, "left shortly after the three of you retired."

"Oh, did he?" Porthos said. "And isn't that just like Aramis? There's people trying to kill us all, some infernal cowards come at us all cloaked and covered up, and yet he goes off all by himself."

"Yes," Athos said, in complete agreement. "I too find Aramis very vexing."

"And D'Artagnan?" Porthos asked Grimaud.

Grimaud shrugged. "I think he too has left," he said. "At least, he's not anywhere else in the house, so I have to believe he has left." He raised the purple missive. "So I don't quite know what to do with this. It was brought over by a servant from the palace, who had gone to Monsieur D'Artagnan's lodging first."

"Why did they come here after his lodging?" Athos asked, frowning.

"Well, Planchet had left word that he would be coming here," Grimaud said. "So they assumed he either was with his master or knew where to find him."

"I take Planchet isn't here, either?" Athos asked.

Grimaud sighed. "Planchet is in the kitchen eating a prodigiously large breakfast." He thought about it a moment. "I think the boy is still growing, which if you permit me saying so, sir, is rather alarming."

"Maybe he is filling out," Porthos said. Both Grimaud and Athos looked at him as if he'd taken leave of his senses.

"You know . . . he's rather too tall and thin, maybe he is . . . growing into his height."

"I doubt it, sir. He has the build that will always be tall and thin," Grimaud said.

"Oh," Porthos said, who was not at all informed on the different builds of youths and in fact didn't remember paying any attention to how people grew up. "So, what should we do with the letter? Perhaps we should send him in search of D'Artagnan?"

Athos covered his eyes with his hand for a moment, then sighed, removing his hand and looking at Grimaud. "Give me the letter," he said.

"But . . ." Grimaud said. "It's for Monsieur D'Artagnan and I"—he hesitated—"think it's from a lady."

"Given the color of the paper and the perfume I can smell from here," Athos said, drily, "I very much hope it's from a woman. Though I'm not absolutely sure anyone who writes in purple deserves to be called a lady. Give it to me, all the same."

"Sir!"

"No, I believe you must. It must be urgent if someone took the trouble of bringing it all the way up to here. So give it to me."

"It's Monsieur D'Artagnan's private business," Grimaud said.

"Quite likely. But that doesn't mean we shouldn't look at it."

"Athos. It indeed does mean so," Porthos said, flabber-gasted by his friend's attitude. Athos was always imperious when he was in pain, be it wound or headache, but today he seemed to be . . . rather more so. Remembering the conversation from the night before, Porthos thought, *Heaven help us. It's Monsieur le Comte.* "Gentlemen do not read gentlemen's correspondence."

Athos gave him a withering look. "Perhaps not. But knowing the trouble that foolish boy can get into, we do indeed read his correspondence. Only think, if your scruples prevented you from following him, and he ended up dead as a result. I know I could not live with it. Could you?" He stretched a hand towards Grimaud and said, imperiously, "The letter, Grimaud!"

Grimaud delivered the letter, managing to look like a dog who cows to his master but does not wish to. Athos frowned at it. And Porthos, still full of misgiving, said, "Athos, should you—"

"Yes, I believe I must." He inserted his fingernail beneath the seal of the letter and pried it open, unfolding the page. For a long time he frowned at the page.

"What does it say?" Porthos asked, and then, thinking that perhaps Athos was having a difficulty he often had, added, "Is the handwriting impossible to decipher?"

Athos said, "No," but his voice was distant and muted, as though he were speaking out of a dream. "It's just . . . there is very little here." He frowned at the page, then cleared his throat. " 'Dear Monsieur D'Artagnan, Just as it had come upon my notice that I might have misjudged you, something happened which I do not feel equal to facing alone. Since it pertains to the maid in which you've shown some interest in the past, I believe it would be a very good thing if you should come to the palace as soon as it may be.' " He frowned. "It is signed Constance B."

"The devil," Porthos said. "Much like the letter she sent

him, which brought him to the palace where he was ambushed."

Athos frowned. "Yes. Do we know if Madame Bonacieux did write that letter? And why is it that she says she realized she might have misjudged him?"

"Boiled if I know," Porthos said, heartily. "But I wonder . . ."

"If our friend got the message by some other means and went to the palace on his own?" Athos asked. He was chewing just on the corner of his upper lip and his moustache, which was always a bad sign with Athos.

Porthos nodded. Athos looked at him, and said something low and soft and shockingly obscene. Then added, "Could Aramis have gone with him?"

Porthos sighed. He wished he could have said that. He hated the idea of D'Artagnan out there alone, possibly falling into a trap, without any of them to stand by him and support him. But he didn't in good conscience think they could surmise that. "Aramis left here late last night, according to Grimaud. He hasn't come back yet. I would be forced to imagine . . ."

"That he's found a softer bed than he could find here. Yes," Athos said, the crease between his eyebrows that he got when he was in pain or worried becoming even more marked. He looked up at Porthos and sighed. "I think, Porthos, that we might have to go to the royal palace and see what has happened with Madame Bonacieux."

"Well, if nothing else," Porthos said, "it will allow us to find out if she was the one who called D'Artagnan to the palace or not, and that must count as a good. Because if it wasn't her . . ."

"Then it must perforce have been someone set on creating a trap, yes," Athos said. "Probably someone who either commanded or was commanded by the men in the black cloaks."

Porthos nodded. Of all of them, Athos was the one—at least when he was not in the mood to go against everything everyone said—to always understand Porthos while requiring him to say the least.

"Very well," Athos said. "Let us go." He pulled his hair back with his fingers, roughly, tying it back with a bit of ribbon. Then he slapped his hat on and reached to the little trunk by the window, for the gloves on top of it.

Thus casually arranged, his appearance made Porthos sigh. Porthos could have spent most of the morning getting ready, and used brushes on his red hair, and set his hat just so, and used his best jewelry, and he'd never look a quarter as noble, as dressed, as full of dignity as Athos. Never. Not as long as he lived. It was a failing he had to learn to live with. But how unfair was it that Athos, who didn't seem to care for any women—except perhaps the criminal he married—who had no interest in court life, who, in fact, did not care what his appearance might be, looked like that while men like Porthos, and even Aramis, had to work for every bit of their dazzling looks.

Out the door of the chamber, and on the landing of the stairs, Athos looked over his shoulder at Porthos. "Are you coming, Porthos?"

"Right away," Porthos said, and followed. They walked side by side, in silence, as profound a contrast as possible. Porthos was taller than Athos, and of a broader build, but that was not what set them so profoundly apart. No, for that, one must take into account Porthos's open, amiable expression, the roving eye that arrested on each pretty woman that walked past. And Athos's focus, which seemed to be not so much inward as somewhere else altogether, cast together with his manner, which seemed to set him aside and enclose him in his own walls that no other human being could penetrate.

When they got to the palace, Athos took the lead.

Porthos watched him, intently. It wasn't that Athos didn't often take the lead. It wasn't even that Athos didn't exude nobility from every pore even while engaged in the most menial of tasks—rubbing down a horse, cleaning a sword, standing guard outside the palace on a cold dark night.

But something else had changed since last night. It was, Porthos thought, as though having admitted who he was— not that his friends hadn't always suspected it—had changed something about him. Looking at him now, it was impossible not to see the count, not to know he was the noblest of the four and their natural leader. Something about the set of his back, the way he squared his shoulders. And this way he had of going straight ahead of whomever accompanied him, and taking the initiative.

Porthos couldn't hear what he was saying, but he saw the musketeer on guard, a young man whom they truly didn't know, shake his head once. Then Athos drew himself up some more. The echoes of his words that reached Porthos were full of disdainful vigor.

The young man looked up at Athos with a stricken expression, very much like a man who finds a serpent under his doormat. Or perhaps a commander where he expected a comrade. Finally he nodded once and stepped aside.

"Come, Porthos," Athos said, and Porthos sighed, knowing that now that Monsieur le Comte had taken over he was, doubtlessly, here to stay. Oh, Porthos would get used to him—a man could get used to anything—but until he did, it was going to be a rough road.

Athos charged ahead into the palace, taking turns with seeming intent. "He said," he told Porthos, "that Madame Bonacieux would be in the little chapel outside the Queen's apartments."

"You asked for Madame Bonacieux?" Porthos said, shocked. After all, the lady was married. If anyone should find out that a musketeer had asked for her . . .

"I told him that I knew her parents and that word had come of an accident in the family. That I might get to her with all possible alacrity." He looked at Porthos. "What? You can't possibly think that anyone would believe me to be interested in the lady."

And the surprising thing was that Porthos knew he was right. No one would think that. Not for one moment. For one thing, no one had ever known Athos to be interested in any woman, no matter how young or how old. For another, if Athos should bestow his favors on someone, no one could imagine him developing any interest in anyone beneath the rank of princess.

And yet, if his story was true, then Athos had married the sister of a village curate. Or someone who passed as one. How odd life was. Either that or the lady must be something special in the way of beautiful and seductive. Something rather in the way of that woman, who was it, who set the towers burning and the ships sailing? Helen of Troy. Aramis had told Porthos of her, in the middle of a very boring sermon on something else, and Porthos remembered thinking that no one was that beautiful and that doubtless the woman would have been found to have protruding teeth, a cast in one eye, but the sort of commanding personality that made everyone think she was beautiful.

And yet, if Athos had married someone with neither title nor connections, she had to be like Helen of Troy and therefore Helen of Troy must have existed, and been flawless. While musing on such things, he'd followed Athos across two small gardens and a sort of terrace, where often the Queen and her ladies would play games in the spring. Set against the edge of that was what looked like a small door into the palace. At that door, another musketeer waited, this one well-known to the two.

He nodded to them and, once more, Athos advanced to talk to him, and once more, after a little resistence the

musketeer went within. Moments later, Madame Bonacieux emerged. She looked like she'd been crying, and she
started a little on seeing them. "Oh," she said. "Monsieur
D'Artagnan's friends. Did he send you? Is he then afraid to
see me?"

Athos bowed, correct and distant, just the sort of look
that tended to make most women fall for him on sight.
Even Athenais, Porthos recalled, had wavered on meeting
him. Though of course, she'd swear she hadn't. "Did you
write to him, then, madam?"

She nodded. "It's just that . . ." And tears started up
again.

"He didn't send us," Athos said, punctiliously. "It's just
that he is involved in a matter of some importance and
could not get away, and therefore we came . . . You said
something about a maid?"

"Oh, yes, yes. It's that poor maid that Monsieur
D'Artagnan talked to this morning. The one that was involved with one of your servants?"

"Hermengarde," Porthos said, unable to help himself.
"What happened to Hermengarde?"

Fresh tears started and it was through them that
madame Bonacieux said, "She was found dead in the garden this morning. She had been run through with a sword."

Coffins and Boxes;
Where When Praying Fails and Threats
Wither, a Good Solid Back and Shoulder
Shall Set You Free

❧

"Monsieurs," Aramis said, very civilly through the keyhole, though he had to control the rage building in him to maintain civility. "Monsieurs. You have the wrong man. My name is Aramis. I am a musketeer of his majesty the King. I'm sure if you open the box, you'll see that you have the wrong man."

Laughter answered him. Distressingly, there was the noise of something that sounded suspiciously like bottles, followed closely by a crackle of something being broken and the smell of bread. Aramis's stomach growled. He hadn't even had a proper dinner the night before. Just wine with Athos.

"Listen, what can I say that will prove it to you that I am not your friend?"

"Nothing, Pierre. We already know your honeyed tongue, and we're not young women whom you can convince. And you were never our friend. Friends don't do things like seduce each other's sisters. You might have friends, I don't dispute that, but we're not them."

Aramis pounded on the lid to the trunk. "Open in, or, God's Teeth, I shall come out and slaughter you."

This one occasioned far more laughter. "Ah, Pierre, if we don't let you out, how do you propose to slaughter us?"

"I am not Pierre and trust me, I will find a way."

For a while there was a silence, and Aramis had time to hope that they were perhaps considering the ways in which he could reach them through the box. But then the two started trading epithets about the supposed Pierre, his brains, his hygiene habits, his morals and—of course—his appearance.

Though none of this applied, in fact, to Aramis, it would be asking more of him than human soul could bear, to hear his supposed self ridiculed in such terms. After a while, in sheer desperation, he let free the voice that had been the pride of his seminary teachers, and launched in a beautiful Te Deum. It wasn't easy, of course, because he was half folded over, and a box didn't exactly have the proper acoustics, but not only did it keep him from listening to the rustics commenting about him, but it also reminded him that the box was not a coffin and that he himself was very much alive.

Reaching the end of his song, triumphant but breathless, he was pleased to note that there was silence from the front. In fact, the silence stretched so long, that Aramis wondered if his singing had finally caused his captors to see the truth.

But instead, he heard at length, one of the miscreants clearing his throat. "Holla, Jean, did you ever know that Pierre could sing that well?"

"No, and in Latin no less. Who would have thought that he paid attention to any of the Mass, even if it was the singy parts."

"Yeah."

"Perhaps we were wrong, Marc. Perhaps Pierre is not a worthless bastard."

"Perhaps not, or perhaps he is a worthless bastard who can sing."

Their roar of laughter managed to push Aramis past whatever the point of insanity had been. He was now furious. In fact, he was sure if he had a mirror, his eyes would be shining with the same light of absolute, concentrated fury he had so often seen in Athos's eyes.

Something like a roar escaped his lips, a roar that was lost in the laughter of his two captors and whatever passed for witty repartee between them. And then Aramis twisted himself around, put his shoulder against the lid of the box, and shoved hard.

Nothing happened. But he was too angry to stop. He'd heard somewhere, though he couldn't remember where, that wood that was still "green," meaning it still had the sap in it, was in fact less resilient than cured wood. He hoped so, but at this point, it did not matter.

Though he had been raised for the monastery, and the soft work of reading the scriptures, preaching, and perhaps writing his own interpretations of it, Aramis had for years now been living by the sword—which is to say by his agility and his strength too. In battle and on guard, and occasionally when he took the holy scriptures to the poor blighted souls who were female and insufficiently able to elude the guard of brothers or husbands, he had often had to lift heavy weights, climb up or down trellises, swing himself from balconies and other feats that demanded one cultivate muscles, as well as brains and piety.

Now his muscles would serve him well, or he would break himself trying. Bracing his feet, he put his now bruised shoulder up once more, and up against the lid of the box. He pushed, as hard as he could, continuously. For a moment he thought the lid was giving, but then he realized that it was his shoulder that had slipped against the wood.

Gritting his teeth, moving around with small movements,

he started to turn himself completely around. It had occurred to him that while his back and his shoulders were strong, his legs had carried him about the length of Paris for several years now, several times a day. And their agility and strength had seen him through several duels. He should be able to break this box with his feet, if his shoulder wouldn't operate.

"Oh, listen, Marc, it sounds like he's slithering around inside the box."

"I'm sure he is, Jean. He's trying to crawl out the keyhole."

The first comedian rapped sharply on the box lid. "Eh, Pierre! You'll have to lose quite a bit of weight to fit through that hole."

"Oh, I'm sure there's a part of him that would fit. If Marie is right, it's not that big."

Right, Aramis thought, and pulled his knees as close to his chest as he could, to give his feet as much chance of hitting the lid with force as could be hoped for. It wasn't as much as he would like to employ, since the space inside the box allowed for very little movement, but all the same, he tried, and pulled back all the way and then he kicked out, with all his might.

The lid of the box splintered under the soles of his boots, the two rustics yelled and rose from what appeared to be a bench seat up front, and Aramis, completely conscious of being at a disadvantage, jumped out of the box and landed on his feet.

He realized he was standing on an oxcart proceeding at a bucolic pace through a landscape of fields and trees. He also realized that his blond, wavy hair, having come completely loose from its bind, was hiding most of his face. He pulled it back, with his fingers, and turned a very angry face onto his captors.

They were portly middle-aged man, attired in the clothes of peasants. And they seemed to be trying to figure out a way to jump off the cart—which was easier said than done, as they were hemmed in by the bench at which they'd been sitting, the box in which Aramis had been, and the oxen. One of them, looking over his shoulder, looked about ready to vault over the oxen.

But the other one had the presence of mind to pull off his hat, and to bow in an awkward, if willing, way. "Your worship," he said. "Oh, Lord help me, your worship. We didn't know it was you. We thought it was our friend Pierre."

Through gritted teeth, Aramis said. "Only because you refused to listen."

"Yes, your worship. That's us all over. I'm always telling Marc here as we're too stubborn for our own goods and one day we'll come a cropper, won't we, Marc? But you see, Marc's sister, Marie, she is with child by Pierre, who came to the country some time ago when his father . . . but that matters not. He came to the country, and he left Marie with child, and it is said he intends to marry a hussy, as works in the palace of the King. And we thought to ourselves, we thought—if we just go into Paris and grab Pierre, we'll make him see the error of his ways, and he won't leave until he's married Marie all right and tight, see?"

Now Marc too was regarding Aramis with a faintly hopeful air and a completely maniacal grin, and holding his hat, squashed, in his blunt-fingered hand. "You can't refuse to acknowledge," Marc said, "that a brother should love his sister, can you?"

Aramis, eyes blazing, was quite beyond controlling his tongue. "No, but I do think perhaps if your ancestors had indulged in a little less of that, you'd have been able to understand my words before now, wouldn't you?" And seeing Marc's mouth open. "And for the love of heaven, don't call me worship and don't agree with me or I shall not be responsible for my actions."

The sad thing was that though his bruised shoulder still hurt like the blazes, and though he felt as though he'd dislocated something moving about in that infernal box, he found the complete and unredeemable cowardice of the two of them very funny indeed. And if he let himself go, he would start to giggle and guffaw, which could not possibly happen. So he spoke through gritted teeth that, they weren't to know, were being held together against laughter. "Do you still have some wine? And some bread? I haven't eaten since yesterday. And turn this infernal cart around and take me back home."

Jean, or perhaps Marc, resumed his place on the bench of the driver, and started executing what seemed to be a complex maneuver of pulling the reins this way and that. It had absolutely no visible effect, and eventually his comrade got tired and said, "Jean, wait. I'll dispose his . . . I mean . . . this person . . . I mean, Monsieur . . ."

"Aramis."

"Monsieur Aramis," Marc said, not even bothering to enquire the provenance of such a strange name. "I'll dispose Monsieur Aramis with something to eat, and then I'll help you turn the animals around, for you know it's going to take a rod on their noses. A more stubborn couple I never met, if very reliable."

Moments later, Aramis, sitting down with a linen napkin—procured from the depths of another box and surprisingly very clean—on his knees, was the sole proprietor of the delights of good dark bread, a glass full of wine that, from wherever it had come, was much better than even Athos's vintage, and a handful of dried figs. As hungry as he was, this seemed to him like a banquet from the gods. And as for the spectacle of watching the two men trying to turn around oxen that were fully as stubborn as they were, it was doubtless as good as anything the theater had to offer.

Aramis, having also found his sword and his lost hat at

the bottom of the cart, was starting to feel very much like himself again. So much so that, when the men had accomplished their purpose of getting the oxen turned around, he'd had time to think of how to take advantage of this very strange situation. He must talk to them. If Pierre was Pierre Langelier, and Aramis was almost sure he was, then Aramis would be able to find out more about the man, more about what interested him, and more about what might have caused the murder of the armorer than he would have otherwise been able to find out.

So when they took their place back on the bench, he said, "So, you took the oxen all the way into Paris?" he was marveling at the feat of logistics, since most streets in Paris were not wide enough for a carriage, much less a broad ox-cart. And the idea of having to turn the oxen at close confines, even in a main street, caused Aramis to shudder.

They shook their heads. "No, your musketeerness," Jean said. "We left it with my cousin, just on the outskirts, you know . . . And we went into the city on our own."

He gave them an appraising look. "And you carried me out in that box by the force of your arms?" They looked sturdy enough, but not that strong. From where they'd been to the outskirts of Paris it would have taken at least an hour's walk and maybe more.

Jean squirmed and Marc cast a significant look at Aramis's sword. "Well . . . it wasn't really like that. You see, we didn't know what we were going to do at first, so we thought, you know, we'll see if we can find Pierre and talk to him. And this we did do last night."

"When you say Pierre, it is Pierre Langelier you speak of?" Aramis asked, taking a bite of the fig and savoring its delicate sweetness. "The armorer whose father was killed?"

"Yeah," Jean said. "You see . . . we heard about it. We have cousins in the city and . . ." He shrugged. "So we knew that Pierre had come into his inheritance. And he's a fine armorer, don't get me wrong your worsh . . . your musketeerness. But he is that fierce for the gaming, that, you know, I think he might have to sell the workshop, and all the swords and all the tools in it, just to be able to pay back his debts. And that's if his father didn't leave a provision in his will for his precious Faustine, which I will promise you he did, because he thought the sun rose and fell out of the brat's crossed eyes.

"So we thought . . . we go and talk to Pierre, like a reasonable human being, no? And we point out to him that Marie won't come to him barefoot, as it were, but well shod, and with a little something on the tip of her shoe."

Marc must have seen Aramis's utterly confused look, as he tried to imagine what the girl's choice in footwear would have to say to the case and particularly what she might have in the tip of her shoe. Everything that he could think of that one might catch on the tip of one's shoe weren't anything to brag about. "What Jean means," he said, in the tone of a man lecturing to the mentally impaired, "is that my sister has a dowry. My parents were wealthy farmers, and friends of Monsieur Langelier. And if Pierre married Marie he would be able to pay all his debts, see? And keep the workshop and his trade and reputation and his means of making more money. So we thought . . . well . . . he cannot resist it, can he?"

"And he didn't resist it . . . in a way," Jean said. "Instead, when we talked to him, he sounded very interested. Many questions about what Marie would bring, and how it would be bound and all."

"He's a mercenary fool," Marc said, in a tone of annoyance. "Any man privileged to enjoy Marie's love . . . but it matters not. Such as he is, he's my nephew's father, and so I said, yes, of course, Pierre, we'll give you anything you want as soon as you marry Marie. And he said he would come with us at nightfall and do it. But, instead, he disappeared, don't you know? Just vanished. We waited and waited for him, and finally we saw you, monsieur, and you see, we thought that with you being roughly the same build, and both of you having straw hair, at least as it appeared to us by moonlight, you would for sure be Pierre."

"For which you felt yourselves justified to hit me on the head and carry me out of the city . . . in your arms? Wouldn't that have attracted attention? Or had you had the providence to carry this charming clothes press in?"

Marc sighed. "No, it was like this—when we saw you looking around we thought of a sure thing it was Pierre. We didn't . . . you don't wear the uniform like the other musketeers wear the uniform, so we never thought that it could be . . ."

"A uniform," Aramis said. "I quite comprehend your point. So you thought it would be a great idea to hit me over the head. And afterwards?"

"Well, afterwards," Jean said. "We thought—what we really need is a good clothes press . . . and we can hide him in it. And then if we can find someone to lend us a wheelbarrow."

"And you found a clothes press and a wheelbarrow in the dead of night, in the middle of Paris? I take my hat off to you gentlemen," he said, though he didn't really, because frankly, he was afraid they might think of something else creative to do with his hat or his head. Like, lift his hat and hit him on his head once more.

"Well," Jean said. "I do have cousins in the neighborhood, so yes. We borrowed a clothes press, and a wheelbarrow."

The idea of himself being wheeled about by these geniuses, in the middle of the night, made Aramis very angry, but it also gave him an incongruous wish to laugh. And behind all this, he was thinking that Pierre Langelier definitely would bear more looking into. Very closely.

Meanwhile, he looked at his erstwhile captors. "Well," he said. "You've made a right muddle of it. For all you know, Langelier is in his workshop, waiting anxiously to tie the knot with your sister, while you two are running about the countryside, ignoring the complaints of the musketeer you've sequestered in a box."

"I wouldn't say we were running," Marc said. "Not with Bossy and Betsy pulling us. They're used to the plow, somewhat, but they're the slowest—" He caught the look in Aramis's eyes and stopped short.

"Right," Aramis said, sighing. "Just get me to Paris as soon as humanly possible, and we will never speak of this debacle again." And he hoped, hoped with all his heart, hoped on the fervent edge of prayer, that he would find all his friends alive and well.

The Etiquette of Visiting a Noble Foreigner;
Where D'Artagnan's Heart and Mind War;
What Planchet Knows

❧

D'ARTAGNAN, coming into his lodgings, was surprised to see Planchet coming in, also, from the other direction. And even more surprised when the young man's spotty, gawky face wreathed in smiles. "Oh, sir, you are well. Oh, sir, *grâce a Dieu*."

D'Artagnan frowned intently at him. "Have you taken leave of your senses? Why shouldn't I be well?"

"It is only," Planchet said, "with the goings on at the palace, and knowing you had been there and alone, earlier in the day, I was afraid you were either dead, or that you'd been taken as Mousqueton was taken."

D'Artagnan decided that Planchet had been listening too much to Grimaud and Athos, who, frankly, both acted as if they were all dancing on the edge of the gallows. "Humor me, Planchet. Explain to me why I should be taken as Mousqueton was taken?"

"Why, for murder!" Planchet said.

"It might interest you to know," D'Artagnan said, as he unlocked his door and allowed Planchet to go in before him, more because he wanted to keep an eye on the young man than because he was so zany as to give his servant precedence, "that I have not in fact murdered anyone. No, in fact, I haven't even come close to murdering anyone. In point of truth, I haven't even seen anyone angry at anyone else. That is, since a minor incident outside the royal palace walls," he added, remembering the incident and wondering if it was the exaggerated report of it that had caused Planchet to take such a fright. "I went to the royal palace and spoke to Madame Bonacieux who was being most unreasonable, mostly because she seemed to think I'd left her to go fight a duel. I'm not even sure what she thought. And then I left there and I went to a tavern." Better not tell Planchet about any alarming incidents. "Where I made a very good dinner on boiled beef. And now I'm home, and I understand the angelic choirs can be heard to rejoice."

But Planchet had stopped on the stairs, just two steps ahead of him, and now dropped on his behind on the step. He looked at D'Artagnan, his face pale. "So, you . . . you did not in fact . . . That is . . ."

"I did not kill anyone?"

"No," Planchet said, and it was almost a wail. "You haven't heard about Hermengarde?"

"What about Hermengarde?" D'Artagnan asked.

Planchet looked up at him, his normally quick eyes now arrested and slow. He reached inside his sleeve for a hand-kerchief and mopped his forehead, though no sweat was visible upon it. "Monsieur, she was found in the little gar-den where . . . where they say you spoke to her. She was run through. They think by a sword. There is talk . . . there were rumors that Monsieur Porthos had killed her to pre-vent her speaking about something with Mousqueton. I had to say that . . . that is, I had to tell them that it could not be so, because Monsieur Porthos and Monsieur Athos too were still asleep when we got the message asking you to come to the palace. Grimaud woke them and I . . ." He shrugged. "I went along to find out what had happened.

Behind them, as it were. And then I came here, because I kept hearing you'd talked to Hermengarde today and I wondered . . ."

"You wondered!" D'Artagnan repeated. He thought of the little maid, her sparkling eyes, her unfailing sense of humor. He couldn't imagine killing her. He couldn't imagine anyone doing it.

"Oh, not if you had done it, sir," Planchet said. "I wondered where you'd been and with whom. And if they . ." He shrugged.

"I was . . . I was on the street and then in a tavern. The Cheval D'Or, you know, where . . ."

"They know you there?"

"Of a certainty they do. I owe them quite a hefty sum on account."

Planchet looked relieved, probably the first time that the estimable young man, who had once been apprenticed as clerk to an accountant, looked relieved at the mention of debt. "Good. Then they know you couldn't have gone back and killed Hermengarde. We were worried . . . I mean . . . I was worried. And perhaps Monsieur Porthos and Athos were worried too."

"Athos thought I might have killed her?"

Planchet looked up and shook his head. "I don't think so. You know, with Monsieur Athos it is sometimes devilishly hard to tell what's passing in his brain."

"Yes. I do know that. And I suspect it's intentional. He'd rather we don't see within."

Planchet nodded, then shrugged. "At any rate, I'm glad you were with people, all three of you, who can vouch for your innocence." He stood up, and started up the stairs again, holding on to the wall. "Though I'm not at all glad about Hermengarde, of course, and I wonder how Mousqueton will take it. He thought the sun rose and set on the girl."

D'Artagnan nodded. It would be hard on Mousqueton. And then he thought over what Planchet had said. "You said the three of us. Where is Monsieur Aramis?"

Planchet shook his head. "He left late at night," he said. "After the rest of you went to sleep."

"The devil!" D'Artagnan said, thinking that it was quite possible his friend had no one to vouch for him. Not that anyone could believe that either Aramis, or indeed any of the musketeers, could have killed the girl, but people would insist on believing impossible things, after all. "Where can he have gone?"

Planchet looked back, a most unbecoming flush on his face. "I don't know, monsieur, but this being Monsieur Aramis, I would say for sure that he's not been alone."

"Oh, of that I'm very sure. I just hope whoever his companion is, she is able to own it."

"There is that," Planchet said.

They'd arrived at the top of the stairs, where Planchet turned around to look at D'Artagnan. "What I don't understand, sir, is why you came here, and not to Monsieur Athos's home. "I thought all of you had agreed that . . ."

D'Artagnan shrugged. "Indeed, I intend to go there, as soon as I've picked some clothes." He looked at the boy. "I've been invited to dinner at the home of a lady for whom I did a trifling favor this morning."

He told Planchet the whole story, as they went within, to D'Artagnan's room. Now, while D'Artagnan knew his servant was inexperienced—at least he hoped he was, though he'd seen the boy eye the tavern wenches with a hungry eye once or twice—he'd never known him to be exactly prudish. So it was odd that, as his story progressed, he found Planchet becoming redder and redder, till presently he was looking at D'Artagnan with an odd, sheepish look.

"Oh, come, Planchet," he said. "You can't be that offended. After all, Madame Bonacieux spends the night here two or three times a week, and you do no more than make sure she's had dinner, before you show her into my room."

Planchet sighed. "And have you thought, sir, on Madame Bonacieux and . . . and what she will feel about all this?"

D'Artagnan, who had thought of scarcely anything else, shook his head resolutely. "Not at all. Her behavior to me—her implication that I had lied to her in order to avoid going to the palace and fighting a duel, her cruelty in sending me way . . . I must say, Planchet, that your loyalty becomes you, but it would be by far a better thing if the lady herself had any notion of loyalty or . . . or care for me."

"She was crying when we got to the palace," Planchet said. "She sent for you to tell you about Hermengarde, and she was crying when we got there."

She was? D'Artagnan thought, as his hopeful heart leapt. But what he said, in restrained tones, was, "Good God, of course she was. You can't think that she's a monster. She might not have known Hermengarde very well, but I'm sure she'd paid special attention to the girl, since the girl was, after all, Mousqueton's lover." And on that he thought that Hermengarde had also, after all, been carrying Mousqueton's child, and his heart turned within him in horror.

"It wasn't that," Planchet said. "I was nearby enough as Monsieur Athos spoke to her, and she said . . . she said she'd been remorseful over what she'd told you."

Remorseful, D'Artagnan's heart said, with relish, cherishing the word, but his mind had control of his mouth, which said, disdainfully, "She very well should be remorseful. She behaved to me as a veritable shrew."

"Yes, but . . ." Planchet said. "From what I understand, women are like that. When they really care, at least. Not that I know much about women, of course, but . . . but . . . I've seen Madame Coquenard take Monsieur Porthos down a peg or two, and he, that giant that he is, he just stands there and takes it humbly, and you know, in the end, she didn't mean to tear him down at all, but was, you know, all in solicitude for him."

D'Artagnan, who had seen it too, could imagine his great giant of a friend standing there, if Athenais told him that he had avoided meeting her to go to a duel. It would all be, "I understand what you're saying, my pigeon." And "I regret having grieved you, my dearest." And in the end, somehow, she would be still, and he would be able to speak, and tell her what had really happened.

Unfortunately, D'Artagnan was not Porthos. His Gascon temper would never allow him to stand meekly by and listen to himself being berated on grounds that were not only untruthful, but which made no sense whatsoever. But in his mind, he very much envied Porthos.

Having selected a bright blue suit from his armoire, he set it on the bed, removed his arm from its sling, and told Planchet, "I'm going to need some help dressing. You see, my arm is very painful still."

"Of course, sir," Planchet said, joining action to words. As he stripped his master of his coat and shirt, and started to slip fresh ones on, he said, "Monsieur?"

D'Artagnan gave him a sharp look. It was obvious that Planchet wanted to tell him something, and was equally afraid of saying anything. The combination was so unusual between the two youths, who, while master and servant, were close enough in age to speak with a disarming lack of ceremony when no one else was present, that it alarmed D'Artagnan.

"Yes, Planchet?" he said, very quietly, trying not to scare away whatever confidence was coming.

"Well, monsieur," Planchet said, and then, as though losing all courage. "Well . . ."

"Planchet, if you say 'well' once more or hesitate to tell me what's on your mind I shall flog you," D'Artagnan said. And, as the young man widened frightened eyes at him, added, "Don't think I can't. A lot of musketeers—a lot of noblemen—thrash their servants."

"You couldn't," Planchet said, softly. "Not you."

"Don't try my patience too high," D'Artagnan said, then seriously, "I know something is eating at you, Planchet. I'm not that cloddish. Tell me what it is. If you feel that much of a need to tell me something, chances are it is something I need to know."

Planchet sighed, a heavy, doleful sigh, full, so it seemed, of the cares of the world. "Monsieur, it is only that I have a bad habit of listening at doors."

D'Artagnan grinned. "Oh, no need at all to tell me that, Planchet. I never say anything with you in the house that I should not wish you to know."

"Yes, yes, monsieur. But the other gentlemen, your friends, do not know that."

"I see. What have you listened to?"

Planchet sighed again. "How castaway were you last night, sir? What is the last thing you remember?"

"Well . . . I remember Athos giving me wine, after all that brandy, which even then, and given the way I felt, seemed to me far less than a good idea."

"And?"

"And then he talked a lot about some duchess that answers to Marie Michon, but I confess there my memory is foggy and I have no clue at all what he meant. He seemed to imply there was a conspiracy on the life of the King."

Planchet shook his head. "No, Monsieur Athos only said that the Cardinal had told him there was a conspiracy on the life of the King, but that he didn't quite believe it, as it were, sir."

D'Artagnan nodded. "I'm not sure I believe it either.

Though there must be a conspiracy on the Cardinal's part. Or at least . . . if there isn't . . ." He shook his head. "He either wants us to be roped in, or he's fighting for his life. Either of those would justify his inventing a conspiracy on the King to get us to defend him."

"Yes," Planchet said. But he bit his lip. "You don't remember . . . that is . . . I'm sure he would want you to know, because he was talking to all three of you, but you must pretend I don't know it, myself."

"Planchet, you make no sense at all."

Planchet sighed again. "It is only that I shouldn't know this, but . . . sir . . . Do you remember Monsieur Athos saying he is a count?"

D'Artagnan shrugged. "Not from hearing it this time, but I've suspected it for a long while. You see . . . I went with him to his friend the Duke de Dreux and it was all '*milord this*' and '*milord that*' and '*Would the Count de la Fere wish water for his shaving?*' I haven't said anything, because I wasn't sure he wanted anyone else to know. I suspect too, though he's only a count, that there is family prestige or other, because the duke treated him quite as an equal."

Planchet nodded. "Well, he told them all he was a count. And that . . . that is . . . that he'd just seen his wife."

"His wife?!" D'Artagnan echoed. "Am I drunk still or were you, Planchet? Athos isn't married."

"Well, Athos might not be," Planchet said. "But the count was. To a beautiful woman who turned out to be marked with the fleur-de-lis."

"The . . . Poor Athos."

"Yes, sir. And he hanged her, and he left his domains. And then . . . And then yesterday he saw her."

D'Artagnan whistled under his breath. "No wonder he was drinking. But it must be all a chance resemblance. I mean, women look like each other, and there are cousins and sisters, and daughters, if it comes to that."

But Planchet inclined his head. "Only he says he never made sure she was dead, after he hanged her, and you know . . ."

"I know," D'Artagnan said thinking he couldn't have been very sure he wanted her dead. Slicing her throat and leaving her in a thicket would have been the way to that. Trying to hang her, no. After all, it took expert hangmen to kill people with a rope and they had traps and deep falls and properly constructed gallows. So Athos can't have been sure in his mind and his heart that he wanted her dead. And he'd left her . . . without checking. "And what does this have to do with me, Planchet?" D'Artagnan asked, curiously.

"Well, sir, Monsieur Athos said that she was called 'milady' by those in the Cardinal's service. And then . . ."

"And then?"

"And then she looked uncommonly like the foreign lady you just described."

"Athos's wife?" D'Artagnan asked, bowled over. "But . . . you said the Cardinal's service?"

"That's where he saw her. At the Palais Cardinal."

"Oh," D'Artagnan said, then, turning around. "Do you mean . . . I mean, does she know who Athos is and what . . ."

"I don't know," Planchet said. "I'm afraid, sir, I would assume the worst."

"Yes. I suppose I must do so," he said. He thought how the lady didn't seem to be truly threatened by the ruffians he'd chased away and how she had invited him to dinner on such small a service. "A fleur-de-lis . . ." he said.

"On her left shoulder," Planchet said. "If you should . . ."

"I hope I shan't," D'Artagnan said, whose heart had never been sanguine over even flirting with a woman not his Constance. Now it was cringing at the idea. And anything more . . .

"I would call it off altogether," he said. "But then, if she is bent on having her revenge on us, that would be the same as putting her on her guard. And besides, if it's her . . . and if she means to entrap us, better myself, with my eyes open, than the others." He thought about it for a moment. "Far better myself than Athos."

Where Athos Tries to Understand
the Impossible;
Porthos Contemplates the Inscrutable;
And Madame Bonacieux Keeps Her Silence

∽

"MADAM," Athos said. "I understand that we had to be informed of Hermengarde's death. In fact, with poor Mousqueton still in the Bastille, and her being killed in the same way that the armorer was killed, I understand our being apprised of it immediately. But why did you ask D'Artagnan to come here? And why with such urgency?"

To himself, Athos was thinking that, in fact, the woman had probably sent for D'Artagnan as part of an attempt at reconciliation. At least, he hoped he wasn't underestimating her, and of course, anyone would shrink from using the death of an innocent girl, almost a child, for such personal purposes. But then, Athos had known enough women to know that women weren't everything. In point of fact, when it came to manipulating circumstances and in any possible way using someone else's misfortune to advantage, there was very little he'd put past a determined woman.

His suspicions seemed to be confirmed by the look of almost fright that Madame Bonacieux darted at him. Then she looked behind him, and around her, as if to ascertain that no one could hear her, and she dropped her voice to a whisper. "Because, Monsieur, D'Artagnan talked to her this morning, and with her friend being the servant of one of you, and with her being . . . well . . . it was rumored, though she denied it when asked, that she was with child. The rumors have already started," she said, looking frightened, "that her killer was one of you. One of the inseparables, they say. Some say that it was because she was with child, and you feared she'd hang on you or ask for support after her friend was executed. And some wonder if she knew something to Mousqueton's detriment and was therefore silenced." She took a handkerchief from her sleeve and wiped at her eyes. "No one has done anything about it, yet, monsieur, but I can tell you that as rumor grows, well, people will start to get some strange ideas about you and . . . and about D'Artagnan. And though I fought with him, I . . . well . . . I wouldn't want any harm to come to him, or any of you."

Perhaps because he felt guilty about having thought ill of her before, Athos forced himself to bow. "No," he said. "No, I understand that. I wouldn't wish any ill to come to any of us, either, and while I'm sure that D'Artagnan is utterly innocent, I also know how rumors can grow and fester. I will . . . warn him. And I will do what I can to solve this."

A look to the side showed him that Porthos looked like he'd heard everything, and his eyes were full of that intent light that showed that Porthos was thinking. This was always a perilous proposition. Porthos could think very well, and indeed very fast, but the things his thoughts could wreak were often far less than orthodox.

Athos himself was not sure what to think, as he bowed over Madame Bonacieux's hands and told her to be careful and that he would do his best to keep D'Artagnan out of the path of harm. "Though you know D'Artagnan, madam, and you know, therefore, how difficult that can be."

And she had given him a little rueful smile. "Yes, indeed, I do know, since I argued with him simply for trying to keep him out of a duel, where, you see, he ended by getting injured."

This brought Athos to with a start. "A duel?" The only time recently that he could think of D'Artagnan's getting injured had been right here, in the gardens of the palace, and there D'Artagnan must be exonerated from recklessness. A fool he might be, and gallant to a fault, and always to rush in defense of others or his own honor. But even D'Artagnan could not have known that he would be attacked by stealth, while walking across the gardens in the royal palace towards an appointment with his mistress.

"Last night," Madame Bonacieux said, "I . . . someone told me that he had a duel, and so I called him to come to me, because I believed, of course, that he would come to me rather than go to the duel. But he didn't. And when he appeared this morning, he was injured."

"But . . ." Athos said at a loss. "He was attacked by stealth while coming to your appointment. From whom did you hear this, madam? It is very important that I know."

Madame Bonacieux was looking at him with intent eyes. "You mean . . ."

"I mean that I think whoever convinced you to send him a note and ask him to come to your chambers on that night, at the hour of the supposed duel, was laying a very clever trap for my young friend."

The lady went pale. "Impossible," she said.

"Why impossible, madam? Who can have told you?"

"She doesn't know I have any relationship at all with him," she said. "She couldn't possibly have guessed."

Athos only raised his eyebrows, a gesture of such imperiousness, that he often found people answering questions he had not yet asked them. This woman was no match for his questioning. She sighed. "It was the . . . it was the

Duchess de Chevreuse," she said. "And she only mentioned it in jest. Because of . . . You know she's friends with your other friend Aramis?"

Athos nodded. He personally would not call it friends but he knew that the lady had some relationship with Aramis, and he would guess—reluctantly, if absolutely pressed on the point—that the relationship probably required close contact. But for the purposes of this conversation, he would call them friends.

"Well, she was talking—not to me, but to a crowd of people, and she said that Aramis would have a duel on his hands—he and his friends both. And I thought . . . She said they would be fighting for their lives that night. And so I thought . . ." She looked horrified at the idea that perhaps D'Artagnan had got wounded because of her attempts to protect him.

"And do you remember, madam, who it was that the lady was talking to?"

Madame Bonacieux shook her head. "Some of her circle, you know. The women she talks to, and some of the men who admire her. But . . ."

"But?"

"I remember little Hermengarde was standing by."

"I see," Athos said, and bowed swiftly, ready to depart. Then stopped. "No, wait, one more question—whom did you tell that you were summoning D'Artagnan to you that evening?"

"Why, no one."

"What did you do after you heard that? You must have been in some agitation. Or at least it sounds as though you were. Which surprises me a little, to own the truth, because the fact that musketeers fight duels should not surprise a lady who is in an intimate relationship with one of them. You know that we—"

"Fight," she said. "Yes, I do. And knowing it doesn't

make it easier to bear, but I understand that men of both honor and temperament . . ." She shrugged as if to express that there was much one could forgive to men of those attributes. "No, this agitated me more than it would just knowing that one—or all—of you were about to fight a duel. You see, there was such malice in her voice, as though . . . as though there were some treason at stake, something horrible about to happen. And I thought . . ."

"You thought you'd preserve my friend, which is very worthy," Athos said, reluctant to admit the, to him, impossible idea that a woman had acted, in fact, from the best of motives. "But what did you do, exactly, madam?"

"I went to my room, and I wrote a note to D'Artagnan, summoning him to come to me. I didn't know the time of the duel, but I surmised that he would be coming home to change or pick up his other sword, or some such thing."

"Yes," Athos said. It was true. All of them usually repaired home before a duel, if for no other reason because one liked to look one's best. "And whom did you send with the note?"

"No one," she said, and blinked in confusion. "I went myself."

"But that means you must have told someone you were leaving or asked someone for permission?"

"Only the Queen, monsieur, only the Queen. And surely you don't mean—"

Athos didn't mean. The thought might cross his mind, dangerous and slick like an iced-over river, but he didn't dwell on it, nor was it something he wanted to encourage. While the Cardinal might suspect the Queen of whatever he might very well want to suspect her, and while the lady, herself, had been known to make less than steady choices or informed decisions, yet it was not to be believed that she had conspired against men who had so often bled in her service. He simply shook his head and bowed.

"Well," Madame Bonacieux said, "I must say I can't conceive how anyone knew of my decision, to choose to bring him here and that I hope . . . I hope I'm not responsible for his wounding. You will tell him that when you see him, will you not?"

Athos nodded. "I will do my best to persuade him you meant him no harm." Which, if nothing else, would make for an amusing change and quite a bit of surprise to D'Artagnan to hear Athos—Athos, of all people—defending a woman. "Meanwhile, madam, may I beg of you to stay silent on the subject of D'Artagnan's visit here, this morning, and to contrive to make it as little known as possible that you . . . that you have an intimate knowledge of him?"

"Yes, oh yes. If indeed it was my fault that he got wounded; that he might easily have got killed, it is dangerous for me to do anything else that might bring a trap upon him. I shall be as silent as the grave."

He felt so guilty for having suspected her of perfidy earlier, that he bowed over the hand she proffered to him, and lightly touched it with his lips. Yet he waited till he and Porthos had gone some distance before deciding to speak. But then, Porthos spoke first.

"The devil," he said. "I wonder what she means by that, that Hermengarde was seen with a musketeer before she was killed."

"Well, she might not have meant anything at all," Athos said. "It seems that D'Artagnan did come to the palace earlier and spoke to Hermengarde, even I have gathered that. So it would seem that he was seen with her. You know what people are like about places and times. Quite likely this is what they refer to, and nothing of more import."

"Quite likely," Porthos said, but he was biting at his moustache. "The devil of this," he said, "is that now everyone will naturally think we are involved. I wish I could see

Mousqueton and ask him what exactly was happening and what he thought he was doing, to be getting in this sort of trouble."

Athos felt a sudden stab of enlightenment. "I wish you wouldn't try to talk to Mousqueton, Porthos, not unless you can arrange it through Monsieur de Treville." This because he could think of many other ways for Porthos to manage the thing—ways that were more in keeping with Porthos's peculiar mind. They could involve all or anything, including fomenting an armed revolt that took over the Bastille. Porthos's capacity for admirable and transforming action was only comparable to his inability to understand the world at large.

"Well," he said, dolefully. "I don't think Monsieur de Treville is going to arrange for me to see him at all. And the devil of it is, we might likely find out who killed the armorer by talking to Mousqueton."

Athos mentally added to his excellent friend's qualities—or lack thereof—his complete inability to imagine how his words sounded to other people. "You cannot possibly mean that," he said. "The only way for us to discover that would be to find that Mousqueton had murdered the armorer."

"What? No. What I mean is that clearly there are other circumstances surrounding this, including Mousqueton's proposed marriage. It's all inscrutable without his view of the matter."

Athos was so surprised that he stopped, stock-still. "Porthos, my friend, did you just say it's inscrutable?"

"Yes, yes, I did. It means it can't be penetrated with eye or mind, depending on whether it's a physical darkness or a darkness of the spirit." He looked at Athos's expression, and Athos must have looked back in total shock, because Porthos guffawed. "It's this new plan of Aramis.' "

"Oh?" Athos said, somewhat fearful, because when a

plan of Aramis's involved Porthos in it, the results were usually incalculable and often bizarre.

"Yes. He thinks that if I learn a new word every week, soon I will not feel about long words the way I do, and I won't confuse their meanings either. So this week, he taught me the word inscrutable, and he has told me to make sure I use it in all possible cases. I presume I used it correctly."

"Admirably so," Athos said, suppressing a smile. The friendship between Aramis and Porthos was in itself one of the inscrutable mysteries of life. The two men could not be more different if they'd been knit from entirely different clay, on opposing shores of different continents. And yet, they bore each other's quirks with greater kindness than the rest of them often could.

They were now at the gate through which they had come, and Athos demurred. "Porthos, I believe I should go and talk to . . . to the duchess the lady mentioned, but I am not sure any of us should be outside alone. We can't help that Aramis and D'Artagnan are, though we can hope they met with each other and that one is guarding the other, but . . ."

"I see," Porthos said. "This is what I propose to do. You go and speak to your duchess, and then you come and talk to me in the kitchens of the palace."

"The kitchens?" Athos said. He knew from their previous adventures—though it had never fully been explained to him—that Porthos had conceived an almost fear of one of his majesty's head cooks.

Porthos sighed resignedly, and combed his moustache with his fingers so that the tips pointed upwards. "It is a cross to bear," he said, "to be so handsome that women fall in love with one at a glance. The cook was more than usual importune. But I am hoping that I can get information from her without . . . without its going too far."

Half amused, though he had to admit that maids, cooks

and peasant women did indeed seem to fall in love with Porthos at a first glance at his shining head of red hair, his strong features and his sparkling eyes, Athos nodded. "Well, I'll come and find you in the kitchens, then, when I'm done interviewing the duchess.

The Disadvantages of a Hot Day;
Many Ways to Slacken Thirst;
Evangelists and Pigs

⚜

ARAMIS had realized, about an hour into the drive—no, the journey, for it was epic and involved shades of odyssey—that he probably could get to Paris earlier if he got down and walked. This because not only did the oxen move at a snail's pace, but also the two men in charge of the oxen felt it incumbent upon them to stop at every roadside stall and every isolated farmhouse to purvey themselves with the necessities of life.

There were two reasons he hadn't actually jumped off the oxcart. The first was that while the oxen were probably slightly slower than Aramis could walk, by sitting in the cart he was sparing his legs, for what he expected would be a run all over Paris to locate his friends, once he got to town. The second, and no less pressing, was that the necessities of life—according to his ex-captors—included a great deal of food and wine, which, of course, they shared freely with him, by way of reparation.

On the road so far, he had tasted some very good ham, some excellent bread, a strong-smelling cheese and a dozen boiled eggs. All of this—the day being hot for the end of winter—had necessitated washing it down with a great deal of wine.

So, by the time they stopped on the farm at the edge of town, where his amiable hosts had friends or contacts or cousins, or whatever it was they had, Aramis was feeling quite at ease with the world and, indeed, of a warm and glowing disposition, where all would be forgiven.

They let him off and explained they were about to go back to the neighborhood where they'd first mistakenly importuned him, so they could capture the original miscreant.

"Well," Aramis had said airily, "only, be sure to take a box with you, in case he resists."

This had resulted in many laughs, which had eventually dissolved into giggles and a never end of "your musketeerness," and Aramis was never to understand exactly how, but he found himself walking along the street with Jean and Marc in the best of understandings.

Or at least, he hoped they understood him correctly, since he was attempting to lecture them on the biblical significance of their names and explaining that if they were evangelists, and his name were Luke, they would be three of a set of four. This seemed to impress them profoundly, and Marc expressed the earnest hope that, if he had his life to live again, he could become knowledgeable in Latin and Greek "and all that horse manure." Forgiving his way of expressing himself, which was clearly due to his lack of exposure to the belles lettres, Aramis said, "My friend, Porthos, he has the same problem. That's why . . . that's why we have this plan." He walked along for a while in silence, his mind assuring him that he'd said absolutely everything he needed to say, until Jean said, "Your musketeerness?"

"Yes, *mon bon* Jean?"

"You never told us your plan."

"Oh, it's simple. You take a word, any word. The word

this week is *inscrutable*. And you learn that word for a week. And when the word is—" Aramis stopped because his intended audience had run in opposite directions, away from him, as fast as their legs could carry him.

Looking forward, Aramis discovered the cause of their fright. There were not one, not two, but at least six men, wearing dark cloaks and armed with swords. "I knew you would come back," the leader of them said, advancing towards Aramis with drawn sword.

Aramis had a vague idea of having met with this treatment before, but the adventure he'd just undergone had given him fresh insight into the possible causes of this. "I think," he said, as he crossed his arms, "that you have quite the wrong man. You see, I'm not Pierre."

"Not Pierre?" the leader said, and looked so confused that, for a moment he halted his advance and lowered his sword. "What do you mean by this, that you're not Pierre?"

"Well, I would think that is glaringly obvious," Aramis said, hearing creep into his voice the peevish tone that he normally used to explain some point of theology to his religion-blighted friends. "If I were Pierre, I would be Pierre. But as it chances, I'm not Pierre. I am Re—I mean . . . I am Aramis." He took his hat off and bowed, very correctly.

At which point the furies of Hell broke loose. At least that's what Aramis thought at the time, though later on, on reflection, he realized that someone had got into the backyard of one of the nearby houses and opened the pens containing the usual collection of domestic animals. Or perhaps more than one backyard, since a veritable bedlam of pigs, chickens, and a few very frightened goats rushed onto the street at the same time.

Bewildered, not quite sure where he was, thinking that perhaps he had gotten off at one of the various isolated farmhouses they'd stopped at, Aramis heard, through the din of bleating, oinking and cackling, a familiar voice saying "Run, your musketeerness. Run."

It seemed like as good an idea as any, and, besides, Aramis had always had a horror of living poultry, since, at the age of two, he'd been attacked by the family farm's very territorial rooster. He ran.

He dodged a pig, stepped over a chicken, might possibly have stepped on another chicken's neck, and thought it was a pity that Mousqueton wasn't there to put it out of its misery and bring it to his friends, and then, running along a broad thoroughfare, realized that he was supposed to go to his friends. He was supposed to warn them that something was very seriously wrong.

From the color of the sunset, in the horizon, he suspected that his friends might very well be home, that is, if whoever she was—this woman—hadn't got their heads, as she wished to. Either that, or Paris was burning, and Aramis hoped Paris wasn't burning, otherwise all the chickens would get roasted before they were plucked and cleaned.

Vaguely recognizing the area he was in, he changed directions, and ran towards Rue Ferou, where Athos's residence was. He arrived there out of breath, and knocked on the door, until it was opened by a very disapproving-looking Grimaud.

Aramis thought someone might overhear him, since he was outside, on the doorstep, so he leaned in close and said in what he thought was a whisper, and yet boomed confusingly in his ears, "Grimaud, fetch your master."

"Monsieur Aramis!" Grimaud said.

"Yes, yes," Aramis said. "I'm out of breath. I was running. The thing was, she's out to kill us all, and the chickens are about to get roasted." At which point and unaccountably, he lost his hold on verticality and started tilting forward. Grimaud stopped his fall and yelled, "Bazin, curse you, leave your rosary beads, your master needs you!"

And then the world went a long way away from Aramis.

Where Athos Is Inspected;
The Lady Is the Tiger;
And Porthos Disappears

❧

ATHOS separated from Porthos, taking only the time to ask a passing gentleman in what appeared to be the livery of the Queen's house, where exactly the duchess lodged. She was, as he should have expected, quite close to the Queen's own chambers, in the sort of spacious apartments that were the envy of late-arrived provincials come to Paris to beg for royal favor.

It wasn't till Athos found himself outside her door that it occurred to him to wonder if perhaps she wasn't in at all. But a knock on the door brought him a sharp command to identify himself, and Athos, deciding that obfuscation was the best part of value and that he wasn't actually technically lying, said, "The Comte de—" and mumbled the rest.

The door flung open, and he stood staring at a child who could be no more than eight, attired in a becoming maid outfit, with a much-beribboned apron. She looked up at him with huge eyes, and he made her a very correct bow, all the while conscious of being watched. He knew, without looking up, that the duchess was just on the edge of the door and looking at him, evaluatingly. "Mademoiselle," he said, using his most polished accents, which were very polished indeed. "I crave the favor of a word with the Duchess de Chevreuse."

Fast footsteps approached the door, and an amused voice said, "Don't be silly, Josephe, let the count in."

The woman who appeared fully in Athos's field of vision was, quite frankly, a vision to behold. She was blond, and had the sort of rounded face with perfect features that always makes its possessor look very young and very innocent. Wide open grey blue eyes and a slightly tilted-up nose contrasted with a full, luscious and very adult mouth, to make the countenance bewitching. What followed beneath the neck was bewitching as well, as the pink and white neck gave way to the pink and white, rising breasts, nestled in a dress that was so low-cut that all it did was hold them up without covering them in the least. Athos could quite easily see the pink edges of her aureolas, and turned his head away before his eyes might discern that he could catch a glimpse of pink nipples amid the cream lace.

Looking away and up, he found himself being scrutinized with equally intent gaze and, from the lady's slightly parted lips just breaking on the edge of a smile, he had to assume that she approved of what she saw. Her eyes shone appreciatively as she took in the wealth of very slightly wavy silk-fine black hair and she said, "You're the Comte de . . . I'm sorry. I didn't catch the rest."

Athos smiled back, one of his practiced smiles that meant very little. "I would prefer not to give my family name. In the musketeers I am called Athos."

"Athos!" Her hands met, in an almost clap at her chest. "You are a friend of a very great friend of mine, then.

"Aramis, madam, if that is whom you mean."

"Aramis, exactly." She smiled at him, almost mockingly. "While I completely understand, monsieur, the need to go into hiding and wear an assumed name—in fact I'm sure if I were a man, I'd have killed a great many men in duels—I cannot understand why both of you must choose such strange names. And there is a third to your group of odd names, isn't there?"

"That would be my friend Porthos, madam."

"Oh, yes, the big one that everyone says is seeing a foreign princess. He always scares me a little. Too much man there, if you know what I mean."

Athos had not the slightest idea what she meant, and, as in all such situations, contented himself with bowing deeply.

She giggled as if he'd performed a particularly clever trick. "Please, come in, Monsieur le Comte," she said.

Athos thought that lately everyone seemed obsessed with his dignity, but he went in, all the same, and bowed again to the bewitching duchess who, while watching him as if he had been a particularly luscious pastry, said, "You may close the door."

Full of misgiving, considering all he had heard about the duchess and her approach to men, Athos closed the door and turned around, trying to keep his face utterly impassive. "Madam, in the last two days, your name has been mentioned to me a great deal, in a variety of circumstances, some of which must give rise to the liveliest concern, insofar as—"

"Turn around," the duchess said.

"I beg your pardon?"

"Turn around," the duchess said, and twirled her pink and white fingers in a motion, as though indicating in which way he could best please her.

Athos, never before having been ordered to twirl, except by his dancing master in the now very distant past, turned around slowly, hands at his waist. "What I mean, your grace," he said, "is that—"

"Do you ride, milord?"

"I beg your pardon?"

"Do you ride?" she asked. "Horses."

"I know how to ride, if that's what you're asking, but I've found a horse is not much use to me in Paris, and a lot of extra expense to stable, so I only borrow a horse when I need to, and I only do that on service to the King or for emergencies."

"Do you dance, then?"

This was getting somewhat past the point of ridiculousness. "Not for many years now, your grace."

"So, there is no accounting for it."

"Madam?"

"Your shape. The way your legs are so well-muscled and your back . . . You must know it's very unusual in a man of your age, for I'd wager despite very few grey hairs that you will not see thirty again."

"I don't—"

"No, of course not. No use at all giving me details, though I daresay I could find them, you know? It is not hard, when you are well-formed and female, to ask whatever questions cross one's mind. People will tell you the strangest and most absurdly intimate things, all in the absolute conviction that you have not a brain in your head. Why is that?"

Athos was starting to wonder if perhaps he were drunk—if the monumental drinking spree of the night before could have clouded his mind to the point where he couldn't make sense of a simple conversation.

"Why is what?" he asked. "I don't have the pleasure of understanding you."

"No, I quite see you don't. Sorry to disturb you." She walked around him, clockwise, eyeing him with a most intent expression. "Do you have any sons, milord?"

"No!" Athos said.

She sighed heavily. "Pity." And then in an undertone, as though speaking to someone else altogether. "The devil of it is, I'm starting to understand why Aramis refused to present you to me. I'd only seen you from afar before, and I couldn't understand it. As you know, Aramis is not in the habit of mind of being insecure. But now . . ." She sighed again, and picked up a fan from a nearby table. "Now I wonder what he could mean by telling me you don't like women. Do you not like women, Monsieur le Comte?"

Athos didn't know what to do. He wasn't stupid, and despite his hangover headache, he knew very well that he was being made fun of. The problem was how he was being made sport of and by whom. If the countess had been a man, he could have challenged her to a duel three times over by now. But, alas, as his body was telling him rather insistently, she was not a man. And alas also, she was following no conventions of discourse, neither man's nor woman's.

He couldn't imagine how to respond to her without violating more than a few societal laws. And he didn't want to spin on his heels and leave her behind, because then, somehow, she would have won. And Athos would be damned if he allowed De Chevreuse to have the best of him.

"I like women well enough," he said.

She gave a pointed look. "Yes, I can see that." And with utter suddenness, sat down on a blue-upholstered armchair and raised her feet to rest on a little padded stool, so that her skirts fell back, revealing tiny slippered feet and a pretty, well-turned ankle.

He couldn't avoid looking. He would not have been human, had he managed it. She followed his look and smiled up at him. "Delightful slippers, are they not. The embroidery was done by little Yvette, one of my maids. It is the birth of Venus."

Squinting, Athos could see a lot of flesh tone, embroidered on black satin. To see the nude lady on the slippers would mean getting rather closer to the nude ankle, and then the lady would make some remark about his liking women well enough and the evidence of it being plain.

Athos clenched his hands by his side, and turned away, towards the window, where he stood for a moment, looking out, trying to collect his thoughts, and hoping that both the evidence of his interest in the fair sex, and the pounding of blood through his temples that seemed to beat a rhythm to his headache, would subside.

"You asked to see me," the duchess said. "I assume it was not to allow me to inspect your physique?" There was something pointed to the question, as though she very much hoped that he would yield to temptation and tell her that yes, it had been exactly that, and then proceed to remove his clothes.

Athos, who knew his Bible, knew that Christ had been led by the devil to a pinnacle, and from such height, been shown all the kingdoms of the world. He wasn't prepared to compare himself to his savior, but he would be willing to bet that Christ's refusal would compare to his in the Herculean strength needed to avoid temptation. He clenched his fists and took deep breaths, and, at length, managed to extract words from the dark ocean of thoughts rushing through his mind. "I said, your Grace, that in the last two days your name seems to always be on the lips of someone, relating to something suspicious."

She took a deep, satisfied breath. "I like a good deal of intrigue, you know? Of all types. Life, otherwise, can be so horribly boring."

Athos turned around. There had been a note of sincerity there, and when he looked at her, her eyes were quite serious. He had heard De Chevreuse described as many things. Most often, people thought her a voluptuary. They thought she lived for the senses and that the senses alone interested her. Others thought that she loved playing with men—their minds as well as their bodies, and making herself the queen of a little male harem. Others, yet, thought she was more the victim than the victimizer, that she led men astray and enjoyed their pathetic attempts to escape but that she was so attracted to them she couldn't help herself.

Athos saw through all that, and to something else. In other days, he'd been often too reckless. The becalmed existence in his domains, much as he enjoyed the land and its inhabitants, had seemed flat. He remembered days of staring out over the still landscape, and wishing he could go somewhere, and do something dangerous and pulse pounding. Perhaps all young people felt like that. Or perhaps his craving was extraordinary.

In the still hours of the night, when he was being exceptionally honest with himself, which usually happened right after he'd drank enough not to flinch from the truth, but not quite enough to make himself sodden drunk, he would admit to himself that he'd fallen for Charlotte because she was dangerous. Oh, he hadn't known it openly, but he was sure there had been signs, signs that his thoughts had missed, but his body hadn't.

Since then he'd found that this distressing tendency followed him. The only women to whom he reacted—or at least reacted strongly enough to forget his reserves and his pain, were dangerous somehow—hoydens or hussies, hedonists or viragos, *religieuses*, or painfully sharp.

It was quite possible, he thought, narrowing his eyes at the duchess, that the Duchess de Chevreuse, at least if half the rumors about her and her alter ego, Marie Michon, were true, was all of those with the exception of being a professed nun. Though he would not put even that past her, should she ever find herself unencumbered by a husband. Not that she would stick to it. It would bore her after a very short time. He looked into those blue grey eyes locked on his, and felt for just a moment that he wished he were

someone else—someone who could, impunely, get involved with her. He would have traded quite a lot to put his
hands on either side of that dainty waist and carry her to
the bed on the other side of the room.[7]

But he had duties to his friends, and more than that,
should the woman involve him in some intrigue, not only
could he be caught, but he could drag his name through the
mud in all its splendid glory, when the details came out.

To protect his name, he had hanged his wife. To protect
his name, he had given it up. Great as the temptation was,
he was not about to discard his care for his name over this
woman's lovely body or even her madcap, raging mind,
that loved adventure and danger more than even he did.

"Madam," he said, making his voice very cold and very
correct. "What I meant to say is that in the last couple of
days you've been mentioned to me as running part of a plot
that might involve regicide, and also that you might have
been the instigator of a plot against my friend D'Artagnan."

"D'Artagnan! At least he uses his real name!" she said,
then shrugged. "As for regicide, what fool can have told
you that? Everyone knows I love the Queen as a sister, and
as for the King"—she shrugged—"he is my sovereign and
lord. Surely you would not accuse me of wanting to subvert the entire order of the court."

He looked into her eyes and sighed. "Madam," he said.
"I would suspect you of wishing to subvert the entire order
of the world."

She laughed, as though his words delighted her. But

---

[7] We know from both Monsieur Dumas and from the rest of these
diaries—despite extensive water damage—that indeed Athos gratified
this ambition during one of Marie Michon's precipitate flights from court
that coincided with one of his travels on behalf of the King. The result
of that wayside night was Raoul, Viscount de Bragelone.

strangely, her face acquired a grave look immediately after. "I see," she said, "exactly why Aramis didn't introduce you to me earlier. Where were you five years ago, Monsieur le Comte."

"Here. As a musketeer. As you see."

She raised an eyebrow. "Have you a wife?"

"That is . . . complicated."

"I see." She nodded. "Tell me at least that you were not free to offer for me ten years ago. Do tell me."

Ten years ago, he thought. She looked like ten years ago she would not have left her nursery. But he knew that she probably had. "I was not free," he said. "I was very far from free."

"Oh, good. That at least is one less complaint against fate," she said. And smiled archly. "And now you were telling me that someone had told you I wanted to get rid of the King. I don't know who it might be. If I would venture a guess, I'd say Richelieu, but I know you like him as much as I do, or possibly less. You must understand, though, I would never try to get rid of the King. Oh, I think as a man he is a bore and a burden. And also that he leads the Queen a very miserable life. However, he is my King." She shrugged. "There is a respect for the crown, if not for the man, and besides, you must believe I am, most sincerely, the Queen's friend. If the King were to die, then the Queen would be in effect deposed. Surely you can't suspect me of wishing that?"

Athos wasn't sure about the rest of the torrential flow of words, but he was sure those last were true. She would not wish to leave her friend dispossessed, without a country. And, if the worst happened, the Queen would very likely be sent back to her parents' house, a dowager daughter, with no position and no power. She had never had a child. Her importance would be very small, and she might not marry ever again.

No. He didn't think De Chevreuse wished that for her friend the Queen. He'd heard that she had caused one of the Queen's many miscarriages by inducing the Queen into racing her along the hallways of the palace. That he could believe. It was the sort of reckless amusement that would come to her at a moment's notice. But the idea that she would deliberately set out to depose a friend . . . no. That he could not believe. Madcap and in love with adventure the duchess might be. Ill-intentioned, never.

He inclined his head, conceding the point. "It was the Cardinal," he said. "But he said, first, that you intended to kill him, and then that you intended, perhaps, to kill the King. I will say I believed the first and not the last."

Her eyes danced with amusement. "Oh, if one were to be punished for wishing to kill someone, then I would have lost my head on the gallows twenty times over." She paused. "Possibly twenty times each day. I do wish to kill the Cardinal, though I must say I don't think any of my plans has ever been good enough to achieve such a noble purpose." She looked at him and raised a perfectly shaped eyebrow. "Monsieur le Comte doesn't think the purpose worthy?"

Athos raised an eyebrow, matching her gesture. "Monsieur le Comte," he said, "would have agreed with you in the heat of his early twenties. But he is now, as you've said"—he bowed his head at her—"past thirty. And being past thirty, he's started to wonder if all his best-intentioned actions have the effect he desires. Madam, we might get rid of Richelieu and saddle ourselves with something far worse."

"How so?" she asked, staring intently at him. "How might someone be worse than Richelieu?"

"He could be less intelligent, your grace. Anyone less intelligent would not only be worse for France, but he would not be nearly as good an adversary."

She laughed again, that delightful laughter, as though he had surprised her in the most wonderful way. "Perhaps, yes. That would be a pity. However, perhaps maybe a slightly less intelligent adversary would be good too? He wouldn't come so close to hitting the mark, quite so often. And Monsieur le Comte, you must know I am not at all sure of the Cardinal's being good for France."

Athos shrugged. "I'm never sure. Some people . . ." He shrugged again. "I am sure he thinks he's doing what's best for France. Not sure if it's truly the best. He's either a more far-seeing statesman than I could hope to be, even had my bend of mind run that way, or he is more ambitious than anyone I've ever read about, and more reckless. Think, though—who could have guessed the result of Brutus's assassination of Caesar. Brutus was—at least according to some—trying to preserve the republic, and yet he ushered in one of the most famous empires in the world. History is a tricky thing, when one is trying to write it."

She shifted her dainty feet, displaying yet more of her ankle in the process. "Milord, I have never wanted to write history. Just to make it go the way I wish it to for a very short time. If history is a river, I'm the boy floating sticks on it, milord. I don't think it will make any difference, in the long run."

He looked her over. "I would hope not, Madam," he said. "I would hope not. Most influence one can have on history seems to be bad."

She smiled at him. "What a dreary philosophy." And smiled wider when he bowed. "Let me tell you, though, that I have no intentions of having the King killed, so if what you wished was to ask me that . . . I have answered." She looked at him, impish and challenging.

"Well, someone else," Athos said, knowing he was skating on thin ice, but unable to stop, because he must ascertain how involved in this she was, "has told me that you had a letter addressed to the Duke de Vendôme, the King's brother . . . and I wondered . . . since yet someone else has told me, that you have an interest in preventing monsieur's marriage to Mademoiselle de Montpensier."

"Certainly," she said, a little hot flush rising to the rounded cheeks. "Certainly I have an interest in preventing monsieur's marriage. The King's younger brother and heir to the throne is seventeen. How will it look if he has children? Everyone will then know that the royal line will continue that way. The King . . . Ah, the King is the King and he will retain his court. But the Queen will become utterly irrelevant—a woman without children, without a stake in the future. Both King and Cardinal mistreat her and ignore her now, when not actively planning to divorce her and set her aside. How do you think they will view her then." She finished the speech, her little fists tight in her lap, and she looked at him, as though thinking she must have scared or shocked him. "I beg your pardon," she said. "I told you I am loyal to my friends."

"It does you credit," Athos said, finding his voice unaccountably hoarse. "To be loyal to your friends."

"So are you," she said. "From what I heard, and if I recall from your list, one of the accusations against me was that I had, somehow, managed to entrap your friends."

"Madam . . . The friend of another of my friends says that she heard you say that we would have a duel or a fight on our hands, and that you said it with such malice, she understood we were to fight a duel that night."

For just a moment, the duchess looked baffled. It was not a put-on, but the surprised, utterly blank face of a woman who is struggling to recollect something and cannot find even a hint of it in her memory. Then, unexpectedly, her laughter pealed forth like a ringing of bells. She looked at Athos with a lopsided smile. "My dear sir, if what I referred to were a duel, the swords involved would be quite fleshy." And to his shocked expression, "Monsieur le Comte, if you must know, your friend, Aramis, had thrice put off a meeting with me. Once because—he said—the young Gascon needed him to be a second in a duel. The next time, because your friend, Porthos, was in need of comfort and company, his friend having put off her own meeting with him, because her husband was suspicious of their relationship. And the third time,"—with a little bow towards Athos—"because, you, monsieur, seemed troubled and were drinking and he was afraid you would again gamble money you do not have."

"Oh, last week," Athos said. "He was an infernal nuisance, I recall, and clung to me like a wet shirt."

The duchess laughed, once more. "Aramis can be very earnest. It is easy to ignore that because he is also . . . well, wild and naughty in many ways. But it is the naughtiness of a good man, you know. His instincts are for good. And his broken heart troubles him more than he wishes anyone to know." She sighed. "Monsieur Athos, when I said you would have a fight on your hands, it was because I felt as if your friendship was wresting him, to be blunt, from my bed. It was that fight I referred to, and if your kind informer had listened more closely, she would have heard what weapon I intended to employ in bringing him to beg for quarter." She smiled, her lips slightly parted and moist. "But you spoke of conspiracy. Surely that could be no more than an idle threat. How did you think I had conspired?"

He longed to kiss her lips, to take her in his arms, to feel the round firmness of her breasts against his chest. But he did not and could not even speak of it. Instead, he bowed a little. "I'm sorry. If you did not mean anything about a duel by that, it is highly unlikely you were implicated in a conspiracy." In truth, he wasn't at all sure of it, but he felt as if he couldn't think clearly until he got out of her presence. And yet, a part of him did not want to leave her at all.

"I am sure I am implicated in several conspiracies, most of them private, but I promise you I have no intention of hurting you or your friends. I am loyal to my friends, remember. And Aramis is my friend."

Athos looked at her and asked the question he had not meant to ask—in fact the question he had meant to never ask, no matter how long he stayed. "How close a friend is Aramis? Are you . . . are you very fond of him?"

She laughed. "Aramis is a good friend, but not . . . that close. He has a disturbing habit of preaching theology in the most awkward of situations, did you know that?"

"Heavens, yes, often in the middle of a duel."

"It wasn't a duel I was thinking of, Monsieur le Comte. But yes. He is, as I said, a good man. And I am not a good woman. But I am . . . very fond of him. And he is very good at providing that excitement that has little or nothing to do with danger." Her eyes were veiled and challenging. "Besides there is something in me that makes me long, very much, to corrupt the innocent. Aramis was only a seminarian, not a priest, but it is close enough for corruption purposes."

Athos wished to despise her for her desires, or at least for speaking of them so freely, but instead, all he could find himself thinking was that he was very much— passionately, in fact—jealous of Aramis.

He bowed to her, abruptly, feeling suddenly very old. Old enough to be past the temptations of the flesh. At least that was what his mind insisted on telling him, even if his body refused to listen.

"Your grace," he said, softly. "I believe it is time I should leave. You've answered all my impertinent questions. I should thank you and leave."

She rose from her chair and came up to him, till she was so close that his nose was full of a cloying perfume of violets and something else that he could only think was her own, unique smell. "Must you go?" she asked. "Without dueling?"

"Lady," he said, feeling his heart heavy as lead within him, even as it pumped madly in his chest, even as his arms longed to envelop her. "You don't wish to engage in that sort of duel with me. I blight all I touch."

And then, without warning, she was on her tiptoes and stretching. She just managed to touch her soft, moist lips to his, but the touch of her lips was like the feel of a branding iron, and her hands, on his shoulder, were like the touch of rain after a long and parched summer.

The last of Athos's self-control fled him. His hands, like mad things, too long confined, escaped him, and settled themselves on either side of her waist. He lifted her. She was scarcely heavier than a small child. He pulled her against himself, raising her, so that her breasts rested, heated and firm, against his hard chest, so that their mouths were at the same level, and his lips could meet hers, and his tongue penetrate the moist haven of her mouth. Her tongue met his, and entwined with it, in a long kiss in which—for Athos—time stopped and breath became something not at all necessary.

He breathed through her, and lived from her touch, and their hearts beat together, one beat echoing each other. Only the moan that escaped him—long and painfully drawn, like the lament of a lost soul, woke him from the idyll. He knew better than to allow his body sway, for every time he did, it meant his heart was yet more bruised. Presently he should grow as much scar tissue on his heart and soul as would make his ability to feel love or friendship even vanish utterly.

He put her down, almost abruptly. She looked bewildered and also a little stunned, as though she'd expected anything but that passionate kiss. Athos bowed, not daring speak, not daring look at her again. And bolted for the door like a man escaping a great danger. Not danger to himself, he thought, but danger to her. He should not be trusted when he got past all his self-controls.

Out in the hallway, he was aware of her gaze burning a hole into his back and looked back, for just a moment, to see her framed in the doorway of her lodgings, her hair askew, her hand covering her mouth, either to not allow the sensation to escape, or to hide her dismay.

He realized he could still taste her in his mouth—a hint of honey, a scent like rosemary. Shaking his head, he thought that he was indeed very jealous of Aramis.

Some moments later, climbing down a staircase, he noticed that passing valets and maids looked very oddly at him, and realized that his hair was all askew.

He'd just managed to comb it with his fingers and re-bind it, when he reached the kitchens.

And there, in the midst of the steam, the confusion, the screams and instructions that accompanied the tasks of making dinner for all the inhabitants, permanent and temporary, of the royal palace, he saw no Porthos.

He looked again, but it wasn't as though Porthos could hide himself easily. On the best of days, in the middle of a company of identically dressed musketeers, Porthos stood out like an oak in a field of daisies. Though he wasn't that much bigger than everyone else, he was large enough to call attention, his height allowing him at least a head advantage over the next tallest man, and his shoulders easily twice the width of anyone else's shoulders. And his flaming red hair and beard weren't exactly discreet in a world that had a lot more drab brunettes and dull blonds.

After the third sweep of his gaze through the kitchens, he motioned a young man, who looked like he might be a cook's aid, to come close, and asked, in a shout, to be heard against the din of the kitchen, "Have you seen a redheaded musketeer, about this tall?"

The man looked a little confused, then smiled. "Oh, yes, he came in and wanted to talk to the head cook, but it turned out it was the old head cook. The new one doesn't know him. So he said, he said, thank you and never mind and somehow—none of us knows how—he disappeared with a dish of pigeons stewed with apples. He said . . ." He frowned a little. "That he was going to the Bastille. And, you know, the cook, though he is very stern, said that the musketeer must be crazy. He wasn't about to denounce him for the theft of a dish of pigeons."

But Athos wasn't about to devote any time to the pigeons. Instead, his mind was telling him the madman had gone to the Bastille. Exactly what he had promised Athos he wouldn't do. And why should Athos have believed him? No one else seemed to be listening to Athos's warnings.

Standing there, aware he had gone pale, staring at the young cook's aid, he wondered if Porthos would need him. Should he go to the Bastille, anyway, and try to extricate his friend?

But then a thought formed that God looked after madmen and children, and that Porthos could combine a good deal of both. Athos was starved and didn't wish to steal a dish of pigeons.

At any rate, his imagination was beggared to think what role that dish might play in Porthos's cunning plan. Was it simply something to eat on the way, to keep his strength up for the ordeal of breaking into the Bastille? Or else, did Porthos assume he would be arrested for at least some time, and in that spirit had decided to take some food with him till his friends could spring him? Alternately, was it the bribe with which he wished to gain his way in to Mousqueton?

Athos could not imagine, and was sure—in fact, would stake his life on it—that no matter what strange ideas he might conjure, they wouldn't approach the amazing and bizarre simplicity of Porthos's plan.

He hoped the god of madmen was on duty and had a close watch on his friend, but right now, hungover, confused and hungry, Athos wouldn't be any use to Porthos. He would go home and see if Grimaud could prepare him a simple meal. And then, if night advanced and Porthos did not return, then Athos would go looking for him.

Monsieur D'Artagnan's Social Scruples;
A Guard's Conscience;
Where a Good Head Is an Unreliable Asset

ᐤ

D'ARTAGNAN had allowed himself to rest a little before he finished dressing to go to his dinner. Or rather, he'd meant it to be only the shortest of rests, and then to go to his dinner early, and perhaps to give some excuse. But he was still hungover, and the inside of his head felt as though it were entirely covered in cobwebs.

His rest prolonged itself, so that when he woke up the sun had almost set completely and a deep shadow prevailed the room. And Planchet stood by his bed, shifting his weight from foot to foot, as nervous as a cat in a circle of dogs.

As he opened his eyes and gave the boy a puzzled look, Planchet said, in an anxious half whisper. "Monsieur," he said. "Milady has sent a carriage. It is waiting at the door. Her footman is in the entrance room."

D'Artagnan felt his heart skip, both because being picked up in a carriage was a novel experience, and because he couldn't like it. His dreams had been tormented by images of a fleur-de-lis branded into soft, female flesh, and by the look on Athos's face when he spoke of women—that desolate look that was like land after fire, when everything has burned, even the stubble of the fields, and nothing remains behind but barren expanses of nothing.

His wakening mind seemed to have decided that not only did he not want to go to dinner with this beauty with the English title, but he would go a long way to avoid it. Even if she weren't Athos's wife, after all, she was a lady—titled. And while he had nothing against titled ladies, he thought that he would much prefer to keep his affairs simple. Or rather, his affair, as he only had one.

He thought, as he sat up, of how he would feel if he were to find that his Constance had gone to dinner with some British earl. He rather suspected his sword would come out of its sheath and the earl would better be very good with his own sword, or the world would be one English earl to the less. So how could he do this to Constance? It wasn't as though she could fight a duel with the English countess.

But here was Planchet, informing him that the carriage was waiting, and he told himself his feelings were only the result of the shadows in the room, and of the remains of his hangover. He would probably find she was not Athos's wife at all, but merely some woman who resembled her. Possibly even an Englishwoman.

And while he had no intention at all of betraying his Constance—for all his Constance had ripped up at him like a fishwife at her errant husband—it wouldn't hurt to go and have dinner in the best of society. Nor would it hurt him to know someone with title and more power than Constance.

He'd been long enough in the capital to know that much of what happened was the result of whom you knew, and who might be willing to vouch for you. As such, he thought that he would do well to expand his circle. "Tell the footman I will be there as soon as may be," he said.

Rising from bed, he put on the blue venetians that Aramis had enjoined him to buy only last week, and he

slipped on the doublet that went with them. He saw his reflection in the lead-paned window, cut up by the lead
panes, and didn't see a dazzle of gold and lace shining
back at him, and so he hoped that the suit looked distinguished and expensive but not Porthos-like dazzling, as he
would hate to appear vulgar.

Pulling his hair back and tying it tightly, he stepped out
into the sitting room, where the footman—a tall English-
man with pale blond hair—dressed all in livery was waiting for him. He led D'Artagnan, without a word, and
D'Artagnan followed him, thinking that this was all very
foolish, but he felt like he was a prisoner.

And even though milady's carriage was deep and
comfortable—a vehicle fashioned on the latest mode, with
arms he didn't recognize painted on the door, and the most
cushiony seats he'd ever had the honor of occupying—her
black horses perfect and perfectly trained to work with
each other, and her driver and the footman absolutely ob-
sequious and formal, he went on feeling as though he were
under arrest.

Nor did the impression diminish when he stopped in
front of a handsome town house, and he was led down a
vast hallway, lined all with candles, to a sitting room where
she waited.

She offered him both her hands and greeted him as her
savior, the man who had rescued her from a fate worse than
death. Wearing a green dress trimmed in different tones of
green lace, she was beautiful and elusive as a forest creature. The hair she'd worn loose when he'd last seen her
was now gathered in a net of spun gold that shone just
slightly darker than the hair it confined. A smell rose from
her, heady and subtle like the scent of a summer night. Her
bare arms were unornamented save for a simple circle of
gold. And she smiled, just enough.

When he had greeted her, bending over her hands as he

knew was expected of him, she allowed him to take her in to dinner. There were no other guests.

Her dining room like the rest of the house was perfectly appointed. The servants circled, serving dishes that D'Artagnan had never tasted before, and they all filled his mouth with wonderful flavors.

She asked him questions—about his mother, about his father, about his friends. He tried to answer in a way that wouldn't compromise anyone, should she be, in fact, Athos's wife and an agent of the Cardinal himself. But as the night went on, she dismissed the servants, and he started finding his tongue considerably more difficult to control.

Perhaps it was the wine. After she dismissed the servants, she'd start serving him the wine herself, cup after cup of some sparkling vintage, that tasted deceptively sweet and light. He'd tried to refuse it, but she'd laughed at his gesture, and just added more wine to his cup. And she'd cajoled him and smiled at him, till he did not know what he was doing.

His mind became more clouded than he ever remembered wine making it. Perhaps it was the fact that he'd drunk so much just the day before. Perhaps the drunkenness built on his so recently disordered senses. Or perhaps he simply had no head for liquor, or not such a head as he'd always assumed he had.

He never understood how, but he found himself in her bed, quite stripped and under the covers, next to her. And she was under the covers too, her hair loose down her back, wearing a nightgown of the sheerest silk.

He tried to speak and said something about Constance. Even he wasn't sure what he'd said, or what it meant, and all it got him in return was laughter. "Your village lass back in Gascony," milady said, ruthlessly, "wouldn't know how to do this." And in saying it, she touched him in a way he didn't even know it was possible to be touched.

Her hands were knowing, as was her mouth, and his confused mind managed to form the thought that there couldn't possibly be any courtesans, any women who lived by the trade of pleasure who were more skilled at the arts of love than this Englishwoman.

And yet not all her efforts could cause him to rise to the occasion. He'd have liked to think that it was his fidelity to Constance, but he was very much afraid it was his excess of alcohol.

When he tried to apologize, milady laughed at him. "Don't worry. It will wear off, and you will still be here, in the morning."

And then she'd blown out the candle, and D'Artagnan had fallen asleep. Naked, in milady's bed.

The Many Uses of a Dish of Pigeons;
A Parlor Boarder in the Bastille;
A Confused Tale of Young Love

⌒

PORTHOS walked along the darkening streets, a dish of pigeons held firmly in his right hand. Fortunately, it was the type of dish they used in the palace kitchens, designed to be carried from the depths of the palace to attics of the palace on the opposing side—that is, designed to preserve as much as possible of its heat and quality even though some poor valet or maid might have to carry it the equivalent of many, many city blocks, before it ever reached its destination. It was made of heavy clay and covered with a lid of heavier clay.

This was part of the reason Porthos had taken it, of course. Had it been in some silver chafing dish, or hidden away in some concoction of painted porcelain, he would have known it was a dish destined for some high personage who had brought his own dishes with him to the palace.

Personages high enough to do that would make life very uncomfortable for the poor valet or maid who waylaid the food. And worse, the plate often being worth far more than the food, they might very well bring up charges against the musketeer who took them.

But this humble clay dish meant that the food was

meant to go to one of the palace guests who was either a minor nobleman or perhaps, even, with some luck, an accountant or an artist brought in to serve the court. Which meant it was safe to take.

As for why he'd taken it, Porthos couldn't have explained that exactly until he was well away from the palace and working at a fast clip towards the forbidding facade of the Bastille. Truthfully, his ideas were normally like this, and he rarely knew what he meant to do till he did it, and this time was no different. It was as though some better informed Porthos thought things through up in the depths of Porthos's mind, and, being as unable to translate thought to words as the real Porthos, he only revealed his plans to the musketeer as they came up to the instant when he had to know.

This time, by the time he reached the Bastille, he had a fairly clear idea of what he meant to do—he approached the nearest entrance, carrying his dish of pigeons, and hailed the guard—a dark-haired man whose dingy uniform looked as though it hadn't been washed in several lifetimes. On seeing Porthos so near, he straightened from his previous position of lolling, bonelessly, against the nearest wall. "Holla," he said, and before he could get to the qui vive, Porthos answered back boomingly, "Holla."

And then before the man could say anything more, he launched into a hearty explanation of his circumstances. "I wish to see my servant Boniface, who also answers to Mousqueton, before this dish of pigeons with apples grows cold."

The guard frowned at him, a squinting expression that seemed to indicate a long-unused brain made some attempt to become active behind the small, porcine eyes. "A . . . a dish of pigeons?" he asked, quiveringly.

"Certainly," Porthos said. "A dish of pigeons. It was prepared expressly by the Princess de—But one must not be indiscreet. The thing is that my dear friend the Princess is very fond of Mousqueton and she prepared him this dish with her very own hands. In the circumstances, you must realize, my dear man, it would be quite fatal if the dish should grow cold before Mousqueton enjoys it."

The guard looked at Porthos with a disoriented expression, then looked around himself, as if to ascertain his surroundings, and, finally, turning to Porthos said in an outraged voice, "Monsieur! This is the Bastille!"

"Of course," Porthos said, reassuringly. "I was counting on that, because, you see, Mousqueton is held in the Bastille. Indeed, it would be very inconvenient if I were to find I was somewhere else altogether."

"Monsieur!" the man said disbelievingly. "People get . . . get tortured here. There are people who disappear in here and are never heard of." He hissed out these words with a dramatic flair that seemed to indicate his own place of employment awed him. "And you come in with a dish of pigeons for an inmate."

Porthos disciplined his face to slight annoyance. "Oh, I know, it seems fantastical, but as I said, my dear friend, the Princess de—well, she has made this dish of pigeons because she knows Mousqueton favors it. Her own recipe." He smiled, foolishly. "And you know, her husband the Prince de—but no. I can't tell you. Suffice it to say he would have the head of any man who displeased her. For he dotes most forcibly on her. And if she hears I was barred from taking her own special recipe to her own dear Mousqueton . . . well . . . I can't swear how she'll react." He looked sheepish. "I wouldn't swear to it that she won't react badly. A very uncertain temper, has my dear Princess."

The man looked caught between two uncomfortable decisions. He stared at Porthos, then at the dish in Porthos's hand. "Open it up, you. To show there is nothing there but food."

"But . . ." Porthos said. "The Princess. If the dish grows cold or congeals . . ."

"Never mind the Princess. If you don't show us there's nothing dangerous in there, you shall never get in."

Sighing and with a show of much reluctance, Porthos opened the dish. The aroma of the stewed pigeons wafted up. The guard took a deep breath, and Porthos decided it was time for more foolish expatiating. "See how good it looks and how well it smells. She has never told me the recipe, but I believe she uses little currants and just a dash of brandy."

The guard sighed. "You may cover it," he said, then looked at Porthos. "The thing is, monsieur," he said, "that no matter what your Princess thinks, I'm not supposed to let just anyone come in and visit the prisoners. I suppose you don't even know when he was arrested."

"On the contrary," Porthos said. "He was arrested three days ago and a friend of mine has spoken to the Cardinal and ensured that nothing bad will happen to Mousqueton until . . . that is, until his eminence has ascertained a few things relating to the case."

He thought that showing that the Cardinal and Porthos had common friends could not possibly hurt his case, and, in fact, the guard looked at him very intently for a moment, then said, "Oh, one of the parlor boarders! Why didn't you tell me that?"

He walked towards the back of his guard booth, and pulled on a handle on the wall. From somewhere, deep within the bowels of the fortress turned prison, came the sound of a bell tolling. Moments later, a man who looked like he hadn't shaved in at least three years, and whose uniform made the first guard's appear a model of cleanliness and pressing, came to the door at the back of the booth.

"Holla, Gaston," the first guard said. "This gentleman here is here on behalf of a Princess, to see one of the parlor borders—the one they call Boniface or Mousqueton."

"The rat!" Gaston said, which seemed like an odd enough comment, since neither Porthos, nor Mousqueton could be in any way confused with small rodents. He looked Porthos up and down, and shrugged, with a sort of resigned look that seemed to say it wasn't any of his business, and besides, he was there to follow orders. He motioned with his hand, and turned.

Porthos followed, holding onto his dish of pigeons with both hands, to prevent the top from falling off. He followed the guard, noting with interest that they were in a dark, narrow passageway and that Porthos had to lower his head at some spots. He heard raucous voices from elsewhere, and there was the sort of smell that suggested that somewhere, not far away, a stream of open sewage flowed. But he didn't see anything really shocking here. The lanterns that illuminated the corridor, at not nearly sufficient intervals, showed dark golden stone wall, marred here and there by what could be moss. There were doors inset in the wall, but no bars and no obvious cells. Somewhere else, someone appeared to be rattling chains.

The guard stopped in front of one of the doors and, slow and deliberate, reached to his belt for a very large key ring. As he selected a key—which seemed to Porthos an impossible task, since they all looked exactly alike—he looked up at Porthos. "They say as he's in for murder, and I must say, sir, I have trouble believing that."

Porthos smiled. "We're quite sure he's innocent," he said. "So you should have trouble believing it."

"It's not that, sir," the man said. "It's just that they said he killed to hide his theft, and I don't think that's possible."

Porthos raised his eyebrows.

The man opened his hands wide. "Well, the thing is, see, sir, that he is such an accomplished and efficient thief that should he choose to steal something, I don't think anyone would have found out. Why, since he's been here, there have been bottles missing from the guard's . . . that is, the place where we keep our bottles and our food. Everyday something else disappears."

Porthos thought this sounded eerily familiar, but did not wish to admit it. Instead he said, in an outraged tone, "How can you know it's him?"

The guard looked at him with a slow, patient look. "Well, sir . . . if we didn't keep finding empty bottles in his cell it would help. But we've looked all over the room for how he might be managing to get up and go to the storage area, and we can't find it. We also cannot understand how he can possibly decide to remain in here, if he has the ability to get out that easily. Some of the men think he's a sorcerer. I, myself, think he's the best thief I've ever met. So I don't believe he would have to kill to conceal a theft."

Porthos nodded, and didn't dare say anything. Part of this, because he was afraid he would laugh if he opened his mouth. The guard sighed, and opened the door. "I don't suppose you're here to free him or to allow him to escape?"

"No, you see, there is this dish of pigeons."

"Pity, because we are starting to feel the loss of wine," the guard said. And, with that, he threw the door open.

What greeted Porthos was not nearly so shocking a spectacle as he expected. In fact, it was not much different from some lodgings he'd endured in wartime. In fact, it was probably better than many such lodgings. It was at least well covered and the narrow bed, up near the tiny, barred window, looked like it had a mattress and at least one set of sheets. And there was no visible vermin jumping off the sheets.

Mousqueton, who had been sitting on the bed, holding a bottle, looked up, in surprise. "Master!" he said, and almost dropped his bottle. "Monsieur Porthos!"

Porthos looked at him and smiled. "I've brought you a plate of pigeons, my dear friend, which the dear Princess prepared for you."

"Madame de C—"

"Discreet, Mousqueton, discreet. And yes, the Princess herself made you these."

Mousqueton smiled. "And I didn't even know she could cook," he said, as he received the covered platter from Porthos's hand.

"I'll stay while he eats," Porthos told the guard, waving him away. He didn't know if it was the bottle in Mousqueton's hand, which had given the guard a pained expression, or if it was the fact that he was being ordered like a lackey that made the man sigh heavily.

"I'll leave the door unlocked," he said, in a tone of great hopefulness. "Perhaps monsieur will be so kind as to take the rather large rat away."

"A rat?" Mousqueton said, puzzled, looking up from his platter.

"Never mind," Porthos said. "I believe the gentleman is being what Monsieur Aramis calls metaphorical."

Mousqueton raised his eyebrows but said nothing, as he tucked into the pigeons with apples. Presently, Porthos removed a large, clean handkerchief from his sleeve, and handed it to the servant. "You're going to need it for your fingers," he said. "They don't seem to have provided you with silverware."

"No. I don't know, perhaps they're afraid I'll use it to escape."

"I daresay by now they are afraid of you on principle. Mousqueton, must you be so abominable? How drunk are you?"

Mousqueton looked puzzled. "Oh, not at all, sir," he said. "I've nursed the bottles I get off and on. Though I've been known to pour some out the window, if they've been particularly trying. They hate it when I waste their wine."

"You don't mind if I ask, but how did you manage to get access to the wine? And why the wine?"

He grinned at Porthos. "Walk all the way to that wall," he said.

Porthos did, walking to the point indicated. "And now?" he asked.

"Now kneel and count three flagstones from the corner."

Porthos obeyed.

"Now pry up the third flagstone."

"Mousqueton! I have no tools."

"None needed. Try it, sir."

Porthos tried it. To his surprise, the flagstone, not very big at all, came up handily. Beneath it was a subfloor of wood, which presumably rested on top of beams. There was a neat hole in the wood. Broken, now sawed, but all the same too regular in shape for it to be the result of rotting. And looking through that hole, Porthos could see, beneath them, what looked like a well-stocked cellar. He sat back, whistling softly.

"You found it like this?"

Mousqueton gave him a jaundiced look. "Monsieur! No. I was bored. I tried every flagstone and found that one somewhat loose. After working at it for some hours, it came up, handily. Then I found that the bottom of my bed's legs also came off," he pulled up the covering to show that each of the sturdy legs of his plain bed had a metal surrounding. "I used that to dig through the subfloor. That the bottles were right underneath was mere coincidence."

"And you reach them how?"

Mousqueton shrugged. "I happened to have some cord in my sleeve," he said.

Porthos nodded, still bewildered. Mousqueton's ability to not only carry the oddest objects about his person, but to keep them there despite very thorough searches had long since become one of the musketeers' jokes. What he couldn't understand was how the rope might have helped the young man get the bottles.

Mousqueton grinned, and taking a looped cord from inside his sleeve, showed Porthos how he had a sort of noose at the end of it. Dropping it through the hole, he got the neck of a bottle. The very process of pulling up the rope tightened the noose, and this brought the bottle, wobbling and shaking, up to the hole in the floor.[8]

"You are extraordinary," Porthos said.

Mousqueton blushed a little. "To own the truth," he said, "the hardest part about the whole thing is to put the flagstone back, and make sure some dirt is swept back into the crevice, so they don't look there." As he spoke, he put the stone back in place, and dragged his foot to sweep some dirt into the crevice. Then he returned to his dish. "But you did not come here," he said, pulling the cork out of the bottle by means of the little thread inserted there for the purpose, "to ask me about my ways of getting wine, and probably not either, to bring me pigeons, though I thank you, and Madame Coquenard for the thought."

Porthos shook his head. "Nothing to do with her. I got it from the palace kitchens. It was lying on a table, and no one was guarding it."

"Monsieur Porthos, I am proud," Mousqueton said, bowing, a little humor in his eyes. "And all for my sake?"

"No. Or rather, yes, but . . ." In a tumble, he related everything that had been happening, omitting only Hermengarde's death. He tried, but when it came to it, he couldn't bring himself to tell Mousqueton that story. The thing was, in recent times, he'd seen Aramis survive the death of his lover—if indeed he had survived it. There were still

---

[8]He repeats this trick later on, in the quite different circumstances that Monsieur Dumas related. It must have seemed incredible to Monsieur Dumas, who perhaps lacked the access to these documents, because he found it necessary to explain such a brilliant piece of deductive theft by relating it to the customs of the North American continent.

days that Porthos wondered. And he suspected that Aramis wondered too. And he'd seen the look on Athos's face when speaking of his long-lost wife. He simply couldn't face seeing Mousqueton's expression crumple like that. Not while the poor man was here, away from Porthos and from all his friends who might support him and comfort him.

So, absent that one distressing fact, Mousqueton listened to everything intently. "She was going to accept my proposal, then?" he said.

"You didn't know that?" Porthos asked.

"She'd never yet told me," he said. He looked somewhat worried. "Is she . . ."

"I think she is well," Porthos said, crossing his fingers as much as might be, and telling himself that he was after all speaking of Hermengarde's soul, which would, doubtlessly, be in heaven.

Mousqueton frowned, which seemed like a very odd response to such a question. "The thing is, monsieur, you see, that Pierre Langelier is a very good-looking man. He looks a lot like Monsieur Aramis, in fact. And though I was willing to marry her, to . . . you know, raise her child as mine, I wanted to make quite sure that *that* was all over before I did. One thing is to marry someone knowing they made a mistake once, and another and completely different to marry her and know you are going to be cuckolded lifelong. One I was ready to accept, the other one never."

"Hermengarde said—says that you were suspicious of her relationship with the armorer's son, but that, in her heart, there was never any other but you."

"In her heart . . ." Mousqueton said, and shrugged. "Perhaps not. But in her arms there was."

"Are you sure of this?" Porthos asked. "Or is it just your unfortunately suspicious nature?"

"Oh, my nature, surely, but my nature is greatly bolstered

by my having walked in on her, in her sleeping room at the palace, in Langelier's arms. He has this uniform . . . at least it is not really a uniform, but a blue suit, of such cut and style that it makes him look like a musketeer. I suspect this makes it easier for him to get into the palace, and he'd got into the palace, and when I came in . . ." He shrugged. "I don't wish to describe it. Let us just establish the child could be either of ours."

Porthos thought that Athos would say that women were, after all, the devil. But Porthos could not echo it. The thing was, with the lives they lived—the lives they all lived—they might be alive in a month and they might not. Porthos knew how much women craved security. Even his Athenais, whom his death would not leave either destitute or abandoned in the world, was known to scold him most fiercely for his perceived failings—particularly those that regularly put him in the way of men animated by a murderous intent and armed with sharp, pointed objects. She was, for some reason, convinced that Porthos did it only to vex her.

How much more would a woman feel that way, if she were dependent on the man for her chances at a future and at her child's future at that?

Mousqueton seemed to read Porthos's mind in his eyes. "It wasn't, you know, that I didn't understand her. Of course, I did. He might be a gambler and a bit wild, but he was the heir to a thriving business, a man with something to himself, some substance to spend."

"And were you talking to his father when . . ." Porthos started. "I mean, what do you remember happening? Exactly?"

Mousqueton rubbed the top of his head. "The devil of it," he said, "is that I only remember very confused things. I remember waking up, of course, and the corpse right here, and Faustine screaming her damn fool head nearby. And then, before I could fully open my eyes, for the infernal pain in my head, the Cardinal's Guards were there, holding me. It was a devilish thing."

Porthos nodded in understanding. "But nothing before that?" he said.

Mousqueton sighed. "I remember going in with sword and . . . working out some terms."

"Terms?"

"Oh, he wanted . . ." Mousqueton shrugged. "He wanted one of us to find out exactly where and how much his son owed. It seems his gambling habit is worse than I'd thought, and his father wanted to know everything he owed. Of course . . ." He hesitated. "He was couching it all under the terms that if Pierre had truly blotted his copy book that badly, he would disinherit him. Something about sending him to the country, to be a smith, which I know for a fact he wouldn't do, since Pierre is one of the best armorers in the country and his father was very proud of it. But he was saying that he would, you know, like people talk when they're very upset. And he said that all his money and his business would then go to Faustine." He rubbed his hand backwards through his hair, as though trying to comb it. It did nothing but increase the wildness with which it fanned around his face. "As though, you know, I could marry her for a few more coins . . ." He shrugged. "And as though I had any idea what to do with an armory. He was telling me, I remember, something about how the man he had trained—not Pierre, but the apprentice—could run it for me very profitably, and all I'd have to do was keep Faustine happy." He frowned. "Which wouldn't be such a bad deal, if only I thought anyone could."

Where Monsieur D'Artagnan Wakes Up;
The Strangeness of a Strange Bed;
Fleur-de-Lis

∽

D'ARTAGNAN woke up. The bed felt wrong. Too soft beneath him, and too hot too, as he appeared to be sinking halfway into a feather bed. The covers above him were far too suffocating, also. They increased his feeling of being hot, and also made him feel as if he could barely breathe.

He threw them back from his body and tried to think. He'd gone to dinner with milady, last night. That much he remembered. And also that milady had given him far too much wine. But how had he come to be naked on her bed? He could not remember. Probably the wine.

A look to the side showed him that she was under the covers, awake, looking at him. "Are you ready now, Monsieur le Guard?" she asked, her voice seductive, rising from the welter of sheets, her high breasts all the more prominent-seeming by being encompassed in a froth of silk.

But D'Artagnan was fully awake now, and fully alive to the possibilities and to everything that might have happened and might happen.

He remembered Planchet's story. It seemed impossible that this blond beauty was Athos's lost and infamous wife. And it seemed impossible that she might have drugged his wine, but unless D'Artagnan's head for alcohol had inexplicably failed, drugging it was what she had, undeniably, done.

And while he could appreciate her beauty—which seemed even more pronounced under the light of day, the question remained of why she would want to sleep with him. Oh, he could understand Constance, at least at first, before she had—as he hoped she now had—found better reasons to care for him. Constance, in her confined life, shuttling between palace, where she was under the eye of her godfather, and her home, under the aegis of her much older husband, could not possibly have met anyone more dazzling than D'Artagnan—such as he was.

She had met a young, wild man, and had been attracted to him for that youth, which she did not share with her husband, and for the wildness which she'd spent most of her life trying to suppress. The love—and D'Artagnan truly hoped she loved him, because he surely loved her—had come later. But that had been the initial attraction.

Now he was sure—as sure as he was of breathing—that milady had her share of acquaintances who were far more dazzling and interesting than D'Artagnan. Noble, beautiful and doubtlessly connected, she could have her share of titled heads. Even if callow youth were what she wanted, there were a good many young bucks of good family and better looks than D'Artagnan, men she could exhibit abroad, displaying her court and her conquests.

So why had she decided upon D'Artagnan, on the glance of a moment, on the pretext that he had saved her? Why had she conceived such a strong desire for him that she must drag him to her bed and attempt to have her very complex, and rather more knowing than he expected, way with him?

Unless, D'Artagnan thought, she was indeed Athos's wife and had informed herself of the friendship that united the four inseparables, that friendship which had, at many times and different places been the saving—both physical and spiritual—of all of them.

If it were so, doubtlessly she also knew that Athos had stood in D'Artagnan's heart in place of a father since D'Artagnan had lost his own father, or possibly before. And he thought—though he'd never dared ask—that Athos thought of D'Artagnan as a son.

What greater revenge was there, D'Artagnan thought, than to seduce the adopted son of the man who had tried to kill her, the man who had repudiated her? Having seduced D'Artagnan, she could either utterly destroy him or turn him against Athos, whichever offered. And even with his eyes open, in the full light of day, D'Artagnan wasn't sure she could not do either of those. Even now.

She looked at him, her luminous blue eyes sparkling with mischief. And he thought that were it not for his love for Constance, he would be succumbing even now. He thought of Constance's image, her beautiful face, and that smile she gave him when he had particularly pleased her.

He managed to look away from milady, and the way her hair fell, moonlight-like, outlining her shoulders, her breasts. She breathed deeply, and her breasts rose and fell. He started sliding his legs off the bed, a risky proposition, since he had not the slightest idea how far the floor was from here. But he was determined to find out. "I must be going," he said. "I am sorry my stupid head made it so difficult for you last night that I must sleep in your bed, but truly I must be going. I have guard duty," he remembered, with a pang that, in fact, he'd had guard duty the night before. He hoped someone had covered his lack and, though he counted on Monsieur de Treville to smooth things with Monsieur des Essarts, his brother-in-law, he wasn't absolutely sure he could explain this to Monsieur de Treville.

As he was about to slip off the bed, she grabbed his shoulder in a surprisingly strong hand. "Stay," she said. And giggled. "You've been no trouble at all."

Her other hand, insinuatingly, curled around his neck and onto his chest, to rake nails very lightly over his heart and head downwards.

Gritting his teeth together, he thought, suddenly, clearly, that the nightgown, mostly transparent as it was on the front, was nonetheless utterly closed in the back, covering it up all the way to her neck. Which, if he understood, was not the sort of design used for this sort of garment.

While her hand explored parts of him he'd never meant anyone but Constance to touch—or at least not for a great many years—he pulled himself up onto the bed by the force of his arm, so that he was more firmly seated. This had the side effect of dislodging her from her position, half-draped over him.

She took it in good part. Now, facing him, she grinned, and lunged forward to kiss him.

D'Artagnan could no more have stopped what he did than he could have willed himself to stop eating or sleeping. Curiosity, his desire to know what was happening and what things meant, was his defining characteristic, his strongest need. Even as her lips met his, as he kept his mouth resolutely closed against her assault, he reached back and, with a strong hand, tore the flimsy cloth that covered her shoulders.

And then just as quickly, he pulled away from her and looked back there, to see, faded and obviously covered in cosmetics, a smaller than normal brand, in the shape of a fleur-de-lis. He blinked at it, and, shocked that he must still, after all, be under the influence of whatever she'd given him, heard himself say, under his breath, "The fleur-de-lis. You are Athos's wife."

If the woman who had shared the bed with him had

suddenly transformed into a tigress, the change couldn't have been more startling or more obvious.

She came at him, claws and teeth, tearing at his face, at his still wounded shoulder. He grabbed at her wrists. She pulled out of his grasp. Screaming in fury, she dove for her pillow, to emerge holding a long and vicious looking dagger.

Addled still by the aftereffects of whatever she'd given him, D'Artagnan only managed to roll out of her way just in time. But she pulled the dagger that had embedded in the bedclothes, and came after him again.

He rolled off the bed, hitting the floor with more force than he'd expected, because the bed was almost as high as his hips. On the floor, he crawled forward, until his head cleared and he could walk.

And then he realized she was right behind him. Stooping, to grab a bundle of clothes and a hat on a nearby chair, he picked up a pretty little statuette of Cupid, on a writing desk by the window, and used it, held in his good hand, to smash the window, then half jumped and half fell through the window onto the roof below.

Milady didn't seem able to follow that action, or perhaps wasn't willing to follow, as D'Artagnan ran, with more desperation than grace across the roof of the house next to milady's lodgings, clothing firmly held in his hand. Instead, she stood at the window and screamed, "Murder, thief, rape!"

Any second, her desperate screams would attract the neighbors from their beds, and they would come after D'Artagnan. What else would they do, seeing him running naked along the roofs.

Desperately, he aimed for a corner of the roof, aware that he was still fully in her sight, and looked down at an intertwining network of stone-bordered balconies. He stepped on one, then swung onto the one below it, suspending himself by his good arm, which was already holding clothes.

It was slow progress, but progress, and he went from balcony to balcony, moving to the other side of the building as he did so, so that by the time he landed, in the dark alley beneath, he was in quite a different location than where milady would have seen him disappear.

It was only when he alighted in the alley and took a deep breath that he took a look at the clothes he was holding. They'd been resting on a chair, on the way to the window—and they were not even vaguely his. They consisted of a dark red dress, and a matching hat, with a very slight veil.

D'Artagnan looked at them in dismay. Well . . . he couldn't walk naked through the streets of Paris.[9]

---

[9]Some will note that in Monsieur Dumas' *Three Musketeers* the whole "affaire milady" was rather more complex and drawn out, and while the scene at the end of it was roughly similar, it involved the complicity of a little maid named Kitty. I trust I don't need to explain to the readers who have been faithfully following these chronicles how unlikely it would be that young, romantic D'Artagnan would be involved not only with one woman but with three. Indeed, it would be somewhat wrenching to think of him betraying Constance—whom even in Monsieur Dumas's embellished chronicle, he mourned lifelong—with the seductive but brittle milady, who might be experienced but cannot help but appear non-genuine.

We'll leave Monsieur Dumas's account, enjoyable and well crafted as it is, in the realm of a pleasant fiction concocted to accord to the morals and manners of his time and the idea that a brave and strong man must, of course, also be promiscuous.

Where Monsieur le Comte
Receives Several Surprises;
The Difference Between a Roasted
Chicken and a Live Countess;
Athos Loses his Battle with Reality

～

By the time Athos got home, he could have truthfully said that not much was on his mind, other than his desire for some dinner and for the comfort of his bed. He was telling himself he needed to shave, and wondering if he should do it now or leave it till tomorrow morning. His beard and moustache, which he wore carefully trimmed and shaped, depended for their look on his keeping the rest of his face hair free, which he was sure it wasn't now.

If he had been in an introspective mood, he would have admitted that another part of him was thinking of the duchess's soft breasts pressed against his chest, of the feeling of her, light and lively, in his hands, of the taste of her mouth against his, of the sheer joy of their kiss. But he shut out any such thoughts and told himself that if he dwelt on them it would only mean he would turn his feet towards the palace once more. And then, where that led no one knew, save that Athos was not one to share, and he was not one to take kindly to his ladylove exposing herself to danger. So

their affair would be of very short duration and end with
his heart broken.

Instead, he walked along and thought that he would
have to ask Grimaud to ask of Planchet to make sure his
master returned Athos's doublet and shirt. Or if not, Athos
would have to procure new ones, an activity he found so
distasteful that he tended to avoid doing it more than once
a decade.

In this mood, divided, he reached his lodgings and unlocked the door and went in. The sight of Grimaud standing in the small vestibule was so unexpected that, for a
long moment, Athos did not realize he was there. And
when he did, it was to blink, bewilderedly. "Grimaud!" he
said. "What has happened?"

The second because his old retainer had his arms
crossed, and his legs planted, as though ready for a battle.
His eyes were blazing and his face pale, and he looked altogether as though he were preparing to challenge Athos
on something, which was always a very strange and rare
event. The poor man submitted to using sign language and
uttering not a word for months at a time, when Athos was
in such a state of mind that the sound of a human voice disturbed him. He submitted to leaving behind the estate in
which he had a good many friends, and even more syco-
phants. All for the sake of Athos.

But now the light of battle was in his eyes, and he was
treating Athos as if Athos had never left behind his dignity,
which was always a very bad sign. "If you think I'm going
to allow you to cede your bed to your friends night after
night, and sleep all cramped up in some corner, or worse—
I know you!—rolled up on a cloak on the floor, let me tell
you, milord, it will not do. And as for Bazin telling me that
his master has been out doing holy work, that won't be believed either. Bazin can pray all he wants to, and lard all his
conversations with Latin, but you won't get me to believe

that Monsieur Aramis can come in smelling of liquor and with straw matted in his hair, and talking about dangerous chickens and have been out in the service of the Lord."

For Grimaud this speech was an epic oration, comparable to other men going on for hours on end, and yet Athos could make neither head nor tail of it.

He frowned at his servant. "Grimaud, I do not have the pleasure of understanding you at all. What happened, and why am I the bout of your wrath?"

"Monsieur Aramis. He came in dead drunk, smelling of wine, and behaving in such a way . . . well . . . he could not stay on his own two feet, and our only choice was to strip him to his shirt and put him in your bed. But if you think I intend to let you pass another unquiet night—"

"Oh, now I see," Athos said. "Your concern is for how I shall sleep, because in your mind I am still the sickly boy whom you watched for through the long nights. But Grimaud, I'm an adult now, and I would thank you—" His mind had caught up with his mouth, and it was informing him rather urgently of something that Grimaud had clearly said. He looked at the weather-beaten face of his servant, and he took a deep breath. "Grimaud, did you say that Monsieur Aramis told you to beware of dangerous chickens?"

Grimaud glared. "He said that she was intending to kill us all, and that if the fire caught all the chickens would be roasted, or something like that, and then, when he became more or less conscious again, as we were putting him to bed, he informed me with the utmost urgency that the chickens might set fire to the sun and kill us all. What was I to make of all this, pray?"

Athos almost chuckled. He couldn't help it. He'd seen Aramis drunk quite a few times, in their years of friendship. But what operated there is that he'd never yet seen Aramis drunk when he, himself, hadn't been drunk. And, in company, when Aramis had got drunk, he had usually amused himself in long arguments with Porthos—or occasionally Athos, though considering that Athos tended to go monosyllabic when drunk, that was a hard feat to achieve—about theology or the manufacture of drinking cups, or whatever else struck his fancy. At the end of it, Aramis would do his best to duel someone, only by that time he was so far gone, he couldn't take his sword out of its sheath. "So Monsieur Aramis is drunk," he said. "Given what we've gone through in the last few days I can hardly make a comment on that. Besides, last night, it was Monsieur Aramis and Monsieur Porthos who put me to bed."

"But didn't strip you down. They didn't even take your sword."

Athos, thinking that this was true and also that it betrayed a naivete as touching as it was dangerous, said, "Yes. I daresay they were a bit gone into their cups, as well." He shook his head. "Don't worry about it, Grimaud. The bed is large enough to accommodate half a dozen people, and at least a normal person and Monsieur Porthos. It is more than large enough for myself and Monsieur Aramis."

But Grimaud's arms remained crossed on his chest. "It's just no use at all thinking that I will countenance your spending another disturbed night, because I won't. When you stop sleeping, it is always the beginning of a troubled time, and I have no intention of allowing you to do that again."

There was this thing about being raised by a male, Athos thought—which in many ways, between his sickly mother and his unbending father, he had been—that should frighten everyone. Mother lions could be scary, but father lions, who had condescended to take notice of their offspring, and devote time to them, could be terrifying.

Still, he knew what lay at the back of it, and he was sure that over the years he'd given the poor man quite a few sleepless nights himself. So, instead of protesting, he put his hand on Grimaud's shoulder, gently. "Don't worry. I can let Monsieur Aramis sleep here. I don't know what he meant by chickens being after him, but I am sure it is nothing but one of those drunken alarms that mean nothing. He will wake tomorrow, and he will be in a better mood, and then we will talk to him and find out what he meant. And meanwhile his taking up a quarter or less of my bed will not disturb me."

"He is snoring fit to wake the saints," Grimaud said. "He is snoring louder than the final trumpet."

"Well, then I shall snore in competition with him," said Athos, feeling like he might very well do that, because his late night the night before, the alcohol ingested, and the emotional shocks of the last few hours had all dropped on his shoulders like a heavy burden, making him totter. The duchess had reminded him that he would not see thirty again and, right then, he felt it. He said, "But first, if you could procure me some broth, or a slice of meat, or something. Just to take the edge off the hunger. I don't think I can sit through an entire dinner just now." At any rate, he had a dread of sitting alone and eating at that polished table, where Grimaud would attend to him as though he were still the Count de la Fere in his ancestral estate.

Grimaud's mouth grew thinner and harder. "I have," he said, speaking while barely decompressing his lips, "prepared you a chicken, and a soup of mutton and lentils, and a sweet of . . ."

Oh, there would be no use arguing with this. When Grimaud took the time to prepare a full meal—when they had enough money to warrant preparing a full meal—there was no gainsaying him. Athos sighed. "Very well. Bring me water to my room, so I can at least wash my hands and face." Because sitting in estate while covered in dust and feeling like he still smelled of his drunken sweat—which was true—would be insupportable. He must at least wash his hands and face, comb his hair and change his shirt.

He was in the middle of combing his hair, when Grimaud came up and, silently, his lips still compressed, poured warm water into the basin in the room. Athos splashed it on his face, and washed his face and neck, his hands and arms, and turned to find Grimaud holding out a clean shirt for him.

The servant left while Athos was tidying his doublet over his shirt, which was the first time that Athos dared cast a look at his friend, on his bed—mostly because he was afraid doing so while Grimaud was there would have caused some withering comment about straw or chickens.

Aramis was indeed snoring, something else that Athos was not aware Aramis could do—and they had often shared lodgings on campaign and in travel. Never before had he seen Aramis lying like this, faceup, his mouth slightly open, snoring in loud, prolonged bursts. Were it not for the stubble, glimmering on his face by the light of the five candles that stood on the nearby table, and for the creases around his eyes that spoke of recent dissipation, Aramis might, in fact, have looked like a young child.

The light of the candles was also more than enough for Athos to catch sight of a few bits of straw stuck to Aramis's normally impeccable hair. What had he been doing? Out tumbling farm girls? While he had the duchess? And could bed her at will or close to it?

Athos shook his head, pityingly. "Ah, Aramis. You don't know what you are ignoring."

And on that, Aramis half sat up and stared at Athos with bewilderingly intent green eyes. "She means to kill us all," he said. "She has asked for our heads as her reward."

In a moment of sick feeling, his stomach lurching within him, Athos felt as though Aramis were answering his innermost thoughts and warning him against the Duchess de Chevreuse. He took a step forward. "Who? Who means to kill us all, Aramis? To whom did she ask for our heads?"

Aramis looked at him, bewildered. Or rather, did not look at him, but at something that appeared to be on a parallel line with Athos's face, but possibly some miles distant. "The chickens," he said, very firmly. "And the goats." He made a gesture with his hand, flat, palm downward, and swept it from left to right, in a circular half motion, as though indicating all the expanse of the room, or possibly of the Earth. "All of it in the service of the Cardinal."

And then, he fell back on his back, and resumed snoring. Athos smiled and shook his head. His verdict to Grimaud, as Grimaud served him some sort of compote, which he said was "made from pears from the north orchard, sent to me by my daughter, for you, milord," was, "Monsieur Aramis is drunk as a wheelbarrow and you know, Grimaud, if you wish me to sleep well, you might not insist I sleep on that bed."

Grimaud narrowed his eyes and made his lips very thin indeed, but, before he could start on his tirade, Athos sighed. "It's no use, Grimaud. We can move him, but if we put him on one of the chairs, or even on the floor, he'll not sleep well, and will be more likely to get up and get into some mischief than otherwise. So, I recommend we leave him on my bed, and you can take my thickest cloak and make me a sleeping area in the sitting room."

Grimaud didn't say anything, but the glare of his eyes said everything. Notwithstanding which, when Aramis was done drinking a small glass of brandy after his dinner, he found that Grimaud had in fact made him an admirable sleeping area, with cloaks and cushions and who knew what else. He stripped down to his shirt, threw clothes and sword over the back of a nearby chair, and climbed into it, too tired to care if by rights he should have had his bed or not. He was bone tired—weary with a weariness that mere physical tiredness couldn't explain.

For what seemed like a few minutes, he was blessedly,

happily unconscious. Only to be brought awake again, by loud, repeated pounding on the door. From the sound of it, it seemed very much like it would be Porthos. Athos, hearing Grimaud hastening down the stairs and calling out, "I'm coming, I'm coming, wait," assumed that he could go back to sleep.

He relaxed in his nest of cloaks and cushions, and started to close his eyes again. Which is when, upon his sleeping ears, there erupted the oddest sound in the world—Grimaud, yelling at a stranger. Or at least the words sounded like they were directed at a stranger. "Get away you hussy, you strumpet. This is a respectable household and we want none of your tricks."

In Athos's recently awakened mind, these words mingled with images of the duchess and more alarming images of his long-lost wife, and he realized he was bolt upright and moving, as he ran down the stairs, towards the front door.

The woman at the front door could not be the duchess, she was not rounded enough. And she could not have been Charlotte. She was much too short. A short, flat little woman, with disproportionately broad shoulders, attired in a dark red dress that would be in the latest fashion, except for the fact that it was much too long on her, and broad and narrow in all the wrong places. She looked, in fact, not so much like a strumpet, as like someone who wore another woman's discards. And the bits of scraggly black hair that peeked from underneath her broad brimmed hat with its veil didn't help at all.

She was bravely resisting Grimaud's attempts at pushing her out and, considering her previous pounding on their door, Athos had to consider the possibility that this was, after all, if not a hussy, at least a madwoman. He wasn't sure which one he would have liked better. And then the woman advanced a foot, and Athos realized that she was barefoot.

He was about to step forward and intervene, when Grimaud, reaching widely, managed to knock the intruder's hat off. His words of "Monsieur D'Artagnan" hit Athos's ear at the same time as the sight of that pale face, those staring, horrified dark eyes, the hair standing all on end, the two-day growth of scraggly eighteen-year old beard, all of it above the satin and silk of a very expensive dress.

The sound of his own laughter, ringing out, surprised Athos, but not enough to make him stop. In fact, once he had started laughing, he who rarely indulged in display of emotion of any kind, could not stop. His laughter rang out louder and louder, while he sat down on the steps—his knees gone too weak to support him—and tears ran down his face in rivulets.

He calmed down sometime later, with D'Artagnan grasping him by the arm and saying, "Athos, for the love of God, you must listen to me."

He looked up at the boy's face, and read the very real terror in it. Looking for a handkerchief in his sleeve and not finding it, because he was not wearing his doublet but solely his shirt left loose to fall almost to his knees, he wiped his streaming eyes and soaked face to the sleeve itself. "Yes, D'Artagnan," he managed, swallowing to maintain his composure. "You must forgive me, it was your looking so male and . . ."

Grimaud had closed the front door and now went by them, on the stairs, cleaving to the opposite wall. The look he gave Athos made Athos aware that if he got his sleep any more disturbed, it was, after all, Athos's fault in allowing his insane musketeer friends the liberty of the house.

Athos looked up and managed to keep his countenance— barely. The boy's fear made that easier. It wasn't something to sport with. "What happened? How come you here, in this attire."

"It is the only clothes I could find on my way out of her

bedchamber. She was after me with a dagger." D'Artagnan shuddered.

"She?" Athos asked.

"Milady. Your . . . wife."

Athos felt as if an ice-cold hand had clutched at his innards, but all he could say was, "I see." And then, louder, "Grimaud, if you could bring some water to my room. I'll help Monsieur D'Artagnan dress, while we speak." And, ignoring Grimaud's mumbled complaints, as he came towards them on the stairs again, Athos helped his friend up the stairs to his room. The only reason D'Artagnan needed help at all was that he appeared to have been running barefoot through shards of clay. "Some tiles that fell from a roof," he said.

By the time Grimaud had come back with warm water in a jug, Athos had found D'Artagnan some underwear, and was digging through one of his clothes presses for a shirt. He didn't see any point giving the boy doublet and hose now, since he would, doubtless, be going to bed. "Here," he said, extending a shirt to D'Artagnan, only to find it rudely ripped off his hands by Grimaud, who went to the trunk and brought out quite a different shirt. "We can send for your clothes in the morning. I assume you left Planchet in your lodgings?"

D'Artagnan nodded. And added, half under his breath, "I hope he's safe."

And Athos looked up, helplessly, at Grimaud, who huffed. "I'll go, and take Bazin and collect the boy. And we'll get you your clothes for tomorrow."

"Thank you, Grimaud," Athos said.

"But first I'm going to bring you another jug of water, Monsieur D'Artagnan, and don't you dare put those feet on Monsieur Athos's bed. You left a trail of mud all up the stairs and across the floor."

After Grimaud left to collect more water, Athos said,

"You must forgive him. He's anxious lest I should be disturbed. I have a feeling this is a truly bad night for him to feel this way."

D'Artagnan gave him a serious look. "I'm afraid so," he said, and proceeded to pour into Athos's ears a tale as chilling as it was unbelievable.

"You believe," Athos said, "that she set it up so you came upon her just as the ruffians appeared to be threatening her? Why? And how?"

"The how wouldn't be difficult," D'Artagnan said. "I suspect she has had us followed. If she is one of the Cardinal's creatures, this can't be wholly difficult."

"No," Athos said, but still felt the cold, clamped on his guts.

Water was delivered, and Athos told D'Artagnan, "I believe it would be best if you laid down and attempted to sleep. I don't know how well you may do next to Aramis, since he alternates between snoring and telling people about the danger of chickens." He smiled a little at D'Artagnan's expression. "I assure you it's true, and I assure you I have no more idea what he means than do you. I'm sure he means something, at least in his own mind, but what that might be, I cannot tell you. He is, needless to say, drunk."

D'Artagnan looked at the blond musketeer curiously, as he snored, faceup on the bed. "It seems like something Aramis . . . I mean, it doesn't seem like him."

"Indeed," Athos said. "And after your story, I'm beginning to wonder whether he did in fact get drunk or whether something was added to his food or drink, and, in that case, what that might be."

He helped D'Artagnan rinse his feet, and then saw him climb onto the bed, on the opposite side of Aramis, before he headed out the door.

"I might yet come and try to sleep on a chair," D'Artagnan said.

"You're welcome to," Athos answered and was, by that time, so tired that he couldn't ever remember getting to the sitting room or crawling into his mound of cushions and cloaks.

He could however remember being startled awake by a loud knocking. For a long time, it seemed, he lay there, wishing that Grimaud would answer. But after a while, it occurred to him Grimaud couldn't answer, since Grimaud had gone to fetch D'Artagnan's Planchet. He grabbed a candle, which he'd forgotten to blow out, from the little table in the corner, reached for his sword, and pulling it from its sheath, held it in his hand, as he went down the stairs and threw the door open.

To find Porthos, holding what seemed to be a covered clay dish, staring at him. Athos blinked at the sight then tried to sheathe his sword, realized that he wasn't wearing a sheath, and bowed slightly. "Come in, Porthos," he said, stepping around his friend as he did so, and closing the door. "I presume that's a dish of pigeons?"

Porthos looked down at the vessel in his hands and seemed for a moment quite confused. Then he said, "Oh. No. That is, it used to be. Now it's just the empty dish." As he spoke, he set it on the last step of the stairs, and looked up at Athos, who had gone up half a dozen steps, candle in one hand, sword in the other. "I used it to break into the Bastille."

"I see," Athos said, thinking that, in fact, those words were starting to have an apposite meaning to him.

"And I must tell you what Mousqueton said," Porthos said. "Because I think it is deucedly important and in fact it might solve the whole mystery for us . . . only . . . only I'm not sure how. You know I'm not good at seeing the picture until it is all completed."

"Yes," Athos said. "Yes, of course." And, making a sudden decision added, "Here, take my sword and candle up, Porthos. Put the sword with my clothes, then go in and

wake D'Artagnan and Aramis on my bed. I can see all efforts at sleeping tonight will be blighted, and that I might
as well give up and stay awake. Tell them it is time for a
war council. And if Aramis speaks of chickens, for the love
of heaven, pour a jug of water over his head. I believe there
is still half a jug left from D'Artagnan's washing."

"But . . ." Porthos said. "Where are you going?"

"Myself? Only to the cellar to get a bottle of wine. So-
briety has proven much stranger than I can endure, and I
believe a bottle might improve my feelings."

A Head Like a Case of Rapiers;
Where Some Ladies Must Be Protected
and Others Delight in Danger

❦

ARAMIS did not like being awakened. He tried to protest, as Porthos, ignored twice, finally grasped him by his shirt, at the nape of the neck, and bodily lifted him from the bed, carried him to the window, threw the window open and poured a good half a jug of water over his head.

While this worked admirably to clear Aramis's head, it also left him spluttering, shivering, and with his wet hair and wetter shirt clinging to him.

"What is the meaning of this?" he asked Porthos, even as every one of the words he pronounced echoed inside his head in a fiendish way, coming back at him as both sound and pain. "Why did you pour water over my head?"

"You should thank the saints it's water," Porthos said. "Only because I didn't have time to look and see if there is a chamberpot about the place. You tried to hit me."

"You yelled in my ear," Aramis said.

"Hardly, I merely told you to get up. It is not my fault that you are hungover."

Aramis regarded Porthos with full disbelief, aware at the same time that they were both being watched by D'Artagnan with something very akin to the fond amusement of the adult watching two children fight over trivial things. Aramis knew he could not be hungover. He had not gone out drinking. Or at least, he didn't remember going out drinking. He remembered, however, the long hot ride in the agonizingly slow oxcart. And he remembered the many farms each with a vintage worth sampling.

He also remembered—and he was fairly sure this had to be the result of drunken hallucinations—a scene that involved several armed men and a profusion of livestock, including something about chickens roasting in the setting sun. He groaned deep in his throat, "I have," he said, "a head like a case of rapiers, too full and close together, so that every movement brings about a frantic clanking."

Porthos regarded him with a jaundiced eye. "All the same," he said, reaching for the towel that Athos kept near the washbasin, "Athos has said we must have a council of war. Dry your hair. He'll be waiting in the sitting room."

Athos was waiting, with an open bottle of wine and a cup, and an expression of bewildered amusement on his refined features. Aramis looked at him, remembering vaguely that Athos had addressed him with a sort of gentle reproach, but not having any idea at all what Athos had told him. He thought he had warned Athos about milady, too, which probably explained the crease of worry between his eyebrows.

It was possibly the strangest council of war the four of them have ever held. At least, it was the first one where three of them were in their shirts, their bare legs hanging out beneath. Also, the first one of them to which Aramis was so ridiculously hungover that he could barely speak beyond a whisper.

To his shocked disbelief, Athos handed him a cup about a quarter full of red wine. "Drink," he said.

The smell of the wine climbed into Aramis's nose and put a knot of nausea at his throat. He pushed it away.

Athos pushed it back, "Drink!" he said. "I beg you to believe I know how to treat hangovers."

And when Aramis merely looked up at Athos, in horror, Athos grasped his hair, at the nape of his neck, causing him to both tilt his head back and open his mouth. At which point Aramis, coughing and spluttering, remembered the story of someone or other who had drowned in a barrel of malmsey, and swallowed frantically to avoid the like fate. As his mouth cleared, he said, "I' faith, Athos, I should challenge you to a duel."

"Probably," Athos said, in all seriousness. "But by the time you sober up enough to do it, I'd have defeated and disarmed you, and if you think I'm going to kill you and save you from feeling this hangover, you are sorely mistaken." And with his aplomb unshaken, he returned to his seat, where he looked at Aramis, as he swallowed and coughed, and squinted at the light of the candles, to determine how many candles there really were and how they burned. He was fairly sure, in fact, that each of the candles did not support a roaring fire, but that was how he saw them, their light augmented by several extraneous auras.

"Over the past few hours," Athos said, as he passed cups of wine around, "I have been awakened three times, each by one of you, and each time I've been greeted with a stranger story. It has become quite obvious to me that my best efforts to protect this group and keep you from harm have only spurned you to greater and more ridiculous feats of lunacy. So now I would like to know what each of you has discovered. Why don't we start with you, Aramis, since you are the one who left this house earliest?"

Aramis, whose head still reverberated at every sound, looked at Athos in mute resentment. He was, alas, all too aware that Athos, in this mood, could not be gainsaid. Plus, he would be quite likely to grab Aramis by the nape of the neck again, and force yet more wine into him. There was that glint of amusement in his eyes, closely followed by a look of hard determination. It was a combination Aramis had never seen in Athos. D'Artagnan, yes, but Athos never.

"When I left here," he said, "I decided to follow up on your impression that you had, in fact, seen your dead wife." He unraveled the whole story of his meeting with Huguette, followed by his forced travel into the countryside, in the belly of a wooden box. He was in the sort of mood where he couldn't think how to leave out the embarrassing parts—possibly because his hangover made him as awkward with words as must be Porthos's normal predicament. He told the story morosely, including the insults that Jean and Marc had leveled at him, before he burst out of the box, and everywhere they had stopped afterwards and what they'd eaten.

Porthos had tried to interrupt, twice, only to have Athos hold his hand up for silence, so that Aramis had to continue unreeling the tale. Only when he got to the part where he'd arrived back at the city and been attacked by swordsmen again did he falter. "Only," he said, "I don't know if there were really any swordsmen, because to believe that, I have to believe, also, that there were several pigs and chickens and goats and that this was what allowed me to get away."

"Well," D'Artagnan said, "people in that neighborhood do keep livestock."

Aramis could have warned D'Artagnan not to talk, because that would only bring Athos's attention on him, but by the time he thought of it, of course, D'Artagnan had spoken and it was too late. Athos turned to him with a slow smile and said, "Why don't you tell us where your follies have taken you, D'Artagnan?"

D'Artagnan told. Some of his words still boomed in Aramis's head, but either Aramis's headache was getting better, or D'Artagnan's voice was not as loud and offensive to the strained cranium as Porthos's and Athos's could be.

The story he told was hard to piece together, mostly

because Aramis felt as though he were trying to understand things through a field of blades. "You mean," he finally said, "that Madame Bonacieux thought you had avoided her for the sake of fighting a duel? Why?"

Athos interrupted. "I believe I have the answer to that, but meanwhile, please finish your story, D'Artagnan."

D'Artagnan finished it, and then Porthos was allowed to explain where he'd been and what he'd been doing. Since part of his efforts included listening to the conversation between Madame Bonacieux and Athos, something about it tickled Aramis's mind.

"So," he said. "Was the . . . No, I can't believe it. I know I was suspicious that Marie might have sent the swordsmen after me—but it would be after me, because I insulted her. Never after the rest of you. And when this conversation happened, the insult couldn't have happened yet."

"It hadn't," Athos said. "I've . . . spoken to the duchess. What?" he said defensively towards Aramis. "A musketeer may speak with a duchess, you know?"

"Of course. Of course he may," Aramis said, appeasing, not sure what had set off a storm of Athos's always uncertain temper. "And she told you she hadn't done it?"

"It seems hardly to matter, since you've asserted at the time she hadn't any reason to be angry at you, yet. But, indeed, she said the duel she meant was . . . metaphorical," Athos said, and had the grace to blush.

For the first time, in this very odd war council, Aramis had to repress a great impulse to chuckle. He could well imagine how Marie Michon's odd sense of humor had played on Athos's repressed, not to say prudish mind. The older musketeer fidgeted and looked away from Aramis's eyes as if he saw something in them that made him uncomfortable. Aramis wished he could have witnessed that encounter. He would have given something. He would have paid money for the chance.

Porthos had been deep in thought. He finally said. "It's inscrutable, of course, particularly Hermengarde's behavior."

"What is inscrutable?" Aramis said, regretting rather having given Porthos the word, which could be very much like giving a young child a loud whistle.

"The whole thing," Porthos said. "But particularly Hermengarde." He looked towards Athos. "I believe you'd say that all women are the devil, but I don't think it was that. I think it was . . ." he sighed. "That she wanted security of a type that Mousqueton couldn't give."

"Porthos, what's inscrutable is what you might be talking about," Aramis said.

"No, no, that's quite clear," Porthos said. "The problem is that I haven't told you yet of my conversation with Mousqueton." And he proceeded to do that, as he always told stories, in a spare, straightforward style. At least, every time he tried to interject some odd observation or some strange idea of his own about what might have been happening, Athos would make a gesture as though sending him back on track, and Porthos would go back, and describe exactly what he had said, and what Mousqueton had said.

When he finished, he sat there, biting his lip. "You understand all of it, right? Including why there were swordsmen when Aramis came back into town?"

"I think I do," Athos said. "However, if you wish to explain . . ."

Porthos nodded. "Hermengarde told Pierre. I'm sure of it. I'm sure that her relationship with him was such, she told him without the slightest idea what he would do with it."

"But I don't understand," Aramis said.

"I do," Athos said. "The mystery of the ambush can be laid at the feet of Pierre Langelier. You see, he heard from Hermengarde that Madame Bonacieux had taken alarm at the words of the duchess. It was probably told as a jest. You must remember, of all of them, only Hermengarde knew what sort of hold Madame Bonacieux had on D'Artagnan. And if she saw Madame Bonacieux leave in a hurry . . . well, Langelier and Hermengarde too, could figure her misunderstanding and what she'd set out to do. They knew she had probably sent a note summoning D'Artagnan to her, as a means to stop a presumed fight. All he had to do was ambush D'Artagnan in that part of the palace—in the most secluded area he could do it."

"But why would he want to?" Aramis asked.

"Well, by that time, doubtless, he would have heard of the ghost in his father's workshop. You have to remember, that though we didn't deal with him, I'm sure Monsieur Langelier fils was often present while we talked to his father. I'm sure he knew us all by look and by description too, from Hermengarde's story. He would hear of it and, I think, gather some friends and try his chance at catching us in the palace. Because that was his chance to put an end to our investigations. I'm sure by now there are rumors of how we solve crimes," Athos said.

"But . . . it would be tight timing, and where would an armorer find seven fighters who could outmatch us on the sword?"

Porthos sighed. "Aramis, surely you remember my saying that armorers are all sword experts. They have to be, in order to make good swords. They have to know what makes a sword work, and be a good sword. They practice as much as we do, and perhaps more. They certainly understand their weapons better."

"I was wounded by crafters?" D'Artagnan asked, shocked.

"Good crafters," Porthos said, in the tone of someone who thought this ought to console the young Gascon.

"But why?" Aramis said. He was sure he would think more clearly once his headache was gone, but all he could do for now was to walk step-by-step past each of the hurdles in his way. "Why would Pierre Langelier choose to not let us investigate?"

"Well, your story and Porthos's too told us that. He was a gambler, and deep in debt. This was never about his rivalry with Mousqueton, and only glancingly was it about Hermengarde's pregnancy. It was all about his need for money. What Mousqueton said he remembered last, about—you know—the armorer saying he would disinherit his son. I don't think this conversation was the sort that happened in front of the whole workshop. So, I presume it was just Monsieur Langelier and Mousqueton talking. And because Monsieur Langelier was probably repeating threats he'd made many times in person, he did not stop as his son came into the workshop. That his son was carrying a sword would occasion no shock, either. He probably, I think, hit Mousqueton on the head with the hilt, then ran his father through before he could reach for a sword himself. Possibly, before he felt any real alarm."

He shook his head. "The thing is, you see, that if he had hit him with a hammer, he might very easily have killed him without meaning to. The hilt of a sword is more controllable."

"And we should have known it from the beginning, because who else could have told the guards of the Cardinal that the hammer must have fallen on Mousqueton's head, and been believed. The fact is that anyone else would have prompted the guards to look up, and at least see if there were hammers hanging. But the new owner of the place . . ." Porthos said, opening his huge hands.

"And Hermengarde?" Aramis asked, his headache forgotten in the wave of curiosity. "Why would he kill her?"

"Oh, you told us that yourself. Because he has another girl, whom he also impregnated."

"But . . . if he impregnated them both, why would he prefer the other? And why kill Hermengarde?"

"First," Porthos said, counting on his huge fingers, "because Hermengarde was a living danger to him. At any moment, she could have told us of her relationship with him, and then we might have thought that perhaps he was the one attacking us. Second, because the other girl was more sure of carrying a child of his siring. And third, because the other girl brought him money, which made it easier for him to pay off his debts and not sell his business."

"Admirably put," Athos said.

"The question remains," Aramis said, "why would they ambush me when I came back from the country?"

"I would guess they had heard of your prowling about the night before," Porthos said, "and were waiting for you to return. Only someone who had heard of your being around the workshop, and desirous to prevent your return, would set a watch there—which to some extent exonerates other suspects."

"So this has nothing to do with a conspiracy against the Cardinal?" Aramis said. "Or the King?"

"No," Athos said. "I think that was all—"

"I wouldn't dismiss it so quickly," Porthos said. "First because the Cardinal honored his side of the pledge and is keeping Mousqueton in some relative comfort at the Bastille. Second because there is some mightily smokey intrigue happening. What, with the duchess writing to the illegitimate brother of the King, and what with milady trying to kill us, and having obtained permission from the Cardinal by promising to do something. I wouldn't consider this a total impossibility yet, but . . . I would say it has nothing to do with this crime."

"So you're saying," Aramis said, "that while I was being hit on the head and taken for a long, slow ride into the country, it was because Langelier, who was supposed to be the one hit and kidnapped, had gone to kill Hermengarde?"

"I'm afraid so," Porthos said.

"It's infamous," Aramis said. "Does this villain truly look that much like me?"

Porthos narrowed his eyes at Aramis. "Only from the back, or perhaps from a distance. His hair is yellower, and his shoulders are a little broader, and his features are considerably coarser. Besides, though I believe he is a flashy dresser, he is not, in any sense a good dresser, like you are, my dear Aramis. His suits are of cheaper material and cheaper cut."

Aramis, realizing that Porthos was trying to soothe him, and also very afraid that the word inscrutable would make an appearance, sighed, as his headache returned. "Well, at least we know. Although we could never have a hope of proving it."

"No," Porthos said, just as gloomily. "If only we had someone who had seen something and who could say . . ."

"What if we had someone who says he's seen something?" Athos said, suddenly.

"Someone?" Aramis asked.

"Some lady, an inmate of the palace, who claims they've seen the murder of Hermengarde up close," he said. "And who is willing to confront Langelier and pretend to blackmail him, while we wait right by, and intervene when needed. We'd have to have witnesses, of course . . ."

"Don't even think on it," D'Artagnan said. "I mean to make peace with Constance as soon as possible, and I'm sure she's very brave and she would gladly offer to help, but the truth is, my friends, she is a delicate lady, gently nurtured and—"

"I know a lady who would delight in it," Athos said. "She lives for danger and madcap defiance of odds."

"You do?" Aramis asked, looking at him, at the same time that the other two echoed him, and D'Artagnan continued, "You know a lady?"

"Well," Athos said, and smiled a little, with his old irony.

"Certainly that can't be any stranger than Aramis knowing a man." And without giving them time to realize he'd made a joke, "The Duchess de Chevreuse would, I'm sure, lend herself to our schemes. If only Aramis asks her nicely. And you see, because she knows Aramis so well, if Pierre Langelier tried to tell her she'd mistaken them one for the other . . ."

"Her denial would carry force," Aramis said. "By the Mass, Athos, I believe you are right! Get me writing paper," he said, to the room at large. "And a pen. And ink. I shall send her a note right away.

"Shouldn't you find out what you are supposed to tell her, first?" Athos asked, his voice vibrating with amusement. "Like . . . where she should meet us, and what we should do?"

"Not at the workshop," Porthos said. "Too many swords, and those hammers, and perhaps his friends too. We could never guarantee her safety."

"No," Athos said. "It must be someplace that he thinks he's utterly safe."

"I've got it," Aramis said, and his own shout set his head aching again.

Where His Musketeerness Discusses a Plan;
The Advantages of Dealing with
a Shifty Character

❧

"**S**o you didn't talk to him that night?" Aramis asked. "Yesterday night? After we went back." He had tracked Marc's and Jean's farms—they were brothers-in-law, and their farms adjoined each other—after he'd found the place on the edge of town where they'd dropped off the oxcart. The family there, distant cousins of Marc's, had been able to direct him.

On horseback, and at his speed, he'd gotten there in an hour instead of ten, and now he stood by the black horse he'd borrowed from Monsieur de Treville's stables, and discussed the matter of their plan and their need of a place with the two rustics.

"Well, we talked to him, in fact, and he's supposed to marry Marie. We didn't tell him that we'd thought we'd put him a box," Jean said, looking sheepish.

"No, I imagine you didn't," Aramis said. And he didn't imagine that Pierre knew that part either, else he would not have had his friends waiting for Aramis—he would have sent someone to find what he'd learned from his acquaintances in the country. Or to kill him halfway home.

He looked at the two of them, in their smocks and clearly in the middle of their working day. Would they be able to understand him? They hadn't struck him as stupid.

A little . . . different perhaps, but in no way worse than Porthos. Their curious approach to life, in any case, had probably saved his life.

Deciding, suddenly, he poured out the story to them, of how they'd realized it was Pierre's doing, and of what they proposed to do about it. After he was done, they were silent a long time, and then Jean looked at Marc, "I knew it. Or at least I suspicioned it all along, because, you know what Marie is like. She always falls for bad lots. Remember what she was like with that one-legged peddler."

Fascinating as the idea was, Aramis did not wish to pursue the case of the one-legged peddler. Instead, he said, seriously, "I know you'll think that I should, in fact, do my best to find one of his armed friends who would be willing to confess, but . . ."

"Oh, no, your musketeerness," Marc said. "That would be fatal, because it would tell Pierre you know. It would not at all do. After all, he owes them money. They wouldn't want him arrested till he can pay."

"But you want him to marry your sister," Aramis said. "Wouldn't that be the same situation?"

"Not at all," Jean said. "As your musketeerness knows, or you would not have come to us, would you? With us, as long as Marie marries him, she's all right, as far as her reputation is concerned. What happens afterward . . ." He shrugged. "In fact, if Pierre is the sort to go about murdering people, I'd much rather he doesn't stay around, after he marries Marie. What if he decided he could use my money too? I could be mortal in a tomb, before I knew what hit me. No, your musketeerness, you can count on our help."

"We'll bring him over," Marc said. "To discuss the details of the wedding, we'll say. And the settlements. Of course," he said, "we'd best have the priest on hand to marry them before you take him off to face justice. That of a certainty we must do."

Where Athos Courts Danger;
And a Lady Takes Up Arms

ॐ

ATHOS intercepted the lady as she came out of her carriage. He'd managed to do it by telling Aramis that he, more subtle and experienced at the nuances of such things, should keep an eye on the discussions within, with Pierre Langelier, who looked like a rather coarser Aramis, sitting at the table and arguing that he needed far more money to take the hapless Marie for his wife.

Besides, Athos had told Aramis, quite mendaciously and remorselessly, Aramis was needed on hand in case one of the two farmers needed reassurance and came through the door from the kitchen into the little pantry, where the musketeers hid behind vast jars that Athos presumed contained butter, but might very well contain wine.

And so, while Porthos, Aramis and D'Artagnan stayed in the pantry and followed the negotiations that were little more than delay tactics, Athos—whose anxious ears had picked up the faintest sound of wheels in the yard—went out to receive the lady.

She had driven in very quietly, so that the sound of her horse's hooves, the noise of the wheels, could be mistaken for nothing more than a carriage going by on the nearby road. But it was her carriage, with the De Chevreuse arms on the door. She descended from it, heavily cloaked, but in a cloak of cream satin, and when she threw the hood back from her head, her blond hair glimmered under the moonlight.

He bowed to her. "He is a murderer," he whispered. "But we will be in the pantry and ready to come to your rescue. I hope you're not afraid."

She turned her head up to look at him, her eyes glimmering insolently and shimmering with excitement. "If I told you I was afraid, would you kiss me for courage, Monsieur le Comte?"

He felt like a knot at his throat and managed a quickly stifled chuckle. "I'm not that brave," he said.

He escorted her to the door to the kitchen—not the door to the pantry, to which he hurried, to rejoin his friends.

When he got into the darkened pantry again, she had knocked and been admitted, and Marc was saying, "But I'm not sure I want you to marry our sister, at all. Not unless this lady is mistaken in her report."

"What report, what?" Pierre said, half rising from the table.

"That I saw you kill Hermengarde in the palace gardens," Marie Michon—for Athos could not doubt it was her, and not the more proper, or at least more socially conscious duchess that stood there—said. "You asked her to meet you and then you ran her through with the sword."

"Bah," Pierre said, and an ugly flush came to his cheeks, and made him look very much not like Aramis. "And who will listen to you?"

"I think everyone," Marie Michon said, drawing herself up, and supplementing her scant inches with the force of her personality. "Do you know who I am?"

"A busybody?"

"No. I'll have you know I'm the Duchess de Chevreuse."

"Oh, I still say you are a fool of a woman, and that you saw wrong. Everyone knows it was the blond musketeer."

"No. Of a certainty it wasn't. The blond musketeer is a good friend of mine, and I'll be willing to swear to any magistrate that he was with me at the time."

Before she'd finished pronouncing the words, Aramis had leapt forward and towards the kitchen and Athos, who had seen the same ugly glimmer in Pierre Langelier's eyes was racing him towards the man. But it was too late.

He wore a dagger. There had been no way of removing his dagger without making him suspicious. And now he'd grabbed the duchess around the chest, and he had the dagger to her neck. "Very pretty, milady." He looked towards the musketeers. "But who will believe any of this, if you are dead?"

"There is Monsieur le Cure," Marc said, pointing towards the door, where a grey-haired man stood, looking rather shocked. "He has seen it, and people will perforce believe him."

Langelier looked wild, and stared around at the musketeers and at the priest. "Very well, but you'll never take me alive. Come with me, pretty lady. We're going to take a long ride through the country." And with a sneer, at the musketeers said, "Put up your swords, or I slit her throat."

Athos, who had been watching De Chevreuse's face as it flushed, and as her eyes shone with the unmistakable light of battle, wondered what she meant to do. Courting danger was not always a good characteristic. Sometimes danger might court back. He looked at the blade near the pale throat, and wished very much he was in her place.

And with a Moo and a Cackle
and an Oink Oink There

❧

ARAMIS saw Marie Michon—his Marie—looking defiant and madcap. Unfortunately Aramis knew his Marie well. He knew she looked like that when the dice were down and the play definitely against her.

He wanted to rise. He wanted to go to her rescue. She wasn't Violette. He wasn't madly in love with her, as he'd been with Violette. But she was a gallant and brave soul, and he'd brought her into this. It seemed ridiculous that after all her intrigues, all her adventures, she should succumb here, at the hands of a brutish murderer.

And then, looking around, to see if anyone else was in a position to help her, he realized that Marc was gone. *The Devil,* he thought. *I wonder where he has gone?*

And then he heard a confused noise from behind him, in the yard, and realized that the door of the kitchen, into the outside yard, stood fully open. He had barely the time to look over his shoulder, as the noise grew deafening, and he was hit, full in the back, by a charging pig, and, as he fell, a confused chicken hopped up on his head.

Around him bedlam reigned. It took him a moment to locate Marie Michon, but when he found her, he realized in the confusion she had somehow managed to overturn the situation and had a small, dainty knife firmly held to

Pierre's throat. She'd somehow managed to make him drop his knife, and from the way his wrist hung, Aramis didn't think she'd done it with kindness. Now she told him in a stern voice, "And where were you going to take me, pig? You might enjoy going there, yourself."

Aramis smiled despite himself. Looking up, he met Athos's eyes, and was surprised to see him smiling as well.

Of course, their grins were nothing to Marc's and Jean's, whose expressions bordered on sheer, manic glee.

A Surfeit of Roasted Chicken;
A Letter from a Lady

∽

ATHOS looked down the expanse of his dining room table. Very rarely was Grimaud's insistence that they eat in the dining room justified as it was now. The table was, in fact, almost too crowded. In addition to his four friends, all four of their servants were present and sitting at the table. Though after Grimaud's arguments, they had decided to allow the servants to sit at the foot of the table.

And from Grimaud's glare, he would keep the others in place if it killed him.

The top of the table itself was entirely covered in roast chicken, ham, and a multitude of bottles of wine. The chicken and the ham were from the farmers. Jean and Marc had sworn that the chickens—about a dozen of them—had got badly trampled or burned in the hearth after being stampeded into the kitchen, and so, the only thing for them was to kill them, roast them and send them to the musketeers as a gift.

No one had explained why they'd also sent the ham— since it was cured and therefore at least weeks old—and the bread, but Athos, who had listened to the two of them go on, guessed they were quite likely to tell them that these had gotten trampled in the stampede, as well, and therefore must be put out of their misery. They lied with the same glib ease as Mousqueton, on whom the news of Hermengarde's death had fallen like a lead weight. He still looked teary and had that expression of a man whose hopes had come crashing around his head.

All he'd told Athos was, "You were always right, monsieur, women are the devil. I don't know which hurts more, that Langelier had to kill her so she wouldn't insist he marry her or . . . Or that she is dead. But it hurts all the same."

And Athos, knowing himself at risk, could do nothing but silently sympathize.

"It was a lovely wedding, though," Porthos said. "Even if the groom was tied up."

"And gagged," Aramis said. "Don't forget gagged. I had to reassure the *bon cure* that the man meant, indeed, to say yes."

"Well, he scarcely had any other choice," D'Artagnan said, as he disposed of a full chicken, heaped on plate. "You pulled his hair so his head must perforce nod."

"I was only doing my duty, to preserve a poor lady from sin," Aramis said, piously.

"And the ways of the Lord are inscrutable," Porthos said.

"Besides," Aramis said, totally ignoring the proffered bait, "you have to agree there was something in the way of poetic justice, to bringing him back to Paris in a box and presenting him to the Cardinal all tied up."

Athos was about to open his mouth, to say that he wondered if the Cardinal still thought that Athos was working on his behalf, even now, and to remind them there was a good chance he'd already agreed to let Charlotte have her way with him, and that she would be an adversary to reckon with in the future. In fact, for all their present joy at having Mousqueton back, Athos wasn't sure that all—or any of them—could survive long enough to defeat the woman who had briefly been Countess de la Fere.

Before he could speak, there was a loud pounding on the door.

Grimaud, who got up to go answer, came back almost immediately, looking baffled and holding up a sheet of expensive cream paper, from which a delicate perfume wafted.

"Ah, that will be for me," Aramis said.

But Grimaud only directed a glare at him, then a glare at the letter, and finally a glare at Athos, in whose lap he dropped it.

The letter said only, "To Monsieur le Comte de—"

The seal was blank and Athos lifted it impatiently. Inside, a well-formed hand said, "There is a public feast given by the court in a week. Marie Michon would like to meet the count at it. Will he meet her there? She shall be wearing a cream dress, with a blue hat, and a rose at her bosom."

Athos felt as though his hand went nerveless. He dropped the note in his lap.

"What is wrong?" Porthos asked. "Is it from milady?"

Athos shook his head. "No, no. It is nothing, just a silly dare."

And in his heart of hearts, he wondered if he did dare.